THE DRAGON IN THE SWORD
Michael Moorcock

"Rousing . . . inventive . . . thoughtful and literate!"
—*Kirkus*

"Excellent . . . not 'just another' Eternal Champion novel, but a *new* Eternal Champion novel . . . Recommended!"
—*Fantasy Review*

"Enjoyable!"
—*Science Fiction Chronicle*

"Stylish writing and originality . . . a cut above the rest!"
—*Indianapolis News*

"A welcome addition to the canon of the Champion."
—*Pulp & Celluloid* magazine

"Intoxicating . . . Michael Moorcock is a pro's pro . . . not afraid to dream big, to be a little outrageous, to even be preposterous, and as a result (thankfully), the reader never knows what is going to happen next . . . Remarkable!"
—*The Coast Book Review Service*

"His darkest battle . . . a rich Moorcock tapestry!"
—*Voice of Youth Advocates*

Other books by Michael Moorcock

THE CITY IN THE AUTUMN STARS
THE DRAGON IN THE SWORD
THE ETERNAL CHAMPION
THE SILVER WARRIORS

The Elric Saga

ELRIC OF MELNIBONÉ
THE SAILOR ON THE SEAS OF FATE
THE WEIRD OF THE WHITE WOLF
THE VANISHING TOWER
THE BANE OF THE BLACK SWORD
STORMBRINGER

The Chronicles of Castle Brass

COUNT BRASS
THE CHAMPION OF GARATHORM
THE QUEST FOR TANELORN

The Books of Corum

THE KNIGHT OF THE SWORDS
THE QUEEN OF THE SWORDS
THE KING OF THE SWORDS
THE BULL AND THE SPEAR
THE OAK AND THE RAM
THE SWORD AND THE STALLION

The Dancers at the End of Time

AN ALIEN HEAT
THE HOLLOW LANDS
Coming from Ace:
THE END OF ALL SONGS
LEGENDS FROM THE END OF TIME
A MESSIAH AT THE END OF TIME

THE DRAGON IN THE SWORD

**BEING THE THIRD AND
FINAL STORY IN THE
HISTORY OF JOHN DAKER,
THE ETERNAL CHAMPION**

MICHAEL MOORCOCK

ACE BOOKS, NEW YORK

This Ace book contains the complete
text of the original hardcover edition.
It has been completely reset in a typeface
designed for easy reading, and was
printed from new film.

THE DRAGON IN THE SWORD

An Ace Book/published by arrangement with
the author

PRINTING HISTORY
Ace hardcover edition/September 1986
Ace edition/December 1987

ISBN: 0-441-16610-5

Ace Books are published by The Berkley Publishing Group,
200 Madison Avenue, New York, NY 10016.
The name "ACE" and the "A"
logo are trademarks belonging
to Charter Communications, Inc.

PRINTED IN THE UNITED STATES OF AMERICA

10 9 8 7 6 5 4 3 2 1

Rose of all Roses, Rose of all the World!
You, too, have come where the dim tides are hurled
Upon the wharves of sorrow, and heard ring
The bell that calls us on; the sweet far thing.
Beauty grown sad with its eternity
Made you of us, and of the dim grey sea.
Our long ships loose thought-woven sails and wait,
For God has bid them share an equal fate;
And when at last, defeated in His wars,
They have gone down under the same white stars,
We shall no longer hear the little cry
Of our sad hearts, that may not live nor die.

—W. B. YEATS, "The Rose of Battle"

PROLOGUE

I AM John Daker, the victim of the whole world's dreams. I am Erekosë, Champion of Humanity, who slew the human race. I am Urlik Skarsol, Lord of the Frozen Keep, who bore the Black Sword. I am Ilian of Garathorm, Elric Womanslayer, Hawkmoon, Corum and so many others— man, woman or androgyne. I have been them all. And all are warriors in the perpetual War of the Balance, seeking to maintain justice in a universe always threatened by encroaching Chaos, to impose Time upon an existence without beginning or end. Yet even this is not my true doom.

My true doom is to remember, however dimly, each separate incarnation, every moment of an infinity of lives, a multiplicity of ages and worlds, concurrent and sequential.

Time is at once an agony of the Present, a long torment of the Past and the terrible prospect of countless Futures. Time is also a complex of subtly intersecting realities, of unguessable consequences and undiscoverable causes, of profound tensions and dependencies.

I still do not truly know why I was chosen for this fate or how I came to close the circle which, if it did not release me, at least promised to limit my pain.

All I do know is that it is my fate to fight forever and to possess peace but briefly, for I am the Champion Eternal, at once a defender of justice and its destroyer. In me, all humanity is at war. In me male and female combine, in me they struggle; in me so many races aspire to make reality of their myths and their dreams. . . .

Yet I am no more or less a human creature than any of my fellows. I can be possessed as easily by love as by despair, by fear as by hatred.

I was and am John Daker and I came at last to find a certain peace, the appearance of conclusion. This is my attempt to put down my final story. . . .

1

I have described how I was called by King Rigenos to fight against the Eldren and how I fell in love and came to commit a terrible sin. I have told what befell me when (I believed as punishment for my crime) I was called to Rowenarc, how I was induced to wield the Black Blade against my will, how I encountered the Silver Queen and what we did together on the South Ice Plains. I believe, too, I have set down somewhere other adventures of mine (or they have been set down by others to whom I recounted them); I have told a little of how I came to voyage on a dark ship steered by her blind captain. I am not sure, however, if I ever described how I came to leave the world of the South Ice or my identity as Urlik Skarsol, so I shall begin my story with my final recollections of the dying planet whose lands were slowly falling to the conquest of cold and whose sluggish seas were so thick with salt they could virtually sustain the weight of a grown man. Having succeeded in that world of redressing at least to some degree my earlier sins, I had hoped I might now be united again with my one and only love, the beautiful Eldren princess, Ermizhad.

Although a hero to those whom I had helped, I grew more and more lonely. Increasingly, too, I was subject to fits of almost suicidal melancholy. Sometimes I would fall into senseless raging against my fate, against whatever and whoever separated me from the woman whose face and presence filled my hours, waking and sleeping. Ermizhad! Ermizhad! Had anyone ever loved so thoroughly? So constantly?

In my chariot of silver and bronze, drawn by great white bears, I ranged the South Ice, forever restless, full of my memories, praying to be restored to Ermizhad, aching with longing for her. I slept little. From time to time I would return to the Scarlet Fjord, where I had many who were glad to be my friends and auditors, but I found the ordinary business of people's lives almost irritating. Hating to appear churlish, I avoided their hospitality and companionship whenever possible. I would confine myself to my chambers and there, half-asleep, perpetually exhausted, I would seek to place my soul in limbo, to depart from my body, to quest through the astral plane (as I thought of it) for my lost love. But there were so many planes of existence—an infinite number of worlds in the multiverse, as I knew already, a vast variety of potential chronologies and geographies. How was it possible to quest through all of these and find my Ermizhad?

I had been told I might discover her in Tanelorn. But where

was Tanelorn? I knew from my memories of other existences that the city took many forms and was forever elusive, even to one skilled in moving between the multitudinous layers of the Million Spheres. What chance had I, bound to a single body, a single earthly plane, of finding Tanelorn? If yearning were enough, then certainly I should have discovered the city a dozen times already.

Exhaustion gradually took its toll on me. Some thought I might die of it, others that I might go mad from it. I assured them my will was too strong for that. I agreed, however, to accept their medicines and these at last sent me into deep sleep where, to my joy, I began to experience the strangest dreams.

At first I seemed to be adrift in a formless ocean of colour and light which swirled in every direction. Gradually I realised that what I witnessed was something of the entire multiverse. To a degree at least I was perceiving every individual layer, every period at once. Therefore my senses were incapable of selecting any particular detail from this astonishing vision.

Then I became aware that I was falling, very slowly, through all these ages and realms of reality, through whole worlds, cities, groups of men and women, forests, mountains, oceans, until I saw ahead of me a small flat island of green which offered a reassuring appearance of solidity. As my feet touched it I smelled fresh grass, saw little clumps of turf, some wild flowers. Everything looked wonderfully simple, though it existed in that churning chaos of pure colour, of tides of light which constantly changed in intensity. Upon this fragment of reality another figure stood. It was armoured all of a piece, in chequered yellow and black, from crown to heel, and its face was visored so that I could see nothing of the creature within.

I knew him already, however, for we had met before. I knew him as the Knight in Black and Yellow. I greeted him, but he did not answer. I wondered if he had frozen to death within his armour. Between us there fluttered a pale flag, bereft of insignia. It might have been a truce flag save that he and I were not enemies. He was a huge man, taller even than myself. When we had last met we had stood together on a hill and watched the armies of humanity fighting back and forth across the valleys. Now we watched nothing. I wanted him to raise his helm and reveal his face. He would not. I wanted him to speak to me. He would not. I wanted him to reassure me that he was not dead. He offered no such reassurance.

This dream was repeated many times. Night after night I begged him to reveal himself, made the identical demands I had always made and received no response.

Then one night there came at last a change. Before I could begin my ritual of requests the Knight in Black and Yellow spoke to me. . . .

—*I have told you before. I will answer any questions you put to me.*

It was as if he continued a conversation whose beginning I had forgotten.

—*How can I rejoin Ermizhad?*

—*By taking passage on the Dark Ship.*

—*Where shall I find the Dark Ship?*

—*The ship will come to you.*

—*How long must I wait?*

—*Longer than you wish. You must curb your impatience.*

—*That is an insubstantial answer.*

—*I promise you it is the only one I can offer.*

—*What is your name?*

—*Like you, I am endowed with a great many names. I am the Knight in Black and Yellow. I am the Warrior Who Cannot Fight. I am sometimes called The Blank Flag.*

—*Let me see your face.*

—*No.*

—*Why so?*

—*Ah, now, this is delicate. I think it is because the time has not come. If I showed you too much it would affect too many other chronologies. You must know that Chaos threatens everything in all the realms of the multiverse. The Balance tilts too heavily in its favour. Law must be supported. We must be careful to do no further harm. You shall hear my name soon, I am certain of that. Soon, that is, in terms of your own timespan. In terms of mine ten thousand years could pass. . . .*

—*Can you help me return to Ermizhad?*

—*I have already explained that you must wait for the ship.*

—*When shall I have peace of mind?*

—*When all your tasks are done. Or before there are tasks for you to do.*

—*You are cruel, Knight in Black and Yellow, to answer me so vaguely.*

—I assure you, John Daker, I have no clearer answers. You are not the only one to accuse me of cruelty. . . .

He gestured and now I could see a cliff. On it, lined at the very edge, some on foot, some on mounts (not all by any means ordinary horses), were rank upon rank of fighters in battered armour. I was close enough, somehow, to observe their faces. They had blank eyes which had become used to too much agony. They could not see us, yet it seemed to me they prayed to us—or at least to the Knight in Black and Yellow.

I cried out to them: *Who are you?*

And they answered me, lifting their heads to chant a frightful litany: *We are the lost. We are the last. We are the unkind. We are the Warriors on the Edge of Time.*

It was as if I had given them a signal, an opportunity to express their terrors, their longings and their agony of centuries. They chanted in a single, cold, melancholy voice. I felt that they had been standing on the cliff's edge for eternity, speaking only when asked my question. Their chant did not pause but grew steadily louder. . . .

We are the Warriors on the Edge of Time. Where is our joy? Where is our sorrow? Where is our fear? We are the deaf, the dumb, the blind. We are the undying. It is so cold on the Edge of Time.

Their pain was so intense I tried to cover my ears. *—No!* I screamed. *—No! You must not call to me. You must go away!*

And then there was silence. They were gone.

I turned to speak to the Knight in Black and Yellow, but he, too, had vanished. Had he been one of those warriors? Did he lead them, perhaps? Or, I wondered, were they all aspects of a single being—myself?

Not only could I not answer any of these questions, I did not really wish to have the answers.

I am not sure if it was at that point, or at some later time, in another dream, that I found myself standing upon a rocky beach looking out into an ocean shrouded in thick mist.

At first I saw nothing in the mist, then gradually I perceived a dark outline, a ship heaving at anchor close to the shore.

I knew this was the Dark Ship.

Aboard this ship, dotted here and there, orange light glowed. It was a warm, reassuring light. Also I thought I heard deep voices calling from the deck to the yards and back again. I believe I hailed the ship and that she responded, for soon—perhaps brought there in a longboat—I was standing on her main deck, confronting a tall, gaunt man in a soft leather seacoat which reached below his knees. He touched my shoulder as if in greeting and I knew before I looked into his calm, ageless face that he was blind.

My other recollection is that the ship was carved, every inch of her, with peculiar designs, many geometrical, many representing bizarre creatures, entire stories or incidents from all manner of unguessable histories.

—*You'll sail with us again,* the captain said.

—*Again,* I agreed, though I could not recall, just then, when I had sailed with him before.

Thereafter I left the ship several times, in several different guises, and pursued all manner of adventures. One came to memory sharper than the others and I even remembered my name. It was Clen of Clen Gar. I remembered some kind of war between Heaven and Hell. I remembered deceit and treachery and some manner of victory. Then I was aboard the ship again.

—*Ermizhad! Tanelorn! Do we sail there?*

The blind captain put the tips of his long fingers to my face and touched my tears. —*Not yet.*

—*Then I'll spend no more time aboard this vessel....* I grew angry. I warned the captain he could not hold me prisoner. I would not be bound to his ship. I would determine my own destiny in my own way.

He did not resist my leaving, though he seemed sad to see me depart.

And I was awake again, in my bed, in my chambers at the Scarlet Fjord. I had a fever, I believe. I was surrounded by servants who had come at my shouting. Through them pushed handsome, redheaded Bladrak Morningspear, who had once saved my life. He was concerned. I remember screaming at him to help me, to take his knife and release me from my body.

—*Kill me, Bladrak, if you value our comradeship!*

But he would not. Long nights came and went. In some of them I thought I was upon the ship again. At other times I felt I was being called. Ermizhad? Was it she who called? I sensed a woman present....

But when I next set eyes upon a fresh visitation it was a sharp-faced dwarf I saw. He was dancing and capering, apparently oblivious of me, humming to himself. I thought I recognised him, but could not remember his name. —*Who are you? Are you sent by the blind captain? Or do you come from the Knight in Black and Yellow?*

I seemed to have surprised the dwarf, who turned sardonic features on me for the first time, pushed back his cap and grinned. —*Who am I? I had not meant to have you at a disadvantage. We are old friends, you and I, John Daker.*

—*You know me by that name? As John Daker?*

—*I know you by all your names. But you shall be only two of those names more than once. Is that a riddle?*

—*It is. Must I now find the answer?*

—*If you feel you need one. You ask many questions, John Daker.*

—*I would prefer it if you called me Erekosë.*

—*You'll have your wish again. Now, there's a straight answer for you, after all! I'm not such a bad dwarf, am I?*

—*I remember! You're called Jermays the Crooked. You are like me—the incarnation of many aspects of the same creature. We met at the sea-stag's cave.*

I recalled our conversation. Had he been the first to tell me of the Black Sword?

—*We were old friends, Sir Champion, but you failed to remember me then, just as you fail to remember me now. Perhaps you have too much to remember, eh? You have not offended me. I note you appear to have lost your sword. . . .*

—*I shall never bear it again. It was a terrible blade. I have no further use for it. Or for any sword like it. I recall you said there were two of them. . . .*

—*I said that there were sometimes two. That perhaps it was an illusion; that there was in fact only one. I am not sure. You bore the one you shall call (or have called) "Stormbringer." Now, I suppose, you seek "Mournblade."*

—*You spoke of some destiny attached to the blades. You suggested my destiny was linked with theirs. . . .*

—*Ah, did I now. Well, your memory's improving. Good, good. It will be of some help to you I am sure. Or perhaps not. Do you already know that each of these swords is a vessel for something else? They were forged, I understand, to be filled, to be inhabited. To possess, if you like, a soul. You're baffled, I can see. Unfortunately I'm fairly mystified myself. I get intimations, of course. Intimations of our various fates. And those are frequently mixed up. I'll confuse you and very likely myself also if I continue in this vein! I can already see you are unwell. Is it merely a touch of physical sickness or does it extend to your brain?*

—*Can you help me find Ermizhad, Jermays? Can you tell me where lies Tanelorn? That is all I wish to know. The rest of it I do not care for at all. I want no more talk of destiny, of swords, of ships and strange countries. Where is Tanelorn?*

—*The ship sails there, does it not? I understood that Tanelorn is her final destination. There are so many cities called Tanelorn and the ship carries a cargo of so many identities. Yet all are the same or some aspect of the same personality. Too much for me, Sir Champion. You must go back aboard.*

—*I do not wish to return to the Dark Ship.*

—*You disembarked too soon.*

—*I did not know where the ship was bearing me. I was afraid I would lose direction and never discover Ermizhad again.*

—*So that was why you left! Did you think you had found your goal? That there was any other way of finding it?*

—*Did I disembark against the captain's will? Am I being punished for that?*

—*Not likely. The captain's no great punisher. He is not an arbiter. Rather he is a translator, I would say. But all that's for you to ascertain for yourself once you return to the ship.*

—*I do not want to be aboard that Dark Ship again.*

I wiped a mixture of tears and perspiration from my eyes and it was as if I had wiped Jermays from my vision, for he had gone.

I rose and clad myself, yelling for my old armour. I made them put it on me, though I could scarcely hold myself steady on my feet. Then I ordered a great sea-sled harnessed with the mighty herons trained to pull it across those salty, undulating plains, those dying oceans. I snarled at those who would follow me. I ordered them to go back to the Scarlet Fjord. I refused their friendship. I sped from the sight of all humankind, into the brine-heavy night, my head lifted back as I howled like a dog and I cried for my Ermizhad. There was no response. I had hardly expected any. So I called instead to the blind captain of the Dark Ship. I called every God and Goddess I could name. I called to myself—to John Daker, Erekosë, Urlik, Clen, Elric, Hawkmoon, Corum and all the others. I called lastly to the Black Sword itself, but I was received by a most terrible, unkind silence.

I looked into the faded light of dawn and thought I saw a great cliff lined with gaunt warriors. They were those same warriors who had stood upon the edge of that cliff for an eternity, each one with my face. But I had seen nothing but clouds, thick as the ocean on which I sailed.

—*Ermizhad! Where are you? Who or what will take me to you?*

I heard a sly, unpleasant wind whispering near the horizon. I heard the flap of my herons' wings. I heard my sea-sled thump upon the surface of the waves. And I heard my own voice saying that there was only one thing I could do, since no power would come to my aid. It was, of course, the reason I had come out here alone. Why I had clad myself in the full battle-armour of Urlik Skarsol, Lord of the Frozen Keep. —*You must throw yourself into the sea*, I said. —*You must let yourself sink. You must drown. In dying, you will surely find a fresh incarnation. Perhaps you will even be taken back to Erekosë and be reunited with your Ermizhad. After all, it will be an act of faith even the Gods cannot ignore. Perhaps it is what they are waiting for? To see how brave you are prepared to be. And to see how truly you love her.* And with that I let go the reins of those massive birds and prepared to dive into the horrible and viscous ocean.

But now the Knight in Black and Yellow stood upon the platform beside me and he had put a steel glove upon my shoulder. And in his other hand he bore the Blank Standard. And this time he lifted his visor so that I might see his face.

That face was a memory of greatness. It displayed enormous and ancient wisdom. It was a face which had seen far more than I would wish to see in all my incarnations. The bone structure was ascetic and fine, the huge eyes penetrating and authoritative. His flesh was the colour of polished jet and his voice was deep, full of the power of approaching thunder.

—*It would not be bravery, Champion. It would be at best folly. You think you seek for something, but yours would be an act of someone merely wishing to escape torment. There are aspects of the Champion far less tolerable than your present one. And, besides, I can tell you that this particular ordeal will not last for very much longer. I would have come to you sooner, but I had business elsewhere.*

—*With whom?*

—*Oh, with you, of course. But that is a tale being told in some other world and perhaps in your future, for the Million*

Spheres roll through time and space at many differing speeds and where or when they intersect is frequently surprising, even to me. But I can assure you this is a poor time to be doing away with your life—or this body, even. I could not speak for the consequences, though I believe they would not be pleasant. A great and momentous adventure lies ahead of you. If you fulfil your duty as Champion in the most effective way, it could result in your partial release from this doom. It could produce a beginning and an ending of enormous import. Let them call you. Surely you have heard them?

—*I have distinguished nothing from the voices I have heard. It cannot be those warriors who call.* . . .

—*What they call for is release from their particular doom. No, these are others who call, as you have been called before. Have you heard no name? A name new to you?*

—*I think not.*

—*This means you should return to the Dark Ship. It is all I can think. I am deeply puzzled.* . . .

—*If you are puzzled, Sir Knight, then I am truly confounded! I have no wish to give myself up to that blind man and his ship. It increases my sense of impotence. Moreover, I remain in the same flesh. In this flesh, surely I cannot find Ermizhad. I must be either Erekosë or John Daker again.*

—*Perhaps your new guise was not ready. The checks and balances involved in this are extremely delicate. But I do know you must somehow return to that ship.* . . .

—*Can you offer me no more than that?*

—*Forgive me, Sir Champion.* The black giant's hand remained on my shoulder. —*I am not entirely omniscient. Who can be when the very structure of Time and Space is in flux?*

—*What are you telling me?*

—*I tell you no more than I perceive myself. Let the ship take you, that is all I can say. Through this medium, I know, you will be transported to those who most require your help and whose help in turn could gain for you some form of release from your present torment. Also you will be united in such a way to promise further unity. This much I can sense.* . . .

—*But where shall I look for this ship?*

—*If you are willing, the ship will come to you. It will find you, fear not.* Then the Knight in Black and Yellow whistled suddenly and from out of the orange mist there now galloped a great stallion, its hooves striking the water but not penetrating the surface. This beast the Knight in Black and Yellow mounted. Its coat was as black as his skin and I marvelled at how it could stand on those waves without sinking an inch. Indeed, I was so astonished by this apparition that I forgot to ask the rider any further questions. I could only stand and watch as he raised the Blank Banner by way of salute to me, then turned the battlehorse towards the clouds and rode rapidly away.

I remained mystified, yet the Knight in Black and Yellow had brought me a form of hope and had stopped me from continuing in my madness. I would not kill myself, after all, though I did not relish a further passage aboard the Dark Ship, either. Instead, I thought, I would lie down upon my sea-sled while the herons bore me wherever they chose (perhaps back to the Scarlet Fjord, for they must soon reach the limit of their endurance, or perhaps they would come to perch upon the sled with me before continuing their journey out across the ocean). Sooner or later, I knew, they would turn homeward. I had wanted to ask the knight's name. Sometimes names brought with them reawakened memories, intimations of my future, incidents from my past.

I slept and as I slept the dreams returned. I heard distant voices and I knew it was the warriors who chanted; the Warriors of the Edge. —*Who are you?* I begged. I was growing tired of my own questions. I was beginning not to care. There were too many mysteries. All I wanted was to be restored to my lost love, Ermizhad. I did not care how this was done or what I did to achieve it. But then the chanting of the warriors began to change in tone until at last I heard a single name: *SHARADIM! SHARADIM!*

The word was meaningless to me. It was not my name, I knew. It had never been my name. Nor would it ever be my name. Was I the victim of some dreadful cosmic error?

—*SHARADIM! SHARADIM! THE DRAGON IS IN THE SWORD!*

—*SHARADIM! SHARADIM! COME TO US, WE BEG!*

—*SHARADIM! SHARADIM! THE DRAGON MUST BE RELEASED!*

—*But I am not Sharadim.* I spoke aloud. —*I cannot help you.*

—*PRINCESS SHARADIM, YOU MUST NOT REFUSE US!*

—*I am neither a princess nor your Sharadim. I wait to be called, it is true. But it is another you need. . . .*

Could there be another poor soul, I wondered, who was doomed as I was doomed? Were there many such as I?

—*A DRAGON FREED IS A RACE RELEASED! LET US REMAIN IN EXILE NO LONGER, SHARADIM! LISTEN! THE FIREDRAKE ROARS WITHIN THE BLADE. SHE, TOO, WOULD BE REUNITED WITH HER KING. SET US ALL FREE, SHARADIM! SET US ALL FREE! ONLY THOSE OF YOUR BLOOD MAY TAKE THE SWORD AND DO WHAT MUST BE DONE!*

This had a familiar ring to me, yet I knew in my bones I was not Sharadim. As John Daker would have thought, I was like a radio tuner receiving messages on the wrong band. And this was all the more ironic since I currently longed to be drawn from my body and into another, preferably into the body of Erekosë, reunited with his Ermizhad.

Yet I could not dismiss them. The chanting grew louder and now I even thought I could see shadowy figures—female figures—forming a circle around me. But I was still on the raft. I could feel its uneven surface beneath my hands as I slept. Nonetheless the circle continued to move slowly around me, first clockwise, then anticlockwise. And this was an outer circle. The inner circle surrounding me was made of pale flame which almost blinded me.

—*I cannot come! I am not the one you seek! You must look elsewhere! I am needed in another place. . . .*

—*SET THE FIREDRAKE FREE!*

—*SET THE FIREDRAKE FREE!*

—*SHARADIM! SHARADIM! SET HER FREE, SHARA-DIM!*

—*No! It is I whom you must free! Please believe me, whoever you are, that I am not whom you seek! Let me go! Let me go!*

—*SHARADIM! SHARADIM! SET THE FIREDRAKE FREE!*

Their voices seemed almost as desperate as my own. But as much as I called to them they could not hear me above their own chanting. I felt kinship with them. I would have spoken to them and tried to give them the little information I possessed, but my voice continued to be unheard.

For all this, I seemed to recall an earlier conversation. Had I once been told about a dragon in a sword? Was it a conversation with the Knight in Black and Yellow? Or with Jermays the Crooked? Or had the blind captain told me that I had been elected to seek such a blade and had that been why I had decided to leave his ship? I could not remember. All those dreams ran together, just as most of my earlier incarnations were frequently indistinguishable one from the other, rising unbidden to my mind, as debris will rise suddenly to the surface of a lake and sink again as mysteriously.

Now a voice cried *ELRIC!* Now *ASQUIOL!* Another group chanted for Corum. Still others wanted Hawkmoon, Rashono, Malan'ni. I screamed for them to stop. None called for Erekosë. None called for me! Yet I knew I was all of these. All of these and many, many more.

But I was not Sharadim.

I began to run from those voices. I begged for release. All I wanted was Ermizhad. My feet sank a little into the saline crust of the ocean. I thought I would drown, after all, for I had left the raft. I was wading through water up to my thighs, holding my sword above my head. And before me, dark against the mist, was a tall ship with high castles fore and aft, with a good, thick, central mast on which was furled a heavy sail, with woodwork all minutely carved and a massive, curving prow, with large wheels on both high decks, for steering. And I cried out:

—*Captain! Captain! It is I! It is Erekosë returned! I am here to complete my task. I will do what you wish me to do!*

—*Aha, Sir Champion. I had hoped to find you here. Come aboard, come aboard and be welcome. There are no other passengers, as yet. There's much for you to do, however. . . .*

And I knew the blind captain addressed me and that I had left the world of Rowenarc, the South Ice and the Scarlet Fjord, left them behind forever. It would be assumed I had ridden out over the ocean and encountered a sea-stag or had drowned. I regretted only the character of my parting from Bladrak Morningspear, who had been a good comrade.

—*Will my voyage be a long one, Captain?* I climbed the ladder which had been lowered for me and I realised that I was clad only in a simple kilt of soft leather, in sandals and with a wide baldric across my chest. I looked into the blind eyes of the smiling captain, who reached out a muscular hand and aided me to clamber over the side. He was dressed in the same simple clothes as before, including his long calfskin seacoat.

—*Nay, Sir Champion. I think you'll find this particular part of it short enough. There is some business between Law*

*and Chaos and the ambitions of the Archduke Balarizaaf,
whoever he may be!*

—You do not know our destination? I followed him to his
own small cabin under the quarter-deck where a meal had
been laid out on his table for just the two of us. It smelled
excellent. He gestured for me to sit across from him.

He said: *I think it could be to the Maaschanheem. Do you
know that realm?*

—I do not.

*—Then you'll soon be familiar with it. But perhaps I
should not speak. I can sometimes be an erratic compass.
Still, destination's the least of our problems. Eat, for you'll
soon be disembarking again. The food will sustain you in your
task.*

He joined me at the meal. The food was wholesome and
filling, but it was the wine which did me most good. Fiery
stuff, it instilled me with purpose and energy. *—Perhaps you
can tell me something of this Maaschanheem, Captain?*

*—It is a world not far removed from the one you knew as
John Daker. Far closer, in fact, than any you've journeyed to
so far.` The people of Daker's world who understand such
things say it is one of the Realms of their Middle Marches, for
frequently their world intersects with it, though only certain
adepts can pass from one place to the other. Yet that Earth is
not truly part of the system to which Maaschanheem belongs.
There are six realms within that system and they are called by
those who inhabit them the Realms of the Wheel.*

—Six planets?

*—No, Sir Champion. Six realms. Six cosmic planes which
move around a central hub, revolving independently and
swinging upon an axis, presenting different facets to each
other at different points in their movement while, at the same
time, each also goes around a more familiar sun, such as the
sun you are used to seeing in your own sky. John Daker's sky.
For the Million Spheres are all the aspects of one planet,
which Daker called Earth, just as you are a single aspect of
an infinity of heroes. Some call this the multiverse, as you
know already. Spheres within spheres, surface sliding into
surface, realm into realm, sometimes meeting and forming
gateways one between the other. And sometimes they never
meet. Then, of course, it is more difficult to cross, unless you
sail between the realms in a ship like ours.*

—*You paint a gloomy picture, Sir Captain, for one like me who seeks an object in this multiplicity of existences.*

—*You should be joyful, Champion. Were it not for all this variety you could not live at all. If there were only one aspect of your Earth, one aspect of yourself, one aspect of Law and another of Chaos, it would have vanished almost as soon as it was created. The Million Spheres offer infinite variety and possibility.*

—*Which Law would curtail?*

—*Aye, or Chaos leave utterly unchecked. That is why you fight for the Cosmic Balance. To maintain a true equilibrium between the two so that humanity might flourish and explore all its potential. You have a great responsibility, Sir Champion, in whatever guise you take.*

—*And the guise I take next? Can it be that of a woman? Of a certain Princess Sharadim?*

The blind man shook his head.—*I do not think so. You'll discover your name soon enough. And if you are successful in this adventure you must promise to return to me when I come for you. Will you promise?*

—*Why should I?*

—*Because it is likely to be to your advantage, believe me.*

—*And if I do not return to you?*

—*I cannot say.*

—*Then I shall not promise. I am of a mind to demand more specific answers to my questions at present, Sir Captain. All I can tell you is that it is very likely I shall seek out your ship again.*

—*Seek us out? You have a better chance of finding Tanelorn unaided.* The captain seemed amused. *We are not sought. We find.* He then became honestly concerned, shaking his head from side to side. He brought the conversation to a polite but abrupt end. —*It is late now. You must sleep and restore yourself further.*

He led me to one of the large cabins at the aft of the ship. The place was fitted to take many more men than I, but I was alone in it. I picked myself a bunk, washed myself in the water provided and lay down to sleep. I reflected ironically that I could be sleeping within a dream, within a dream, within another dream. How many layers of reality did I currently perceive, let alone those of which the captain had spoken?

Again as I drifted into slumber I heard that same chanting,

those same women, and I tried again to tell them they attempted to summon the wrong person. I knew this now for certain. I had had it confirmed by the blind captain himself.

—*I am not your Princess Sharadim!*

—*SHARADIM! RELEASE THE DRAGON! SHARADIM! TAKE UP THE BLADE! SHARADIM, SHE SLEEPS IMPRISONED, WITHIN THE STEEL THAT CHAOS MADE! SHARADIM, COME TO US AT THE MASSING! PRINCESS SHARADIM, ONLY YOU CAN HOLD THE SWORD. COME TO US, PRINCESS SHARADIM! WE SHALL WAIT FOR YOU THERE!*

—*I am not Sharadim!*

But the voices were fading, their chant to be replaced by another. —*We are the tired, we are the sad, we are the unseeing. We are the Warriors on the Edge of Time.* Fleetingly I saw again the warriors who waited at the Edge. I tried to speak to them, but they had already faded. I was yelling. I was awake and the blind captain stood over me.

—*John Daker, it is time for you to leave us again.*

Outside it was as dark and misty as always. Overhead the sail was swollen like the belly of a starving child. Then, all of a sudden, it grew empty and flapped against the mast. There was a sense that the ship rode again at anchor.

The captain pointed to the rail and I followed his blind gaze, looking down to where another man stared back at me—a man who was identical to the captain, save that he could see. He signed for me to clamber down the ladder and join him in the boat. Now I wore no kilt and bore no sword. I was stark naked. —*Let me find some clothes. A weapon.*

At my side the blind captain shook his head. —*All that you need will be waiting for you, John Daker. A body, a name, a weapon... Remember one thing. It will go best for you if you return to us when we come for you.*

—*I would rather pretend, at least for now, to have some mastery over my own fate,* I told him.

And as I climbed down the ladder and entered the longboat I thought I heard the captain's gentle laughter. It did not mock me. It was not sardonic. But nonetheless it was a comment on my final statement.

The longboat took me out of mist and into a cold dawn. Grey light illuminated streaks of grey cloud. Large white birds flapped over what looked to be a vast fenland, glittering with grey water, with grey tufts of reeds. And standing nearby, on a hummock of land, I saw a figure. It was like a statue, it was so still and stiff. Yet in my heart I knew it was made neither of iron nor of stone. The figure, I knew, was made of flesh. I could guess something of its features. . . .

I could already see that it was clothed in dark, tight-fitting leather, with a heavy leather cape pushed back from its shoulders, a sturdy conical cap upon its head. There was a long-hafted pike in its hand on which it seemed to lean and it bore other weapons whose details were harder to determine.

Yet even as our longboat approached this rigid figure I saw another in the distance. This was a man who seemed inappropriately dressed for the world he traversed. He was weary and had the air of one pursued. He wore what seemed to be the remains of a twentieth century suit of clothes. He was weatherbeaten, with pale blue eyes staring from features affected by something more than just the wind and the sun. He was probably not more than thirty-five years old. His head was bare, revealing light blond hair, and he seemed tall and sturdily built, though somewhat thin. By the look of him he was close to collapse as he waved at the statue and shouted something I could not hear. By what was evidently an effort of will he continued to plod and to stumble across the chilly marshland waste.

The captain's twin gestured for me to get out of the longboat. I was a little reluctant. When I hesitated he offered me a reassuring smile. As I put one naked foot onto the yielding peat he said:

—*John Daker, let me wish you something other than luck. Let me wish instead that, when the time comes, you will be able to call upon your resources of courage and sanity when you most need them! Farewell! I trust you will wish to sail with us again. . . .*

Not one whit improved in spirit by this, I stepped with greater alacrity from the longboat. —*For my part, I hope never to see you or your ship again. . . .*

But the boat, the oarsman and the frozen figure had all vanished. I turned a stiff neck to look for them, aware that I felt suddenly warmer. I realised immediately why the figure had disappeared, at least. It was because I now inhabited and animated him. Yet still I did not know my name or what my purpose was in this new realm.

The other man was still wading towards me, still shouting for my attention. I raised my heavy pike in greeting.

I felt the sharp pang of fear. I had a premonition that in this fresh incarnation I stood to lose everything I had ever possessed; everything I had ever desired. . . .

BOOK ONE

He slept aloft on a sarsen stone
Dreaming to, dreaming fro,
And the more he dreamt was the more alone
And the future seemed behind him;

But waking stiff and scrambling down
At the first light, the cramped light,
The wood below him seemed to frown
And the past deployed before him;

For his long-lost dragon lurked ahead,
Not to be dodged and never napping,
And he knew in his bones he was all but dead,
Yet that death was half the story.

—LOUIS MACNEICE, "The Burnt Bridge"

1.

THE man called himself Ulrich von Bek and he had come out of a camp in Germany called Sachsenwald. His crime had been that he was a Christian and had spoken against the Nazis. He had been released (thanks to well-placed friends) in 1938. In 1939, when his attempt to kill Adolf Hitler had failed, he had escaped the Gestapo by entering the realm we now both occupied. I called it Maaschanheem but he called it simply the Mittelmarch. He was surprised that I should be so familiar with the world he had left behind him. "You look more like a warrior from the Nibelungenlied!" he said. "And you speak this oddly archaic German which seems to be the language hereabouts. Yet you say you were from England originally?"

I saw no point in telling him too much of my life as John Daker, nor of mentioning that I had been born into a world where Hitler was defeated. I had long since learned that such revelations frequently had disastrous consequences. He was here not merely to escape but also to find a means of destroying the monster who had taken possession of his country's soul. Anything I said might divert him from his destiny. For all I knew, von Bek might have been responsible for defeating Hitler! I explained as much of my own circumstances as I thought politic and even this was enough to leave him open-mouthed.

"The fact remains," I told him, "that neither you nor I is any better equipped to deal with this world. At least you have the advantage of knowing your own name!"

"You have no memory at all of Maaschanheem?"

"None. The only thing I seem to have is my usual facility

to speak whatever language prevails on whatever plane I find myself. You said you had a map?"

"A family heirloom which I lost in that fight I told you of, with the little armoured boys who tried to drag me off. It was not very specific. It had been drawn up, I would guess, some time in the fifteenth century. It enabled me to reach this place and I had hoped it would enable me to leave when my reasons for being here were over, but now I fear I'm stuck here for good unless I find someone to aid me in leaving."

"The place is populated, at least. You have already encountered some of the inhabitants. There may be those who can help you."

We made a peculiar pair. I was dressed in clothing which seemed appropriate for the terrain, with tall boots to my thighs, a kind of long-handled brass hook at my belt (like a heavy salmon gaff), a curved knife with a serrated blade and a pouch containing some edible dried meat, some coins, a block of ink, a writing stick and a few rather grubby pieces of rag paper. It gave me no real clue as to my trade but at least I did not have the misfortune to be dressed in a ragged grey flannel suit, a rather loud Fairisle pullover and a collarless shirt. I offered von Bek my cloak but he refused for the moment. He said he had become used to the melancholy weather of this place.

We were in a strange sort of world. The grey clouds very occasionally parted and let down some thin sunshine which illuminated shallow waters in every direction. The world seemed to consist of long strips of low-lying land divided by swamps and creeks. Hardly any tall trees grew there. Only a few shrubs offered cover to the oddly coloured waterbirds and bizarre little animals we occasionally sighted. We sat together on a mound of grass staring around us and chewing on the dried meat I had found. Von Bek (he added with some embarrassment that he was a count in Germany) was ravenous and it was obvious he could scarcely contain himself from devouring the food before he had properly chewed it. We agreed that we might as well stick together, since we were both in similar circumstances. He pointed out that his purpose here was to find a means of destroying Hitler and that this would always be paramount with him. I said that I too was determined to accomplish a particular task but that so long as my self-interest was not directly challenged I would be more than happy to count him an ally.

It was at this point that von Bek's eyes narrowed and he pointed behind me. Turning I saw in the far distance what looked like a building of some description. I was certain I had not seen it there before, but assumed it had been hidden in mist. It was too far away to make out details. "Nonetheless," I said, "we'd be well advised to head in that direction."

Count von Bek agreed enthusiastically. "Nothing ventured, nothing gained," he said. He had improved physically and mentally, thanks to food and rest, and seemed a cheerful, stoical individual. What we used to call "the best type of German" when I was at school all those aeons ago.

It was long, slow going through that marshland. We had constantly to stop, to test the ground ahead with my pike or the gaff which von Bek now held, to look for means of crossing from one clump of solid earth to the next, to rescue one another from plunging waist-deep into deceptive patches of water, from falling into the sharp fronds of reeds which were in the main the tallest plants in the region. And sometimes we could see the building ahead of us, sometimes it seemed to vanish. Sometimes too it had the appearance of a good-sized town or a large castle.

"A definitely mediaeval appearance, I think," said von Bek. "Why, I wonder, am I reminded of Nurenberg!"

"Well," I said, "let's hope the occupants are not similar to those currently in residence in your world!"

Again he showed a little surprise at my detailed knowledge of his world and I made a private resolution to make as few references as possible to Nazi Germany and the twentieth century which we had in common.

As I helped von Bek through one particularly foul section of the mire he said to me: "Is it possible we were meant to meet here? That our destinies are somehow linked?"

"Forgive me if I seem dismissive," I said, "but I have heard too much of destinies and cosmic plans. I am sick of them. All I want is to find the woman I love and remain with her where we shall be undisturbed!"

He seemed sympathetic to this. "I must admit all this talk of dooms and destinies has a somewhat Wagnerian ring to it—and reminds me a little too much of the Nazis' debasement of our myths and legends to justify their own ghastly crimes."

"I've experienced many justifications for acts of the grossest cruelty and savagery," I agreed. "And most of them have a high-sounding or sentimental character to them, whether it be one person flogging another as in de Sade or a national leader urging his people on to kill and be killed."

It seemed to me that the air was growing colder and there was a hint of rain. This time I insisted that von Bek take my cloak and he at last agreed. I leaned my pike upon a hillock, close to a bed of particularly tall reeds, and he placed his fishing gaff on the ground so that he could settle the leather garment better about his shoulders.

"Is the sky darkening?" he wondered, looking up. "I have difficulty telling time here. I've been here for two full nights but have yet to work out how long the days are."

I had a feeling that twilight was approaching and was about to suggest we have another look in my pouch to see if I possessed any means of making a fire when something struck my shoulder a heavy blow and sent me face forward onto the ground.

I was on one knee and turning, trying to reach my pike which, apart from the short knife, was my only weapon, when about a dozen weirdly armoured warriors rose up out of the reed bed and moved rapidly towards us.

One of them had cast a club and it had been that which had thrown me down. Von Bek was yelling, stooping to reach for his gaff, when a second club caught him on the side of the head.

"Stop!" I cried to the men. "Why won't you parley? We are not your enemies!"

"That's your delusion, my friend," one of them growled, while the others uttered unpleasant laughs in response.

Von Bek was rolling on his side, clutching his face. It was livid from where the club had hit him.

"Will you kill us without challenging us?" he shouted.

"We'll kill you any way we choose. Marsh vermin are fair game for anyone and you know it."

Their armour was a mixture of metal and leather plates, painted light green and grey to merge with the landscape. Even their weapons had the same colouring and they had smeared mud on their exposed skin to further disguise themselves. Their appearance was barbaric enough, but worst of all was the noxious smell which came off them—a mixture of human stink, animal ordure and the filth of the swamps. This alone might have been enough to knock a victim off his feet!

I did not know what marsh vermin were, but I knew that

we had little chance of surviving their attack as, with raised clubs and swords, they advanced, chuckling, towards us.

I tried to reach my pike but I had been knocked too far away from it. Even as I scrambled across the wet and yielding grass I knew that another club or a sword would find me before I could get to my weapon.

And von Bek was in an even worse position than I.

All I could think of to do was to shout at him.

"Run, man! Run, von Bek! There's no sense in us both dying!"

It was growing darker by the moment. There was a slight chance that my companion could escape into the night.

As for myself, I threw up my arms instinctively as a mass of weapons was lifted to despatch me.

2.

THE first blow landed on my arm and came close to breaking it. I waited for the second and the third. One was bound to make me unconscious and that was all I could hope for—a swift and painless death.

Then I heard an unfamiliar sound which, at the same time, I recognised. A sharp report swiftly followed by two more. My closest assailants had fallen, evidently stone dead. Without pausing to question my good fortune I seized first one sword and then another. They were awkward, heavy blades of the sort favoured by butchers rather than fencers, but they were all I wanted. I now had a chance at life!

I backed to where I had last seen von Bek and from the corner of my eye saw him rising from a kneeling position, a smoking automatic pistol held in both hands.

It had been a long while since I had seen or heard such a weapon. I felt a certain grim amusement when I realised that von Bek had not come completely unarmed from his realm to the Maaschanheem. He had possessed the presence of mind to bring with him something of considerable use in such a world as this!

"Give me a blade!" shouted my companion. "I've no more than two shots left and I prefer to save those."

Scarcely glancing at him I tossed him one of my swords and together we advanced on our enemies, who were already badly demoralised from the unexpected shots. Plainly they had never experienced pistol fire before.

The leader snarled and flung another club at me, but I dodged it. The rest followed suit so that we received a barrage of those crude weapons, which we either avoided or deflected.

Then we were face to face with our attackers, who seemed to have little further stomach for fighting.

I had killed two scarcely before I thought about it. I had had an eternity of such contests and knew that one must kill in them or risk losing one's own life. By the third man, I had recovered my senses enough to knock the sword from his hand. Meanwhile, von Bek, plainly an expert with the sabre, like so many of his class, had dealt with another couple until only four or five of the fellows remained.

At this the leader roared for us to stop.

"I take it back! You're no marsh vermin, after all. We were wrong to attack you without parleying. Hold your swords, gentlemen, and we'll talk. The Gods know I'm not one who refuses to admit a mistake."

Warily, we put up our blades, ready for any likely treachery from him or his men.

They made a great play, however, of sheathing their weapons and of helping their surviving comrades to their feet. The dead they automatically stripped of their purses and remaining weapons. But their leader growled at them to stop. "We'll unshell 'em when this business is dealt with to everyone's satisfaction. Look, home's close enough now."

I stared in the direction he had indicated to them and saw to my utter astonishment that the building—or town—von Bek and I had been making for was now considerably nearer. I could see the smoke from its chimneys, the flags on its turrets, lights flickering here and there.

"Now, gentlemen," says the leader. "What's to be done? You've killed a good few of ours, so I'd say we're at least even on the score, given that we attacked you but that you have no serious injuries. Also you have two of our swords, which are of fair value. Would you go on your way and no more said on the matter?"

"Is this world so lawless you can attack another human creature at will and not suffer further consequences?" von Bek asked. "If so, it's no better than the one I've recently departed!"

I saw no great point in continuing this kind of argument. I had learned that men such as these, whatever sort of world they lived in, had neither stomach for nor understanding of a fine moral point. It seemed to me that they had characterised us as some kind of outlaw and that, upon finding us to be otherwise, were showing more, if grudging, respect. My own

idea was that we should take our chances in their town and see
what service we could offer its rulers.

The substance of this I whispered to von Bek, who seemed
reluctant to let the matter go. It was obvious that he was a man
of considerable principle (it took such people to stand against
the terror instilled by Hitler) and I respected him for it. But I
begged him to judge these people later, when we knew a little
more about them. "They are fairly primitive, it seems to me.
We should not expect too much of them. Also they could be
our only means of discovering more of this world and, if necessary, escaping it."

Rather like a grumbling wolfhound which desires only to
protect its owners (or in this case an ideal), von Bek desisted.
"But I think we should keep the swords," he said.

It was growing steadily darker. Our attackers appeared to
become more nervous. "If there's more parleying to be done,"
said the leader. "Maybe you'd care to do it as our guests.
We'll offer you no more harm tonight, I promise. You have a
Boarding Promise on that."

This seemed to mean a great deal to him and I was prepared to accept his word. Thinking we hesitated he pulled off
his grey-green helmet and put this over his heart.

"Do you know, gentlemen," said he, "that I be called
Mopher Gorb, Binkeeper to Armiad-naam-Sliforg-ig-Vortan."

This giving of names also seemed to have significance.

"Who is this Armiad?" I asked, and saw a look of considerable surprise cross his ugly features.

"Why, he's Baron Captain of our home hull, which is
called *The Frowning Shield,* accountant to our anchorage, The
Clutching Hand. You have heard of these, if not of Armiad.
He succeeded Baron Captain Nedau-naam-Sliforg-ig-Vor-
tan. . . ."

With a cry, von Bek held up his hand. "Enough. All these
names give me a headache. I agree that we should accept your
hospitality and I thank you for it."

Mopher Gorb, however, made no move. He waited expec-
tantly for something. Then I realised what I must do. I removed my own conical helmet and placed it over my heart. "I
am John Daker called Erekosë, sometime Champion of King
Rigenos, late of the Frozen Keep and the Scarlet Fjord, and
this is my sword-brother Count Ulrich von Bek, late of Bek in
the principality of Saxony in the land of the Germans. . . ." I
continued a little further in this vein until he seemed satisfied

that enough names and titles had been uttered, even if he failed to understand a word of them. Plainly the offering of names and titles was a sign that you meant to keep your word.

By this time von Bek, less versed in these matters and less flexible than myself, was close to laughing, so much so that he refused to meet my eye.

While this had been going on, the "home hull" had been growing in size. It now became apparent that its monstrous bulk was on the move. It was not so much an ordinary city or castle as a lumbering ship of some kind, unbelievably big (though I suppose a deal smaller than some of our transatlantic liners) and powered by some form of engine which was responsible for the smoke I had mistaken for ordinary signs of domestic life. Yet I might have been forgiven for thinking it a mediaeval stronghold from a distance. The chimneys seemed to be positioned at random here and there. The turrets, towers, spires and crenelations had the appearance of stone, though more likely were of wood and lath, and what I had thought were flagposts were actually tall masts from which were hung yards, a certain amount of canvas, a wealth of rigging, like the work of a mad spider, and a rich variety of rather dirty banners. The smoke from the funnels was yellowish grey and occasionally bore with it a sudden gouting of hot cinders, which presumably did not much threaten the decks below but which surely must cover them with ash from top to bottom. I wondered how the people could bear to live in such filth.

As the massive, bellowing vessel made its slow progress through the shallow waters of the marsh I knew that the smell of our attackers was characteristic of their ship. Even from that distance I could smell a thousand hideous stinks, including the cloying smoke. The furnaces feeding those chimneys must burn every sort of offal and waste, I thought.

Von Bek looked at me and was for refusing Mopher Gorb's hospitality, but I knew it was too late. I wished to find out more of this world, not insult its inhabitants so thoroughly that they would feel honour-bound to hunt us down. He said something to me which I could not hear above the shouting and booming of the ship which now towered above us, framed against the grey twilight clouds.

I shook my head. He shrugged and drew a neatly folded silk handkerchief from a pocket. He placed this fastidiously to his mouth and pretended, as far as I could tell, that he had a cold.

All around the gigantic hull, which was a patchwork of metal and timber, repaired and rebuilt a hundred times over, the muddy waters of the swamp were churning and flying in every direction, covering us with spray, a few clumps of turf and not a little mud. It was almost a relief when a kind of drawbridge was lowered from close to the vessel's bottom, near its great curving back, and Mopher Gorb stepped forward to shout reassurance to someone within.

"They are not marsh vermin. They are honoured guests. I believe they are from another realm and go to the Massing. We have exchanged names. Let us embark in peace!"

Some tiny part of my brain was suddenly alerted. There was one familiar word in all this which I could not quite identify.

Mopher had referred to "the Massing." Where had I heard that expression used? In what dream? In what previous incarnation? Or had it been a premonition? For it was the doom of the Eternal Champion to remember the Future as well as the Past. Time and Consequences are not the same thing to the likes of us.

No amount of effort brought me further illumination and I deliberately dismissed the problem as we followed Mopher Gorb, Binkeeper of *The Frowning Shield* (evidently the name of this ship) into the dark, stinking bowels of his home hull.

As we walked up the gangplank the smell was so bad that I was close to vomiting, but I controlled myself. There were lights burning within the vessel. Below our feet were slats and through the gaps in these I could see farther down into the ship, where naked people ran to and fro tending to what I assumed were the rollers on which the great vessel moved. I could make out a series of catwalks, some of metal, some of wood and some which were mere ropes stretched between other gangways. I heard cries and shouts above the slow rumble of the rollers and assumed these men and women must be oiling and cleaning the machinery as it turned. Then we had advanced up another flight of wooden steps and were standing in a large hall full of weapons and armour and tended by a sweating individual of some six and a half feet tall, so fat it seemed a miracle he could move at all.

"You've exchanged names and so are welcome on board *The Frowning Shield*, gentlemen. I am called Drejit Uphi, Chief Weapon Master of our hull. I see you are bearing two of our blades and would be obliged for their return. You, too,

Mopher. And the rest. All blades called in. And all armour returned, too. What of the rest? Must we send heifers to un-shell 'em?"

Mopher seemed shamefaced. "Aye. We attacked these guests, thinking they were marsh vermin. They convinced us to the contrary. Umift, Ior, Wetch and Strote need stripping. They're all fuel now."

This reference to fuel gave me some notion of why the smoke from the chimneys was particularly hideous and why everything aboard seemed covered in a slightly sticky, oily film.

Drejit Uphi shrugged. "My congratulations, sirs. You are good fighters. Those warriors were seasoned and clever." He spoke as politely as he could but it was plain he was strongly displeased, both with Mopher and with us.

They did not think to take von Bek's pistol and so I felt a little more secure as, when Mopher had stripped off his ar-mour to reveal dirty cotton jerkin and breeks, we followed the Binkeeper into the upper levels of the city-ship.

The whole hull was crowded, very much like a mediaeval town, with people in every alley, gangway and boardwalk, carrying burdens, calling to each other, bartering, gossiping and arguing. They were all dirty, all very pale and somewhat sickly looking and, of course, no piece of clothing was free of the ash which fell everywhere and clogged throats as thor-oughly as it covered our skins. By the time we had come out into the open night air again and were crossing a long bridge over what on land I might have thought to be a market square, we were both of us wheezing and had streaming noses and eyes. Mopher recognised what was happening to us and laughed. "Sooner or later your body gets used to it," he said. "Look at me! You'd hardly guess I had half the ship's carrion in my lungs by now!"

And he laughed again.

I clung to the rail of the bridge as it swayed in the wind and shivered from the motion of the ship, which was still on the move. Overhead in the yards I saw figures constantly at work while others swarmed up and down the rigging, all illuminated by sudden gouts of fiery ash from the chimneys. The larger pieces, I now saw, were caught in wire nets surrounding the chimneys and either gathered around the sides at the top or fell back in again.

Von Bek shook his head. "Squalid and ramshackle though

the whole thing is, it's a miracle of crazed engineering. One must suppose it's steam which powers all this."

Mopher had overheard him. "The Folfeg are famous for their scientific devices," he said. "My grandfather was a Folfeg, of the Wounded Crayfish anchorage. He it was made the boilers of the great *Glowing Mosslizard,* who sought to follow Ilabarn Kreym over the Edge. The hull returned, as all of the Maaschanheem know, without a single crew member left alive—yet her engines had not failed. Those engines brought her back to the Wounded Crayfish. In the days of the Wars Between the Hulls she conquered fourteen rival anchorages, including The Torn Banner, The Drifting Fern, The Lobster Set Free, The Hunting Shark and The Broken Pike. And all those hulls besides."

Von Bek was more curious than I. "How do you name your anchorages?" he asked. "I take it these are the strips of firm land between which your hulls sail."

Again the Binkeeper was confused. "Just so, sir. The anchorages are named for what they most closely resemble upon the map. How the land is shaped, sir."

"Of course," said von Bek, replacing his handkerchief over his mouth so that his voice was muffled. "Forgive my naïveté."

"You may ask us any question here," said Mopher, trying to remove the frown from his hairy features, "for we have exchanged names and only what is Sacred may not be communicated to you."

We had come to the end of the bridge and reached a port-cullis, all iron lattice through which we could see a shadowy hall in which lanterns gleamed. At Mopher's shout the massive gate was raised and we passed through. The hall was more elaborately decorated and I realised that the portcullis was covered in fine gauze. Very little of the ash had actually permeated this part of the ship.

A trumpet sounded (a somewhat unpleasant squawk) and from a dimly lit gallery above our heads a voice cried:

"Hail to our honoured guests. Let them feast tonight with the Baron Captain and keep passage with us until the Massing."

We could see little of the speaker, but apparently he was simply a herald. Now down a wide, open staircase on the other side of the hall bustled a short, stocky individual with the face of a prize fighter and the demeanour of an aggressive man who seeks to control a normally short temper.

He held a skullcap across a chest covered in the most elaborate red, gold and blue brocade and on his thick legs were flaring breeches weighted at the bottoms with heavy balls of differently coloured felt. On his head was one of the strangest hats I had ever seen in all my rangings through the multiverse, and it was no wonder he did not choose to use this for the ritualistic covering of the heart. The hat was at least a yard high, very much like an old-fashioned stovepipe but with a narrower brim. I guessed that it was stiffened from inside, yet nonetheless it tended to lean wildly in more than one direction and it was coloured a garish mustard yellow so bright I feared it would blind me. It was all I could do to contain my laughter.

The owner of this costume plainly felt it to be not only perfectly congruous but rather impressive. As he reached the bottom of the stairs he paused, made a small gesture to acknowledge us, then turned to Mopher Gorb. "You're dismissed, Binkeeper. And as I'm sure you'll be aware you'll be responsible for stocking no more bins this tour. It was poor judgement to mistake our guests for marsh vermin. And you lost good hands as a result."

Mopher Gorb bowed low. "I accept this, Baron Captain."

The ship suddenly shuddered and seemed to moan and complain deep within itself. For a few moments we all clutched for whatever support was available until the motion calmed. Then Mopher Gorb continued. "I give over my bins to the one who would succeed me and pray that they catch good vermin for our boilers."

Although only dimly aware of what he meant I found myself again close to vomiting.

Mopher Gorb slunk back through the portcullis, which was wound down rapidly behind him, and the Baron Captain strutted towards us, his great hat nodding on his head.

"I am Armiad-naam-Sliforg-ig-Vortan, Baron Captain of this hull, accountant to The Clutching Hand. I am deeply honoured to welcome you and your friend." He was addressing me directly, a somewhat unpleasantly placatory note in his voice. I was evidently surprised by his response and he smiled. "Know you, sir, that the names you gave my Binkeeper were but a few of your titles, as I understand, for you would not demean yourself to offer your true name and rank to such as he. However, as a Baron Captain I am permitted, am I not, to address you by the name known best by us, at least, in this our Maaschanheem."

"You know my name, Baron Captain?"

"Oh, of course, Your Highness. I recognise your face from our own literature. All have read of your exploits against the Tynur raiders. Your quest for the Old Hound and her child. The mystery you solved concerning the Wild City. And many, many more. You are quite as much a hero amongst the Maaschanheemers, Your Highness, as you are amongst your own Draachenmenschers. I cannot tell you how deeply glad I am to be able to entertain you, without any wish for publicity for this hull or myself. I would like this clear that we are only too honoured to have you aboard."

I could barely control my smile at this unpleasant little man's awkward and somewhat disgusting attempts at good manners. I decided to take a haughty tone, since he expected it of me.

"Then how, sir, do you call me?"

"Oh, Your Highness!" he all but simpered. "But you are Prince Flamadin, Chosen Lord of the Valadek, and a hero throughout the Six Realms of the Wheel!"

It seemed I had learned my name at last. And once again, I feared, more was expected of me than I cared or desired.

Von Bek was sardonic. "You hid this great secret from me, also, Prince Flamadin."

I had already explained to him my circumstances. I glared at him.

"Now, good gentlemen, you must be my guests at a feast I have had prepared for you," said Baron Captain Armiad, pointing with his skullcap to the far end of the hall, one wall of which was slowly rising up to reveal a brilliantly lit room in which was set a great oaken table already covered with a variety of hideous-looking food.

Again I avoided von Bek's eye and prayed that it would be possible, somehow, to find at least a morsel or two that was to some degree palatable.

"I understand, good gentlemen," said Armiad as he led the way to our seats, "that you have chosen to take passage on our hull and that you journey to the Massing."

Since I was more than curious to discover the nature of this Massing, I nodded gravely.

"I must take it that you are upon a fresh adventure," said

Armiad. His huge hat waved dangerously as he seated himself beside me. Although not quite as obnoxious, his smell was not greatly different from his hirelings'.

I knew that this was a man who not only disdained good manners as a rule, he was scarcely familiar with the ordinary rituals involved. Moreover I believed that, if he did not think it served his purposes much better to entertain us as guests, he would as cheerfully have slit our throats and fed our corpses to his bins and boilers. I felt relieved that he had recognised me for this Prince Flamadin (or had mistaken me for him!) and resolved to accept as little of his hospitality as possible.

As we ate I asked him how long he thought it would take before we reached the Massing.

"Another two days, no more. Why, good sir, are you anxious to be there before all are assembled? If so, we can increase speed. A simple matter of mechanical adjustments and fuel consumption . . ."

I shook my head hastily. "Two days is excellent. And does everyone attend this Massing?"

"Representatives of all Six Realms, as you know, Your Highness. I cannot speak, of course, for any unusual visitors to our Massing. We have always held it, as you know, in the Maaschanheem whether the realms come together or not. Every year, since the Armistice, when the Wars Between the Hulls were finally resolved. There will be many coming, all under truce, naturally. Even marsh vermin, those horrid renegades without hull or anchorage, could come and not go to the bins. Yes, there will be a fine company, all in all, Your Highness. And I shall make sure you have a vantage place amongst the most privileged hulls. None would dare refuse you. *The Frowning Shield* is yours!"

"I am greatly obliged to you, Baron Captain."

Servants came and went, putting dreadful dishes under our noses and these, it seemed, it was politic to refuse, for none seemed angered. I noted that, like me, von Bek was making do with a salad of relatively tasty marsh plants.

Von Bek spoke for the first time. "Forgive me, Baron Captain. As His Highness has no doubt indicated I have a condition which has robbed me of much of my memory. Of what other realms than this one do you speak?"

I admired his directness and his method of explaining himself so that I should not be embarrassed.

"As His Highness knows," said Armiad with barely restrained impatience, "we are Six Realms, the Realms of the Wheel. There is Maaschanheem, which is this realm. There is Draachenheem, which is where Prince Flamadin rules (when not adventuring elsewhere!),"—a nod to me—"and Gheesten-heem, Realm of the Cannibal Ghost Women. The other three realms are Barganheem, claimed by the mysterious Ursine Princes, Fluugensheem, whose people are guarded by the Flying Island, and Rootsenheem, whose warriors have skins of glowing blood. There is also, of course, the Realm of the Centre itself, but none comes from there nor ventures there. We call it Alptroomensheem, realm of the Nightmare Marches. Are you fully reminded now, Count von Bek?"

"Thoroughly, Baron Captain. I thank you for your trouble. I have a poor memory for names at the best of times, I fear."

In some relief, or so it seemed to me, the Baron Captain turned his pugnacious, barely polite eyes towards me again. "And shall your betrothed meet us at the Massing, Your Highness? Or does the Princess Sharadim remain to guard the realm while you go adventuring?"

"Aha," I said, taken aback and unable to disguise my shock. "The Princess Sharadim. I cannot say as yet."

And somewhere, even now in the back of my mind, I could hear that desperate chanting.

SHARADIM! SHARADIM! THE FIREDRAKE MUST BE FREED!

It was at that point that I claimed weariness and begged Baron Captain Armiad that I be shown to my bed.

Once in my quarters I was joined by von Bek, whose rooms were next to mine. "You seem unwell, Herr Daker," he said. "Are you afraid you'll be found out in your deception and that the real prince will turn up at this Massing of theirs?"

"Oh," I said, "I've little doubt I'm the real prince, my friend. But what shocks me is that the only name I've heard since I arrived in this world which is in any way familiar is that of the woman to whom I am apparently betrothed!"

Von Bek said: "That at least should save you embarrassment when you eventually meet her."

"Perhaps," I said, but privately I was deeply disturbed and could not be sure why.

That night I scarcely slept at all.

I had come to fear sleep.

3.

NEXT morning, I had no difficulty arousing myself.

The night had been filled with visions and hallucinations, with the chanting women, the despairing warriors, the voices calling not only Sharadim but calling me also—calling me by a thousand different names.

When von Bek found me, as I was putting the finishing touches to my toilet, he remarked again on how ill I seemed. "Are these dreams of yours a permanent condition of the life you've described?"

"Not permanent," I told him, "but frequent."

"I do not envy you, Herr Daker."

Von Bek had been given fresh clothing. He moved awkwardly in the soft leather shirt and trousers and the thicker leather jerkin, the tall boots. "I look like some robber in a *Sturm und Drang* play," he said. He continued to be sardonically amused by his situation and I must admit I was glad of his company. It was a relief, at least, from my doom-filled premonitions and dreams.

"These clothes," he said, "are at least fairly clean! And I see they gave you hot water, too. I suppose we should count ourselves fortunate. You were so distressed last night I forgot to thank you for your help." He held out his hand. "I should like to offer you my friendship, sir."

I shook his hand warmly. "And you are assured of mine," I told him. "I'm happy to have such a comrade. I had not expected so much."

"I've read of many marvels in the Middle March," he continued, "but nothing so strange as this great lumbering ship. I was up earlier inspecting her machinery. It's crude—steam of

course—but it works to achieve its end. You've never seen so
many rods and pistons at so many stages of age! The thing
must be extremely old and there have been few improvements
made, I would guess, in a century or more. Everything is
patched and mended, lashed together, crudely welded. The
boilers and furnaces themselves are massive. And oddly efficient. It moves a tonnage at least the size of your *Queen Eliza-
beth* and is only partially supported by water. It depends, of
course, more on manpower than an ocean liner, and that could
have something to do with it. My engineering background, I
must admit, is limited to a year at technical college, which my
father insisted upon. He was a progressive type!"

"More progressive than mine," I told him. "I know nothing
at all of such things. I wish that I did. Not that I've been
called upon to use skills of that sort in the worlds I've known.
Magic is more the order of the day. Or what we of the twentieth century called magic."

"My family," he said with one of his ironical smiles, "has
some familiarity with magic, also."

Count von Bek then proceeded to tell me of his family
history, going back to the seventeenth century. His ancestors,
it seemed, had always possessed the means of travelling between different realms and to different worlds where different
rules applied. "There are supposed to be reminiscences in existence," he added, "but we've never come across them, save
for one which is very likely a partial fake!" It was because of
this that he had sought out the aid of one he called "Satan" in
his fight against Hitler. Satan had helped him discover the
means through to the Mittelmarch and had said that there was
some hope he might find there a means of defeating the Chancellor. "But whether this Satan was the same as was cast from
Heaven or whether he is a minor deity, an imprisoned godling
of some description, I have never been able to decide. Nonetheless, he helped me."

I was relieved. Von Bek would not, as I had thought he
might, require too much in the way of introduction to what
had become familiar facts of life for me. This realm, however,
seemed to possess little in the way of supernatural marvels,
save that it took the existence of other planes for granted. In
that respect, I found it reassuring.

Von Bek, who had, as he said, already partly explored the
ship, led me down the creaking wooden corridors of what I
suppose I had begun to think of as the Baron Captain's palace

and into a small chamber hung with quilted cloth whose workmanship looked too fine to be from this world. Here a wooden table had been prepared. I tasted a piece of salty, powdery cheese, a little hard bread, a sip of what I took to be very thin yoghurt, and finally settled for a relatively uncloudy mug of tepid water and the egg of some unknown bird, hard-boiled. Then I followed von Bek through another maze of swaying, narrow gangways, out across a flimsy catwalk stretching between two masts. The thing swayed so violently I grew dizzy and clung hard to the rail. Far below, the people of the ship were going about their business. I saw carts drawn by beasts similar to oxen, heard the cries of women calling from window to window in the ramshackle buildings, saw children playing in the lower rigging while dogs barked at their feet. Everywhere the smoke billowed, obscuring some scenes completely; then, occasionally, the wind would lift everything clear and it was possible to smell clean air from off the vast, glittering marsh through which *The Frowning Shield* ploughed with a kind of cumbersome dignity.

Though flat and predominantly grey-green, the Maaschanheem was magnificent in its way. The clouds hardly ever lifted for very long, yet the light which filtered through them was forever changing, revealing different aspects of the lagoons, marshes and narrow strips of land, the "anchorages" of this nomad people. Flocks of strangely beautiful birds could be seen drifting on the water, or wading through the reeds, sometimes rising in a great dark mass to wheel in the air and stream away towards the invisible horizon. Unlikely looking animals would scuttle through the grasses or raise enquiring heads from the water. The most astonishing of these for me was something resembling an otter, yet it was larger than most sea lions. It was called, we learned, nothing more fanciful than a *vaasarhund*. I was learning that the language which I spoke more fluently than von Bek was of Teutonic origin, somewhere between old German, Dutch and to a lesser degree English and Scandinavian. Now I knew what had been meant when I had been told that this world bore a closer relation to the world I had left as John Daker than most I had visited as the Eternal Champion.

The water hounds were as playful as otters and would follow the ship at a safe distance when it entered deeper water (though it never floated entirely free of the bottom), barking or leaping for scraps which the citizens of the hull would throw to them.

I quickly discovered that morning that the hull itself and the people aboard were not inherently sinister, though the present ruler and his Binkeepers were singularly unsavoury. They had learned to live with the filth from the chimneys and were used to the stink of the place, but they seemed cheerful and friendly enough, once they were assured that we meant them no harm and were not "marsh vermin"—a general term, we discovered, for any person who either had no home hull, was outlawed for a variety of crimes, or who had chosen to live on land. Some of these bands would, indeed, attack hulls when they got the chance, or kidnap individuals from the ships, but it seemed to me that not all were characteristically evil or deserved to be hunted down. We learned that it was Baron Captain Armiad who had instigated the rule that all landspeople should be killed and their corpses consigned to the bins. "As a result," one woman told us as she stood scraping a hide, "no land people will trade with *The Frowning Shield* these days. We are forced to forage what we can from the anchorage or depend on what the Binkeepers strip from the marsh vermin." She shrugged. "But that's the new way."

We found that a rapid way of moving about the city was to use the catwalks between the masts. We could thus save ourselves the time of negotiating the winding streets below and not get lost so easily. The masts had permanent ladders with a kind of cage-guard running the length of them, so there was far less chance of losing one's grip and being flung backwards to the buildings below.

We fell in with a group of young men and women who were evidently nobles of some sort, though not very well dressed and almost as grimy as the commoners. They sought us out as we crossed the roof of a turret, trying to see towards the back of the ship and its monstrous rudders, which were used for braking and for turning, frequently gouging deep into the mud. One of them was a bright-eyed young woman of about twenty, dressed in worn leather similar to von Bek's costume. She was the first to introduce herself. "I'm Bellanda-naam-Folfag-ig-Fornster," she said, placing her cap across her heart. "We wanted to congratulate you on your fight with Mopher Gorb and his collectors. They'd grown too used to chasing half-starved outcasts. We hope they'll learn a lesson from what happened yesterday, though I'm not sure his kind are capable of learning."

She introduced her two brothers and their other friends.

"You have the air of students," said von Bek. "Is there a college aboard?"

"There is," she said, "and we attend it when it is open. But since our new Baron Captain took power there's been little encouragement given to learning. He has a hearty contempt for what he says are the softer pursuits. There's been little encouragement to artists or intellectuals over the past three years, and our hull is virtually ostracised by all. Those who could leave *The Frowning Shield* who had skills or knowledge to offer other hulls have already gone. We have nothing but our youth and our eagerness to learn. There's little hope of changing berths, at least for a long time. There have been worse tyrants in the histories of the hulls, worse warmongers, worse fools, but it is not pleasant to know that you're the laughingstock of the entire realm, that no decent person from another ship would ever wish to marry you or even be seen with you. Only at the Massing do we manage to achieve some kind of communication, but that is somewhat formal and too short."

"And if you left the ship entirely . . . ?" von Bek began.

"Exactly—marsh vermin. We can only hope that the present Baron Captain falls into the rollers or otherwise meets his end as soon as possible! I'm no snob, I hope, but he is the worst sort of arrivist."

"Your titles are not inherited?" I asked.

"Usually, they are. But Armiad deposed our old Baron Captain. Armiad was Baron Captain Nedau's steward and came, as frequently happens when a childless ruler grows old, to assume many of the responsibilities of leadership. We were ready to elect a new Baron Captain, from Nedau's immediate family. He is related to my mother, for instance, on the Fornster side. Also Arbrek's uncle," she indicated a redheaded young man who was so shy his face was glowing to match his hair, "was a Lord of the Rendeps, who had an ancient Poetry Bond with the then incumbent ruler. Lastly, the Doowrehsi of the Saintly Monicans had closer blood-claims, though of late a recluse, celibate and a scholar. All of these were to be voted for. Then, in his senility (it could have been nothing else), our Baron Captain Nedau called for a Blood Challenge. Such a ceremony has not taken place since the Wars of the Hulls, all those many years ago. But it is still upon the Lawmast and had to be honoured. Why Nedau should challenge Armiad, we never discovered, but we assumed Armiad had goaded Nedau to it, perhaps through some deep insult, perhaps by threatening to reveal a secret. Whatever the cause, Armiad naturally accepted the Blood Challenge and the two of them fought across the main hanging gangway between the great middle masts. We all watched from below, according to a tradition all of us who still live had forgotten, and though the smoke from a chimney obscured the final moments of the fight, there was no question that Nedau was stabbed through the heart before he fell a hundred or more feet into the market square. And so, because an old Law was never changed, our new Baron Captain is a gross, ignorant tyrant."

Von Bek said: "I know something of such tyrants. Is it not unsafe for you to utter such sentiments aloud and in public?"

"Perhaps," she agreed, "but I know him for a coward. Moreover, he is concerned because the other Baron Captains will have little or nothing to do with him. They invite him to no celebrations. They do not make visits to our hull. We are scarcely part of the hull-gatherings anymore. All we have is the yearly Massing, when all must gather and no contention is allowed. But even here we are offered the very minimum of civility by the other hulls. This *Frowning Shield* has the reputation of being a barbaric craft, worthy of our dimmest Past, before the Wars of the Hulls even. All this did Armiad achieve through calling up that old law. Through murdering, we all think, his master. If he were to commit further crimes against his own people—try to silence the relatives, like us, of the old Baron Captain, he would have even less chance of ever being accepted into the ranks of the other noblemen. His efforts to win their approval have been as ludicrous and ill-conceived as his machinations and his plans have been crude. Every time he attempts to win them over—with gifts, with displays of courage, with examples of his firm policies, such as that with the marsh vermin—he drives them further away from him." Bellanda smiled. "It is one of our few amusements left aboard *The Frowning Shield*."

"And you have no way of deposing him?"

"No, Prince Flamadin. For only a Baron Captain can call a Blood Challenge."

"Cannot the other Baron Captains help you against him?" von Bek wished to know.

"By law they cannot. It is part of the great truce, when the Wars of the Hulls were finally ended. It is forbidden to interfere with the internal business of another city-vessel." This last offered by a stammering Arbrek. "We're proud of that law. But it is not to the advantage, presently, of *The Frowning Shield. . . .*"

"Now do you understand," said Bellanda with a small smile, "why Armiad cultivates you so? We heard he all but fawns upon you, Prince Flamadin."

"I must admit it is not the most agreeable experience I have ever had. Why does he do it, when he does not feel obliged to be civil to his own people?"

"He believes us weaker than himself. You are stronger, as he understands such things. But the real reason for his attempts to win your approval are to do with the fact, I'll swear, that he hopes to impress the other Baron Captains at the Massing. If he has the famous Prince Flamadin of the Valadek at his side when we sail in to the Massing Ground, he believes they must surely accept him as one of themselves."

Von Bek was highly amused. He exploded with laughter. "And that's the only reason?"

"The chief reason at any rate," she said, joining in his amusement. "He's a simple fellow, isn't he?"

"The simpler they are the more dangerous they can be," I said. "I wish we could be of help to you, Bellanda, in relieving you of his tyranny."

"We can only hope some accident will befall him before long," she said. She spoke openly. Plainly, they did not plan to perpetuate their hull's history of murder.

I was grateful to Bellanda for illuminating me on the matter. I decided to seek her help a little further. "I gathered from Armiad last night," I said, "that I am something of a folk hero amongst at least some of your people. He spoke of adventures which are not wholly familiar to me. Do you know what that means?"

She laughed again. "You're modest, Prince Flamadin. Or you feign modesty with great charm and skill. Surely you must know that in the Maaschanheem, as well, I think, as in other Realms of the Wheel, your adventures are told by every market tale-spinner. There are books sold throughout the Maaschanheem, not all originating from our book-manufacturing hulls, which purport to describe how you defeated this ogre or rescued that maiden. You cannot say you've never seen them!"

"Here," said one of the younger men, pushing forward and brandishing a brightly coloured book which reminded me a little of our old Victorian penny dreadfuls or dime novels. "See! I was going to ask you if you'd sign it, sir."

Von Bek said softly: "You told me you were an elected hero in your many incarnations, Herr Daker, but until now I had no proof!"

To my extreme embarrassment he took the book from the boy's hand and inspected it even as he passed it to me. Here was a rough likeness of myself, riding some sort of lizard creature, sword raised high as I did battle with what looked like a cross between the water hounds and large baboons. I had a frightened young woman on the saddle behind me and across the top of this picture, just as in a more familiar pulp magazine, was a title: *Prince Flamadin, Champion of the Six Worlds.* Inside, written in lurid prose, was a story, evidently largely fictitious, describing my courageous exploits, my noble sentiments, my extraordinary good looks and so on. I was both baffled and discommoded, yet found myself signing a name—Flamadin—with a flourish before handing the book back. The gesture had been automatic. Perhaps I was, after all, this character. Certainly my responses were familiar ones, just as I could speak the language and read it. I sighed. In all my experience I had never known anything quite so ordinary and so strange at the same time. I was some kind of hero in this world—but a hero whose exploits were thoroughly fictionalised, like those of Jesse James, Buffalo Bill or, to a lesser degree, some of the popular sports and music stars of the twentieth century!

Von Bek hit the nail on the head. "I had no idea I had been befriended by someone as famous as Old Shatterhand or Sherlock Holmes," he said.

"Is it all true," the boy wished to know. "It's hard to believe you've done so much, sir, and yet still be fairly young!"

"The truth is for you to decide," I said. "I dare say there's a fair bit of embellishment, however, in there."

"Well," said Bellanda with a broad smile, "I'm prepared to believe every word. There's idle gossip says your sister is the real power, that you do nothing but lease your name to the sensational writers. But I can now say, since I have met you, Prince Flamadin, that you are every inch a hero!"

"You're very kind," I replied with a bow. "But I'm sure my sister deserves a great deal of credit, too."

"The Princess Sharadim? She refuses to be mentioned in those pages, I hear."

"Sharadim?" Again that name! Yet only yesterday she had been described as my betrothed.

"Aye . . ." Bellanda looked puzzled. "Have I been too bold, Prince Flamadin, in my humour . . . ?"

"No, no. Is Sharadim a common name in my own land . . . ?" I was asking a stupid question. I had baffled her.

"I cannot follow you, sir. . . ."

Von Bek came to my rescue again. "I had heard that the Princess Sharadim was Prince Flamadin's bride-to-be. . . ."

"So she is, sir," said Bellanda. "And the prince's sister. That's a tradition in your realm, is it not?" She grew further confused. "If I have repeated a piece of stupid gossip or believed too much in these fictions, I really do apologise. . . ."

I recovered myself. "It is not for you to apologise." I went towards the edge of the turret and leaned against it. A wind blew up, dispelling the smoke, and freshened my lungs, my skin, helped me cool my mind. "I am fatigued. Sometimes I forget things. . . ."

"Come," said von Bek, apologising to the young people, "I will help you back to your quarters. Rest for an hour. You'll feel better for it."

I allowed him to lead me away from the thoroughly puzzled group of students.

When we returned to the cabins we found a messenger waiting patiently outside the main door. "My good gentlemen," he said, "the Baron Captain sends his respects. He lunches at your pleasure."

"Does that mean we should join him as soon as possible?" von Bek asked the man.

"If you are so disposed, sir."

We went inside and I made my way to my bedroom, sitting down heavily. "I apologise, von Bek. These revelations should not affect me so. If it had not been for those dreams— those women calling me Sharadim . . ."

"I think I can understand," he said, "but you should try to pull yourself together. We don't want these people to turn against us. Not just yet, my friend. I believe that amongst the intelligentsia they are curious as to whether you are the hero which the story books describe. I think there's a rumour that Prince Flamadin is a mere puppet. Did you sense that?"

I nodded. "Perhaps that's why they call to Sharadim."

"I'm not sure I follow you."

"A suggestion that it is she who holds the real power, that her brother—her betrothed—is a mere sham. Perhaps it suits her to have him a kind of living legend, a popular hero. Such relationships are not unheard of in our world, after all."

"I did not gather as much, but I agree it is a possibility. Does this mean, then, that you and Flamadin of the Valadek are not necessarily of the same character?"

"The shell alters, von Bek. The spirit and the character remain unchanged. It would not be the first time I have been incarnated in the body of a hero who was not all people expected him to be."

"The other thing I'd be curious about in your shoes, as it were, is how I came to be in this world in the first place. Do you think you'll discover that answer soon?"

"I can be sure of nothing, my friend." I stood up and straightened my shoulders. "Let's prepare ourselves for whatever foul experience luncheon is going to bring us."

As we left for the Baron Captain's hall, von Bek said: "I wonder if this Princess Sharadim will be at the Massing. I must say I am becoming increasingly curious to meet her. What about you?"

I managed to smile. "I am dreading such a meeting, my friend. I fear nothing but misery and terror will result from it."

Von Bek looked hard at my face. "I think I would be less impressed," he said, "if you did not have that exceptionally ghastly grin on your lips."

4.

BARON Captain Armiad had a favour to ask me. Since my discussion with the young students, I was not surprised when eventually he came round to asking me if I would do him the honour of accompanying him aboard another hull, just prior to the Massing.

"The hulls come gradually to the Massing Ground, frequently sailing side by side for many miles before the Ground itself is reached. Already the upper lookouts have sighted three other hulls. By their signals they are *The Girl in Green*, *The Certain Scalpel* and *The New Argument*, all from the farthest anchorages. They must have made good time to be so close to the Massing Ground. It is the custom for Baron Captains to make courtesy calls, one upon another, at this time. These calls are only refused in the case of sickness aboard or some other great crisis. I should like to put up flags to *The New Argument*, telling her we wish to pay her a visit. Would you and your friend be curious to see another hull?"

"We'll gladly come," said I. Not only did I wish to compare the hulls, I wanted to get some idea of how the Baron Captain's peers actually regarded him. From what he said it was not possible to refuse even him. And it was obvious to me that he wished to display his guest to the others so that the word would go round before the Massing. By this means he hoped to win their acceptance or, at the very least, increase his prestige.

He was plainly relieved. His little piglike features relaxed. He all but beamed at me. "Good. Then I'll have the signals set."

He excused himself a little while later and left us to our own devices. We continued to explore the city-ship, again

47

finding ourselves in the company of Bellanda and her friends.
These were certainly the most interesting people we had met
so far. They took us high up the masts and showed us the
smoke from the distant hulls, slowly moving together as they
sailed towards the Massing Ground.

A pale-faced boy called Jurgin had a spyglass and knew the
flags of all the ships. He called them out as he recognised
them: "There's *The Distant Bargain*, accountant to The Float-
ing Head. And that's *The Girl in Green*, accountant to The
Jagged Jug. . . ." I asked him how he could tell so much. He
handed me the glass. "It's simple, Your Highness. The flags
represent what the anchorages look like on the map and the
names describe what those representations most resemble. The
way we name configurations of stars. The names of the hulls
are ancient, in most cases, and are the names of old sailing
vessels on which our ancestors first set forth. Only gradually
did they grow into the moving cities on which we now live."

I looked through the glass and eventually made out a banner flying from the tallest mast of the nearest hull. It was a red
symbol on a black field. "I'd guess that's some sort of goblin.
A gargoyle."

Jurgin laughed. "That flag's flown for The Ugly Man anchorage and therefore the hull's *The New Argument* from the
farthest north. She's the hull you'll visit this evening, eh?"

I was impressed by his clairvoyance. "How did you know
that? Do you have spies at Court?"

He shook his head, still laughing. "It's simpler than that,
Your Highness." He pointed up higher to our own main mast,
where a good score of banners flapped in the light wind.
"That's what our signals say. And *The New Argument* has
replied with due courtesy (probably reluctant where our great
Baron Captain is concerned) that you are welcome to visit
them at the hour before twilight. Which means," he added
with a grin, "that you'll have no more than an hour of calling,
for Armiad hates crossing the marshlands at night. Perhaps he
fears the vengeance of all those so-called marsh vermin he's
fed to the bins. Doubtless *The New Argument* is equally aware
of that fact!"

A few hours later von Bek and I found ourselves accompanying the Baron Captain Armiad-naam-Sliforg-ig-Vortan, all
dressed in his most elaborate (and ludicrous) finery, into a
kind of flatboat with small wheels, which was poled by about
a dozen men (also in somewhat flamboyant livery) and which

sometimes floated, sometimes rolled, across the marshes and lagoons towards *The New Argument,* which was now quite close to our own *Frowning Shield.* Armiad could barely walk in all his quilted cloak and padded hose, his vast, nodding hat, his grotesquely stuffed doublet. I understood that he had come across the designs in an old picture book and determined that these were the proper and traditional clothes of a true Baron Captain. He had a fair amount of difficulty getting into the barge and had to hold on to his hat with both hands when the wind threatened it. Very slowly the men poled us towards the other hull, while Armiad shouted to them to take care, to be careful not to splash us, to rock the vessel as little as possible.

Dressed in plain garments and without weapons, we had no particular problems of his sort. Our main difficulty was in hiding our amusement.

The New Argument was no less battered and repaired than *The Frowning Shield,* and if anything was somewhat older, but she was altogether in better condition than our hull. The smoke from her chimneys was not the same yellowish oily stuff and the stacks were arranged so that by and large very little ash fell upon the decks themselves. The banners were rather cleaner (though it was impossible for them to be completely fresh) and the paintwork everywhere was brighter. Some care had been taken to maintain the hull and, I suspect, she had been made especially shipshape for the coming Massing. It seemed strange that Armiad could not tell that his own hull could be cleaner, that its condition reflected both his own failure of intelligence, the poor morale of his people and half a dozen other things besides.

We came up to the bulk of the other hull, moving across cold water until we reached a ramp which they lowered for us. With some effort the men poled the craft up the ramp and into the bowels of *The New Argument.* I looked about me with curiosity.

The general appearance of the hull was the same as that which we'd left, but there was an orderliness, a smartness about it which made Armiad's vessel seem like an old tramp steamer compared to a navy ship. Moreover, although the men who greeted us were dressed much as those we'd first seen, they were considerably cleaner and plainly had no taste for entertaining the likes of us. Even though von Bek and I had bathed thoroughly and insisted on fresh clothing, we had picked up a film of grime on the way from our quarters to the barge. Also, I was sure, all three of us smelled of the hull, though we had become used to it. It was also plain that the complement of *The New Argument* found Armiad's clothing as ludicrous as did we.

It became very clear to us that it was not mere snobbery which made the other Baron Captains reluctant to have Armiad aboard. However, if they were snobs, Armiad's condition and disposition would have confirmed every prejudice they had.

Although apparently unaware of the impression he gave, Armiad was evidently ill-at-ease. He blustered at the welcoming party as we were greeted formally and names were offered. He was the very essence of pomposity as he announced those he brought with him as guests of *The New Argument,* and he seemed pleased when our hosts recognised my name with evident surprise, even shock.

"Yes, indeed," he told the group, "Prince Flamadin and his companion have chosen our hull, *The Frowning Shield,* as their means of travelling to the Massing. They will make our hull their headquarters for the duration. Now, my men, lead us on to your masters. Prince Flamadin is not used to such tardiness."

Greatly embarrassed by his bad manners and attempting to show our hosts that I did not endorse his remarks, I followed the greeting party up a series of ramps which led to the outer decks. Here, too, a thriving town existed, with twisting streets, flights of stairs, taverns, food shops, even a theatre. Von Bek muttered his approval, but Armiad beside him and just behind me said in a loud whisper that he observed signs of decadence everywhere. I had known certain Englishmen who associated cleanliness with decadence and whose opinion would have been confirmed by the additional evidence of thriving arts and crafts on *The New Argument.* I, however, attempted to make conversation with the greeting party, all of whom seemed pleasant enough young men, but they were evidently reluctant to respond to me, even when I praised the appearance and beauty of their hull.

We crossed a series of catwalks to what had the appearance of a large civic building. This possessed none of the fortified appearance of Armiad's palace, and we passed through high, pointed arches directly into a kind of courtyard which was surrounded by a pleasant colonnade. From the left side of this colonnade there now emerged another group of men and women, all of them in middle to late years. They wore long robes of rich, dark colours, slouch hats, each of which bore a different-coloured plume, and gloves of brightly dyed leather. Their faces were dimly visible through fine gauze masks they wore and which they now removed, placing them over their hearts in a version of the same gesture we had first encountered from Mopher Gorb and his binmen. I was impressed by their dignified features and surprised, too, that all but two of them, a man and a woman, were brown-skinned. The party greeting us had all been white-skinned.

Their manners were perfect and their greetings elegant, but it was more than plain that they were pleased to see none of us. They clearly did not distinguish between von Bek and myself and Armiad (which, of course, I found wounding to my pride!) and although not directly rude gave the impression of Roman patricians suffering the visit of some coarse barbarian.

"Greetings to you, honoured guests from *The Frowning Shield*. We, the Council to our Baron Captain Denou Praz, Rhyme Brother to the Toirset Larens and our Snowbear Defender, welcome you in his name and beg that you join us for light refreshment at our Greeting Hall."

"Gladly, gladly," replied Armiad with an airy wave which he was forced to halt in midflight in order to restore his hat to its original position. "We are more than honoured to be your guests, Prince Flamadin and I."

Again their response to my name was not in any sense flattering. But their self-discipline was too great for them to make any open display of distaste. They bowed and led us under the archways, through doors panelled with coloured glass, into a pleasant hall lit with copper lamps, its low ceiling carved with scenes of what were evidently stylised versions of stories from their hull's distant past, largely to do with exploits on ice floes. I remembered that *The New Argument* was from the North, where evidently it sailed far closer to the pole (if indeed this realm possessed a pole as I understood it!).

Rising from a brocaded chair at the end of a table, an old man raised his gauze mask from his face and placed it to his heart. He seemed very frail and his voice was thin when he spoke. "Baron Captain Armiad, Prince Flamadin, Count Ulrich von Bek, I am Baron Captain Denou Praz. Please advance and seat yourselves by me."

"We've met before once or twice, Brother Denou Praz,"

said Armiad in a tone of blustering familiarity. "Perhaps you remember? At a Hull Conference aboard *The Leopard's Eye* and last year on *My Aunt Jeroldeen,* for our brother Grallerif 's funeral."

"I remember you well, Brother Armiad. Is your hull content?"

"Exceptionally content, thank you. And yours?"

"Thank you, we are in equilibrium, I think."

It very quickly became obvious that Denou Praz intended to keep the conversation completely formal. Armiad, however, blundered blithely on. "It is not every day we have a Chosen Prince of the Valadek in our midst."

"No, indeed," said Denou Praz unenthusiastically. "Not, of course, that the good gentleman Flamadin is any longer a Chosen Prince of his people."

This came as a shock to Armiad. I knew that Denou Praz had spoken pointedly and barely within the bounds of accepted politeness, but I did not know what the significance of his statement was. "No longer Chosen?"

"Has not the good gentleman told you?" As Denou Praz spoke the other councillors were gathering about the table and seating themselves nearby. Everyone was looking towards me. I shook my head. "I'm at a loss. Perhaps, Baron Captain Denou Praz, you could explain what you mean."

"If you do not think it inhospitable?" Denou Praz was, in turn, surprised. I guessed that he had not expected me to respond in that way. But since I was genuinely puzzled I had taken the chance to request illumination from him. "The news has been in circulation for some time. We have heard of your banishment by Sharadim, your twin, whom you refused to wed. Your giving up of all your duties. Excuse me, good gentleman, but I would not continue for fear of offending the rules of a host. . . ."

"Please do continue, Baron Captain. All this will help explain some of my own mysteries."

He grew slightly hesitant. It was as if he were no longer absolutely sure of his facts. "The story is that Princess Sharadim threatened to expose some crime of yours—or some series of deceptions—and that you tried to kill her. Even then, we heard, she was prepared to forgive you if you would agree to take your rightful place beside her as joint Overlord of the Draachenheem. You refused, saying that you wished to continue your adventurings abroad."

"I behaved like some sort of spoiled, popular idol, in other words. And thwarted in my selfish desires I tried to murder my sister?"

"It was the story we had from Draachenheem, good gentleman. A declaration, indeed, signed by Princess Sharadim herself. According to that document you are no longer a Chosen Prince, but an outlaw."

"An outlaw!" Armiad rose partially from his seat. If he had not suddenly realised where he was he might well have banged his fist on the table. "An outlaw! You told me nothing of this when you boarded my hull. You said nothing of it when you gave your name to my Binkeeper."

"The name I gave to your Binkeeper, Baron Captain Armiad, was not that of Valadek at all. It was you who first used that name."

"Aha! A cunning deception."

Denou Praz was horrified at this breach of courtesy. He raised his frail hand. "Good gentlemen!"

The councillors, too, were shocked. One of the women who had first greeted us said hastily: "We are most apologetic if we have given offence to our guests. . . ."

"Offence," said Armiad loudly, his ugly face bright red, "has been given me, but not by you, good councillors, or by you, Brother Denou Praz. My good will, my intelligence, my entire hull have all been insulted by these charlatans. They should have told me the circumstances of their being on our anchorage!"

"It was published widely," said Denou Praz. "And it does not seem to me that the good gentleman Valadek has attempted any deception. After all, he asked that I say what these reports were. If he had known them or had wished to keep them secret, why should he have done that?"

"I beg your pardon, sir," said I. "My companion and I had no wish to bring shame on your hull nor to pretend that we were anything more than what we originally said we were."

"I knew nothing of it!" bellowed Armiad.

"But the journals . . ." said one of the women gently. "Hardly one did not have long reports. . . ."

"I allow no such rubbish aboard my hull. It breeds bad morale."

Now it was obvious to me how a story known throughout the Maaschanheem had failed to reach Armiad's philistine ears.

"You are a cheat!" he flung at me. He glowered, glancing around him from beneath frowning brows as he realised he had won further disapproval from these others. He tried to keep his mouth closed.

"These good gentlemen are your guests, however," said Denou Praz, combing at his little white goatee with a delicate hand. "Until the Massing, at least, you are bound to continue extending hospitality to them."

Armiad let out a sudden breath. Again he was on his feet. "Is there no contingency in the Law? Can I not say they have given false names?"

"You named the good gentleman Flamadin?" asked an old man from the far end of the table.

"I recognised him. Is that not reasonable?"

"You did not wait for him to declare himself, but named him. That means that he has not gained the sanctuary of your hull through any deliberate deception of you. It seems that self-deception is to blame here. . . ."

"You say it's my fault."

The councillor was silent. Armiad puffed and blustered again. He glared at me. "You should have told me you were no longer a Chosen Prince, that you were a criminal, wanted in your own realm. Marsh vermin, indeed!"

"Please, good gentlemen!" Baron Captain Denou Praz raised his thin brown fingers into the air. "This is not the proper behaviour of hosts or of guests. . . ."

Armiad, desperate for his peers' approval, took a grip on himself. "You are welcome aboard my hull," he said to us, "until the Massing is complete." He turned to Denou Praz. "Forgive this breach of etiquette, Brother Denou Praz. If I had known what I brought aboard your hull, believe me I should never . . ."

The woman councillor broke in. "These apologies are neither required nor are they within our traditions of courtesy," she said. "Names have been exchanged and hospitality extended. That is all. Let us, I beg you, remember that."

The rest of the meeting was strained, to say the least. Von Bek and I looked at one another without being able to speak, while Armiad grunted and grumbled to himself, hardly responding to the formal remarks which Baron Captain Denou Praz and his Council continued to make. Armiad seemed torn. He did not wish to stay at a place where he had lost face so badly, as he saw it. And he did not want to take us back with

him. Eventually, however, as he became aware that it was
growing dark, he signed for us to rise. He bowed to Denou
Praz and made some effort to thank him for his hull's hospitality, to apologise for the tension he had brought. Von Bek and I
murmured the briefest and most formal of farewells, whereupon Baron Captain Denou Praz said graciously: "It is not for
me to judge men upon what the journals report of their deeds.
My guess is that you did not seek the earlier fame which made
you a hero in the popular imagination and that you are perhaps
made more of a villain now, simply because people saw you
for so long as the personification of all that was brave and
noble. I hope you will forgive my own breach of poor taste,
which made me judge you, good gentleman, before I knew
you or understood anything of your circumstances."

"This apology is unnecessary, Baron Captain. I am obliged
to you for your kindness and civility. If I should ever return to
your hull, I hope it will be because I have proven myself
worthy of treading the boards of *The New Argument*."

"Damned fancy words," grumbled Armiad as we were
escorted down through the swaying walkways and decks to
where our barge stood ready to take us back to *The Frowning
Shield*. "For a man who attempted to murder his own sister!
And why? Because she threatened to tell the world the truth
about him. You're a sham and a scoundrel. I tell you, you are
not welcome aboard our hull for any longer than the Massing.
After that it is up to you to take your chances in the anchorages or choose an accountant hull within twenty hours. If a
hull will accept you, which I doubt. You're as good as dead,
the pair of you."

The barge rolled down the ramp and out into the shallows.
It was close to nightfall and there was a cold wind blowing
across the lagoons, making the reeds rustle and sway. Armiad
shivered. "Faster, laggards!" He struck at the nearest man with
his fist. "You two will abuse the hospitality of no other hull.
All will know of you by tomorrow, when the Massing begins.
You can count yourselves lucky that no blood is permitted to
be spilled at the Massing. Not even that of an insect. I would
challenge you myself if I thought you worthy of it. . . ."

"A Blood Challenge, my lord baron?" asked von Bek, unable to resist this barb. He had remained amused by the entire
affair. "Would you make a Blood Challenge to Prince Flamadin? I believe that is the prerogative of a Baron Captain, is it
not?"

At this, Armiad glared at him so fiercely he might have set the marsh afire! "Watch your tongue, Count von Bek. I know not of what crimes you are guilty, but doubtless they'll come to light soon enough. You, too, shall pay the penalty of your deception!"

Von Bek murmured to me: "How true it is when they say there is nothing which makes a man more furious than the discovery that he has deceived himself!"

Armiad had overheard. "There are conditions to our custom of hospitality, Count von Bek. If you should breach those conditions, I am permitted, under the Law, to exile you or worse. If I had my way, I'd hang you both from the crosstrees. You have to thank those decadent and enfeebled old people of *The New Argument* and their kind for their intercedence. Happily, I respect the Law. As you, evidently, do not."

I ignored the rest of this. I was thinking deeply. I now had some idea of how Prince Flamadin came to be alone in the Maaschanheem. But why had he refused to marry his twin sister Sharadim, since it was plainly what had been expected of him? And had he tried to murder her? And was he really a sham, to be exposed by her when he proved himself a traitor? No wonder the world had turned against him, if it were true. People hated to worship a hero and then discover him to have ordinary human weaknesses!

Grudgingly Armiad allowed us to return with him to his palace. "But be careful," he warned. "The smallest infringement of the Law is all the excuse I need to evict you. . . ."

We went back to our quarters.

Once in my room, von Bek at last released a great belly laugh. "The poor Baron Captain thought to gain prestige from you and discovered that he'd lost further face with his peers! Oh, how he'd love to murder us. I shall sleep with my door barred tonight. I should not like to catch a chill and perish. . . ."

I was less amused, largely because I had still more mysteries to consider. I had at least thought myself fortunate in possessing power and prestige in this world. Now that had been taken from me. And if Sharadim was the true strength of the Draachenheem why had I been summoned to inhabit this body?

I had never experienced anything like it. They (whoever they were!) were calling for Sharadim, my twin, perhaps because they already knew that she was the real force, that I was merely a sham who had lent his name to a series of sensational fictions. That much was logical enough, and credible. Yet the Knight in Black and Yellow, and the blind captain, both had seemed to think it was crucial for the Eternal Champion to come to this realm.

I did my best not to think too much of all this. Instead I tried to consider our immediate problems. "Custom allows us to remain here during the Massing. Thereafter, we are outlawed—fair game for Armiad's Binkeepers. Is that the story in brief?"

"It was my understanding," von Bek agreed. "He seemed to think nobody would hire us. Not that I have much liking to work my passage on one of these hulls." Even as he spoke, the whole cabin gave a great shudder and we were almost jerked against the far wall. *The Frowning Shield* was on the move again. "What chance have we, I wonder, of moving to another realm? I understand it is not difficult in the Mittelmarch."

"Our best plan is to wait here and attend the Massing. There we shall have a good idea of who still thinks Prince Flamadin a prize, who does not believe the Sharadim story, who genuinely loathes me."

"My guess is that you'll find few friends at present. Either you—as Prince Flamadin—were responsible for those crimes or you are the victim of efficient propaganda. I know what it is to be turned into a villain overnight. Hitler and Goebbels are masters at it. But it might be possible at the Massing to prove that you are not guilty of all they say."

"Where could I begin?"

"That we shall not know until tomorrow. Meanwhile we'd be wise to remain where we are. Have you noticed that I rang for a servant as soon as we came in?"

"And none came. They're normally swift. We are to receive only the minimum of Armiad's hospitality, it seems."

Neither of us was hungry. We cleaned ourselves as best we could and retired to bed. I knew that I must rest, but the nightmares were particularly potent. The voices still called for Sharadim. I was tormented by them. And then, as I fell deeper and deeper into that particular dream, I began to see clearly the women who called my twin sister. They were tall and astonishingly beautiful, both in face and body. They had the fine, slender figures I knew so well, the tapering chins, the high cheekbones and large, slanted, almond eyes, the delicate

ears and soft hair. Their costumes were different but that was
all. The women who formed the circle beyond the pale fire,
whose voices filled the darkness, were Eldren women. They
were of the race sometimes called Vadhagh, sometimes called
Melnibonéan. A race who were close cousins to John Daker's
people. As the Eternal Champion I had belonged to both. As
Erekosë I had loved such a woman.

And then suddenly as the white flames burned lower and I
could see more beyond them I trembled in a mixture of ec-
stacy and fear, crying out, reaching out—longing to touch
that face I had recognised.

—Ermizhad! I cried. —Oh, my darling! I am here. I am
here. Pull me through the flames! I am here!

But the woman, whose arms were linked with those of her
sisters, did not hear me. She had her eyes closed. She continued to chant and sway, chant and sway. Now I doubted it was
her. Unless it was the Eldren who called one back to them,
who called Sharadim, thinking they called me. The fire grew
brighter and blinded me. I glimpsed her again. I was almost
certain it was my lost love.

I was dragged away from this dream and into another. Now
I had no idea what my name was. I saw a red sky in which
dragons wheeled. Enormous reptilian flying beasts who appeared to obey a group of people standing upon the blackened
ruins of a city. I was not one of these people, but I stood with
them. They, too, resembled the Eldren, although their costumes were far more elaborate, somehow almost dandified,
though I could not be sure how I knew so much. But these
were Eldren, I was sure, from another time and place. They
seemed distressed. There was a rapport between them and the
beasts above which was difficult for me to understand, although I had an echo of a memory (or a premonition, which is
the same thing for such as I). I tried to speak to one of my
companions, but they did not know I was amongst them. Soon
after this, I found myself falling away from them again and I
stood upon a glassy plain without horizon. The plain changed
colour from green to purple to blue and back to green, as if it
had only recently been created and had yet to stabilise. A
creature of astonishing beauty, with golden skin and the most
benign eyes I had ever looked into, was speaking to me. But
somehow I was von Bek. The words were completely meaningless to me, for again they were addressed to the wrong
individual. I tried to tell this wonderful creature the truth, but

my mouth would not move. I was a statue, made of the same glassy, shifting substance as the plain.

—*We are the lost, we are the last, we are the unkind. We are the Warriors at the Edge of Time. We are the cold, the halt, the deaf, the blind. Fate's frozen forces, veterans of the psychic wars* . . .

I saw those despairing soldiers again, ranged along the ragged edge of a great cliff above an unfathomable abyss. Did they address me, or did they speak whenever they sensed the presence of an audience of any kind?

I saw a man in black and yellow armour, riding a massive black war-charger across a stretch of wild water. I called out to him but either he did not hear me or he chose to ignore me.

Then, briefly, I saw Ermizhad's face again. I heard the chanting, much louder for a few seconds. *SHARADIM! SHARADIM! SHARADIM! AID US SHARADIM! FREE THE FIREDRAKE! RELEASE THE DRAGON, SHARADIM, AND SET US FREE!*

—*Ermizhad!*

I opened my eyes and I was shrieking her name into the face of a concerned and bewildered Ulrich von Bek.

"Wake up, man," he said. "I think we have reached the Massing Ground. Come and see."

I shook my head, still deep within my memories. of those dreams.

"Are you ill?" he wanted to know. "Shall I find some sort of doctor? If they have such people aboard this disgusting vessel."

I drew a series of deep breaths. "Forgive me. I did not wish to startle you. I had a dream."

"Of the woman you seek? The one you love?"

"Yes."

"You cried out her name. I am sorry if I have disturbed you, my friend. I'll leave you alone to recover yourself. . . ."

"No, von Bek. Please stay. Ordinary human company is what I need most at present. You've been on deck already, eh?"

"I find it difficult to sleep because of the movement of the hull. Also the smell. Perhaps I'm too fastidious, but it reminds me just a little of the concentration camp I was sent to."

I sympathised with him, understanding his distaste for Armiad's ship a little better.

Soon I was dressed and as clean as I could get, following

von Bek out to a gallery which ran almost the length of our apartments and which gave a fairly good view to starboard. Through the smoke, the tangled rigging, the banners and chimneys and turrets, I saw that we had effectively beached, prow turned inwards, upon an island of firm land which was almost circular in shape, rising to a central point on which was erected a simple stone monolith, similar to some I had seen in Cornwall as John Daker. Almost fifty hulls had already arrived and their massive bulks dwarfed the human figures who milled about them. They continued to make steam, but in a somewhat desultory fashion. Every so often one of the hulls would give off a great hiss and blow smoke high into the air so that I began to be reminded of a company of beached whales, though these were not accidentally arranged. There was an impressive precision to the almost exact distance between each hull.

The hulls formed a semi-circle about the island. On the far side was a group of slim, elegant vessels reminiscent of Greek galleys, with shipped oars and relatively little sail on their masts. They were beautifully decorated and richly dressed. I would have taken them for the formal boats of a wealthy nation. There were five of these. Next to them were six smaller vessels which in their own way were as impressive as the others. These were painted white from stern to prow. Almost everything which could be white was white. Masts, sails, oars—even the single flags flying from each ship were white, save for a small dark symbol in the left-hand corner. It seemed to be nothing more than a cross, each end of which was completed by a long barb.

Next came three much bigger, bulkier vessels, apparently also powered by steam, though they resembled nothing I had seen elsewhere. They were primarily wooden, with high castles, ports for guns or oars, a single fat funnel in the stern section and a series of perhaps eight small paddle wheels on either side. It was almost as if someone had had an idea of a steam ship and attempted to make it, irrespective of whether it worked well or not. But it was obvious that it was not my place to judge. The cumbersome ships were doubtless perfectly functional. Docked beside these were a number of dish-shaped vessels, apparently carved from a single piece of wood (though the tree would have had to have been enormous), gilded and painted and containing only a flag mast on one edge, together with rowlocks all around, through which were placed long wooden oars. These did not seem designed to negotiate anything but the shallowest of inland waters and I guessed that the people who used them had not had to cross an ocean to be here.

Lastly, between the farthest Maaschanheemer hull on our left and the dish-shaped boats, was one great vessel which looked more like a stylised Noah's Ark than anything I had ever seen afloat. It was of wood, with sharply pointed stern and prow; one single huge house on its deck, also of the simplest design, but four stories high, with windows and doors placed at regular intervals without any attempt at decoration. It was one of the most functional, unimaginative vessels you could find. The only thing which made me curious about it was that the doors seemed a good deal larger than were needed for people of average height. No flags flew from it and von Bek was as incapable as I of guessing who owned it or where it was from.

A few distant figures had landed near their ships, but we could see no details. The people from the white vessels seemed to wear clothing which covered them from head to foot and which was also of an unrelieved whiteness. The people from the very elaborate galleys next to them were, as one might have expected, brightly dressed. The people from the large, open boats had erected tall, angular tents and judging by the smoke from the largest of these were preparing themselves food. There was no sign at all of the occupants of the ark.

I wished that I might have had Jurgin's spyglass, for I was intensely curious about all the occupants of the so-called Six Realms.

We were speculating on the identities of the people and their ships when a voice from above shouted: "Enjoy your leisure, good gentlemen! You'll have little enough after the Massing. We'll see if a deposed prince of the Valadek can run as well as the average marsh mouse!"

It was Armiad, red-faced and spitting, clad in some sort of morning robe of purple and cerise, leaning over a balcony above us and to our right and clenching his fists as if he would squeeze the life from out of us if he could.

We bowed to him, wished him a pleasant morning, and went inside. We had decided to risk leaving our quarters now (though we took all we owned with us) and went to look for our young friends in the hope that they would still wish to spend time in our company.

We discovered Bellanda and her companions seated on a flat part of a high foredeck playing some kind of game with coloured counters. They were a little surprised to see us and got up reluctantly from their game.

"You've heard the news, plainly," I said to Bellanda, whose youthful, pretty face was full of honest embarrassment. "I have been turned from a hero into a villain, it seems. Would you take my word, for the time being, that I know nothing of the crimes they speak of?"

"You don't have the manner of someone who would easily quit his responsibilities or would try to murder his own sister," said Bellanda slowly. She looked up at me. "But you would not have been made into a popular hero if you did not strike people as being honest and upright. It is hard to know a heart from a handsome face, as we say on *The Frowning Shield*. Easier to read the character of an ugly one . . ." She looked away for a second, but when she looked back her eyes were candid. "For all that, Prince Flamadin—or is it ex-Prince?—I think we are agreed between us to offer you the benefit of the doubt. We have to trust ourselves. Better than believing either the fictions of the popular prints or the edicts of our good Baron Captain Armiad!" She laughed. "But why should it matter to you, hero or villain, what our opinion is? We would do you neither harm nor good. We are in a position of almost complete impotence here on *The Frowning Shield*."

"I think your friendship is what Prince Flamadin desires," said Ulrich von Bek softly, "for that offers at least a little confirmation that what we value is of positive worth. . . ."

"You're a flatterer, my lord count?" She grinned at my comrade. It was his turn to show a touch of confusion.

Peering up into the crosstrees I saw young Jurgin, using his glass to observe one of the other hulls. After a brief conversation with the others I began to climb the rigging until I was seated beside Jurgin on the yardarm. "Anything of particular interest?" I asked.

He shook his head. "I was merely envying the other hulls. We're the filthiest, most unkempt, poorest vessel of all. And we used to be proud of our appearance. What I fail to understand is why Armiad doesn't notice what has happened to our hull since he killed the old Baron Captain. What did he want from that act?"

"The miserable frequently believe that possession of power for its own sake is what has made others more content. They grab such power in many different ways and remain baffled as to why they are just as miserable as they were to begin with. Armiad killed for something he thought would bring him happiness. Now perhaps his only satisfaction is that he can make others as unhappy as himself!"

"A somewhat complicated theory, Prince Flamadin. Are we still to call you that? I saw you with Bellanda and I understood that the others have decided to remain your friends. But since you disinherited yourself . . ."

"Call me simply Flamadin, if you will. I came up here to ask if I could borrow your glass. I'm particularly curious about the big, plain ship and the people in white. Can you identify them?"

"The big ship is the only vessel of its kind possessed by the Ursine Princes. They will doubtless remain inside until the true Massing begins. The women in white are said to be cannibals. They are not like other human beings. They give birth only to girls, which means they must buy or steal men from other realms, for obvious reasons. We call them the Ghost Women. They clad themselves entirely in ivory armour, from crown to instep, and one rarely sees their faces. We are taught to be afraid of them and to stay clear of their ships. Sometimes they make forays into other realms for males. They prefer boys and young men. Of course, they'll take nothing at the Massing save what is offered them by way of trade. Your folk are prepared to deal with them and I think Armiad would do so, too, if he was prepared to risk complete ostracism from the other Baron Captains. It is several centuries since any of our hulls traded in slaves."

"So my own people, the people of the Draachenheem, buy and sell men and women."

"Did you not know this, Prince? We thought it commonly understood. Is it only at a Massing that your folk indulge in such business?"

"You will have to assume that I'm suffering from lapses of memory, Jurgin. I'm as mystified as you as to the domestic customs of the Draachenheemers."

"The worst of it," said Jurgin, handing me his glass, "is that the Ghost Women are said to be cannibals. They are like female spiders who eat the males as soon as their work is done."

"They're very elegant-looking spiders." I now had a group
of the women in focus. They were conferring amongst themselves. They seemed to be uncomfortable in their ivory armour which, at closer range, I could tell was not simply white
but had all the shades from light yellow to brown which ivory
possesses when it is used for artefacts. It was covered in fine
engraving which reminded me a little of scrimshaw work. It
was held together by bone pins and leather toggles and was
marvellously articulated so as to enclose the entire body, making the wearers rather resemble elegant insects with unusually
marked carapaces. They seemed taller than the average person
and had a graceful way of moving in the restricting armour
which I thought very attractive. It was hard to believe that
people of such beauty could be slave traders and cannibals.

Two of the women now put helmeted heads together to
speak. One of them shook her head impatiently so that the
other tried to repeat what she had said and then, in frustration,
raised her visor.

I could now see part of the woman's face.

She was both young and unusually beautiful. Her skin was
fair and her eyes large and dark. She had the long, triangular
face I associated with the Eldren and, as she turned towards
me, I almost lost my grip on the spyglass.

I was looking full into the features of one of the women
who had plagued my dreams, who had called for my sister
Sharadim, who had spoken so desperately of a dragon and a
sword. . . .

But what had shocked me so thoroughly was that I had
recognised the face.

It was the face of the woman I had searched the eons to
find again; the woman with whom I longed, night and day, to
be reunited. . . .

It was the face of my own Ermizhad!

5.

IT seemed to me that I remained staring at that face for an age. How I did not fall from the rigging I do not know. I was repeating her name over and over. Then, anxiously, I attempted to follow her with the glass as she moved. She smiled at the other woman, seemed to make some slight joke, then reached up her hand to bring her visor down again.

"No!" I did not want her to hide that exquisite face. "Ermizhad! No! It is I, Erekosë. Cannot you hear me? I have searched for you so long. . . ."

I had the impression of hands trying to help me from the rigging. I tried to fight them off, but there were too many. Slowly I was borne to the deck while enquiring mouths wished to know what was wrong. All I could do was repeat her name and struggle to get free, to follow her. "Ermizhad!"

I knew in my heart that it was not really my Eldren wife but someone closely resembling her. I knew it, yet I resisted the understanding as thoroughly as I resisted the hands of my astonished companions.

"Daker! Herr Daker! What's wrong? Is it a hallucination?" Count von Bek held my face and stared into my eyes. "You're acting like a madman!"

I drew a breath. I was panting. I was sweating. I hated them all for holding me as they did. But I forced myself to grow calm. "I have seen a woman who might be Ermizhad's sister," I told him. "The same woman I saw in my dream last night. She must be related. It cannot be her. I am not so crazed my logic is completely askew. Yet the sight strikes the same chords as if it were really Ermizhad I had seen. I must get to her, von Bek. I must question her."

Bellanda was shouting from behind me. "You cannot go. It

is the Law. All our encounters are formal. The true time of the Massing has not yet come. You must wait."

"I cannot wait," I told her simply. "I have already waited too long." But I let my body relax, felt their grasp grow limp. "No other creature could believe how many lifetimes I have spent seeking her. . . ."

They became sympathetic. I closed my eyes. Then I opened them a slit. I was looking at a likely route down to the shore.

A moment later I was up, diving for the side of the deck, vaulting the rail, flinging myself towards rigging, then sliding and clambering and dropping down, down to the lowest outside deck. While various workers yelled at me in protest, I pushed through gangs of men hauling on ropes, others who carried barrels down towards the rollers and yet others who bore large pieces of timber sheeting of the kind used for repairs. These I ignored, got to the side and found that ropes had been arranged here so that the hull might be inspected. I swung down one rope, dropped onto a swaying plank, jumped from the plank to a tall ladder and slid down this to the ground. Then I was running over the soft turf of the island towards the boats of the so-called Ghost Women.

I was halfway to their camp, passing the monolith which now raised itself above me, when the pursuers (of whom I'd not been aware) caught up with me. Suddenly I found myself struggling in a huge net while beyond the mesh I saw von Bek, Bellanda, some of the young men and a group of Binkeepers.

"Prince Flamadin!" I heard Bellanda call. "Armiad seeks any excuse to destroy you. Cross into another camp before the Massing and the penalty can be death!"

"I don't care. I must see Ermizhad. I have seen her—or someone who will know where she is. Let me go. I beg you to let me go!"

Von Bek stepped forward. "Daker! My friend! These men are commissioned to kill you if necessary. As it happens they have no stomach for Armiad's orders, but they are bound to obey him if you do not pull yourself together."

"Do you understand what I have seen, von Bek?"

"I think so. But if you wait for the Massing to begin, you can approach this woman in a civilised fashion. It is not long to wait, after all."

I nodded. I was in danger of losing my mind completely.

Also I might bring those who had befriended me into danger. I forced myself to recall the ordinary human decencies.

When next I rose up I was in full charge of my senses. I apologised to everyone. I turned and began to make my way back to our hull. From the ground the grouping of hulls was even more impressive. It was almost as if every great transatlantic liner, including the *Titanic,* congregated here, each one neatly beached with her bow pointing inland, each one bearing on its back a complete and complex mediaeval town. This sight took my attention away from Ermizhad just a little. I knew that I was experiencing something akin to a continuing hallucination, an extension of my dreams that past night. Yet there was no question the woman resembled Ermizhad, down to the shape of her mouth and the subtle colour of her eyes. So the women were Eldren. Yet they were not from the same time, probably even the same realm, as the one from which I had been wrenched against my will. I resolved to contact those women as soon as I could. They might have some clue, at least, to Ermizhad's whereabouts. And I might also discover why they called for Sharadim.

Von Bek and I had been wise to take all our possessions with us when we left our quarters. When we reached Armiad's portcullis and called to the guard to open it for us there was a silence. This was followed by some kind of mumbled reply to our third request for the gate to be opened.

"Speak up, man!" cried von Bek. "What's the trouble?"

Finally a guard on the other side yelled that the gate was stuck and that it would be a number of hours before it could be repaired.

Von Bek and I looked hard at one another and smiled. Our suspicions were confirmed. Armiad could not dismiss us from his hull but he could do everything in his power to make life uncomfortable for us.

For my part I was as glad to be out of his company and we made our way back to the part of the ship where our student friends generally congregated. Some of them were there, playing their interminable game with counters, although Bellanda, we learned, had gone to take instruction from a teacher recently dismissed from their school.

With Jurgin's willing assistance, we continued to watch the preparations being made for the Massing. Various stalls, pens, tents and other temporary buildings being erected. Each group from the Six Realms had brought goods they wished to trade, as well as livestock, publications, new tools. The people of the Draachenheem seemed a little disdainful of the others, while the Ghost Women kept themselves thoroughly apart.

One group seemed more used to trading. They had the hardy, simple look of a people who regularly carried on barter in a variety of locations. It was the way in which they set up their stalls, looked at their neighbors, chatted amongst themselves which characterised them. The only surprise, for me, was their inefficient boats. They must be more used to making overland treks for their normal trading, I thought. These were the people whose realm was called Fluugensheem, who were protected, I remembered being told, by a flying island. They seemed singularly ordinary for folk so exotically named.

There was still no sign of those who had come here in the oddly shaped ark, nor of the occupants of the three bulky paddle steamers.

"This evening," Jurgin told me, "they will begin the first ceremony, when all announce themselves and give up their names. Then you shall see them, every one, including the Ursine Princes."

He would say no more. When I asked him why the Ursine Princes were so named he would only grin at me. Since my chief interest was in those they called the Ghost Women, I was not greatly upset by his deliberate mystification.

Needless to say von Bek and I were not among those invited to attend the first ceremony, but we watched from the rigging of *The Frowning Shield* as gradually the various peoples of the Six Realms began to assemble about the monolith. This was called, I was told, the Meeting Stone and had been erected several centuries before, when these strange gatherings first began. Until then, Bellanda informed me, all the various realms had regarded the others with superstitious fear and had fought each other at random. Gradually, with familiarity, they had struck upon this means of trading and exchanging information. Every thirteen and a half months, apparently, the Six Realms intersected so that each realm could enter any one of the others. This period was brief—three days or so—but it was enough for everyone to conduct their business, so long as it was agreed that only the most formal rules were applied. No time could be wasted on anything but the agreed activities.

Now the stolid merchants of Fluugensheem came to take

their places on one side of the monolith. Next the Ghost
Women of Gheestenheem arranged themselves on the other
side of the Meeting Stone. They were followed by six Baron
Captains of the Maaschanheem, six splendid lordlings of the
Draachenheem, and, from the strange steamers, six fur-fes-
tooned and bearded Rootsenheemers, wearing great metal
gauntlets and metal masks which obscured the top halves of
their heads. But it was the last contingent which stunned me.

The Ursine Princes were precisely named. All five of the
great, handsome beasts who marched out of their ark and
down the lowered ramp to the ground were not human at all.
They were bears, bigger than grizzlies, clad in rippling silks
and fine plaids, each wearing upon his shoulders a kind of
delicate frame from which, suspended over his head, hung a
banner—doubtless the banner of his family.

Von Bek was frowning. "I am astonished. It is as if I look
at the legendary founders of Berlin! You know we have
legends. . . . My family has stories concerning intelligent
beasts. I had thought they spoke of wolves, but doubtless it is
of bears. Have you seen anything like the Ursine Princes in
your travels, Daker?"

"Nothing quite like them," I said. I was greatly impressed
by their beauty. Soon they, too, were grouped around the
Meeting Stone and we were able to catch a few words of the
ceremony. Each person gave his or her name. Each described
his or her intention in coming to the Massing. This done, one
of the Baron Captains declared: "Until the morning!"

The response came: "Until the morning!" Then they all
went their separate ways, back to their own ships.

I had strained to hear the Ghost Women announce their
names. I had heard nothing which even remotely resembled
the sound of "Ermizhad."

That night we were guests of the students, sleeping in their
already cramped quarters, constantly inhaling ash, besieged
by drafts, rolled from side to side by sudden movements of the
hull which, although it did not travel, was still subject to peculiar shudderings, like someone in a disturbed sleep. It sometimes seemed to me that *The Frowning Shield* was in tune
with my own state of mind.

Again my sleep was constantly interrupted by nightmares.
I heard the Ghost Women chanting, still, but no longer in my
dreams. I could hear them in their own camp. I longed to go
to them but the one time I rose, with the intention of going

over the side once more, both von Bek and Jurgin took hold of
me and stopped me.

"You must be patient," von Bek said. "Remember your
promise to us."

"But they are calling for Sharadim. I need to know what
they want."

"They want her, surely. Not you." Von Bek's voice was
urgent. "If you left now Armiad and his men would be bound
to see you. They'd feel within their rights to kill you. Why
risk that when tomorrow you can approach them under the
terms of the Massing?"

I agreed that I was being childish. I forced myself to lie
back down again. I lay there, looking up through the gaps in
the roof at the occasional spurt of glowing cinders, and the
grey, cold sky, trying not to think of Ermizhad or the Ghost
Women. I slept a little, but sleep only allowed the voices to
sound louder in my ears.

"I am not Sharadim!" I cried out at one point. It was dawn.
Around me the students were stirring. Bellanda made her way
through the sleeping bodies. "What is it, Flamadin?"

"I am not Sharadim!" I told her. "They want me to be my
sister. Why is that? They do not call me? They do call me—
but they call me by my sister's name. Could Sharadim and
Flamadin be the same person?"

"You are twins. But one is male, the other female. You
could not be mistaken for her. . . ." Bellanda's voice was a
little sluggish with sleep. "Forgive me. I suppose I'm talking
nonsense."

I put out my hand and touched her. I was apologetic. "No,
Bellanda, it is I who should apologise. I talk nonsense a great
deal of the time at present."

She smiled. "Then, if you think that, you cannot be completely insane. You say those women were chanting all night
for Princess Sharadim? I could not hear them so clearly. It
sounded like an incantation. Do they believe Sharadim is a
supernatural creature?"

"I cannot say. Until now I have always recognised the
name I hear in my dreams. I have responded to it. I was Urlik
Skarsol, then I was a variety of other incarnations, then Skarsol again and now Flamadin. The fact is, Bellanda, that I
know in my bones they should be calling me!"

But because this sounded like egomaniacal ravings (and
might have been) I stopped myself from continuing. I

shrugged and lay back in my blanket. "Later," I said, "I shall have the chance to answer them face to face."

And I slept a little longer, dreaming only pleasantly of my life with Ermizhad when together we had ruled the Eldren.

By the time I awoke again everyone else was already up. I stretched, stumbled to the communal washing stands and tried to clean oily grime from my body.

When I next looked towards the Massing Ground I was surprised and impressed by what I saw.

In some parts little groups of people stood engaged in eager conversations. I saw two bears squatting beside a Ghost Woman displaying charts and all three talking vigorously. Elsewhere the bright awnings of market stalls offered an illusion that this was no more than an ordinary country fair, while the lie was given by a pen in which two awkward and bad-tempered lizards, standing upright on their hind legs and resembling a kind of dinosaur, snapped with red mouths at two Maaschanheemers who were pointing out aspects of the saddles and harness on these beasts and questioning their owner, a tall Draachenheemer. Doubtless the lizards gave that folk its name.

All manner of weird livestock was on display, as well as animals more familiar to me. There were certain goods which I failed completely to identify but which plainly were in great demand.

The noise of all these exchanges was loud but reasonably good-humoured. Many people walked in small groups, neither buying nor selling, but merely enjoying the spectacle.

Over near the great ark, vessel of the Ursine Princes, a less pleasant aspect of the day could be seen. Here were frightened teenage boys, stark naked and chained together, being inspected by Ghost Women. I could scarcely believe that the Eldren had become so corrupt as to be slave owners and cannibals.

"Is that the people you claim are so much nobler than human beings?" said von Bek. He spoke sardonically, but he was plainly disgusted by the sight. "I can hardly find help for my own mission here, if such things are commonly permitted."

Bellanda joined us. "The Ursine Princes rule a realm where the humans are savages. They kill and eat one another. They buy and sell one another. So the Princes feel it is an ordinary custom amongst humans and do not see why they should not benefit. The boys are well treated—by the bears, at least."

"And what do the women do with them?"

"Breed from them," said Bellanda. She shrugged. "It's no more than a reversal of a situation commonly found amongst our people."

"Except that we don't cook and eat our wives," said von Bek.

Bellanda said nothing.

"For all that," I said, "I am now going down there. I intend to approach the Ghost Women and ask them some questions. Surely that is permitted?"

"Permitted to exchange information," said Bellanda. "But you must not interrupt a bartering while it is in progress."

We disembarked from the hull with a crowd of others who were interested in the sights and who casually inspected the variety of goods for sale. With von Bek in my wake, I headed directly for the area near the white ships where the Ghost Women had pitched their tents and enclosures of tightly woven silk. Finding no one outside, I walked to the largest of the pavilions. The opening was unguarded. I entered. I stopped in some consternation.

Von Bek behind me said: "My God! A cattle market indeed."

The place stank of human bodies. Here the slavers had brought their wares to be inspected. Some were presumably embarrassed or ashamed by their calling. Others preferred to strike their bargains in relative privacy.

In the gloom of the tent I saw at least a dozen pens, their floors covered with straw, and within the pens were boys and youths, some of whom bore the marks of every kind of cruelty, while others were proud, holding themselves with straight shoulders and glaring into the unseen faces of the Ghost Women who looked them over. Many more were simply passive, as docile as calves.

But what really shocked me was the sight of Baron Captain Armiad, evidently in the process of striking a bargain with one of the ivory-clad women. A ruffian, who was plainly not of the usual hull's complement, held a string of about six boys in a kind of continuous rope halter about their necks. Armiad was pointing out their virtues to the woman, making jokes to her which plainly she neither understood nor cared to hear. Doubtless he had discovered a more lucrative means of rid-

ding himself of some of his surplus population and, since the
other Maaschanheemers hated trading in slaves, felt himself
safe enough from scrutiny.

He looked up in the middle of a greasy grin, saw von Bek
and me looking at him, and shouted with fury. "Spies as well
as outlaws! So this is how you'd be revenged on me, when I
discovered your perfidy!"

I held up my hands, trying to show him that I was not
about to interfere with his business. But he was incensed. He
knocked the rope from the hand of his hireling. He strode
towards me. And he would not stop yelling.

"Keep the damned slaves!" he screamed at the surprised
Ghost Woman. "Have them for your supper tonight, with my
compliments. Come Rooper, we have changed our plans." He
stopped when he reached me. His face was bright red. He
glared up into my eyes. "Flamadin, you renegade. Why did
you follow me? Did you hope to blackmail me? To shame me
further in front of my fellow Baron Captains? Well, the truth
is that I was not selling those lads. I had hoped to free them."

"I am not interested in your affairs, Armiad," I said coldly.
"And I am even less interested in your lies."

"You say I lie?"

I shrugged. "I am here to speak with the Ghost Women.
Please continue with your business. Do whatever you care to
do. I have no wish to have anything further to do with you,
Baron Captain."

"You still take a haughty tone for a would-be kin-killer and
a disgraced exile." He lunged at me. I stepped back. From out
of his uncharacteristically simple tunic he drew a long knife.
Weapons were banned at the Massing, I knew. Even von Bek
had left his gun with Bellanda. I reached out to grab his wrist.
He dodged back. He stood there panting like a crazed dog. He
glared. Then he rushed me again, the knife raised.

By this time there was cacophony in the Ghost Women's
pavilion. Half a dozen age-old Laws had been broken at once.
I tried to hold him off me, calling to von Bek to help.

My friend, however, had been attacked by Armiad's ruffian and had another knife to contend with.

We found ourselves backing from the great tent, yelling for
help and at the same time trying to make Armiad and Rooper
see some kind of sense. They were serving themselves badly
and attracting unwanted attention.

Suddenly a dozen men and women had fallen on us and

dragged Armiad and his henchman back, twisting the knives from their hands.

"I was defending myself," said Armiad, "against that villain. These knives were carried by the pair of them, I swear."

I could not believe that anyone would accept his story, but now a thickset Draachenheemer spat on the ground at my feet.

"You know me, I think, Flamadin. I was one of those who chose you for our Overlord. But you spurned us. And worse. It is good for you, Flamadin, that no blood may be spilled here. If it were not for that, I'd take a knife to you myself. Traitor. Charlatan!" And he spat again.

Now virtually all of the gathered people were staring at me with loathing.

Only the women, their emotions unreadable behind their ivory masks, looked at me in a different way. I had the impression that they had suddenly recognised me and were taking a considerable interest in me.

"When the Massing's done, we'll find you soon enough, Flamadin!" said the Draachenheemer. He strode back into the tent which hid the slave pens.

Armiad was plainly almost as surprised as I had been that people were prepared to believe his story. He gathered his clothing together. He drew himself upright. He snorted and cleared his throat. "Who else would dare to break our ancient Laws?" he asked of the crowd in general.

There were some, evidently, who did not believe him. But I think they were outnumbered by those who already hated me and would believe me guilty of a dozen additional crimes, as well as those already published!

"Armiad," I said again, "I assure you I had no intention of meddling in your business. I came to visit the Ghost Women."

"Who but a slaver pays a visit to the Ghost Women?" he asked of the crowd in general.

A broad-beamed old man made his way through to us. He carried a staff almost twice his height and his ruddy features were stern with the importance of his office. "No arguments, no fights, no duels. These are our rules. Go you your ways, good gentlemen, and bring no further disgrace upon us."

The Ghost Women were no longer interested in anyone but me. They were staring hard now. I heard them talking amongst themselves. I heard the name "Flamadin" on their lips. I bowed to them. "I am here as a friend of the Eldren race."

There was no response. The women remained as impassive as their ivory masks.

"I would speak with you," I said.

Still there was no response. Two of them turned away.

Armiad was still blustering, accusing me of beginning the whole affair. The old man, who called himself the Mediator, was adamant. It did not matter who had begun the dispute. It must not continue until after the Massing. "You will both be confined to your hulls under pain of death. That is the Law."

"But I must speak with the Ghost Women," I told him. "It is what I came for. I had no intention of getting into a brawl with that braggart."

"No further insults!" insisted the Mediator. "Or there will be further punishment. Return to *The Frowning Shield*, good gentlemen. There you must remain until the Massing is done."

Von Bek murmured. "You can do nothing now in sight of all these people. You will have to wait until tonight."

Armiad was giving me an unpleasant grin. I thought he had already planned my demise. I guessed that few now would blame him if he was forced to imprison me and sentence me to death as soon as the Massing was over. His thoughts were so primitive they were not difficult to read.

Reluctantly, however, I walked back towards the hull with Armiad. We were escorted by the Mediator and a mixed group who had evidently been elected by the whole assembly to uphold the Laws. It was not easy to see how I was going to be able to leave the hull and find the Ghost Women.

I looked back over my shoulder. They were standing in a group staring after me, all other dealings forgotten. It was plain that they would be more than interested in a visit from me. But what they wanted of me and what they expected to do with me, I had no idea.

In the hull Armiad let the Mediator's people lead us to our original quarters. He was still grinning. Matters had gone well for him, after all. I did not know how von Bek and I were to be accused or what we would be accused of, but I knew that Armiad already had a plan in mind.

His final words as he stalked away to his own rooms were a gleeful: "Before long, good gentlemen, you'll be wishing that the Ghost Women had kept you and were stripping the flesh from you before your eyes and eating your parts while the rest of you slowly roasted."

Von Bek raised an eyebrow. "Anything would be more enjoyable than your own cuisine, Baron Captain."

Armiad frowned, failing to understand the reference. Then
he glared, almost on principle, and was gone.

A few moments later we heard the outer bars go down over
our doors. We could still get to our balcony, but it would be a
long and difficult climb to the decks below and no certainty
that Armiad had not deliberately left that means of escape
open to us as a way of trapping us. We would have to plan
carefully now and see if there was a less obvious means of
escape. It was likely we had a night to ourselves, but we could
not be sure.

"I doubt he's as subtle as you think," said von Bek. He was
already casting about for something he could use as a rope.

For my part I needed to think. I sat on the bed, automatically helping him knot the blankets together, while I reviewed
the events of the morning.

"The Ghost Women recognised me," I said.

Von Bek was amused. "So did most of the entire camp. But
you do not seem to have a great many here who approve of
you! Your refusal to honour tradition seems a worse crime, to
many here, than your attempt to murder your sister! I am
familiar with such logic. My own people are often guilty of
the same thing. What chance do you think you'll have, even if
you get off this hull? Most of the others, with the possible
exception of the Ursine Princes and the Ghost Women, would
be in full cry after you. Where would we escape to, my
friend?"

"I must admit I have thought of the same problem." I
smiled at him. "I had hoped you might have a solution."

"Our first task must be to review all possible escape
routes," he said. "Then we must wait until nightfall. We'll
achieve nothing before then."

"I'm afraid it was not greatly to your advantage," I said
apologetically, "throwing in with me."

He laughed. "I do not believe I had a great deal of choice,
my friend. Did you?"

Von Bek had a way of improving my spirits, for which I
was enormously grateful. Once we had debated all routes to
freedom (there were none which seemed very useful), I lay
back on my bed and tried to fathom why the Ghost Women
had looked at me with such curiosity. Had they, ironically,
mistaken me for my twin sister Sharadim?

Night fell. We had decided on our original means of escape, via the balcony and across to the nearest mast, from there down the rigging. We had no weapons of any kind, von Bek having given his pistol to Bellanda. All we could hope for would be to escape our pursuers even if we were seen.

So it was that we found ourselves in the chilly air, seeing a hundred different fires off in the distance, hearing the sounds of people of all different races and cultures, some of them not even human, as they celebrated this strange Massing. Von Bek had made a kind of grappling hook from some wooden furniture. The intention was to throw this into the nearest tangle of rigging in the hope that it would hold. He whispered to me to be ready to pay out our homemade rope as soon as he gave the word, then he swung the thing out into space. I heard it hit, hold for a moment, then fall free. Another four or five casts and it seemed to find good purchase. I let the rope run through my hands until von Bek gave the order to stop. He began to tie the remainder to the gallery rail.

"Now," he murmured, "we must trust to luck. Shall I go first?"

I shook my head. Since this affair was a result of my obsessions the least I could do would be to take the chief risk. I clambered to the other side of the balcony, took hold of our rope and began to swing, hand over hand, towards the rigging.

It was at that point that a voice from above shouted triumphantly.

"The thieves are escaping. Capture them, quickly!"

And the whole hull seemed to come alive with men exposing the beams of dark lanterns and training them on von Bek, who was half over the rail, and on me where I hung helplessly, unable to go forward or back.

"We surrender!" cried von Bek lightly, making the best of it. "We'll go back to our prison."

And Armiad's answering hiss was full of malicious glee. "Oh no you will not, good gentlemen. You must fall to the decks and break a few bones before we recapture you. . . ."

"You're a cold-hearted bastard as well as a mannerless parvenu," said von Bek. He was loosening the knot holding the rope to the rail. Did he mean to kill me? Then he had jumped, grabbed the rope just below me and yelled: "Hang on, Herr Daker!"

The rope fell free of the rail and we swung with enormous

force towards the rigging, striking tarred ropes, which cut our faces and hands, but also shaking our enemies from their posts nearby. We began to scramble down.

But the whole hull was acrawl with armed men and even as we set foot on a firm deck two or three sighted us and attacked at a run.

We rushed to the next balustrade and looked down. There was no way in which we could jump, nothing we could even hope to hang on to.

I heard a peculiar rattle from above and looking up saw to my complete astonishment a tall woman in bone-white armour sliding down a rope. She had a sword under her arm, a war-axe dangling from a thong on her wrist. She landed beside us and moved efficiently forward, slicing and carving apparently at the air.

What in fact she did to the Maaschanheemers I was never sure, but they seemed to collapse to the floor in small pieces. She signalled to us to follow her, which we did gratefully. Now we could see at least a dozen of the Ghost Women here and there on the ship—and wherever they had gone there were no Maaschanheemers to block our way.

I heard Armiad laughing. It was an unpleasant laugh. He seemed to be choking. "Farewell, you dogs. You deserve your fate. It is bound to be worse than anything I could conceive!"

The Ghost Women now formed a sort of moving barrier around us as they moved swiftly through the ship, cutting all down before them.

Within moments von Bek and I were over the side and being borne by the women through the camp towards their own tents.

I knew that they had broken all the old Laws of the Massing.

What could be so important to them that they were prepared to take such enormous risks? Without the Massing, they would be hard put to find more male slaves. Their race must surely perish!

I heard von Bek say to me in a voice which shook: "I think we are their prisoners, my friend, rather than their guests. What on earth can their purpose be with us?"

One of the women said sternly: "Be silent. Our future and our very existence is now in question. We came to find you, not to fight those others. Now we must leave at once."

"Leave?" I felt my stomach begin to turn. "Where are you taking us."

"To Gheestenheem, of course."

I heard von Bek utter one of his wild laughs. "Oh, this is too much for me. I've escaped Hitler's torturers only to be someone's Christmas goose. I trust you'll find me tasty, ladies. I am rather leaner at present than either of us would like."

They had carried us up to one of their slender white ships. Now we were bundled over the side. I could hear oars being unshipped.

"Well, von Bek," I said to my friend. "At least we are to solve the mystery of Gheestenheem at first hand!"

I sat upright in the boat. Nobody restrained me as, supporting myself on a wooden seat, I got to my feet and looked out over black water.

Behind us were the fires and huge shadows of the Massing Ground. I was certain I would never see it again.

I turned to address the woman who had led the raid on the hull. "Why did you risk all you value? You can never attend another Massing, surely? I still do not know if I should be grateful to you or not!"

She was loosening her armour, unstrapping a visor plate. "You must judge that for yourself," she said, "when we reach Gheestenheem."

She removed her visor.

She was the woman I had seen earlier. As I stared at her beautiful features I remembered a dream I had had once. I had been speaking to Ermizhad. She had told me that she could not be eternally reincarnated, as I was, but that when her spirit came to inhabit another form, the form would always be the same. And she would always love me. I saw no recognition in this face, yet tears came to my eyes as I looked at her.

I said: "Is it you, Ermizhad?"

The woman regarded me in some surprise.

"My name is Alisaard," she said. "Why are you weeping?"

BOOK TWO

Not unremembering we pass our exile from
the starry ways:
One timeless hour in time we caught from the
long night of endless days.
With solemn gaiety the stars danced far
withdrawn on elfin heights:
The lilac breathed amid the shade of green
and blue and citron lights,
But yet the close enfolding night seemed on
the phantom verge of things,
For our adoring hearts had turned within
from all their wanderings:
For beauty called to beauty, and there
thronged at the enchanter's will
The vanished hours of love that burn within
the Ever-living still.
And sweet eternal faces put the shadows of
the earth to rout,
And faint and fragile as a moth your white
hand fluttered and went out.
Oh, who am I who tower beside this goddess
of the twilight air?

"AE" (GEORGE RUSSELL), "Aphrodite"

1.

I REMEMBER little else of that voyage until dawn of the next day. There the sun was rising, red, massive and insubstantial, wavering in watery haze and giving a kind of pink and scarlet glaze to the wide waves. There was a wind up, filling the white sail, and the sun touched us also so that we were all of the same subtle colourings, blending with the ocean as we drove on towards the east.

Then, gradually, I made out something else ahead. It was as if the sea had thrown up a series of gigantic waterspouts. Then I realised this was not water, but light. Great columns of light plunging down from the sky and illuminating a vast area of water. Behind them were mist, foam and clouds. Within the area the columns surrounded, the water was calm.

Von Bek was in the prow, one hand on a taut rope, the other shielding his eyes. He was excited. There was fresh spray on his skin. He looked as if he had come alive again. I, too, was grateful for the salt water which had washed the oily grime from me.

"What a marvel of Nature!" von Bek exclaimed. "How do you think it's formed, Daker?"

I shook my head. "My assumption is always that it is magic." I began to laugh, realising the irony of my remark.

Shaking out her dark red hair, Alisaard came from below decks. "Ah," she said seriously, "you have seen the Entrance."

"Entrance?" said von Bek. "To what?"

"To Gheestenheem, of course." She plainly found his naïveté charming. I felt an uncalled for pang of jealousy. Why should this woman not favour whom she chose? She was not my Ermizhad. But it was hard to bear that in mind, the resemblance was so strong. She turned to me. "Did you sleep? Or did you weep all night, Prince Flamadin?" Her tone was one of amused sympathy. I found that I could not easily believe these women to be cruel slave owners and cannibals. Nonetheless I felt I had to bear in mind my own experience, that often the most urbane, civilised and humane cultures have at least one aspect to them which, though ordinary in their eyes, may seem perfectly hideous to others. For all that, these women had the grace I associated with my own Eldren.

"Do you call yourselves 'Ghost Women'?" I asked her, as much to have her attention as anything.

"No. But we've long since discovered that our best weapon of defence lies in turning the human's superstitions to our advantage. The armour has a number of practical functions, especially when we are in the vicinity of those smokey hulls, but it maintains a kind of mystery, frightens those who would offer us all kinds of insult and aggression."

"Then what do you call yourselves?" I asked, scarcely wanting to hear her answer.

"We are women of the Eldren race," she said.

"And your people dwell in Gheestenheem?" My heart had begun to pound.

"The women," she said. "They dwell in Gheestenheem."

"Only the women? You have no men?"

"We have men, but we are separated from them. There was an exodus. The Eldren were driven from their original realm by human barbarians who called themselves the Mabden. We sought refuge elsewhere, but in seeking it we were parted. Thus we have perpetuated ourselves for many centuries by means of human males. We, however, may only bear girl children from such a union. It maintains our blood, but it is a distasteful process to us."

"What becomes of the males when they've served your purpose?"

She laughed, flinging back her fine head so that the sun seemed to set her hair on fire. "You think we intend to fatten you for a feast, Prince Flamadin? You'll have an answer to your question when we get to Gheestenheem!"

"Why did you risk so much in order to rescue us?"

"We had not intended to rescue you at all. We did not know you were in danger. We wanted to talk to you. Then, when we saw what was happening, we decided to help you."

"So you came to capture me?"

"To talk. Would you rather we returned you to that smelly hull?"

I was quick to deny any desire to see *The Frowning Shield* ever again. "When do you intend to offer me an explanation?"

"When Gheestenheem is reached," she said. "Look!"

The columns were high overhead now, though our ship had not yet reached them. The white ship was ablaze with reflected light. At first I had thought the columns white, too, like marble, but in fact they were alive with all the colours of the rainbow.

In the stern, the helmswomen leaned hard on their steering oars, moving the ship carefully between the columns.

"It's dangerous to touch them," Alisaard explained. "They could burn a ship like ours to ashes in seconds."

Now I was half blinded by the dazzling light. I received an impression of massive waves rising up around the base of the columns, of the ship being swept upwards, of us being hurled towards first one pillar of light and then another. But our crew were experienced. Suddenly we were through and bobbing gently on calm water in total silence. I looked upwards. It was as if I was in a massive tunnel which extended into infinity. I could see no end to it. There was an atmosphere of tranquility within it, however, which dispelled any terror I might have felt on entering it.

Von Bek was astounded. "It's magnificent! Is this really magic?"

Alisaard said: "Are you as superstitious as those others, Count von Bek? I had assumed otherwise."

"This goes beyond any training I had in science," he told her with a smile. "What else could this be but magic?"

"We think of it as a perfectly natural phenomenon. It occurs whenever the dimensions of our realms intersect with another. A kind of vortex is formed. Through this, if one has sufficient reason or curiosity or courage, it is possible to reach the Realms of the Wheel. We have charts which tell us when and where such Entrances materialise, where they are likely to lead and so on. Since they are both regular and predictable, we would not define them as magical. Does the definition make sense to you?"

"Perfect sense, madam." Von Bek raised his eyebrows. "Though whether I could convince even Albert Einstein of the existence of this tunnel, I am not sure."

His references were meaningless to her, yet she smiled.

There was no doubt that Alisaard found von Bek to her liking. With me she was much warier and I could not really understand why, unless she, too, believed the stories of my crimes and betrayals. Then it came to me! These women wanted Sharadim, my twin sister. Did they plan to offer me, a wanted outlaw, in return for her help? They were used, after all, to bartering males. Was I merely an item of currency?

But all these thoughts were driven from my mind as suddenly the ship began to whirl. We were flung back against the timbers as she spun round and round, never so rapidly as to fling us out, and then gradually began to lift into the air. It seemed that the tunnel was drawing us up, sucking us through into the next dimension! The ship tilted and I was convinced we would be hurled into the water, but somehow our gravity remained the same. Now we were sailing down the tunnel just as if we followed the swift current of a river. I half expected to see banks on either side, but there was nothing save the glittering rainbow colours. Again I found myself close to weeping, but this time for the beauty and the marvellousness of it.

"It is as if the rays of more than one sun have all been focussed together," said von Bek, coming to stand beside me. "I am curious to learn more of these Six Realms."

"There are, as I understand it, dozens of differently constituted groupings in the multiverse," I told him, "just as there are different kinds of stars and planets, obeying a variety of physical laws. To most of us on Earth these are not readily perceptible, that is all. Why that is so, I do not know. Sometimes I think our world is a kind of colony for an underdeveloped or crippled race, since so many others take the multiverse for granted."

"I would happily live in a world where such sights as these are familiar," said von Bek.

The ship continued to travel rapidly along the tunnel. I noticed, however, that the helmswomen remained alert. I wondered if there was some additional danger.

Then the ship began to turn again and to shift her position so that she seemed to be diving down into pitch darkness. The crew shouted back and forth to one another, preparing for something. Alisaard told us to hang on tightly to the sides. "And pray that we are come to Gheestenheem," she said. "These tunnels are notorious for shifting their bearings and stranding travellers until the following revolution!"

The darkness was so complete I could see nothing of my

companions. I felt a peculiar surging sensation, heard the
timbers of the ship creak, and then, very slowly, light returned. We were bobbing on ordinary water again and were
still surrounded by the bright columns, though these were
fainter than when we had first seen them.

"Steer through! Steer through!" cried Alisaard.

The ship bucked and jerked forward, heading between the
columns, with the helmswomen throwing all their weight on
the oars. Another wave and we were through, rushing on the
crest, towards a distant shoreline which reminded me, for a
vague reason I could not identify, of Dover's chalky cliffs,
topped with a lush and rolling green.

Here golden sunlight fell upon blue water. Little white
clouds hung in a blue sky. I had almost forgotten the sheer
pleasure of an ordinary summer landscape. It had been, I
thought, several eternities since I had looked upon such sights.
Not since parting with Ermizhad, in fact.

"My God!" exclaimed von Bek. "It is England, surely? Or
Ireland, perhaps?"

These words were without any meaning to Alisaard. She
shook her head. "You are a compendium of alien names,
Count von Bek. You must have travelled very widely, eh?"

At this he was forced to laugh. "Now you are the unwitting
naïve, good lady. I assure you my travels have been very tame
compared to anything you take for granted!"

"I suppose the unfamiliar always seems more exotic." She
was enjoying the breeze in her hair and had stripped off more
of her ivory armour, as had the others, in order to feel the sun
on her skin. "A gloomy world, the Maaschanheem. All that
shallow water makes it so grey, I suppose." She was looking
ahead now. The cliffs were parted here and formed a great
bay. Within the curve of the bay was a quay and behind that a
town whose houses crowded upwards on three sides above the
sea.

"There's Barobanay!" Alisaard spoke in some relief. "We
can be ourselves again. I hate these charades." She rapped her
knuckle on her ivory breastplate.

There were many other sailing ships of all types moored
along Barobanay's quaysides, but there were none like ours. I
guessed that the white ships were part of the trappings which
the "Ghost Women" used to keep other folk at a distance.

The ship tacked in, oars were shipped, ropes were swung
out to young men and women who stood by to receive them

and secure them to capstans. The women were clearly of Eldren blood, while the men were equally obviously human.
Neither sex seemed to possess the demeanour of slaves. I
mentioned this to Alisaard.

"Save that they are not allowed certain specific rights," she
told me, "the men are happy enough."

"You must have some who have wanted to escape, no matter how pleasant their lives?" said von Bek reasonably.

"First they must have the knowledge of our Entrance Tunnel," said Alisaard as the boat bumped against the wall.

We watched as a gangplank was laid from ship to quay.
Then Alisaard led the way onto dry land, into a little cobbled
square and up a steep, winding lane to where, some distance
from the shore, a tall, somewhat Gothic, house stood. It had
the air of a civic building.

The sun was warm on our bodies as we took the final few
steps up to the building.

"Our Council House," said Alisaard. "A modest enough
piece of architecture, but it is the hub of our government."

"It has the unpretentious air of our old German town
halls," said von Bek with approval. "And," he added, "it is
considerably finer than anything we've experienced of late.
Just think, Daker, what one of Armiad's Binmen would make
of a Council House like this!"

I could only agree with him.

Within, the place was cool and pleasant, full of sweet-
smelling plants and flowers. The floor was marble, but fine
rugs were scattered everywhere, and there was nothing chilled
about the green obsidian of pillars and fireplaces. On the walls
were tapestries, mostly nonrepresentational, and the ceilings
were painted with elaborate and exquisite designs. There was
an air of quiet dignity about the place and I found it harder
still to believe that these Eldren women planned to use me for
barter.

An older woman, with silver hair piled above a face which,
typical of her kind, showed none of the less attractive signs of
age we humans so frequently display, emerged from a small
door on the right. "So you were persuaded to come to us,
Prince Flamadin," she said warmly. "I am most grateful."

Alisaard introduced Ulrich von Bek and explained a little
of the circumstances. The older woman wore flowing red and
gold. She welcomed us and said she was known as the An-

nouncer Elect Phalizaarn. "But of course nobody has explained to you why we were seeking you, Prince Flamadin."

"I had the impression, Lady Phalizaarn, that you wanted the help of my sister, Sharadim."

She was surprised. She signed for us to go ahead of her through a door and into a conservatory full of the most magnificent blooms. "How did you know of that?"

"I have a certain sixth sense in these matters, my lady. Is it true?"

She paused beside a purple rhododendron. I seemed to have embarrassed her. "It is true, Prince Flamadin, that some of our number have tried—through unconventional means—to summon your sister to them, or at least ask for her help. They were not forbidden to do this, but in general it was disapproved by everyone, including the Council. It seemed an unlikely and barbaric means of approaching the Princess Sharadim."

"These women do not, then, represent all the Eldren."

"Simply a faction." The Announcer Elect looked a little quizzically at Alisaard, who dropped her gaze. It was clear to me that Alisaard was, or had been, one of those women who sought my sister by "barbaric" means. Yet why had she rescued me from Armiad? Why had she sought me out at all?

I thought it fair to say something on Alisaard's behalf. "I must tell you, madam, that I am used to such incantations." I smiled at Alisaard, who had looked up in mild surprise. "It is not the first time I, myself, have been called across the barriers of the worlds. But what puzzles me is why I should have heard the call for Sharadim."

"Because Sharadim is not whom we sought," said Alisaard simply. "I must admit that until yesterday I was prepared to insist that the oracle had misled us. I was convinced that no human male could have the rapport with the Eldren which was needed if we were to proceed. Of course we knew of you both. Knew that you were twins. We assumed the oracle had spoken of Flamadin in mistake for Sharadim."

"There were many heated debates on the matter," said Lady Phalizaarn gently. "In this very hall."

"The night before last," Alisaard continued, "we attempted once more to call Sharadim. We thought that there was no better place to do this than at the Massing Ground. We were aware of the power flowing in us by then. It was stronger than ever. We lit our fire, we linked arms, we concentrated. And for the first time we had a vision of the one we sought. You can imagine, I am sure, whose face it was."

"You saw Prince Flamadin," said Lady Phalizaarn, evidently trying to disguise the satisfaction in her voice. "And then you saw him in the flesh. . . ."

"We remembered that you had commissioned Helmswoman Danifel to approach Prince Flamadin if he was at the Massing. We went to her and admitted that we had been mistaken. Together, as you can see, we went to visit Prince Flamadin. We were forced to go secretly because of the nature of the Massing and the character of the brute who is Baron Captain of the particular hull where Prince Flamadin and his friend were guesting. To our complete astonishment we arrived to discover that Prince Flamadin and Count von Bek were in the process of attempting escape. So we helped them."

"Alisaard," said Lady Phalizaarn softly, "did you think to invite Prince Flamadin to Gheestenheem? Did you give him the choice?"

"In the heat of the moment, I forgot, Lady Announcer Elect. I apologise to all. We thought we might be pursued."

"Pursued?"

"By the bloodthirsty enemies from whom Alisaard saved us," said von Bek quickly. "We owe you our lives, madam. And, of course, we should have accepted your invitation had it been extended."

Lady Phalizaarn smiled. She, too, was evidently charmed by my friend's old German courtesy. "You are a natural courtier, Count von Bek. Or perhaps a natural diplomat is a better choice."

"I would prefer the latter, my lady. We von Beks have never been overfond of monarchs. We even had one member of our family serve in the revolutionary French National Assembly!"

Again the words were meaningless. I could understand them but they were like a foreign language to the others. One day von Bek would learn, as I had learned, to carry on a conversation without reference to the existence of our Earth or its twentieth century.

"I still have no notion of what you want from me," I said politely. "I assure you, my lady, I am here most willingly, given that all others appear to be against me, but I will be frank with you. I have no real memory of being Prince Flamadin. It is only a matter of a few days since I inhabited his body. If Flamadin has knowledge that you need, then I am afraid I'm likely to disappoint you."

At this the Lady Phalizaarn beamed. "I am most relieved to hear that, Prince Flamadin. The accuracy of our 'oracle,' as Alisaard insists it be called, is further confirmed. But you shall hear all when the full Council convenes. It is not for me to speak until I am given instructions to do so."

"When does the Council convene?" I asked her.

"This afternoon. You are at liberty to explore our capital if you will, or to rest. We have chambers here which have been set aside for you. Anything you need in the way of food or clothing, please let us know. I am exceedingly pleased to see you here, Prince Flamadin. I had thought it almost too late!"

On this mysterious note we were dismissed. Alisaard showed us to the rooms which had been prepared for me. "You were not expected, Count von Bek, so it will take a little while to make ready your accommodations. Meanwhile there are two adjoining chambers, a couch large enough for even a man of your size."

I opened a door. "This is what I'm interested in," I said delightedly. It was a huge bathtub, rather reminiscent of the old Victorian kind, though it had no obvious plumbing attached to it. "Is there perhaps some way we can obtain hot water?"

She indicated something I had mistaken for a bell-rope hanging to one side of the tub. "Two tugs for hot," she said. "One for cold."

"How does the water reach the bath?" I wanted to know.

"Through the pipes." She pointed at a peculiar kind of plug near one end of the bath. "And up through there." She spoke to me as if I were some kind of barbarian being introduced to civilised amenities.

"Thanks," I said. "No doubt I'll soon learn how to work it."

The soap she handed me was a kind of abrasive powder, but it softened well enough in the water. My first blast of hot water almost killed me. I learned that she had forgotten to tell me that it was three tugs for a mixture. . . .

Von Bek had been talking to Alisaard while I bathed. She had left by the time it was his turn to use the tub. He had the benefit of my new wisdom where the water was concerned. As he soaped himself he rattled on cheerfully. "I asked Alisaard if her race and humans can normally interbreed. She thinks it unlikely, though she can only speak from her own experience. Apparently this method they have isn't all that simple. She said that 'a great deal of alchemy' is involved. Presumably they make use of chemicals, other agents. Some form of artificial insemination, perhaps?"

"I've no understanding of such matters, unfortunately. But the Eldren were always clever with medicines. What puzzles me is how the women came to be separated from the men and if these people are the descendants of those I knew or are they, perhaps, their ancestors?"

"Now I find you hard to follow," von Bek admitted. He began to whistle some popular jazz song of his time (which was a few years before my own, as John Daker).

The rooms were furnished in much the same style as the rest of the Council House, with large pieces of carved hardwood furniture, tapestries, rugs. There was a great quilt flung across my bed which, by the workmanship, must have taken fifty years to make. More flowers filled the place and the windows looked down into a courtyard with a gravel walk, a green lawn and a fountain at the centre. The mood of tranquility was thus maintained. I felt I could cheerfully settle amongst these people. But I knew it was not to be. Again came a pang of almost physical agony. How I longed for my Ermizhad!

"Well," said von Bek later as he towelled himself, "if I did not have urgent business with the Chancellor of Germany, I would find this Barobanay an excellent place for a holiday. Eh?"

"Oh, indeed," I replied absently. "However, von Bek, I think we'll be busy soon enough. These women seem to think it a matter of urgency, our coming here. I still find it hard to understand, however, why Sharadim was called and not me. Did Alisaard offer you any further explanation?"

"A matter of principle, I think. She did not wish to believe that a human male could be of any use to them at all! I suppose that's based on her experience. And then, of course, there was the business of the murder, or the probable murder."

"What? The murder they say I attempted? Do they think now that I actually succeeded in killing my twin sister?"

"Oh, no, of course not." Von Bek rubbed at his hair. "Weren't you present when Alisaard mentioned that? Apparently Prince Flamadin is almost certainly dead. The story put out from the Draachenheem is a reverse of the truth. Flamadin seems to have been murdered on the direct instructions of Sharadim!" Von Bek found this amusing. He laughed and slapped me on the shoulder. "It's a turning world, eh, my friend?"

"Oh, aye," I agreed as my heart began to pound again. "A turning world indeed. . . ."

2.

"WE should first tell you," said the Lady Phalizaarn, rising from amongst the seated women, "that we are in grave danger. For many years we have been attempting to seek out our own folk, the Eldren, and rejoin them. Our method of maintaining our race is, as I am sure you can imagine, distasteful to us. Admittedly our purchased males are well treated and given almost all the privileges of the community, but it is an unnatural business. We would rather procreate through union with those who had a choice in the matter. Of late we have embarked upon a series of experiments, designed to locate our people. Once we have located them, we believe we will find a means of rejoining them. However, we have made a number of unlikely discoveries. What is more, we have been forced to compromise and, finally, some of our number have taken a wrong direction. Now, for instance, your sister Sharadim knows a great deal more than we would have revealed, had we understood her character."

"You must illuminate me as to that," I said. Von Bek and I were seated, cross-legged, in front of the women, most of whom were of a similar age to Phalizaarn, though some were younger and one or two were older. Alisaard was not present. Neither were any of the others who had rescued us from Armiad's hull.

"We shall," the Announcer Elect promised. But first she intended to describe briefly her people's history; how as a handful of survivors they had been driven farther and farther into hiding by the numerous forces of barbarian humans. Eventually they decided to escape into another realm where the Mabden could not follow. There they would begin life again. They had explored certain other worlds. Yet they wished to find one where humans had not settled. They devised a means of reaching such a world. Earlier explorers had brought back with them two great beasts whose own curiosity had led them to follow the explorers. It was already known that these beasts had some means of returning to their own world—of creating a gateway through the barriers. The Eldren planned to release the beasts and then follow them through. The creatures were not antagonistic towards the Eldren. Indeed, there was a kind of mutual respect existing between them which was hard to define. The Eldren felt they would have no difficulty living in the same world as the beasts. So it was that one party followed the male beast through the gateway it made. The second party, of women, were to follow a little later, when the men had made certain it was safe. So they waited and, hearing of no danger, they sent the female beast through. However, they were following in her wake when suddenly she vanished. There was a sense of a struggle, a sense that the beast was trying to warn them of something, and then they found themselves in this world. It soon became clear that the Eldren men were not here. Somehow the beast which was to lead them to safety had either lost her way or been abducted.

"Somehow the gateway had shifted. The multiverse intersects like cogs in a clock. One tick of the pendulum and you find yourself in an entirely different world, perhaps many times removed from the one you sought. That is what happened to us. Until recently we never knew what had become of the beast who was supposed to lead us through. In order to survive we were forced to use our knowledge of alchemy so that we could breed with males who had wandered here from human dimensions. At length we discovered we could buy such males from various traders in the Six Realms. Only at the Massing do all the realms intersect. At times, however, it is not difficult to visit perhaps one or two others whenever we choose. Meanwhile we have devoted ourselves to a study of what constitutes the multiverse, of how and when certain realms cross each other's orbits. By means of our psychics, the same as those who contacted you, mistaking you for Sharadim, we have communicated very occasionally with our menfolk. It became clear that the only way to reach them was to find the beast which had intended to lead us through in the first place. Then a further disturbing problem came a few years ago. We discovered that the herbs we use in our alchemy to perpetuate ourselves were becoming rapidly scarcer. We do not know why. Perhaps a simple climatic change. We can grow plants very similar to them in our special gardens, but they do not have exactly the same properties. Therefore we have very few sources of supply left to us. We have almost no children. Soon we shall have none. Our race will perish. That is why our quest for help grew more urgent. Then came one to us who said that he knew where our beast could be found, but that only one creature in the whole universe was both fitted and fated to find her. He called this creature the Champion Eternal."

Another woman spoke from where she sat on the floor. "We did not know if it was male or female, human or Eldren. All we had was the Actorios. The stone."

"He told us we should find you by means of that stone," said Phalizaarn. From a pouch at her hip she drew it out, displaying it on the flat of her hand. "Do you recognise it?"

Something within me knew the stone, but no memory would come to me. I made a helpless gesture.

Phalizaarn smiled. "Well, it appears to know you."

The jewel, all smokey darkness, full of restless, nameless colours, seemed almost to writhe in her palm. I felt a great need for it. I wanted to reach out and take it from her but I restrained myself.

"It is yours," said a voice from behind me. Both von Bek and I turned. "It is yours. Take it."

No longer in black and yellow, but in enfolding purple, the black giant Sepiriz looked down at me with a kind of amused compassion. "It will always be yours, wherever you see it," he continued. "Take it. It will help you. It has served its turn here."

The stone was warm. It felt like flesh. I shivered as I held it in my fist. It seemed to send a thrill of energy through me. "Thank you." I bowed to the Announcer Elect and to Sepiriz. I placed the stone in my belt purse. "Are you their oracle, Sepiriz? Do you bind them about with mysteries as you do me?" I could only speak with affection.

"That Actorios will one day sit in the Ring of Kings," said the giant. "And you shall wear it. But for now there is a more immediate game to play. A game, John Daker, which could earn you at least part of what you most desire."

"Not a very specific promise, Sir Knight."

He accepted this. "It is only in certain matters that I dare be specific. The Balance is singularly fine just now. I would not tip it. Not at this stage. Did my Lady Phalizaarn describe their lost she-beast?"

"I can remember the incantation very clearly," I told him. "It was a firedrake. A dragon. And it is held prisoner, I take it. They seemed to want me—or Sharadim—to release the creature. Is it trapped in some world which only I can visit?"

"Not exactly. It is trapped in an object which only you are entitled to handle. . . ."

"That damned sword!" I stepped backwards, violently shaking my head. "No! No, Sepiriz, I will not bear it again! The Black Sword is evil. I do not like what it makes of me."

"This is not the same sword," he said calmly. "Not in this aspect. Some say the twin blades are the same. Some say they have a thousand forms. I do not believe that. The blade was forged to accept what we would call a soul—a spirit, a demon, whatever you like—and it was by unhappy coincidence that the she-dragon became trapped there, filling the vacuum, as it were, within the blade."

"Those dragons are surely monstrous. And the blade—"

"Simple matters of space and time are scarcely relevant to the forces of which I speak and of which you must know something," said Sepiriz, raising his hand. "The sword had but lately been forged. Those who had made it had not quite finished their work. The blade was, as it were, cooling. There was a massive movement throughout the multiverse. Chaos and Law even then fought for possession of the blade and its twin. Dimensions were warped, whole histories were altered in a space of moments, the very laws of nature were changed. It was then that the dragon—the second dragon—attempted to fling herself through the barriers between the realms and burst through to her own world. It was an unaccounted for coincidence. As a result of those huge disturbances, she became trapped within the sword. No incantation could release her. The blade had been designed to be inhabited. Once possessed it could only release that which dwelt within it under certain portentous circumstances. The blade was designed to be wielded by you, Champion. And only you can release the dragon. It is a very powerful object, even without you. In the wrong hands it could damage everything we value, perhaps destroy it forever. Sharadim herself believes in the sword. She heard the voices calling her. She asked certain questions and received certain answers. Now she would own that thing of power. Her plan is to rule all Six Realms of the Wheel. With the Dragon Sword she could easily have her way."

"How did you learn that she was evil?" I asked Sepiriz. "Amongst the folk of the Six Realms—or at least most of them—she is regarded as a paragon of virtue."

The Lady Phalizaarn spoke. "That is very simple. We made the discovery recently, after a trading expedition to the Draachenheem. We bought a batch of males, all of whom had been employed at Court. Many were nobles. To silence them, Sharadim had sold them to us. It frequently happens—since we are supposed to eat the men we buy—that we become a convenient means of disposing of unwanted people. Some of those men had actually witnessed Sharadim poisoning the wine she offered you on your return from whatever quest it was you had been on. She bribed some of the courtiers to side with her. The others she had arrested as conspirators, henchmen of Flamadin, and sold to us."

"Why did she want to poison me?"

"You had refused to marry her. You hated her cunning and her cruelty. For years she had encouraged you to go adventuring abroad. This suited your temperament and she assured you that the kingdom was safe with her. Gradually, however, you began to realise what she was doing, how she was corrupting everything you believed noble in order to prepare the Draachenheem for war against the other realms. You swore you would tell all at the next Massing. Meanwhile she understood something of what the Eldren women had said. She realised that it was you they really sought. She had several motives for murdering you."

"Then how am I here now?"

"That is puzzling, I agree. Several of the men here saw you in death. Stiff and bloodless, they said."

"And what became of my corpse?"

"Some believe Sharadim still has possession of it. That she practises the most disgusting rites upon it . . ."

"That leaves the question 'Who am I?'" I said. "If I am not Prince Flamadin."

"But you are Prince Flamadin," said Sepiriz. "All agree on that matter. What they cannot decide is how you escaped. . . ."

"So you wish me to seek out this sword? And what then?"

"It must be brought to the Massing Ground. The Eldren women will know what to do."

"Do you know where the sword may be found?"

"We have rumours only. It has changed hands more than once. Most who have attempted to put it to their own purposes have died quite terrible deaths as a result."

"Then why not let Sharadim find it. When she is dead, I can bring the sword to you. . . ."

"Your jests were never your strength, Champion," said Sepiriz almost sadly. "Sharadim may have some means of controlling the blade. She may have devised a method by which she can make herself invulnerable to the sword's particular curse. She is neither stupid nor ignorant. She will know how to make the best use of the sword once she finds it. Already she has sent out her minions to gather information."

"She knows more, then, than you do, Lord Sepiriz?"

"She knows something. And that is more than enough."

"Am I to try to reach the sword before she does? Or am I to stop her by some means? You are unclear as to what you expect of me, my lord."

Sepiriz could tell that I was resisting him. I had no wish to set eyes on another sword like the Black Sword, let alone put a hand upon one.

"I expect you to fulfil your destiny, Champion."

"And if I refuse?"

"You shall never know even a hint of freedom for eternity upon eternity. You shall suffer more terribly than those whom your selfishness will consign to everlasting horror. Chaos plays a part in this. Have you heard of the Archduke Balarizaaf? He is a most ambitious Lord of Chaos. Sharadim presently negotiates with him, offering an alliance. If Chaos claims the Six Realms it will mean nothing but hideous destruction, frightful agony for the conquered peoples, Eldren or human. Sharadim cares only for power, whereby she can indulge all her perverse whims. She's a fitting medium for the Archduke Balarizaaf. And he, better than she, understands the significance of the sword."

"So this is a matter between Law and Chaos?" I said. "And I am chosen to fight for Law this time."

"It is the Will of the Balance," said Sepiriz with a note of unwonted piety in his deep voice.

"Well, I trust you as cheerfully as I trust any of your ilk," I told him. "I can do very little else. But I will do nothing unless you tell me that what I do will aid these Eldren women, for it is to the Eldren, not any great cosmic force, that I feel my greatest loyalty. If I succeed, will they be reunited with their men?"

"That I can promise you," said Sepiriz. He seemed impressed by my statement rather than resentful of it.

"Then I shall do my best to find the Dragon Sword and release its prisoner," I agreed.

"I have your oath on that now," said Sepiriz with satisfaction. He seemed to be making a mental note. He also seemed somewhat relieved.

Von Bek stepped forward. "Forgive this interruption, gentlemen, but I would be much obliged if you could tell me if I, too, have a preordained destiny or if I am to do my best to make my own way home?"

Sepiriz placed a hand on the Saxon count's right arm. "My young friend, matters are far simpler where you are concerned and I can speak plainer. If you continue with this quest and aid the Champion to fulfil his destiny, you will, I promise, achieve what you most desire."

"The destruction of Hitler and his Nazis?"

"I swear it."

It was difficult for me to remain silent. I already knew the Nazis had been defeated. But again it occurred to me that perhaps they might succeed, that it had been von Bek and myself who had been responsible for the destruction of the fascists. I had some faint understanding, now, of why Sepiriz was bound to speak in mysteries. He had more than a knowledge of the Future. He had a knowledge of a million different Futures, a million different worlds, a million ages. . . .

"Very well," von Bek was saying, "then I shall continue with this, at least for the time being."

"Alisaard will also go with you," said the Lady Phalizaarn. "She has volunteered, since she was one of those responsible for revealing too much to Sharadim. And, of course, you will take the men."

"The men? Which men?" Foolishly I looked about me.

"Sharadim's exiled courtiers," she said.

"Why should I want them with me?"

"As witnesses," put in Sepiriz. "Since your first task is to go at once to Draachenheem and face your sister with an accusation and your evidence. If she is ousted from power, it will make your task considerably easier."

"You think we could do that? Three of us and a handful of men?"

"You have no choice," said Sepiriz gravely. "It is the first task you must accomplish if you would find the Dragon Sword. There is no better beginning. By confronting your evil twin, Sharadim, you will set the pattern for the rest of your quest. Remember, Champion, we forge Time and Matter as a consequence of our actions. That is one of the few constants in the multiverse. It is we who impose logic, for our own survival. Make it a good pattern and you shall come a step closer to achieving the destiny you most desire...."

"Destiny!" My grin had no humour in it. For a moment I rebelled. I almost turned and walked from the hall, telling Sepiriz that I would have no more of it. I was sick of his mysteries and his destinies.

But then I looked into the faces of those Eldren women and I saw, hidden beneath the grace and dignity, both anguish and desperation. I paused. These were the people I had elected to serve against my own race. I could not refuse them now.

For my love of Ermizhad, not for Sepiriz and all his oratory, I would take the road to Draachenheem and there give challenge to evil.

"We shall leave in the morning," I promised.

3.

THERE were twelve of us in the small boat as it entered the columns of light and was drawn back into the tunnel between the worlds. Alisaard, again in her ivory armour, steered while the rest of us clung to the sides and gaped. The other nine were all nobles of Draachenheem. Two of them were Land Princes, rulers of whole nations, who had been abducted the night Flamadin was apparently murdered. Four others were elected sheriffs of great cities and three had been squires at Court who had seen the poison administered. "Many others are dead," the Land Prince Ottro, an older man with heavy facial scarring, told me. "But she could not make everyone a corpse, so we were sold to the Gheestenheemers. Just think—we shall be the first to return."

"Though sworn to secrecy," young Federit Shaus reminded him. "We owe these Eldren women more than our lives."

All nine agreed with this. They had taken an oath to say nothing of the true nature of the Gheestenheem.

The boat raced on through the weird rainbow light, occasionally bucking and swerving, as if it had struck resistance, but never slackening her speed. Then quite suddenly we were bobbing on blue water again, surging between two columns and then the wind had caught our sail and we were upon an ordinary salt ocean, with a clear sky overhead and a good strong breeze behind us.

Two of the Draachenheemers consulted a map with Alisaard, giving her some idea of our position. We were going straight to Valadeka, land of the Valadek, home of Sharadim and Flamadin. Some of the Draachenheemers had wanted to return to their own lands, to gather up their armies and march against Sharadim, but Sepiriz had insisted we go directly to Valadeka.

Now a coastline came in sight. We saw great black cliffs framed against the pale sky. They were almost like the cliffs in my dreams. We saw spray and rocks and very few places where a boat could land.

"It is Valadeka's great strength," Madvad of Drane, a black-haired fellow with enormous eyebrows, informed me. "As an island she is virtually invulnerable to sea attack. Her few good harbours are well guarded."

"Must we land in one of them?" Von Bek wished to know.

Madvad shook his head. "We know of a small cove where, at certain tides, it is possible to land. That's what we seek now."

It was almost nightfall by the time we were able to land on the cold shingle of a narrow beach surrounded by black granite crags and overlooked by the ruins of an ancient castle. The boat was dragged into a cave and one of the squires, Ruberd of Hanzo, led us through a series of secret openings and up a flight of old steps until we were standing amongst the crumbled stone of the abandoned fortress.

"One of our noblest families once lived here," Ruberd said. "Your own ancestors, Prince Flamadin." He paused as if in embarrassment. "Or should I say simply 'Prince Flamadin's ancestors.' You say you are not yourself, my lord, yet I would still swear you are our Chosen Prince. . . ."

I had seen no point in deceiving these honest people. I had told them as much of the truth as I felt they could comprehend.

"There's a village nearby, is there not?" asked old Ottro. "Let's get there quickly. I could do with some victuals and a jug of beer. We plan to rest overnight, do we not, and continue on horseback in the morning?"

"The early morning." Gently I reminded him of our plan. "We must reach Rhetalik by noon tomorrow, when you said Sharadim is to have herself crowned Empress." Rhetalik was the capital of Valadeka.

"Certainly, young quasi-prince," he assured me. "I'm well aware of the urgency. But one thinks and acts better if one is fed and rested."

Alisaard and I swathed ourselves in cloaks so that we should not excite the villagers' curiosity overmuch, and we found a tavern large enough to accommodate our party. Indeed, the innkeeper was delighted at this unseasonal bonus. We had plenty of the local money and were generous with it. We dined and slept in great comfort and had our pick of the best horses the next morning. Then we were riding for Rhetalik. We must have made a strange enough sight to the Valadekans with myself in the leathers of a marsh-hunter, von Bek in a shirt, jacket and trousers roughly resembling what he had worn when I first saw him (made for him by the Eldren who had also furnished him with gloves, boots and a wide-brimmed hat), two of the Draachenheemers in the full, multi-coloured silks and woollens of their clans, four others in borrowed ivory armour, and three wearing a mixture of clothing selected from the store offered by the Eldren. I rode at the head of this strange little band, with von Bek on one side and Alisaard on the other. She was wearing her helm almost as a matter of habit. The Eldren rarely showed their faces to people from other realms. They had made a banner for me to carry on my lance, but this was presently furled and covered. I also took pains to pull my cloak's cowl over my head whenever we met others on the road. I had no intention of being recognised at that stage.

Gradually the earthen track began to widen. Next we discovered that it was paved with great stone flags. Now more and more people were joining us, all heading in the same direction. They seemed in holiday mood and were drawn from all walks of life. I saw men and women evidently of a monastic disposition and others who were as plainly secular in their tastes. Men, women, children, all in their best, all in brightly mingled shades. These Draachenheemers were fond of rich plaids and patchworks and thought nothing of wearing a score of different colours. I found their taste attractive and began to feel extremely dowdy in my dull leather gear.

Soon the road began to be lined on both sides with great gilded statues, of individual men and women, of groups, of beasts of every persuasion, though with a preponderance of those large lizards I had first seen at the Great Massing. These beasts were plainly not in common use. For the most part the horse, the ox and the donkey were the ordinary beasts of burden, although here and there was a large piglike creature which people rode upon and carried goods on by means of a sturdy wooden saddle.

"See!" Land Prince Ottro said to me as he came riding up. "It is the best time to arrive unnoticed in Rhetalik, as I said."

The city was surrounded by very high walls, of warm, reddish sandstone topped by huge spikes of rock, similar to the crenelations on a mediaeval castle, but of an entirely different shape. Each of these spikes had a hole at the centre and I guessed a man could stand behind the spike and shoot without much chance of being hurt himself. The city had been built for war, though Ottro assured me there had been peace throughout Draachenheem for many years. Within, it consisted of similarly fortified buildings, of rich palaces, market arcades, canals, temples, warehouses and all the other varied buildings of a complex trading city.

Rhetalik seemed to slope inwards, all her narrow streets leading down towards a lovely lake at her centre. There, upon an artificial island of some age, stood a great palace of slender marble, quartz, terra cotta and limestone: a palace which glittered and shone in the sunlight, which reflected a score of exquisite colours from the tall obelisks surrounding the island's perimeters. From the palace's central turrets there flew a hundred different banners, every one of which was a work of art. A curving, slender bridge crossed the moat to the delicately carved stonework of the gateposts, which were guarded by sentries in elaborately inefficient armour of the most fanciful design. The baroque effect of this armour was further increased by the hulking beasts which, in harness and trappings to rival that of their masters, stood beside the guards and were equally stiffly at attention. These were the giant riding lizards I had seen before; the dragons which had given this world its name. Ottro had explained how, in ancient times, these creatures had been plentiful and his people had to fight them for the land.

We brought our horses to a halt beside a wall which overlooked the lake and the castle. All around us the streets were filled with bunting, with scintillating banners and little mirrors, with polished shields and plates so that the entire place seemed ablaze with silver light. The people of Valadeka were celebrating the coronation of their Empress. There was music everywhere, crowds of jubilant men and women, feasting in the twitterns and lanes.

"Innocent enough, this festivity," said von Bek, leaning forward in his saddle to ease his back. It had been several years since he had ridden a horse. "Hard to believe that they celebrate the elevation of one who is supposedly the personification of evil!"

"Evil flourishes best in disguise," said Ottro grimly. His companions nodded in assent.

"And the best disguise is simple," said the youth, Federit Shaus. "Honest patriotism. Joyful idealism . . ."

"You're a cynic, lad," von Bek smiled at him. "But sadly my own experience would support your view. Show me a man who cries 'My country right or wrong,' and I'll show you one who'd cheerfully murder half his own nation in the name of patriotism."

"I once heard someone say that a nation was merely an excuse for crime," said Ottro. "In this case I might find myself in agreement. She has misused the love and trust of her people. They have made her Empress of this whole realm because they believe she represents all that is best in human nature. Moreover she now has their sympathy. Did not her brother try to kill her? Has it not been proven she suffered for years to try to preserve his reputation, letting people think him noble and good when all the while he was the very essence of self-indulgence and cowardice?" Ottro spoke bitterly.

"Well," I said, "since her brother is supposedly dead and you his victims"—that had been the tale put out—"think how overjoyed she will be to discover that she was not wrong in trusting him!"

"She'll kill us on the spot. I still say it." Von Bek did not believe our plan could work for a second.

"I doubt if even Sepiriz, with all his plots and cunning, would have sent us to a certain death," said Alisaard. "We have to trust his judgement. It is based on more than we can know."

"I have no relish for feeling myself a pawn in his mighty chess game," said von Bek.

"Nor I." I shrugged. "Though you would think I'd grow used to it. I still believe that individual will can achieve at least as much as all these alliances of men and gods Sepiriz speaks of. It has occurred to me more than once that they have become so engrossed in their game, in their cosmic politics, that they have lost sight of any original goal."

"You have little respect for gods and demigods, then," said Alisaard with a quick movement of her fingers to her face, as if she had forgotten she wore her visor beneath her cowl. "I must admit we do not think much of such creatures in Gheestenheem. Too often what we hear of them sounds like the activities of little boys at play!"

"Sadly," said von Bek, "those little boys care more for power than most of us. And when they achieve it, they can destroy all those of us who don't wish to join in their games."

Alverid of Prucca pushed his cloak away from his shoulders. He was more taciturn than most of the others. His principality was in the far west, where the people had a reputation for saying little and judging much. "Be that as it may," he said, "we should get on with this business. It will soon be noon. Do we all remember the plan?"

"It is not a difficult one," said von Bek. He jerked at his steed's reins. "Let's get on with it."

Making slow progress through the happy crowds we eventually came to the bridge. On this side it was also guarded by dismounted lizard-riders who saluted us as we approached.

"We are the invited delegation from the Six Realms," said Alisaard. "Come to pay our respects to your new Empress."

One of the guards frowned. "Invited, marm?"

"Invited. By your own Princess Empress Sharadim. Shall we wait here like trinket sellers or shall we proceed to the tradesman's entrance? I had expected a warmer greeting from a sister. . . ."

They exchanged looks and somewhat sheepishly let us pass. And because the first guards had admitted us, the others let us through without any form of challenge.

"Now follow me," said Ottro, riding ahead. He was most familiar with the palace and with protocol. He urged his horse forward, under a high arch which must have been twelve feet across and some six feet thick, of solid granite. This led us into a pleasant courtyard of turf surrounded by gravel. We crossed this, again unchallenged. I looked around me. The high walls of the palace reached up everywhere, ending in beautiful, almost ethereal, spires. Yet I felt I was entering a trap from which escape was impossible.

Under another arch, then another, until we came upon a group of young men in green and brown livery which Ottro recognised. "Squires," he cried. "Take our horses. We are late for the ceremony."

The squires ran forward to do his bidding. We dismounted and Ottro now marched without hesitation through a central door and into what was plainly a private apartment, though unoccupied. "I used to know the lady whose rooms these are," he said by way of explanation. "Hurry, my friends. We've had luck with us so far."

He opened a door and we were in a cool corridor with high ceilings and more of the colourful wall hangings enjoyed by these people. A few boys in the same green and brown livery; a young woman in a white and red gown, an old man in fur-trimmed plaid looked at us with casual curiosity as we walked purposefully in Ottro's wake, turned a corner, then another, mounted three flights of marble stairs and eventually came to a heavy wooden door. Ottro opened the door carefully, then signed for us to follow him.

This chamber was dark, unoccupied. Shades were drawn across all the windows. Cloying incense burned here. Great thick-leaved plants grew in profusion, giving the place something of the air of a huge greenhouse. There was the same sticky humidity, reminiscent of the tropics.

"What is this place," said von Bek shuddering. "It is so different in atmosphere from all the rest."

"It is the room where Prince Flamadin died," said one of the squires. "On yonder couch." He pointed. "It's evil you can smell, sire."

"Why should it be kept in darkness?" I wanted to know.

"Because they say Sharadim still communicates with the soul of her dead brother. . . ."

It was my turn to feel a chill. Did they refer to the soul of the body I now inhabited?

"I heard she keeps his corpse in these chambers," another said. "Frozen. Uncorrupted. Exactly as it was the minute the last breath went out of him."

I grew impatient. "These are mere rumours."

"Aye, Your Highness," said a squire in swift agreement. Then he frowned. I felt sympathy for him. He was not the only one who felt confused. I had been murdered in this room, by all accounts—or, at least, something which was almost myself had been murdered. I put my hand to my head. My senses seemed momentarily to leave me.

Von Bek caught me. "Steady, man. God knows what this can mean to you. It's bad enough for me."

With his support I was able to collect myself. Now we followed Ottro through the chambers, every one as dark and as unwholesome as the last, until we came to another outer door. Here he stopped.

We could hear sounds from the other side of the door. Music. Shouts. Cheering.

I understood our plan, but I still found it hard to believe we had already gained so much. My heart began to pound. I nodded to Ottro.

With a sudden movement the old man drew back the bolts from the double doors and kicked them outwards with a crash.

We stared into a sea of colour, of metal and silk, of faces already turning towards us in curiosity at the sound.

We stared into the great, vaulted ceremonial hall of the Valadek, at lances and banners and armour and every kind of finery, a predominance of rose-red and white, of gold and black. From the huge windows set at both ends of this hall poured great shafts of sunlight, half blinding us.

Mosaics, tapestries and stained glass contrasted magnificently with the pale, carved stone of the hall and seemed to be designed to lead the eye towards the very centre where, from a throne of blue and emerald obsidian, a woman of astonishing beauty was rising, her glance meeting mine the moment I reached the first step down the wide staircase which ended at the dais on which her throne was set.

Flanking her were men and women in heavy robes. These were the religious dignitaries of the Valadek, also married siblings as had been our custom for two thousand years. She wore the ancient Robe of Victory. It had not been settled on a member of the Valadek for centuries. We had never wanted to wear it again, for it was a War Robe, a robe signifying conquest by force of arms. She had offered it to me and I had refused it.

She held in her hands the Half Sword, the old broken blade of our barbarian ancestors, said to have killed the last of the Anishad bloodline, a girl of six, establishing the reign of our family until the reformation of the monarchy, when princes and princesses were chosen by the people. Sharadim and Flamadin had been chosen. We had been chosen because we were twins and this was thought a perfect omen. We should marry and bless the nation. The nation knew we would be lucky for them. They had not understood how much Sharadim had wanted this chance at power. I remembered our arguments. I remembered her disgust for what she saw as my feebleness. I had reminded her that we were elected, that any power we had was a gift of the people, that we were answerable to parliaments and councils. She had laughed at this.

—*For three and a half centuries our blood has waited to be revenged. For three and a half centuries our family spirits have held their peace, knowing the moment must come, know-*

ing that the fools would forget—knowing that if they had wished to see the last of their rightful masters, the Sardatrian Bharaleen, they should have done what we did to the Anishads and killed every last one of them, to the most distant cousins. We are fully of that blood, Flamadin. Our people cry out for us to fulfil our destiny. . . .

"NO!"

Her eyes widened as, slowly, I began to descend the steps.

"No, Sharadim. You shall not come so easily to this power. Let the world know, at least, by what foul means you achieved it. Let them know that you will bring disorder, horror, bloody torment to this realm. Let them know that you plan to ally yourself with the darkest powers of Chaos, that you would conquer first this realm and then make yourself Empress of the Six Realms of the Wheel. Let them know you are even prepared to let down the barriers which hold back the forces of the Nightmare Marches. Let this great assembly know, Sharadim, my sister, that you feel only contempt for them because they had thought our old blood mellowed, when actually it had gained a fierce intensity for being constrained so long. Let them know, Sharadim, who sought first to seduce me and then to slay me, what you think of their simple enthusiasm and their good will. Let them know you aspire to be immortal, to be elevated into the pantheon of Chaos!"

I had planned for the huge effect my words would have in that vast hall. My voice boomed. My words were knives, each one going directly to its target. Yet, until that moment, I had not known what I was going to say.

The memory had come to me suddenly. For a little while, it seemed, I had possessed Flamadin's mind, his own recollection of his sister's statements to him.

I had thought to make some revelation before the gathered nobles of a dozen nations. But I had not for a second suspected that it would be so specific or so accurate! I had begun by possessing the body of Prince Flamadin. Now Prince Flamadin had taken possession of me.

"Let them know all your thoughts, my sister!" I began a further descent. Now I waded through heaped roses, red and pink, and their sweet perfume filled my nostrils almost like a drug. "Tell them the truth!"

Sharadim flung down the Half Sword which, a moment since, she had caressed like a lover. Her face was alight with hatred and, at the same time, a kind of exultant joy. It was almost as if she had rediscovered an admiration for her brother which she had long since forgotten.

Some rose petals drifted lazily in the great shafts of light from the stained glass. I paused again, my hands on my hips, my whole body challenging her. "Tell them, Sharadim, my sister!"

Her voice when at last she spoke held not a trace of uncertainty. Indeed, it bore a cold and horrible authority. It was contemptuous.

"Prince Flamadin is dead, sir. Dead. And you, sir, are a crude imposter!"

4.

I HAD left it until now to throw off my cowl. From every part of the hall there came a murmur of recognition. Some backed away in fear, as if I were a ghost; others pushed forward to see me better. And out of the crowd near the dais, at Sharadim's signal, came half a hundred men at arms, with ceremonial pikes in their hands, to surround her and the throne.

I pointed behind me. "And if I am an imposter, who are these? My lords and ladies, do you not recognise your peers?"

Ottro, Land Prince of Waldana, came to stand beside me. Then Madvad, Duke of Drane; Halmad, Land Prince of Ruradani and all the other nobles and squires.

"These are the men you sold into slavery, Sharadim. You must wish now that you killed them when you killed the others!"

"Black magic!" cried my twin. "Phantoms conjured by Chaos! My soldiers will destroy them, never fear."

But now many more nobles were rushing forward. One tall old man in a high crown made of coloured shells raised his hand. "No blood is to be spilled here. I know Ottro of Waldana as if he were my kin. They said you went adventuring, Ottro, to look for fresh gateways to the other realms. Is that so?"

"I was arrested, Prince Albret, as I tried to take ship to my own land. The Princess Sharadim ordered the arrest. A week later all whom you see here were sold to the Ghost Women as slaves."

Another wave of murmuring from the crowd.

"We bought these men in good faith," said Alisaard, still

112

wearing her visor. "But when we learned of their circumstances, we decided to release them."

"There's your first miserable lie," cried Sharadim, seating herself upon her throne again. "When have the Ghost Women cared about the source of their slaves or of their circumstances? This is some plot hatched between rebellious nobles and foreign enemies to discredit me and weaken the Draachenheem...."

"Rebellious?" Prince Ottro took a step or two farther until he was standing below me. "Pray, madam, what do we rebel against? Your authority is purely ceremonial, is it not? And if it is not, why do you not reveal that fact?"

"I spoke of common treachery," she said. "To all our realm and its nations. They disappeared not because they were captured, but because they sought an alliance with the Gheestenheemers. It is they who seek to corrupt our traditions. It is they who hope to gain power for themselves over us all." Sharadim's face was the picture of outraged virtue. Her fair skin seemed to glow with honesty and her large blue eyes had never seemed more innocent. "I was elected to be Empress of the Realm by the suggestion of various barons and Land Princes. If it brings disruption rather than added unity to the Draachenheem, I shall of course refuse the honour...."

There was considerable approval of her speech and many cries for her to ignore us.

"This woman deceived almost the entire realm," Ottro continued. "She will bring ruin and black misery to us all, I know it. She is a mistress of deception. See this boy?" He brought young Federit Shaus to stand by him. "Many must recognise him. A squire in the employ of Prince Flamadin. He saw Princess Sharadim place the poison in the wine with which she intended to murder her brother. He saw Prince Flamadin fall...."

"I murdered my brother?" Sharadim turned astonished eyes on the assembled nobles. "Murdered him? I am confused. Did you not say that this was Prince Flamadin?"

"I am he."

"And you are murdered, sir?"

There was laughter in the hall.

"The attempt failed, madam."

"I did not murder Prince Flamadin. Prince Flamadin was exiled because he attempted to murder me. The whole world knows that. Every one of the Six Realms knows that. Many thought I should have killed him. Many thought me too lenient. If this is Prince Flamadin returned from exile, then he is breaking the Law and should be placed under arrest."

"Princess Sharadim," I said. "You were too quick to judge me an imposter. Any normal response would have been for you to have assumed I was your brother returned. . . ."

"My brother had his weaknesses, sir. But he was not evidently a madman!"

This drew further approving laughter from the crowd. But many were wavering.

"This will not do," cried the old man in the crown of shells. "As Hereditary Master of the Rolls I must use my authority in this matter. All must be put to Law. Let everyone be given the proper opportunities to speak. One day is all it will take, I am sure, for everyone to be heard. And then, if everything is still in order, the Coronation can commence. What do you say, Your Majesty? My lords and ladies? If the matter is to continue to the satisfaction of us all, let us call a Hearing on it? In this Hall at midafternoon."

Sharadim could not refuse and, as for us, it was better than we had hoped for. We agreed at once.

I cried: "Sharadim! Will you grant me an audience in private? You and three chosen companions. I and three of mine?"

She hesitated, looked over to one side of the hall as if in quest of some guidance. Then she nodded. "In the antechamber in half an hour," she said. "But you cannot convince me, sir, that you are my exiled brother. Surely you did not think I would accept you as my own flesh and blood?"

"Then what am I, madam? A ghost?"

I watched as she and her guards left the hall in a billowing wave of silks and bright metal while the Master of the Rolls signed for us to accompany him through another side door and into a cool chamber, lit by a single large round window above. Once he had closed the door, he sighed. "Land Prince Ottro, I had feared you slain. And you, also, Prince Flamadin. There have been uncomfortable rumours here and there. For me, your words today confirm what I suspected of that woman. Not one of the nobles who voted to make her Empress is the kind I'd willingly invite to my own house. Ambitious, self-serving, foolish fellows all, who believe themselves deserving of greater power. That must be what she offers them. Of course, other, more innocent people, followed suit out of ordinary, if misguided, idealism. They see her as a kind of living goddess, a personification of all their highest dreams and hopes. Her beauty, I suppose, has much to do with that. However, it did not need your melodramatic declarations of today to convince me that we are a whisker from complete tyranny. Already she speaks (albeit sweetly) of those in neighbouring realms who envy us our wealth, how we should protect ourselves more thoroughly. . . ."

"Women are always underestimated by men," said Alisaard, a note of satisfaction in her voice, "and this enables them sometimes to gather far more power to themselves than the men suspect. I have noticed this in my own studies of history, in my own travels about the realms."

"Believe me, madam, I do not underestimate her," said the Master of the Rolls, closing the door behind him and motioning us to be seated at a long table of polished oak. "You'll remember, Prince Flamadin, that I warned you to be more cautious. But you would not believe in your sister's schemes, her perfidy. She treated you like a favourite child, a wild son, rather than as a brother. And this enabled you to go scampering hither and yon in search of adventure while gradually she amassed more and more allies. Even then, you would have scarcely guessed the level of her evil had she not lost patience with you and ordered you to marry her, to consolidate her position. She assumed she could control you, or at least keep you a good distance from Court. Instead, you objected. You objected to her ambitions, her methods, her very philosophy. She tried to persuade you, I know. Then what happened?"

"She tried to kill me."

"And put it about that you were the would-be murderer. That you were the one who stood against all our ideals and traditions. It is as if she is a reincarnation of Sheralinn, Queen of the Valadek, who regularly filled the moat out there with the blood of those she considered her enemies. I had guessed much of what you said today, but I had not realised she consciously sought to re-establish your dynasty as Empress of the Draachenheem. And you say she seeks the aid of Chaos? Chaos has not entered the Six Realms since the Sorcerers' War, more than a thousand years ago. It is contained within the hub, in the Nightmare Realm. We swore we should never let it through again."

"I have heard she is already in communication with the Archduke Balarizaaf of Chaos. She seeks his help in fulfilling her ambitions."

"And what would an Archduke's price be, I wonder?" The Master of the Rolls was now even more concerned.

"A high one, I would guess," said the Land Prince Ottro quietly. Deliberately, he folded his arms across his chest.

"Do such creatures really exist?" von Bek wished to know. "Or do you speak figuratively?"

"They exist," said the Master of the Rolls gravely. "They exist in uncountable numbers. They seek to rule the multiverse and would use mankind's folly and vice to that end. The Lords of Law, on the other hand, seek to use mankind's idealism against Chaos, and to further their own schemes. Meanwhile the Cosmic Balance seeks to maintain equilibrium between the two. So much is commonly understood by those who recognise the existence of the multiverse and who travel, to some degree at least, between the realms."

"Do you know of a legend concerning a sword?" von Bek asked. "And a creature said to slumber within it?"

"The Dragon in the Sword. Aye, of course I have heard of the Dragon Sword. It is a terrible weapon, by all accounts. Forged by Chaos, they say, to conquer Chaos. The Lords of Chaos would give much for that. . . ."

"Could that be the Archduke Balarizaaf's price?" von Bek suggested.

I was impressed by how swiftly he came to understand the logic by which we presently lived.

"Indeed," said the Master of the Rolls, his eyes widening, "it could be!"

"And that's why she wants it. And that is why she was so glad to hear of it from us!" Alisaard clenched her ivory fists. "Oh, what dolts we were to tell her so much. We should have guessed that the person we really sought would not ask so many questions."

"You communicated with her that successfully?" I was surprised.

"We told her all we knew."

"And doubtless she had information of her own to add to yours," Ottro said. "But surely you do not want the Dragon Sword in order to strike a bargain with Chaos?"

"We wanted it so we might rejoin our own people in a far realm. The Eldren have no truck with Chaos."

"Is there anything else I should know?" asked the Master of the Rolls. "We must call a Hearing and we must try to prove Sharadim evil. But if we cannot, if the vote goes against us, we must consider other means of stopping her."

"Surely our evidence will sway the Court?" said Alisaard.

Von Bek looked at her almost as if he envied her innocence. "I have but lately come from a world," he said, "whose rulers are masters at turning lies to truth and making the truth seem the foulest lie. It's easily done. We cannot expect to be believed simply because we know we do not lie."

"The problem is," added the Master of the Rolls, "that so many wish to believe Sharadim the paragon they all desire. Often people fight hardest of all to preserve a delusion. And they will frequently persecute those who challenge that delusion."

We debated the matter further until the Master of the Rolls told us that the time had come for our meeting with Sharadim. Alisaard, von Bek, Land Prince Ottro and I left the chamber and were escorted through the now-deserted hall, still full of rose petals, and up a short flight of stairs into a series of rooms, some of which formed a kind of aviary, and finally to a circular room whose windows overlooked flower gardens and formal hedgerows and lawns, the inner courtyard of the palace. Here the Princess Sharadim sat. On her right was a long-jawed fellow with thin, unkempt, light-coloured hair. He wore a surcoat of orange and a jerkin and breeches of yellow. On her left, leaning a little on her large chair, was a bulky, plump creature whose tiny eyes were never still and whose jaw moved slowly, like a goat chewing cud; he wore a mauve surcoat and dark blue underneath. The last was a youth of such decadent appearance I could hardly believe my eyes. He was almost a grotesque parody of the type, with thick wet lips, drooping eyelids, pale, spotted unhealthy skin, twitching muscles and fingers, and reddish, curly hair. They announced themselves in a sulky, challenging manner. The first was Perichost of Risphert, Duke of Orrawh in the distant west; then Neterpino Sloch, Commander of the Befeel Host, and lastly Lord Pharl Asclett, Hereditary Prince of Skrenaw, but better known as Pharl of the Heavy Palm.

"I know of you all, gentlemen," said Ottro with poorly disguised disgust as he introduced us. "And you know Prince Flamadin. This is his friend Count Ulrich von Bek. Lastly Alisaard, Legion Commander of Gheestenheem."

Sharadim had waited impatiently through all this. Now she rose from her chair and pushing through her companions walked straight to where I stood and looked up into my face. "You are an imposter. You can admit it here. You know, as do most of those who came with you, that I slew Prince Flamadin. True, his body is not corrupted and lies even now in my cellars. But I am lately from where I left that body. It is still there! I know you for the one called The Champion, who those foolish women prayed to, mistaking myself for you. And I can guess what you are attempting by this essay into playacting. . . ."

"They hope to get to the sword before we do," interrupted Pharl, scratching at his palm. "And make their own bargain with the Archduke."

"Be quiet, Prince Pharl," she said contemptuously. "Your imagination is notoriously poor. Not everyone holds identical ambitions to your own!" Ignoring his flushing features, she continued: "You either wish to oust me from the throne and rule in my place," she said, "or you merely wish to bring my plans to an end. What? Do you all serve Law? Are you employed to give battle to Chaos and his allies? I know a little of your legend, Champion. Is that not your function?"

"I'll allow you your speculations, madam, but you cannot expect me to confirm or deny them. I am not here to give you more power."

"You are here to steal what I have, eh?"

"If you would give up your schemes, if you would refuse any further dealings with Chaos, if you would tell us what you know of the Dragon Sword, then you would receive no further conflict from me. If, as I suspect, you do not accept my terms, then I shall have to fight you, Princess Sharadim. And that fight would almost certainly bring about your own destruction. . . ."

"Or yours," she said calmly.

"I cannot be destroyed."

"I had heard otherwise." She laughed. "This disguise, this flesh you assume, can be destroyed easily enough. What you love can be destroyed. What you admire can be corrupted. Come now, Champion, it is unworthy of either of us to mince words when we know exactly what we are dealing with!"

"I offered you a fair bargain, madam."

"I have been offered better elsewhere."

"The Lords of Chaos are notoriously treacherous. Their servants have a tendency to die in horrid circumstances. . . ." I shrugged.

"Servant? I'm no servant of Chaos. I am in alliance with a certain party."

"Balarizaaf," I said. "He will cheat you, lady."

"Or I him." Her smile was all pride. I had seen many like her in the past. She believed herself cleverer than she was because it suited others to let her maintain that delusion.

"I speak sincerely, Princess Sharadim!" I was more urgent now. I should have felt less fearful if she had been a little more clever. "I am not your brother, it is true. But I have something of your brother's soul mixed with mine. I know that I lack the strength to counter Chaos when it turns against you!"

"It will not turn against me, Sir Champion. Besides, my brother knew little of my dealings with Chaos. You have gathered that information from elsewhere!"

This set me back a little. If I was not tapping her brother's memories, then I must be receiving my knowledge by some other means. Then it occurred to me that I was in some sort of telepathic communication with Princess Sharadim. That was how I had known what she meant to do. I found the thought unpleasant.

Flamadin and Sharadim had been twins, after all. I inhabited a body which was the exact counterpart of Flamadin's. Therefore it might be possible that communication existed between us. And if that were so, Sharadim was as much party to my secrets as I was to hers.

What further disturbed me was knowing that a corpse identical to me was still stored in Sharadim's cellars. I was not sure why I found this so distasteful, but it made me shudder. At the same time I had a sudden image: A wall of pale red crystal, and within the wall a sword which seemed to glow green and black and which at other times seemed to be on fire.

"How will you cut the crystal, Sharadim?" I said. "How will you tear the sword from its prison?"

She frowned. "You know more than I guessed. This is foolish. We should consider an alliance. They will all believe Flamadin restored. We shall marry. The folk of the Draachenheem will be overjoyed. What celebrations! Our power would increase immediately. We would share equally everything we gained!"

I turned away. "These are the self-same proposals you made to your brother. When he refused, you killed him. Now that I refuse, will you kill me, Sharadim? On the spot? Here and now?"

She all but spat in my face. "Moment by moment I gain in strength. You shall be swallowed up in the storm I shall release. You shall be forgotten, Champion, and all who are with you. I shall rule the Six Realms and with my chosen companions shall indulge my every whim. That is what you refuse— immortality and an eternity of pleasure! What you have chosen is prolonged agony and certain death."

She was foolish and because she was foolish she was exceptionally dangerous. I recognised that. I was afraid, as she had hoped I would be afraid, but not because of her threats. If she allied herself with Balarizaaf there was no anticipating the danger we faced in our search for the sword. And if she were thwarted, I thought, she was the kind who would willingly drag all down with her as she went. I preferred a more knowing foe.

"Well," said von Bek from behind me. "We shall see what the Hearing brings. Perhaps the people will decide this issue."

A look of secret calculation crossed Sharadim's face.

"What have you done, madam?" cried the Land Prince Ottro. "Be careful, Prince Flamadin. I can see the meanest treachery in her eyes!"

At this Prince Pharl of the Heavy Palm uttered a peculiar snigger.

Then there came a hammering on the door of our chamber and I heard a voice cry from the other side: "My lady Empress! My lady. A message of the utmost urgency!"

Sharadim nodded and Perichost, Duke of Orrawh, stepped forward to draw back the bolt.

A frightened servant stood there, one hand to his face. "Oh, madam. Murder has been done!"

"Murder?" She displayed horrified surprise. "Murder, you say?"

"Aye, madam. The Master of the Rolls, his wife and two young pages. All cut down in the Silver Auditorium!"

Sharadim turned to me with a look of exultation in her huge blue eyes. "Well, sir, it seems that violence and terror accompany you wherever you go. And they visit us only when you—or the one you resemble—come amongst us!"

"You have killed him!" cried Ottro. He made a motion to his hip before he realised that he, like the rest of us, were without weapons. "You have killed that fine old man!"

"Well?" asked Sharadim of the servant. "Do you have any idea who was responsible for these crimes?"

"They say it was Federit Shaus and two others. That they obeyed the Land Prince Halmad of Ruradani."

"What? The ones who came with the rest of this party?"

"That is what they say, madam."

I was furious. "You planned this. Within an hour you have spilled further blood in pursuit of your appalling lie. Neither Shaus nor Halmad nor any of our companions was armed!"

"Tell us," said Sharadim softly to the servant, "how did that good man and his wife come to die?"

"By the ceremonial blades kept in the Auditorium," said the servant, darting bewildered glances at me and my friends.

"We had no reason to kill Prince Albret," bellowed Ottro in perplexed outrage. "You killed him to silence him. You killed him to provide yourself with a motive for destroying us. Let us continue with the Hearing. Let us speak our evidence!"

She spoke softly and triumphantly. "There'll be no Hearing now. It is obvious to all that you came here on a mission of assassination, that you had no other motive."

It was at this moment that von Bek sprang for Sharadim and seized her from behind, his arm across her windpipe.

"What good can that do?" cried Alisaard, confounded by all this villainy. "If we use violence, we resort to their methods. If we threaten her, we prove her case against us."

Von Bek did not loosen his grip. "I assure you, Lady Alisaard, that I do not act thoughtlessly." As Sharadim struggled von Bek forced her to be still. "I have had enough experience of such plots to know that everything is already planned. We will not receive a fair Hearing. We will be lucky if we are able to leave this room alive. As for leaving the palace alive, I think we have only the poorest of chances now."

Her three lieutenants were moving uncertainly towards von Bek. I stepped between them and my friend. My head had grown muzzy. I had a series of images, of emotions, which I knew were not mine. They were doubtless coming from the captured princess. I saw the crystal wall again, the entrance to a cave. I heard a name which sounded like *Morandi Pag*. More fragments of words. Another that was complete—*Armiad*—then *Barganheem* . . .

Ottro came up beside me, then Alisaard. The three made feeble motions in our direction but did not dare advance. Noticing Neterpino Sloch slip one hand beneath his surcoat, I moved suddenly forward and struck him hard on the jaw. He went down like a stunned pig. I bent over him as he moaned and drooled on the ground. I tore back his surcoat, revealing a knife of some nine inches long set between the double row of buttons on his jerkin. I pulled the blade free.

Next I inspected the other two. They glared and objected, but did not resist. I found two more knives.

"What contemptible creatures you are!" I handed a knife to Ottro and another to von Bek. "Now, Sharadim, you'll tell that poor servant who currently bangs on your door to fetch those of our friends that remain alive. Bring them here and leave them here."

Almost choking, she did as I ordered. Von Bek carefully placed a knife-point at her side and relaxed the tension on her throat.

A few minutes later the doors opened. In came Federit Shaus, looking dazed and frightened, followed by all the others who had accompanied us to Rhetalik.

"Now send a message to your guards to search in the Eastern Wing of the palace," I said. Scarlet with fury, she issued the command.

To my companions I said: "You must return to the courtyard and have our horses saddled at once. Tell them you seek fleeing assassins. Then wait for us or, if you think your chances are better, head for wherever you think you'll be safest. Try to convince your own people of Sharadim's evil ambitions. On her instructions, Prince Albret and his wife were murdered, to silence him and create a crime for which she can blame us. Armies must be raised against her. Some of you must succeed. Prepare your people for what she plans. Resist her. Ride away from here at once, if you desire. We'll follow in a short while."

"Go," said Prince Ottro in agreement. "He is right. There is no other way. I shall stay with them. Pray that at least some of us are successful."

When they had disappeared, Prince Ottro looked quizzically at me. "But how long can we hold off all the forces of the Valadek? I say we should kill her now."

She uttered a great groan and tried to break free again, but felt von Bek's knife at her ribs and thought better of it.

"No," said Alisaard. "We cannot resort to her methods. There is no justification for cold-blooded murder."

"True," I agreed. "By acting as they would act, we become

what they are. And if we are what they are, then there is little point in resisting them!"

Ottro frowned. "A fine point, but I do not think we have time for such niceties. We'll be dead within the hour if we do not act soon."

"There's nothing for it," I said. "We must use her as our hostage. We have no other choice."

Sharadim moved her body against von Bek, trying to draw back from the knife. "You would do best to kill me now," she said fiercely. "For if you do not, I will hound you through the Six Realms, and when I find you I shall . . ." Whereupon she uttered a series of intentions which chilled my blood, made Alisaard look as if she were about to vomit and turned Prince Ottro white as a Ghost Woman's armour. Only von Bek seemed unmoved. He had, after all, witnessed much of what she threatened, as an inmate of Hitler's camps.

I made a decision. I drew a deep breath. "Very well," I said, "we shall probably kill you, Princess Sharadim. Perhaps it is the only way to ensure that Chaos shall not conquer the Six Realms. And I think we can kill you as imaginatively as you would dispense with us."

She looked hard at me, wondering if I spoke the truth. I laughed in her face. "Oh, madam," I said, "you have no idea what blood is already on my hands. You cannot possibly begin to guess what horror I have looked upon." And I let her find my mind. I let her know something of my memories, my eternal battles, my agonies, of the time when, as Erekosë, I had led Eldren armies in the utter destruction of the human race.

Sharadim screamed. She began to collapse.

"She has fainted," said von Bek in bewilderment.

"Now we can leave," I said.

5.

SPEED and desperation were our only allies. We left Sharadim's henchmen bound and gagged in a large chest. We took the insensible princess with us. I held her in my arms as I might hold a loved one. Every time we came upon a guard we would call out that she was sick and that we were hurrying her to the hospital wing of the palace. And very soon we were back in the courtyard, running for our horses.

Sharadim was now bundled into a cloak and slung over Prince Ottro's saddle. We had crossed the bridge and were galloping through the town within minutes. Still there was no pursuit. Doubtless they were still shocked by the murder of the Master of the Rolls and it had not yet registered that their princess had been kidnapped.

Through the town! And now she was waking. I heard her muffled protests. We ignored them.

And then at last we were on the open road again and heading for where we had hidden our boat. We looked back all the time, but none came after us. Von Bek grinned.

"I had thought us as good as dead. There is something to be said for experience!"

"And quick thinking to make use of it," I pointed out. I, too, was surprised that we had managed to get away before a hue and cry was raised. Apart from the murder of Prince Albret, the other factor in our favour was that the entire palace had been geared for a peaceful celebration. Most ordinary guards were on ceremonial duty. Many strangers were coming and going all the time. By now they would have found Neterpino Sloch, Duke Perichost and Prince Pharl and would be attempting to discover what had happened to Princess Sharadim. These people seemed to have no sophisticated methods of long-distance signalling. If we could reach the boat in time, we had every chance now of getting completely clear of Valadeka.

"But what of our captive?" said Prince Ottro. "How will we dispose of her? Take her with us?"

"It would prove an unwelcome encumbrance," I said.

"Then I suppose we shall have to kill her," said Ottro, "if she is of no use to us. And if we are to save this realm from Chaos."

Alisaard murmured an objection. I said nothing. I knew that Sharadim was now awake again and could hear our conversation. I knew, too, that I had frightened her sufficiently—if momentarily—to make a little further use of her.

Two hours later we had released our horses into a field and were climbing down the cliffs to where we had left our boat. Sharadim was over von Bek's shoulder. Ottro led the way. Eventually we stood on the shingle. The sky was grey now and the whole beach seemed dead. Even the ocean had a lifeless quality to it.

"We could take the body with us," Ottro argued, "and dump it in the sea. That would be the end of her forever. The nobles would pick up the pieces soon enough."

"Or would they seek revenge on my murderers, I wonder." She was on her feet, shaking out her lovely golden hair. Her eyes were blue flints. "You could bring our realm to civil war, Prince Ottro. Would that be what you want? I promise unity."

He turned away from her, untying cords from the mast and settling it in the centre of the boat.

"Why did you not go yourself to Barganheem and try to take the sword?" I asked her. I was bluffing. I was using the few words I had found in her mind.

"You know as well as I why that would be folly," she said. "I can enter Barganheem at the head of an army and take what I want."

"Would not Morandi Pag object?"

"What if he did?"

"And Armiad?"

She drew her beautiful brows together in another glare. "That barbarian? That parvenu? He will do what he is told. If he had come to us a few hours before the Massing we could have settled this once and for all. But we had not known where you would be."

"You sought me at the Massing?"

"Prince Pharl was there. He offered to buy you both, dead or alive, from Armiad. So he would have done, had not the Ghost Women found you first. Armiad is a poor ally, but so far he is the only one I have in the Maaschanheem."

I realised now that her schemes already extended beyond her own realm. She was gathering accomplices everywhere she could. And Armiad, of course, in his hatred for me, was perfectly willing to be of service to her. Now I knew, too, that the Dragon Sword was probably in the Barganheem, that someone called Morandi Pag knew its exact location, or was its protector, and the Sharadim felt he was powerful enough for her to require an army to aid her against him.

Federit Shaus, Alisaard and Prince Halmad by now had readied the boat and were preparing to push it into the water. Prince Ottro drew out the long knife I had taken from Neterpino Sloch. "Shall I do it? We must get it over with."

"We cannot murder her," I said. "She's right in one thing. A civil war could result from that. If we leave her, some will realise we're not the killers she says we are."

"Civil war's inevitable now," said Prince Ottro feelingly. "More than one country will refuse to acknowledge her as Empress."

"But many others will accept her. Let our actions be witness to our humanity and honesty."

Prince Halmad and Alisaard were both in strong agreement.

"Let her be brought to Law," said Alisaard. "I for one shall not descend to her methods. Flamadin is right. Now many will suspect her. Her own people might insist upon a trial. . . ."

"That last I doubt." Von Bek spoke soberly. "Or let us say that those who do insist on a Hearing will be silenced soon enough. There is a monotonous pattern to the rise of tyrants which, I suppose, is reflected in the general pattern of human folly. Depressing though it is, we must accept the fact."

"Well, she'll be resisted now," said Ottro with satisfaction. "Come, we must set sail at once for Waldana. There, at least, I will be believed."

Sharadim was laughing at us as we shoved off into the water. Her wonderful hair whipped in the wind and her cloak snapped and flapped as she clasped it around her body. I stood in the stern, looking back at her, staring into her eyes, perhaps trying to will her to put a halt to her evil. But her laughter grew stronger. I could still hear it when the boat rounded the headland and she was lost from sight.

I think some big schooners came after us. We saw them on the second day but happily they did not see us. By then we were almost at the coast of Waldana. We let Ottro and the others ashore in a small fishing harbour, at night. The prince saluted us. "I go to rouse my people. We, at least, shall oppose the Princess Sharadim."

We had no time for rest.

"North," said Alisaard. She had a kind of compass on a thong about her neck. "But quickly. By morning it will be gone."

We sailed north, the black of the ocean gradually turning to pewter as the sun rose, and then, on the horizon, we saw the Entrance. Already it appeared to be fading. Expertly, Alisaard moved the sail to catch the full benefit of the breeze. The boat tugged forward. It seemed to bring von Bek and myself alive again. Eagerly we stared at the great columns of soft light which plunged from an unseen source and descended to an unseen destination.

"I'll have to risk a more rapid approach," cried Alisaard. "It's now only seconds before the eclipse is over." And with that she directed our little boat between two of the columns which had grown so close together that I thought we must be crushed by them. The whole temple of light was contracting, the columns moving to form a single faint beam.

But we were through, and even though this tunnel was considerably narrower than the last, we knew we were safe. For a moment we knew a little relief on tranquil water, then the ship was tilting, moving along the corridor at enormous speed.

"We are taught to know where and when to find all the gateways between the realms," Alisaard informed us. "We have charts and calculators. We can anticipate when one gateway opens and another closes. We know exactly where one will lead and another will not. Never fear, soon we shall be in Barganheem. We shall arrive about noon."

Von Bek was weary. He fell back in the boat, a weak smile on his face. "I have to trust your judgement, Herr Daker, but I'm blessed if I know how you decided we should find this sword in Barganheem."

I told him how I had come by the knowledge. "I have the advantage over Sharadim that I can consciously read something of what is in her mind. She can only guess. That is, she has the same power but she does not know how to use it. I was able to let her see my whole mind for a moment—"

"And that was why she fainted so suddenly? Aha! I am glad you do not let me enjoy such a privilege, Herr Daker!" He yawned. "But this means if she ever learns the secret, Sharadim will be able to read something of your thoughts, also. She will have the same advantage."

"Even now she could well be determining which of her intuitions she should trust. There's every chance she'll pick the right ones."

The boat shivered. We looked forward. Ahead was a bright green mass of light, almost a ball, like a sun. Slowly it turned to blue and then to grey. Then the corridor seemed to narrow dramatically and we found ourselves ducking. There was a noise like wind chimes, random yet musical, and we were jerking painfully, the whole boat bumping up and down on what, evidently, was no longer water.

Below us were clouds. Above was a blue sky and a sun at zenith. The columns had disappeared. We were not on water at all, but in a soft, green mountain meadow. A little way from us, in another field separated by a drystone wall, three black and white cows were grazing. Two of them looked with mild curiosity in our direction. Another made a noise as if to indicate she had no interest in us whatsoever.

In all directions were these same steep meadows, walls and mountain peaks. It was impossible to see anything of the land below the clouds. There was a strange, pleasant quietness here. Von Bek put his leg over the boat and smiled at Alisaard. "Is all of Barganheem so peaceful, my lady?"

"Much of it," she said. "The river traders tend to be quarrelsome, but they never bother to climb so high."

"And what of the farmers? Will they object to finding a boat in one of their fields?" Von Bek spoke with his usual dry humour.

Alisaard was removing her visor completely. Once again, as she shook out her long hair, I was struck by her resemblance to my Ermizhad, both in mannerisms and looks. And again I felt that pang of jealousy when she gave von Bek an answering smile which held, I was sure, at least a hint of an emotion that was stronger than casual friendship. I controlled myself, of course, for I had no right to feel as I did. If Alisaard found von Bek sexually attractive and my friend reci-

procated her feelings, I should feel pleased for them. Yet still
the little nagging devil remained. I would have cut him from
me with a white-hot knife if that had been possible.

"You'll notice that the farmers have placed no livestock in
this particular field," said Alisaard. "They are as aware as any
that this is, in their terms, a magic place. They have had cows
disappear when the Pillars of Paradise materialise! They've
seen stranger things than boats. However, we cannot expect
them to be of much help to us, either. They have no experience of travelling between the realms. They leave such adventures for the traders of the river valleys far below."

"How shall we begin to look for Morandi Pag?" I asked,
breaking rather curtly into her speech. "You said you could
guess, by the name, where we should begin looking, Lady
Alisaard."

She looked at me curiously, as if she sensed an emotion
which had something to do with her. "Are you in pain, Prince
Flamadin?"

"Merely anxious," I told her briefly. "We cannot let Sharadim gain another minute. . . ."

"You don't think we have made time for ourselves?" von
Bek reached down and wet his hands on the lush grass. He
patted at his face and sighed.

"Gained some and lost some," I reminded him. "She must
either consider bringing an army into Barganheem or she must
plan fresh strategy. If she's as impatient for power as I believe, she will now be willing to risk more than she ever did in
order to get to the Dragon Sword before we do. So, Lady
Alisaard, where would you think it wise to begin looking for
Morandi Pag?"

Silently, she pointed down the steep hillside towards the
clouds. "Unfortunately we must descend to the river valleys.
That name has an inhuman ring to my ears. But be warned—
when we reach the valleys you must allow me to speak. They
have traded with the Gheestenheemers for several centuries
and we are the only people who have not at some point offered
them violence. As much as they trust any outrealmer, they'll
trust me. They will not trust you, however, for a moment."

"A xenophobic race, eh?" said von Bek cheerfully,
readying himself for the long walk down.

"Not without reason," said Alisaard. "You Mabden are the
unlikeliest of evolved species. Most of us learn to enjoy and
understand the differences between cultures and races. Your

history appears to be a long tale of persecution and destruction of anything not like yourselves. Why is that, do you think?"

"If I had that answer at this moment, my lady," said von Bek with some force, "I do not believe I would be here discussing the problem. All I can assure you is that a few of us 'Mabden' are as concerned by the truth you state as anyone. I sometimes think we are born of a monstrous nightmare, that we live perpetually with the horror of our hellish origin, that we seek to silence any voice which reminds us of what ill-formed intelligences we are!"

She was evidently impressed by his passion. I wished that I had said as much and been as eloquent. I forced myself to take a keen interest in the surrounding view as we tramped rapidly downhill towards the calm plateau of cloud.

"Once below that layer," said Alisaard, "we shall no longer be in the territory of the farmers. Look, there's one of their houses. . . ."

It was a rather tall, conical building, with a chimney and thatch almost to the ground. I saw two or three figures nearby, going about the ordinary business of farming. However, I was struck by the oddness of some of their movements. Our descent took us closer to the farm. The people did not look up as we went by, though they had plainly seen us. Evidently, they preferred to pretend we did not exist. As a result I could stare without much rudeness at them. They seemed oddly bent. At first I attributed this to the nature of their work, to some unusual cut to their clothing, but it soon became obvious, from the glimpse I had of their faces, that they were not human at all. I was reminded at first of a kind of baboon. And now I understood a little better what Alisaard had meant. Another close glance and I saw large, solid, cloven hoofs where the feet would be on a human. What else were these quiet, harmless farmers but devils from the superstitions of Daker's world? "Why," I said with a laugh, "I do believe we are marching through Hell, von Bek."

My friend offered me a sardonic glance. "I assure you, Herr Daker, that Hell is not nearly as pleasant."

Alisaard called out a greeting in her clear, sweet voice. It was as if a beautiful songbird had suddenly begun its call. Hearing it the farmers looked up. Their strange, wizened faces beamed in recognition. Now they waved and shouted something to us which was in such a thick dialect I could barely understand a word. Alisaard told me they were wishing us good fortune "below the sea." "They think of these layers of cloud as an ocean and the people beneath it possess almost a mythological character to them. They have, of course, never seen a real sea. There are large lakes below, but they will not go beyond their own shores. So this is the sea." And it was at that point that I began to realise we had entered the clouds, that visibility was rapidly growing less. I looked back. Already I could barely see the farmhouse. "Now," Alisaard told us, "we had best link hands. I shall continue to lead. The path is marked by cairns, but frequently animals will destroy them. Be wary, too, for the smoke snakes. They are predominantly dark grey and frequently cannot be seen until they are at your feet."

"What do they do, these smoke snakes?" Von Bek stretched his hand out to Alisaard. He put his other hand in mine.

"They protect themselves if you step on them," she said simply. "And since we have no weapons save the knives, we must be more than usually careful to avoid that. I shall watch for the cairn. You two watch the ground. Remember, they are of a darker grey."

In all that white and grey, with rocks and the remains of abandoned walls sometimes emerging from the fog, I wondered how anyone could spot such a creature. Nonetheless I scrupulously did as she had instructed me. I had come to trust Alisaard both as a comrade and a guide. This fact increased my misery on one level, particularly when it seemed to me she gave von Bek a further admiring glance.

The going was slower and slower, yet I continued to concentrate on looking for the dark grey of a smoke snake. From time to time I saw something moving; something which curled lazily upwards like a snake and then sank down again, which seemed to possess a vast number of coils, like the old pictures of sea serpents on mariners' charts. I thought I heard a faint noise, too, like the rise and fall of surf on a gentle beach.

"Are those the sounds the smoke snake makes?" I asked Alisaard. I was astonished at the echoing effect of the fog. My voice sounded completely unreal in my own ears.

Ahead, concentrating on finding the next cairn, she nodded.

It had grown very cold and our clothing was either soaked or running with water. I could not imagine it would be much warmer when we emerged from the fog, since it was thick enough to blot most of the sunlight. Von Bek, too, it seemed was feeling the chill, for he appeared to be shivering.

I looked ahead, wondering if Alisaard's ivory armour offered her any protection at all from the fog. As I did so, I saw a great grey coiling shadow rise up not three feet from the Ghost Woman. I cried out in warning. She did not respond, but stopped. The three of us watched as the thing writhed slowly into the fog. I had still not made out any features. "They are not to be feared when they poise themselves like that," Alisaard told me. "They are merely looking at us. If they can see us then we are in no danger. It is only the young ones, and usually only then when they are disturbed in sleep, who strike. But I remind you—do not step upon a smoke snake. They react violently when startled. These old fellows have seen many travellers and know they are not in danger. Am I clear?"

She sounded almost impatient, as if she dealt with a slow-witted child. I apologised for my panic. I said I would remember what she said and keep my concentration only on the ground ahead of me.

Von Bek understood that I had received a mild reprimand. He turned to look at me just as we started off again. He winked.

And it was at that moment that I saw his foot stepping directly upon the tip of a grey coil.

"Von Bek!"

He looked at me in horror, realising what I had seen. His eyes widened further in pain. "My God," he said softly, "it has my calf. . . ."

Then Alisaard was flinging herself downwards, knife poised, left hand stretching full ahead of her.

The dark grey coils were moving slowly but surely up von Bek's leg. I could see no head, no mouth, no eyes, yet I knew the creature was crawling up his body, seeking the upper parts, the head and face. I reached out to try to tug the thing off and there came a savage, metallic hiss from somewhere within the beast. Another coil seemed to detach itself from the main body and cling to my wrist. With my knife I cut at it, trying to slice it, but somehow the knife made no impression at all. Von Bek also used his knife. And with equal impotence. I saw Alisaard's figure very dimly through the fog. She was still on the ground, growling to herself, cursing in frustration, as if she sought something she had lost. I heard the

ivory armour clattering against rocks. I thought I saw her arm
rise and fall. And still the smoke snake continued to climb my
arm and von Bek's leg at the same time. I was close to being
sick with the horror of it while von Bek's face was paler than
the mist surrounding it.

I looked at the tip of the coil, where it was almost at my
shoulder. Now I thought, somewhere within the creature, I
saw the faintest suggestion of features. It darted at my face
then, as if in outrage at my discovery. I felt a sharp pain in my
cheek. I felt blood begin to run down my cheek. Almost at
once the smoke snake's head revealed a scarcely visible but
distinct mouth full of long, thin teeth, of vibrating nostrils, the
suggestion of a tongue.

And, thanks to my blood, the head now glowed a delicate
and horrifying pink.

6.

WITHIN seconds the smoke snake had begun to turn a darker red. Its other head reached von Bek's face and struck, as it still struck at mine, taking tiny, almost dainty, bites of my flesh. I knew it would continue to bite in this way until my head was nothing but a white skull on my body. I believe I screamed something, but I cannot remember the words. It was a prospect of death all the more terrifying because it would not be quick. I waved my knife in front of the head, which now displayed glaring crimson eyes, hoping somehow to distract it. But it had a strange kind of patience. It was as if it waited until it perceived a gap in my defence then it would dart through again. And again my face would sting from a further wound. I remembered scars on a traveller's face at the Great Massing. I remembered wondering what had pocked him so. At least, I thought, it was possible to escape the smoke snake. That man had done so, though it had cost him an eye and half his face.

Von Bek was screaming, too. There was an appalling inevitability about the creature's attack. As our arms grew more tired, as it became steadily more and more visible, thanks to our blood, it merely waited, maintaining its grip on our limbs and occasionally giving vent to that awful metallic hissing.

What made the experience worse for me was that the creature no longer seemed angry. It was a simple enough organism, I supposed. It only reacted when it believed itself attacked. When it had its coils about something, that something was then tasted. If the taste was good, that something simply became the smoke snake's ordinary prey. It probably could not even remember its initial reason for attacking von

Bek. It had no reason to hurry now. It could take a leisurely meal.

I tried to stab the fanged maw with the knife again. All logic suggested that the creature which could inflict such wounds must therefore to able to receive such wounds. But it was not so. My knife, cutting and slashing wildly, found only the tiniest resistance and a faint, pinkish dust seemed to surround the head like a halo for a moment before being reintegrated into the bulk of the animal.

All this, of course, in a matter of seconds.

Meanwhile, Alisaard continued to curse and shout. I could not see her at all. I could only hear, as if in the back of my mind, her rattling armour and her animal-like grunts and howls of frustrated action.

Von Bek's face looked as if he had been weeping tears of blood. Streamers of blood ran down his cheeks. Part of his left ear had been torn away. He had a bite, swollen with blood, in the very centre of his forehead. He drew rapid, sobbing breaths. His eyes spoke not so much of a fear of death but of the horror and pointlessness of the manner of his death.

Then I heard Alisaard's cry change. It was almost a howl of triumph. A kind of ululation. I still could not see anything of her, save a white hand grabbing for the insubstantial main body of the smoke snake. She uttered a sort of prolonged groan. I saw her knife dart out of the fog and her other hand seemed to strike at the identical spot.

The smoke snake reared back. I was sure it would take one of my eyes. I brought my hand up to shield myself. Unable to see the snake I might easily have believed the thing did not exist, save in my imagination. It had virtually no weight. Yet it held me tight.

I heard von Bek give vent to a huge roar. I thought the thing had struck some vital spot and, still without looking, threw myself forward, even while I knew I was incapable of saving him. But there would be some value, I remember thinking, if one died in such an attempt. There is consolation for certain souls, even in the moment of the most hideous and violent death.

I felt two arms embrace me. I opened my eyes. The smoke snake's coils no longer writhed around half von Bek's body. I wondered if he and I were already dead, if this were some anodyne illusion of safety as our lifeblood bloated the belly of our antagonist.

"Herr Daker!" I heard von Bek say in some surprise. "He appears to have fainted, my lady."

I lay on the ground. I saw my friends staring down at me. There was amusement as well as anxiety there. I looked at them. I felt tremendous relief that they lived. And I felt again that demeaning pang of jealousy as I saw their heads come together above mine. "No," I murmured. "You must be Ermizhad. Be Ermizhad if only for a moment while I die. . . ."

"That is the name he spoke before," said Alisaard.

I thought them rather unconcerned that their friend was dying. Were they already dead?

"It is the name of an Eldren woman, like yourself," I heard von Bek say. "He loves her. He has sought her across the aeons; he has searched for her in so many realms. He thinks you resemble her."

Her features softened. She removed a glove and touched my face. I moved my lips and said for a second time: "Ermizhad, before I die . . ." But already reality was returning and I knew I hovered on the edge of playacting, willing to pretend I was still in a swoon if I could prolong that moment, that feeling of receiving goodhearted and honest sympathy, such as I had once received from Ermizhad and which, I hope, I had given in return. Then I made a great effort and said firmly: "Forgive me, my lady. I am recovered. My senses are about me again. Perhaps you would be good enough to tell me how Count von Bek and myself are still amongst the living!"

Von Bek helped me into a sitting position. The fog did not seem quite so dense now. I thought I could see some distance down the hill, to where wide, silver water awaited us.

Alisaard had seated herself upon a rock. She had something small and unlovely at her feet, placed on a flat shard of flint. It, too, seemed to possess thousands of coils, but these were tiny and of no possible danger, unless they were poisoned. She poked at the little black thing with her knife-point. It seemed completely lifeless. Indeed, beneath her knife it began to crumble. Parts of it rapidly turned to fine, black dust.

Unbelievingly I said: "Surely that cannot be the remains of the smoke snake?"

She looked up at me, sucking in her lower lip, raising her eyebrows. She nodded.

Von Bek stared down at the fossilised fragments. "It was defeated by the commonest of substances in the hands of a most uncommon woman."

She was pleased by his praise. "I knew only one way of killing a smoke snake. You must find its centre. Cut it, and you create as many new creatures as there are fresh pieces. You must make it bleed and kill it at the moment before it can divide. The blood carries that which you use to destroy it. Happily I remembered that. Happily, too, like all Gheesten-heemers I travel with my own supplies."

"But what killed it, Lady Alisaard? How did you save our lives when our weapons had no effect on the thing?"

Von Bek interrupted her. He was laughing. "You'll see the humour of it, when she tells you. Please, Alisaard, let him not stay in suspense any longer. The poor man's exhausted!"

Alisaard showed me the palm of her left hand. It had a faint crust of white near the centre. "Salt. We always carry salt."

"The thing responded as swiftly as any ordinary garden slug!" Von Bek was exultant. "As soon as she found that core —and that was where her courage was unbelievable—she had to strike with her knife to draw blood and apply the salt at the exact same second. The core shrivelled immediately. And we were saved." He dabbed at the little scabs on his face. The wounds were already healing. They would leave few marks. I supposed myself lucky. "Nothing to show for it," my friend added, "but what appears to be the remains of a bad case of acne."

He helped me to my feet. I presented myself to the Lady Alisaard. Now she resembled my Ermizhad even closer than she had at first. "I thank you from the bottom of my heart, Lady Alisaard. I thank you for my life."

"You would have given yours trying to save Count von Bek," she said gently as she flipped the dead core out into the mist. "Luckily I had a little more knowledge of these things." She looked with a mixture of merriment and sternness at von Bek. "And let us hope a certain gentleman does better at watching his feet rather than his comrade if he comes this way again."

Chastened, von Bek became an exemplary German nobleman. He drew himself upright and at attention. He clicked his heels and bowed in acknowledgement of what he regarded as a just condemnation of his folly.

Both Alisaard and I found it difficult to hide our amusement at his sudden adoption of formal manners.

"Come," she said then, "we must haste to reach the lower

slopes. There we shall be out of the domain of the smoke snakes and can rest without much fear of any further attacks. It is too late now to approach the city, for it is their custom to refuse all visitors after dark. But in the morning, refreshed, we can go there and hope they will agree to help us find Morandi Pag."

With the mist at last above us and twilight bringing further chill, the three of us drew close together for warmth as we stretched out on the springy and rather comfortable turf of the slope. I remember looking down into the valley where it widened out into a kind of bay overlooking the lake. In this bay and along the river bank for some distance inland I could see lights winking, fires blazing. I thought I heard voices, although these could have been the sounds of flocks of jet-black carrion birds as they crowded home to their nests in the upper crags. I wondered at the city. I could see no buildings of any kind. I could see no ships, though I thought there were some quays and piers at the water's edge. Further along the shore of the lake there grew a deep, thick wood whose trees primarily resembled oaks. From this, too, now emerged some lights, as if foresters made their way homeward. Again I looked in vain for buildings. I wondered vaguely as I fell into a deep and exhausted slumber, if, like the smoke snakes, the city and its residents were invisible to the human eye. I remembered something of another people who had been called "ghosts" by those who refused to understand them and I tried to bring the memory into sharper focus. But as often happened with my overcrowded brain, I could not quite grasp the full recollection. It had something, I thought, to do with Ermizhad. I turned my head. In the last of the light I looked directly into Alisaard's sleeping face.

And in the privacy of the night I believe I wept for Ermizhad before sleep came to fling me into further torment. For I dreamed of a hundred women: a hundred who had been betrayed by warlike men and heroic folly, by their own deepest feelings of love, by their romantic idealism. I dreamed of a hundred women. And I knew each of them by name. I had loved each of them. And every one I had lost.

At dawn I woke to see that out near the horizon of the lake the clouds had parted and great red-gold waves of sunlight were pouring through, staining the water where they struck. Elsewhere this explosion of light stood in heavy contrast to the black and grey of the surrounding mountains and waters, giv-

ing them an added dramatic value. I half expected to hear
music, to see the people of the river valley come rushing out
into the morning, cheering in that magnificent dawn. But the
only sound from the settlement below us was the occasional
clank of domestic pots, the yap of an animal, a thin voice.

I could still not see where the city itself was. I supposed
these people to be cave dwellers who camouflaged the entrances to their houses. This was a common enough custom in
all the realms of the multiverse I had visited. Yet I was somehow surprised that the traders who risked the journey through
the Pillars of Paradise to barter with neighbouring realms did
not live in what I would think of as more civilised buildings.

Alisaard smiled when I voiced this puzzle. She took me by
the arm and looked into my face. "All the mysteries will be
solved in Adelstane," she promised. Then she linked her arm
in von Bek's and, like a schoolgirl on a picnic, led us down
the grassy hill towards the settlement. I paused for a moment
before following. For a moment I had lost any notion of where
I was or, indeed, who I was. I thought I smelled cigar smoke.
I thought I heard a double-decker bus in the nearby street. I
forced myself to stare at the blossoming dawn, the huge tum-
bling clouds on the far side of the lake. At last my head
cleared, I remembered the name of Flamadin. I remembered
Sharadim. A tiny shock went through my body. And then, for
my present purposes, I was whole again.

I caught up with my friends when they were almost at the
bottom of the hill, passing through a gate in a low wall and
looking back as if they realised for the first time that I was not
with them.

We walked together down a winding track to where the
water was shallow, forming a ford. I could see now that this
weir had been artificially built to do away with the need for a
bridge which could be easily seen from above. I wondered at
this strange precaution even as we waded through the cold,
clear water and eventually stood on the other bank, staring up
at a series of mighty openings in the cliff face, each one of
which had been cunningly fortified and then disguised as natural rock. Now I was beginning to realise that these people
were not bereft of architectural and building skills.

Alisaard had replaced her visor. Now she cupped her hands
and called up. "Friendly visitors here to throw themselves
upon the mercy of Adelstane and her lords!"

There was a sudden silence. Even the tiny sounds of cooking could no longer be heard.

"We bring news in the common interest," called Alisaard. "We have no weapons and we are neither loyal to nor serve any of your enemies."

This had begun to sound like a formal declaration; a matter of necessary courtesy, I supposed, if we were to be granted an audience with the troglodytes.

All at once the silence was broken by a distinct thud. Then another. Then a louder sound, as if metal struck metal. Then the long booming note of a gong came rolling from the higher entrances of the cave system.

Alisaard lowered her arms as if in satisfaction.

We paused. Von Bek made to speak but she motioned him to hold his tongue.

The note of the gong died away. Next came a kind of breathy roaring as if a giant failed to find a note on a monstrous trumpet. Then part of the nearest cave entrance seemed to fall inwards, revealing a dark, jagged opening; it might have been a natural fissure in the rock.

Alisaard led us forward and, with an easy movement of her body, slid herself through the opening. Von Bek and I followed, with rather less grace and some complaint.

And then we were turning and looking in awe at what was next revealed to us.

It was perhaps the most graceful city of spires and slender architecture I had ever seen in all my wanderings. It was white, glistening as if the moon shone upon it. It was stark against the surrounding semi-darkness of the vast cave. Above we heard the breathy noise again, then the booming, and we realised that the sounds had been created through natural acoustics in the cave, which had to be more than three miles in circumference and whose roof was lost from sight. It was so delicate, that city, with its traceries of marble and quartz and glittering granite, that it seemed a breeze would waft it away. It had the fragility of a wonderful illusion. I felt that if I blinked it might not be there when I looked up again. I had been right to be suspicious of apparent primitivism, but I had been wrong to think for a moment that the river traders were barbarians.

"It's like a city made of lace," said von Bek almost in a whisper. "A thousand times more beautiful even than Dresden!"

"Come," said Alisaard, beginning to walk down the large, polished steps which led to a road which in turn led to Adelstane. "We must now proceed without a hint of hesitation. The lords of this city are over-quick to detect spies or scouts from an enemy."

Behind us little fires were burning in the rocks. I saw white faces peering from the shadows of crude shelters. These people shuffled and scuffled and muttered to themselves before gradually returning to their interrupted tasks. I found it very difficult to associate such obvious savages with the people who dwelled in and had built the city.

I asked Alisaard who the people of the walls were and she apologised for not telling me more. "They're Mabden, of course. They are afraid of the city. Afraid of almost everything. And being permitted no weapons with which they can attack what they fear, they are reduced to what you see. It seems the Mabden can only kill or run away. Their brains are of no use to them."

Von Bek was sceptical. "They look to me like the useless economic units of some over-rigid political system, driven out here so that they will not be a burden on the others."

Alisaard frowned. "I cannot follow you."

Von Bek was smiling, almost to himself. "You have great experience of magic and scientific marvels, Lady Alisaard, but it appears there are very few economically complex civilisations in the whole of the multiverse!"

She appeared to understand him. Her brow cleared. "Ah, of course! Yes, your assumption is more or less accurate. This is not the right sector for those societies."

I looked with private pleasure on von Bek's face as he realised that not only had he been guilty of intellectual arrogance, he had been put in his place by someone who was undoubtedly his mental superior.

Von Bek looked at me and saw that I had recognised his response. "It's odd how easily we slip into the assumptions and follies of our own cultures when we are faced with the alien and inexplicable. If ever I come through this and am successful in my ambition, if Germany is ever free of war and insane terror, I have it in mind to write a book or two on the subject of mankind's reactions to the novel and the unlikely."

I clapped him on the back. "You are avoiding one trap and falling into another, my friend. Never fear, when the moment comes you'll decide against those treatises and get on with the business of living. It's example and effort which improve our lot, not any number of learned volumes."

He took what I said in good part. "You are truly a simple soldier at heart, I think."

"There are probably few simpler than I," I told him. "Few more ordinary. It baffles me why I should have become what I am."

"Perhaps only a fundamentally sane creature could accept the amount of experience and information you have accumulated," said von Bek. His voice was almost sympathetic. Then he cleared his throat. "However, there's a danger in too much sentimentality as well as too much intellectuality, eh?"

We had arrived at the glowing, circular gate of the city. A ring of fire, it seemed to me, burned steadily and without heat. It shone so brightly that we were half blinded, unable to see beyond the gateway into Adelstane herself.

Alisaard did not pause but walked directly up to the mighty circle and stepped through it at the point where it touched the rocky surface. We could do nothing else but follow her example. Closing my eyes I stepped into the fire and immediately found myself on the other side, unscathed. Von Bek was next. He found the whole thing, he said, remarkable.

Alisaard said: "The fire burns cold only for friendly visitors. The Lords of Adelstane have extended to us their most trusting welcome. We can feel flattered."

Now we saw about five figures ahead of us on the white road, which still reflected the firelight behind us. The figures were dressed in billowing robes, heavy weaves of sober colours, lighter silks and lace to rival the exquisite complexity of the city's architecture. Each figure held a staff on which a small, stiffened linen banner stood. Each banner was a finely detailed picture in its own right. The pictures were extremely stylised and I could not immediately recognise the subjects. My attention was quickly drawn away from the banners, however, by the faces of the waiting five. They were not human. They were not even the eldritch faces of Alisaard's people. I had not realised that Barganheem was the realm dominated by those strange beasts, the Ursine Princes. These people resembled bears, though it was plain there were many differences, particularly about the hands and legs. They stood upright with no difficulty whatsoever. Their black eyes were like rain-washed ebony, yet they did not threaten.

"Be welcome in Adelstane," they said in chorus.

Their voices were deep, vibrant and somehow to me they were also comforting. I wondered at those who had made themselves this people's enemies. I felt that I could trust any one of them to do exactly what he claimed. I stepped forward, extending my arms in greeting.

The bear-folk moved back a step, their nostrils quivering. They attempted to recover themselves and it was plain they thought they had been discourteous to us.

"It is our smell," said Alisaard softly in my ear. "They find it revolting."

7.

I HAD expected to find myself and my friends in some vast receiving room, an auditorium where guests could state their business and be seen by all the Ursine Princes and their retinues. Such ceremony would have been suitable for the city.

Instead we were led by the five dignified creatures through streets of exceptional cleanliness, filled with buildings of astonishing beauty, until we came to a small domed hall which, in its simplicity, reminded me somewhat of an old Baptist church. Within we found warmth, comfortable chairs, a library—all the accumulated treasures which, say, a university don might come by in a lifetime of quiet appreciation of the world.

"This is where we live much of the time," said one of the bearlike people. "We have domestic quarters, of course. We conduct our business from this place. I hope you will forgive the informality. Will you have wine? Or another drink?"

"We appreciate your hospitality," I said awkwardly. I was going to add that we were rather anxious to see the great princes as soon as they could spare time to see us when Alisaard, doubtless anticipating me, interrupted.

"We all appreciate it, my lords. And we are honoured to find ourselves in the company of those who are called the Ursine Princes throughout the Six Realms."

I was surprised, even while I was grateful to her. It seemed completely wrong to my expectations that such a wonderfully decorative city should not indulge the most elaborate of ceremonies. And I had thought we were to be inspected by a whole host of noble bears. Now I could only presume that these were the only ones. Certainly the only ones we should meet.

The large room was heavily perfumed. From the fireplace in the centre of the left-hand wall great gusts of incense billowed. I realised that our odour must be inconceivably disgusting to them for them to go to such pains.

"Ah, that," said one of the princes, seating himself and his complicated arrangement of clothing in a great armchair, and pointing at the fire with his pole. "That is our custom. I trust you will forgive our fads. We are all somewhat old and set in our ways. I am Groaffer Rolm, Prince of the North River, successor to the Autuvian family which, sadly, ceased to produce issue." He rubbed at his snout and sighed. The closer I came to them, the more I realised they only superficially resembled bears. It seemed to me this species had existed long before the advent of the bear. "And this is Snothelifard Plare, Prince of the Big South River and the Little East, hereditary head of the Winter Caravan." A wave of silk and lace at the creature beside him. "Over there is Whiclar Hald-Halg, Prince of the Great Lake Spill, last bearer of the Flint. Glanat Khlin, Prince of the Deep Canals, Bat Speaker. And lastly, my wife, Faladerj Oro, Prince of the Shouting Rapids and Regent of the Western Seasonals." Groaffer Rolm made a small, polite grunting noise. "I am, I'm afraid, the last male prince left."

"Are your people so depleted by aggressors?" von Bek asked sympathetically, after we had returned the introductions. "Is that why you were so cautious, Lord Prince, to admit us here?"

Prince Groaffer Rolm paused, raising a hand. "I have misinformed you, it seems. Until lately, this realm knew peace for century upon century. We grew used to persecution, certainly, and we built our cities away from the envious eyes of Mabden and others. But we have so successfully hidden ourselves from enemies we have only the habit of caution left!" He pretended to turn his head and inspect the fire. Actually he was inhaling more of the incense.

His wife, Prince Faladerj Oro, spoke. "Most of what we mine is too precious, too beautiful, to trade. You see before you five decadent old creatures in the decline of their race's age. We have lived without stimulus for too long now. We are dying."

"Though," said one I took to be younger, Whiclar Hald-Halg, "we have seen four full cycles of the multiverse come and go. Few others survive one." She spoke proudly. "There are few with histories as long as those you call the Ursine Princes. We call ourselves Oager Uv. We have almost always been a river people." She began to seat herself, fluffing her lace and her heavy wools as she did so.

Prince Groaffer Rolm waited with attentive stillness until Whiclar Hald-Halg had completed her speech. "There you have us," he said. "We have a few family left, but that is the sum of our race. We had expected to end our days in peace. The Mabden offer us no trouble. Sometimes they trade one of their young for whatever it is they have decided they need from us. We, in turn, pass the boys on to Gheestenheem, where we know no harm will come to them. But then came news of this army of liberators, apparently sworn to release the Mabden from imprisonment here. Is it this you would warn us of?"

Alisaard was puzzled. "I know nothing of such an army. Who leads it?"

"A Mabden. I cannot remember his name. They are coming through on the Eastern Banks, apparently, in large numbers. Of course, it is many years since we were there ourselves. If all they wanted were those shores, we would have given them up. We want nothing but this city and tranquility. But, thanks to a Mabden more honourable than most, we learned of this invasion in time. And so our allies will arrive here shortly, to defend us in our last years. It seems an unlikely irony. And, moreover, it is a familiar one, eh? The remnants of an ancient aristocracy defended by those who were once their fiercest enemies?"

I was suspicious as, I could see, were Alisaard and von Bek.

"Pardon, Prince Groaffer Rolm," said Alisaard. "But when did you learn of this holy war against you?"

"Not thirty breaks since."

"And do you remember the name of the honourable Mabden who has offered to help you?"

"That I can remember easily, aye. Her name is the Princess Sharadim of Draachenheem. She has become a good friend to us, and asks nothing. She understands our principles and our customs and she has made it her business to learn much of our history. She is a good creature. It is a blessing for us that all our other cities are long since abandoned. She only has the

one to defend. We anticipate her soldiers during the next con-
junction."

Alisaard flushed. Like me, like von Bek, she did not know
how best and with what formal manners, to disabuse the Ursine Princes.

At last von Bek said brutally, "So she deceives you also.
As she deceives so many in her own land. She means you ill,
my lords, and that is certain."

There came a considerable snuffling, throat clearing and
not a little cracking of joints.

Alisaard spoke passionately. "It is true, my princes. This
woman plans to league herself with Chaos and destroy the
barriers between the realms, turning the Worlds of the Wheel
into one vast and lawless place where she and her allies of
Chaos shall establish a perpetual tyranny!"

"Chaos?" Prince Glanat Khlin waddled to the fire and
breathed in the smoke. "No Mabden can league themselves
with Chaos and survive—not in their original form, at any
rate. Or does she hope to be made a Lord of Chaos herself?
That is sometimes the ambition of such people...."

"I would remind my Sister Prince," said Snothelifard
Plare, "that we have only heard charges from this trio. We
have been offered no evidence. I have, for my own part, an
instinctive trust of the Mabden female Sharadim. I have a way
of understanding her kind. These emissaries could be from
those who march against Adelstane!"

"On my word," cried Alisaard, "we are not your enemies.
We serve neither Sharadim nor the jehad you speak of. We
came to you for help in our own quest. We seek to stop the
spread of evil, to halt Chaos and its schemes for our realms.
We came to you because we hoped to find Morandi Pag."

"There you have it!" Snothelifard Plare pulled back her
muzzle and clicked at her teeth with her nails. "There you
have it!"

Alisaard looked from face to face. "What do you mean?"

Groaffer Rolm inhaled an enormous mouthful of smoke.
Even as he spoke the fumes began to escape from his nostrils
and add to those already in the room. "Morandi Pag has gone
mad. He was one of us. An Ursine Prince, you would say.
Prince of the Southeast Rushers and the Cold Ponds. A great
trader. Always his own steersman. Friend. Oh!" And Groaffer
Rolm raised his snout to the painted ceiling and gave a
mournful groan.

"His childhood friend," explained Faladerj Oro as she stroked her husband's wrinkling head. "His great sharer." And a little whimper escaped her mouth. "Yes. He is with them, we are informed. We sent for him. Urgently, we told him we must see him in Adelstane, so that he could tell us he does not serve the Mabden. But he did not come. He did not send a message. Amongst our people that is more than a statement that what is rumoured is true."

"Morandi Pag has an odd mind," said Glanat Khlin. "Always an odd mind. Took action, he did. Always action following his delicate and unreadable logic. As a trader he was the last of the true River Princes. As a seer he had trained himself to look into a thousand times and places. As a scientist his theories were of exquisite intricacy. Oh, Morandi Pag was what our ancestors were. An odd mind which could foresee unimaginable possibilities. So he left for his crag at last. But we did not know he disapproved of our treatment of the Mabden. He had only to make it clear. We do merely what the Mabden say they want. We offered them one of our loveliest cities for themselves. They refused it. If we are guilty of obtuse reasoning, we should be told. We would change. If the Mabden want to return to a Mabden realm, we can take them. But they would not consider any of our suggestions. Now this comes. We did no wrong, I think."

"Perhaps we did wrong," said Snothelifard Plare. "If so, Morandi Pag of all the princes could have told us how. Yet that is done. We have a barbarian force marching against us. It means killing. We cannot defend ourselves entirely without employing death. These other Mabden know death and how to deal it. We are without resources in the matter of tools, even."

"Aye," agreed Groaffer Rolm, recovering himself slowly. "No weapons, and Sharadim has the means of finding these. She defends beauty, she says. That, we think, is worth defending. But we could not easily kill. Mabden can easily kill, as we all recognise here, I think. Ah! Morandi Pag. He will not send even writing to us. No. We do not want the Mabden. They are fleas. Ah!" And he turned his head into the fireplace, leaving his wife in great confusion, offering us a glance of apology for her husband's description of those she considered our kind.

"They are worse than fleas, Prince Faladerj Oro," I said quickly. "They are perhaps the worst sort of flea, at any rate. Wherever they bite, they leave disease and ruin behind. But I suspect both Mabden armies to be commanded by Sharadim. She uses one to frighten you, one to reassure you. We know she planned to bring an army here. But we thought she marched against Morandi Pag. If so, how can she be in league with him?"

"Someone should visit that crag, as I said." Groaffer Rolm puffed smoke from his nostrils again. "If he is dead or ill, then much is explained. And I agree with these, Mabden, fellow princes. Sharadim cannot any longer be trusted. I suspect we waited so long to find Mabden whose morality we could respect that we deceived ourselves. . . ."

"The Princess Sharadim is an honourable creature," said Prince Snothelifard Plare. "I know it in my bones."

"Why did you not send someone to this crag before?" I asked. "If you suspected Morandi Pag to be ill."

Groaffer Rolm's snout grew wet and he sniffled. He coughed and pushed his head so far into the fireplace it almost disappeared. "We are too old," he said. "There is none can make the journey."

"Is the crag so far away?" von Bek's voice took on a new urgency.

"Not so far," said Groaffer Rolm, re-emerging from the incense. "About five miles, we used to reckon."

"You could send nobody five miles?" von Bek began to sound contemptuous.

"It is across the lake," Glanat Khlin spoke defensively. "The lake he himself explored, looking for the mythical Central Passage, which is said to pass permanently through all realms at once. All he found, they say, was his crag. But there is often a maelstrom there. And often big winds. We have no boats for it. Nothing made. And we can make nothing ourselves now."

"You, the great River Princes, have no boats? I have seen your ark at the Great Massing." I could not believe they were lying. "You do have boats."

"A few. The ark is mere trickery so that no Mabden will look greedily on our artefacts. The Gheestenheemers have similar strategies, which is why we have always been allies. A few little boats left, yes. But we are too old."

"Then lend us one of those," said Alisaard. Hesitantly she put her hand on Groaffer Rolm's massive arm. "Lend us a boat and we will cross the lake to find Morandi Pag. Perhaps we shall find that he does not work against you. Perhaps the Mabden lied in this as in everything else?"

"The Princess Sharadim has psychic gifts," growled Snothelifard Plare. "She knows Morandi Pag schemes our finality."

"You will let them prove this?" Groaffer Rolm rose up from his chair in a great hissing and whispering of fabric. "You will let them prove it, lord prince. What bad can that bring us?"

Snothelifard Plare bent with fastidious slowness towards the fireplace and drew in the fumes by means of a long, loud sniff.

"Take the boat, but be careful," Faladerj Oro said, sounding almost like a mother to her children. "The crag lies beneath the sun. It is hot and the water acts strangely. Morandi Pag went there for solitude, to study. But he stayed. Only he knew the exact way the sea runs. It was one of his golden strengths. We watched him as young females, scenting for the currents lying in the deepest reaches. Then he would take his rafts and race through. Half our charts were drawn before the birth of Morandi Pag. Half our charts have been drawn since he came to us. And even a long-lived people like ours do not pass through four full cycles of the multiverse. He was our last great pride. If he had been a leader, I think we should have survived even a fifth cycle." She did not seem greatly upset by the prospect of her race's extinction. "Morandi Pag has derived his knowledge from the whole of the multiverse. Compared to him the rest of us are ignorant and parochial. We have boats below. They can be floated up to the old mole. Will you wait for the boat there? We shall give you charts. We shall give you provisions. We shall give you messages of friendship and concern for Morandi Pag. And then, if he lives, he will reply."

Not an hour later we stood in the grey light beneath those massive cliff walls, on a worn stone quayside, watching as from the depths there drifted a pale golden boat, with a mast all ready and a sail wrapped against the wet; with oars and little watertight boxes full of sweet pastes and grains, the water pouring from her as she rocked beside the stone mole, ready to receive us.

"I have seen these boats of theirs once before," said Alisaard, stepping confidently into it and arranging a seat for her comfort. "They cannot fill with water. It is a system of vents and valves, but so cunningly hidden in the design that they cannot be discovered by anyone save their makers."

The boat was much wider than the last one we had used. This boat was plainly designed to accept the weight and bulk of the bear-folk. But the boat responded with subtle ease to the tiller and the breeze.

We saw no more of the Ursine Princes as we set off towards the vent in the clouds, where light still poured, almost violently, upon water which, as we approached, was evidently foaming furiously and sending up occasional geysers of steam.

"Scalding water," said von Bek wearily. He seemed ready to accept defeat. "That's what defends Morandi Pag's crag. Look at the charts, Herr Daker. See if there are alternative means of approaching."

But there were none.

Soon, picked out by that vast funnel of sunlight, we saw through the steam and the foam a tall spike of rock, rising at least a hundred feet above the turbulent waters. Upon this spike, just visible now, was a building resembling those we had just left behind. It might even have been a natural formation, worked by thousands of years of elemental forces, but I knew it was not. It could only be Morandi Pag's house.

We slowed our boat's progress, heaving to before we were caught up in the swirling currents. The steam was so hot that we were soon all of us perspiring. There were other crags, other vicious spikes of rock, surrounding Morandi Pag's, but none was so tall. We stood upright in the boat and waved in the hope that he had some means of guiding us in. There was no sign of life from the white lace palace on the crag.

Alisaard had the charts beside her. "We can go through this way," she said, pointing. "It is a slab of rock which the sea has worn through. It offers the best protection from the geysers. Once through that we have to steer between the crags, but the water, according to the chart, is cooler there. At Morandi Pag's crag, there is a small bay, apparently. This is what we must reach before we are crushed against the rock walls. We seem to have only this choice. Or we can return to Adelstane and tell them we were unsuccessful. We can wait until Sharadim comes with her army. What shall we do then?"

She had answered her question. We would go forward. She scarcely waited for us to agree before, the chart in her teeth, one hand on the tiller and the other on the boom cords, she was driving towards the roaring, unsettled heat.

I hardly knew what happened to us in those few minutes while Alisaard steered our boat. My impression was of wild, dangerous waves, hurling us back and forth so that we rocked as we surged up and down, of sharp rocks passing an inch from the hull, of the wind tearing into the sail and of Alisaard singing a strange, ululating song as she took our craft towards the crag.

The black opening of the sea-worn tunnel came in sight and we were swallowed at once. The sea boomed and screamed at us. The boat scraped first one wall and then the other. Alisaard's song continued. It was a beautiful song. It was a defiant song. It was a challenge to the entire multiverse.

And then we were on a fresh current, being drawn out of the tunnel and towards Morandi Pag's towering shard of rock. I looked up. The intense sunlight seemed to have been concentrated by some cosmic lens. At its strongest point it shone directly upon the white palace, revealing whole parts of it to be utterly ruined.

I was furious. I slammed my fist against the side of the boat. "We have risked all that for nothing. Morandi Pag is dead. Nobody has lived in that place for years!"

But Alisaard ignored me. With the same delicate precision she steered the dancing boat towards the crag. And there, suddenly, we saw a pool of placid water, surrounded by high walls, with only a single narrow entrance. It was through this that Alisaard aimed our boat, and we found ourselves at last in a little enclave of tranquility. The boat rocked gently against the harbour wall. Beyond that wall we could hear the roaring water, the screaming geysers, but it was muffled, seemingly a long way distant. Alisaard finished her song. Then she stood up in the boat and she cheered.

And we joined in. Never has anyone cheered so thankfully.

The adrenaline was still running through us. Even Alisaard showed no sign of exhaustion. She clambered rapidly up the rungs of the harbour wall and stood watching as we left the boat more carefully and eventually joined her.

"There," she said, indicating a flight of steps and an opening beyond. "We are at the entrance of Morandi Pag's castle."

Ulrich von Bek looked out to where the sea still foamed. He said quietly: "I pray this Pag has devised a better way of leaving his stronghold. I am already feeling anxiety about our return voyage!"

Alisaard strode ahead of us, her ivory armour shedding the last of the sea water. She began to call Morandi Pag's name.

Von Bek laughed suddenly. "She should tell them we're from the funeral company. That old bear has been dead for years. Look at the condition of this place."

Alisaard began to speak a version of the same proclamation she had made outside the caves of Adelstane. "We are peaceful travellers, enemies of your enemies. We shall enter your home, knowing that you have not forbidden us that privilege."

She paused. There was no response.

Together the three of us passed through the cracked and mildewed entrance which, to our surprise, led immediately upon a set of steps going downwards into the rock.

The steps crept steadily down. Outside we could hear the distant groaning and murmuring of the waves. The place had a musty smell. I thought I detected a snuffling sound, of the kind Groaffer Rolm had made. It came from below.

And then, all at once, I grinned. My grin was shared by my companions.

For from the darkness at our feet there began to curl a thick, greenish smoke, its perfume so strong we were almost sickened by it.

"I think an Ursine Prince makes ready to bid us welcome," said von Bek. Alisaard chuckled appreciatively. I thought her response excessive.

Through this voluminous cloud we now progressed until we had at last reached a small archway. From the other side of this we made out tables, other furniture, books, ladders, instruments of all kinds, several different orreries, strange light from odd-shaped lamps. And emerging slowly with a rolling, energetic kind of shuffle, came the huge bulk of Morandi Pag himself. He wore few clothes—a little decorative lace and embroidery—and was almost entirely white. His fur had once been black, I suspected. Now there was only grizzled black hair on his head and down the middle of his back.

His large, dark eyes held an alert, perhaps sardonic, curiosity missing in his peers. Yet there was also a strange light in them, a tendency for his gaze to wander away from what he had begun to look at, to focus on sights invisible to us. His voice was deep and comforting, though vaguer and richer than those of the other princes. His manner was, in short, evidently absent-minded. It was, however, as if he deliberately fostered this in himself; as if he feared to let his mind cohere. This was a great intelligence, but one which had received an enormous blow. I had seen such looks on the faces of survivors from a thousand different forms of outrage. Von Bek, also, noticed this. We exchanged a glance.

Morandi Pag seemed amiable. "More Mabden explorers is it? Well, Mabden, be welcome. Do you chart these waters, as I once charted them?"

"We are not merchant adventurers, my lord," said Alisaard calmly. "We are here because we hope to save the Six Realms from Chaos."

There was a flash of awareness in those mild eyes. Then it was gone. Morandi Pag mumbled a tune through the remains of his teeth. He shuffled back towards his books and retorts. "I am old," he said, without looking at us. "I am too old. I am probably half-crazed with knowledge. I am not of use to anyone." He turned very quickly, almost glaring at me. And it was at me that he shouted. "You! It will come to you. It will come to you yet. My poor little Mabden." He leaned against a bench on which a dozen burners had been placed. It was these which gave off the heavy perfume. "Knowledge ceases to be wisdom when one has no method for making sense or use of what one learns. Eh? It was probably inevitable. Eh?"

"Prince Morandi Pag," said Alisaard urgently. "Our mission is what we say it is. Against Chaos and all that brings. Surely you would not hide something from us? Something crucial to our quest!"

"To protect," he said, moving his snout up and down in confirmation of his own statement. "Only that. Yes."

"Do you know where the Dragon Sword is?" von Bek asked him.

"Oh, yes. That. Of course I know. You may see it, if you wish. Below." He sighed deeply. "Is that all? The old hell-sword itself, hm? Yes, yes." But his eyes had already wandered to a jar of blue glass on his table. Within it, some sort of firefly seemed to be dancing. The noise Morandi Pag made was one of gentle pleasure.

After a moment, he turned that enormous head towards us again. He seemed to deliberate for almost a minute. Then he said soberly, his voice quavering a little with age, "I am extremely frightened by what is happening. How can you three not be afraid, also?"

"Because, Prince Morandi Pag, we have yet to confront anything," said von Bek. He spoke very softly indeed, as if he were gentling a horse.

"Ah!" said Morandi Pag, as if he found the explanation satisfactory. "Ah, you cannot imagine, cannot imagine. . . ." He became distracted again. He began to murmur names, scraps of equations, lines of verse, much of it in languages we could not begin to understand. "La, la, la, la. Would you three share a little of what I have? Food was never the problem, as you may have heard. But . . ." He scratched at his left ear. He looked at us enquiringly.

"The Dragon Sword, Prince Morandi Pag," Alisaard reminded him.

"Yes. You wish to see it? Yes. It is below."

"Will you take us to it? Or shall we go ourselves?" she asked slowly. "What shall we do, Prince Morandi Pag?"

"See what you think." He had forgotten our conversation already. He tapped at tubes and bottles. "La, la, la, la."

Von Bek motioned towards a door on the other side of the room. "We must see what is through there. I am sorry to seem impolite, but we have little time." He strode through parchments and tomes, abandoned instruments and piles of jars, each of which contained a mysterious substance, and put his fingers out towards the handle. He paused, looking enquiringly at Morandi Pag.

Eventually the old bear spoke. Again his voice was controlled, full of wise awareness. "You may go through there to look for it, if you wish."

We had joined von Bek by the time he had begun to turn the handle. The door was not made of wood but of pockmarked rock, like pumice, multicoloured. There were designs carved into it. The designs were in the same style I had seen on the banners of Adelstane. I could not quite make out what they represented.

Without a creak or a protest, the door opened smoothly. The room beyond was small and circular, virtually a cupboard. Lamps flickered from within it. On shelves were packets, scrolls, boxes, jars, strawbound bottles and a number of objects whose function was obscure.

However, it was what hung from the central beam by means of a big brass hook which drew our attention. It was an ornamental cage, which, judging by the droppings on its sides and bottom, had once been used to hold an enormous bird.

But it no longer held a bird. Instead the captive who stared at us through the narrow bars was a small man. Dressed in what closely resembled mediaeval motley, he seemed thankful that we had come. There was no telling how long he had been there.

From behind us, Morandi Pag's voice had grown vague again.

"Ah, yes," he said. "Now I remember where I hid the little Mabden."

8.

THE man in the cage was Jermays the Crooked. He recognised me almost at once and laughed aloud. "Well met, Sir Champion! I am glad to see you."

Morandi Pag came shuffling up to fumble at the complicated lock. "I put him in there when I sighted your boat. That way any enemy would think him a slave or a pet and not necessarily wish to destroy him."

"Put me in there, I might add," said Jermays without malice or anger, "against my protests. That's the fifth time you've had me in that damned cage, Prince Pag. Don't you ever remember?"

"Have I put you there before?"

"Almost every time you've spotted a boat." Jermays clambered with his usual agility from the cage and dropped to the floor. He looked up at me. "Congratulations, Sir Champion. Yours is the first to get through undamaged. You must be a skilled helmsman."

"The credit is all the Lady Alisaard's. She is an expert at the tiller."

Jermays bowed to the Gheestenheemer. The young dwarf, on his bandy legs and with his thin, ginger beard, managed a certain dignity. She seemed charmed by him. Next he presented himself to Ulrich von Bek. The two exchanged names.

"You already know my little Mabden?" said Morandi Pag in tones of absolute normality. "It will be wonderful for him to have others of his kind for company. You're the Champion, I know. Yes, I know you are the Champion. Because . . ." And his eyes became strangely blank. He stood with his muzzle gaping, staring into the middle distance.

Jermays darted forward and took the old bear's arm, leading him back to his chair. "He has too much in his head. Sometimes this happens."

"You know him well?" asked Alisaard in some surprise.

"Oh, indeed. I have been his sole companion here for almost seventy years. I had no choice. In my present circumstances I do not seem to be able to roam through the realms at will, as I sometimes can. I have found every day stimulating, I must say. Now, you were looking for something." He helped Morandi Pag slowly resume his seat. "I should like to assist."

"Morandi Pag said he would show us the Dragon Sword," von Bek told him.

"Oh, so he has spoken of the Scarlet Crystal? Yes, I know where that is to be found. Well, I can easily lead you down there, but we shall have to take Morandi Pag with us. For I am useless where spells are concerned. Will you give him a while to rest?"

"We are upon a desperate quest," said Alisaard softly.

"We shall go now!" Morandi Pag rose suddenly, full of energy. "At once! It is urgent, you say? Very well. Come, you shall see the Dragon Sword!"

There was a narrow doorway at the back of the cupboard where we had found Jermays. Morandi Pag led us through it, down two more spiralling flights. Now we could hear the sea booming and crashing all around us. It was so violent that we felt it must break down the rock walls and come flooding through.

Jermays the Crooked lit a brand and by means of the light from this he bent and with his long-fingered hands pulled on a chain set into the damp floor. He had opened a manhole. Misty light now came from below. Jermays disappeared down the hole, having signed for us to follow.

Morandi Pag said: "Go first. It will take me longer because of my age and my bulk."

I saw von Bek hesitate. He suspected a trick. But Alisaard urged him forward. I followed her down the somewhat slippery ladder.

The ladder descended directly into a cave which was actually a hollow pinnacle of rock. We stood on a long slab overlooking a swirling and foaming pool of water formed by rushing streamers which poured from what looked almost like windows set at fairly regular intervals above us. The water seemed to leave by an unseen series of vents at the bottom. It was a marvellous natural sight and we looked at it in silence for some while, wondering where we could possibly go from here.

I felt the bear's paw upon my shoulder. Turning, I saw that his eyes were melancholy. "Too much knowledge," he said. "It will happen to you, unless you take action. Our minds are finite in their capacity to accept information. Yes?"

"I suppose so, Prince Morandi Pag. Is the sword likely to do me harm?"

"Not yet. The harm it has done you and the harm it will do are not part of your current destiny, I think. But actions can change courses, naturally. I am not sure. . . ." He cleared his throat. "But you would see the sword, eh? Then you must look down there, into that pool."

"They'll not see it, Prince Pag," said Jermays the Crooked, speaking loudly over the sound of the ocean. "Not without your incantation."

"Ah, yes." Morandi Pag looked disturbed. He scratched at his white chest. He patted reassuringly at my arm. "Never fear. It is a peculiarly complicated arrangement of logic. A mental equation I must form. It helps me to sing something. You'll forgive me?" And he raised his snout and gave vent to a singular kind of wailing and grunting, a musical howling and a series of sharp barks.

"Has he gone crazy again?" asked von Bek.

Jermays pushed at his back. "Go to the edge. To the edge. Look into the waters. Think of nothing. Quickly. He is making the incantation!"

Now all four of us stood at the very end of the slab, peering through the spray into the swirling grey-green water as it poured relentlessly into the pool. The water had a hypnotic effect. It almost immediately captured our attention and held it. I felt myself swaying, felt little Jermays reach out and steady me. "You must not fear falling," he said. "Simply concentrate on the pool."

With some trepidation I did as he ordered. I could hear Morandi Pag's voice blending with the sound of the sea and the sound seemed to form an image, something substantial. Gradually the waters began to glow with a crimson lustre. Outside the tower the wind howled and the sea continued to assault the rocks. But within the spray was hardening, turning to tiny fragments of quartz fixed in space, and the crimson ocean had become an entire chamber of crystal. And suddenly I no longer heard Morandi Pag's voice. I no longer heard the natural sounds beyond those walls. A mighty stillness had fallen.

Now we looked through the crimson crystal to where something green and black seemed frozen, imbedded deep within the rock, like a fly in amber.

"It is the Dragon Sword," murmured Alisaard. "It is exactly as it was in our visions!"

Black blade, green hilt, the Dragon Sword seemed almost to writhe in its prison of crystal. And I thought I saw a tiny yellow flame moving deep within the blade, as if something else were imprisoned in the sword, just as the sword was imprisoned in the crystal.

"Can you let me hold it, Morandi Pag?" asked Alisaard in a whisper. "I know the spell to release the dragon. I must bear it back to Gheestenheem."

The Ursine Prince was as rapt as the rest of us. He seemed not to have heard her. "It is a thing of great beauty, I think. But so dangerous."

"Let us take it, Morandi Pag," begged von Bek. "We can make good come out of it. They say the sword is only as evil as the one who bears it. . . ."

"Aye, but you forget. They say it instills evil into whoever takes hold of it. Besides, it is not for me to say if you should or should not have the Dragon Sword. It is not mine to give."

"But it is in your cave. Surely it is in your possession." Alisaard began to look suspicious.

"I can summon it to this cave, because of our location. Or what do I mean? I mean that I can bring the shadow. . . ."

Quite suddenly Morandi Pag slid down onto the stone and seemed to fall into a peaceful sleep.

"Is he unwell?" said Alisaard in alarm.

"He is tired." Jermays stood over his friend. He placed a hand on the bear's wrinkled head, another near his heart. "Simply tired. He is these days in the habit of sleeping more than half the day as well as the night. He is naturally nocturnal."

Von Bek shouted urgently. "The sword! The sword is fading. The crystal wall is disappearing!"

"You said you wanted to see it," said Jermays, standing upright as best he could. "And see it you did. What else?"

"We need to release the dragon from the sword," Alisaard told him. "Before the blade can be forced to serve Chaos. The dragon seeks only her homeland. Keep it there, Jermays. Give us time to break it free of its prison! Please!"

"But I cannot. Neither could Prince Pag." Jermays seemed genuinely baffled. "What you saw was an illusion—or rather a vision of the Dragon Sword itself. The wall of crimson crystal is not in this cave any more than the sword can be found here."

The crimson glow had faded. The spray had become ordinary moisture again. The sea thumped and pounded and roared. Jermays begged us to help him get Morandi Pag to his feet. The old bear began to revive as we helped him as far as the ladder.

"But we had understood from you that it was physically here," von Bek spoke in an aggrieved tone. "Morandi Pag said it was here."

Alisaard corrected him. For a moment there was a sardonic smile on her features. "He said we could see it," she told von Bek. "That was all. Well, that's better than nothing. Now perhaps, when he revives, he'll tell us where we must go to find it."

Morandi Pag mumbled something as Jermays put his shoulder under the bear's rump and tried to push him up the ladder. Quickly I climbed up on the other side, then swung over so that I could take the old prince's paw and haul him from above. Eventually we got him back into the chamber, by which time he seemed to have grown alert again. He it was who seized the flambeau and led the way up the stairs. "Here!" he cried. "Follow me. This is where we go."

When we had all rejoined him in his main chamber he had already reached his armchair, fallen into it and was sleeping, as if he had never left.

Jermays looked down at him affectionately. "He'll sleep for a whole day now, I think."

"Shall we have to wait that long before we can continue with our search?" I asked.

"It depends what you want," Jermays said reasonably.

"You told us we had been granted a vision of the sword. But where is the crimson crystal wall? How can we get to it?" Alisaard wanted to know.

"I think we had assumed you knew the whereabouts of the sword," said Jermays. "And that you had decided not to pursue it."

"We had not the merest clue," Alisaard told him. "We do not even know which realm it is in."

"Ah," said Jermays, apparently illuminated by this information. "That explains much. What if I were to tell you that the Dragon Sword is held in the Nightmare Marches, that it has been there almost as long as the Barganheemers have dwelled here? Would that alter your intention of seeking it out?"

Alisaard put her head in her hands. The news had not merely confounded her. Temporarily, at any rate, it had robbed her of her resolve. "What chance have three mortals of finding anything there? And what chance have we of surviving?"

"Very little," said Jermays in a matter-of-fact tone. "Unless, of course, you had an Actorios. Even then it would be extremely dangerous. You are welcome to remain here with us. For my own part I would be glad of the additional company. There are few interesting card games for two players. And Morandi Pag tends to lose attention these days, even in a game of 'Snap.'"

"Why should the possession of an Actorios stone give us an advantage in the Nightmare Marches?" I asked him. Even as I spoke I was reaching into my belt-pouch and touching the warm, fleshlike stone of the Actorios which had been given me by the Announcer Elect Phalizaarn in Gheestenheem and whose destiny, according to Sepiriz, was intimately linked with mine.

"It shares something in common with a runestaff," Jermays said to me. "It can have an effect on its surroundings. To some slight extent, of course, compared with other more powerful artefacts. It will stabilise that which Chaos has touched. Moreover it has a certain affinity with those swords. It could help lead you to the blade you want. . . ." He shrugged his crooked back. "But what good would that do you? None, I suspect. And since it will be a good few ticks of the cosmic pendulum before you have an Actorios in your possession, Champion, there's no real point to this discussion."

I took out the pulsing, writhing stone and showed it to him on the flat of my palm.

He stared at it in silence for a while. He seemed suddenly subdued, almost frightened.

"Well," he said after a bit, "so you do have such a stone. Aha."

"Does that alter your estimate of our chances in the so-called Nightmare Marches, Master Jermays?" asked von Bek.

Jermays the Crooked darted a look at me that was oddly sympathetic. He turned around, pretending to interest himself in Morandi Pag's collection of alchemical glass. "I could do with a pear," he said. "I get a craving. Or a good apple would do at a pinch. Fresh food's scarce here. Unless you like fish. I have a feeling I'll be able to pick something for myself soon. The Balance is wavering. The Gods wake up. And when they begin their play, I shall be tossed about as usual. Here and there. But what will become of Morandi Pag?"

"There is an army on its way," said Alisaard. "It plans either to torture information from him or to destroy him, we are not absolutely sure. Princess Sharadim will lead the army."

"Sharadim?" Again Jermays looked directly at me. He had turned round in a flash. "Your sister, Champion?"

"Of sorts. Jermays, how can we enter the Nightmare Marches?"

He waved his unnaturally long arms and went to stand beside the sleeping Ursine Prince. "Nobody's stopping you," he told us. "It is not usually a question of the Nightmare Marches refusing visitors. Most visitors to those Marches are to say the least unwilling. The place is ruled by Chaos. It is where Chaos was exiled in the old battles of the Wheel, so many centuries ago that almost everyone has forgotten. It could have been at the very beginning of this cycle. I can't remember. The Nightmare Marches lie at the very hub of the Wheel contained by the self-same forces which maintain the Six Realms, almost as if compressed by a kind of gravity. Is it not Sharadim who will seek to release those forces? Who will attempt to free the ruler of the Nightmare Marches, Archduke Balarizaaf? Why go to him? Soon he could come to you?" And Jermays shuddered.

"You know of Sharadim's movements?" asked Alisaard eagerly. "You can predict what she will do?"

"My predictions are never accurate," Jermays said. "They are useless to anyone. I dart from place to place. I see a little of this, a little of that. But I haven't the mind or the temperament to fit anything together. That could be why the Gods permit me to travel as I do. I am a shadow-creature, lady, for the most part. You see me at present in one of my most solid roles. And I know it cannot last too long. Sharadim has huge and evil ambitions, I know. But nothing I can say will help you counter this. The pattern, such as it is, could already be set. She seeks the Dragon Sword, eh? And by means of it will bring the Chaos Lord to his fullest power, perhaps. Aye . . ."

Then suddenly Morandi Pag was grunting in his sleep, shaking his huge head, fluffing his whiskers and, lastly, opening wide, intelligent eyes. "Princess Sharadim leads an army against my kind. That is what you have to tell me, eh? She threatens what? Adelstane? The other realms? Chaos involved? I can hear her. Where is she?—*Now, Flamadin, my false brother, you shall not defeat me. My power increases by natural momentum as yours declines.* Does she believe me still in Adelstane? It seems so. She'll storm our gates. Will she break through? Who knows? My sisters are there! My brother. My old friend Groaffer Rolm is there! Did they send you to find me?"

"They sent a message, Prince Morandi Pag, that they are concerned for you. And that they are in danger and need your help. Mabden attack them. More Mabden than they know."

"Not you?"

"For better or worse, Prince, we are your allies against a common enemy."

"Then I must think what to do."

And he had closed his eyes and was asleep again.

"You know how we can reach the Nightmare Marches, Jermays?" von Bek asked. "Will you tell us?"

Jermays the Crooked nodded absently and rummaged about on Morandi Pag's bench. Then he went under the bench and began to throw old pieces of parchment about, willy-nilly. Then he crawled across the floor and opened a chest. Within the chest were dozens of neatly rolled parchments, numbered as far as I could tell. He looked down on these and beamed. Then, very delicately, he selected one, being careful not to disturb the others. "These are Morandi Pag's charts. Charts of so many realms. So many configurations and complexes, conjunctions and eclipses." He unrolled the parchment. "This is the table I hoped to find." He began to run his finger down it. "Aye. It seems there's a gateway about to open in the Northwest. Near the Goradyn Mountain. You could go that way. It will take you into the Maaschanheem. From there you would have to travel to The Wounded Crayfish and wait for the gateway which will take you into the Realm of the Red Weepers. Good. From there, within the volcano they call Tortacanuzoo, you will find a direct route into the Nightmare Marches. Or so

I believe. However, if you wish to wait five days, seven hours and twelve seconds, you could go from near Adelstane itself, into Drachenheem, through Fluugensheem, and still be near the Wounded Crayfish at almost the same time you arrived from Goradyn. Or you could return to the upper mountains, wait for the Sedulous Urban Eclipse, which is rare enough anyway and worth experiencing, then go directly to Rootsenheem by that method."

Alisaard silenced him at last. "When is there a direct gateway from Maaschanheem?"

He paused, studying the tables for all the world like a man of the twentieth century looking up the train timetables. "Direct? From Maaschanheem? Another twelve years . . ."

"So we have no choice but to make for The Wounded Crayfish anchorage?" she said.

"It seems not. Though if you were to travel to The Torn Shirt . . ."

"It seems in your world as in mine," said von Bek dryly, "it becomes increasingly difficult to get into Hell."

Alisaard ignored him. She was committing Jermays's words to memory. "Wounded Crayfish—Rootsenheem—Tortacanuzoo. That's the shortest route, eh?"

"Apparently. Though it seems to me that Fluugensheem should be crossed, if only briefly. Perhaps it is by-passed. There is said to be a cross-warp around there. Did you ever discover it?"

Alisaard shook her head. "Our navigating is fairly simple. We do not risk the swift-leaping journeys. Not since we lost our menfolk. Now, Master Jermays, can you tell us where to find, in the Nightmare Marches, the Dragon Sword?"

"At their very core, where else!" This was Morandi Pag, heaving his bulk from his chair. "In a place called The World's Beginning. This is the heart of the Nightmare Marches. And that sword sustains them. But it can only be handled by one of the blood, Champion. One of your blood."

"Sharadim is not of my blood."

"She is enough of your blood to serve Balarizaaf's purpose. If she only lives long enough to drag the sword from its crystal prison, that will suffice."

"You mean none can remove it from the crystal?"

"You can, Champion. And so can she. Moreover, I would guess she knows the risk she takes. Which is not a simple death for her. She might succeed. And if she does, she ascends to immortality as a Lord of Hell. As powerful as Queen Xiombarg or Mabelode the Faceless or Old Slortar Himself. That is why she risks so much. The stakes are the highest she can imagine." He put his paws to his head. "But now the ages all congeal into one agonising lump. My poor brain. You understand, I know, Champion. Or you will. Come, we must leave this place at last. We must return to the mainland. To Adelstane. I have my duty. And, of course, you have yours."

"We can use the boat," said Alisaard. "I believe I can steer a course out of the rocks."

At this Prince Morandi Pag chuckled with genuine humour. "You will let me take the tiller, I hope. It will do me good to sniff the currents again and guide us clear to Adelstane."

9.

"SOME say there are no more than forty-six individual folds in the configuration of the waves," said Morandi Pag as he seated himself heavily in the boat. "But that is a statement made by those who, like the feudal islanders of the East, honour simplicity and a kind of unholy neatness over complexity and apparent disorder. I say there are as many folds as there are waves. But it was once a matter of pride that I could smell them all. Waves and multiverse are, I would agree, one. However, the secret of steering any course, no matter where you are bound, is to treat each aspect as fresh-minted and utterly new. To formalise, in my view, is to perish. The folds are infinite. The folds have personalities." His nostrils quivered. "Can't you sniff the currents again? And all the intersecting realities, all the thousands of realms of the multiverse. What a wonder it all is. And yet I was not wrong to be afraid." With that he gave the sign for Alisaard to slip the rope, turned the sail a touch, made a small motion with the tiller and we were riding the roaring waves again, heading for the hollow rock by which we had entered.

There was never a moment when any of us felt in danger. The boat danced lightly across the enormous, threshing waters. She turned as gracefully as any bird in flight, sometimes upon the crest of the waves, sometimes in the gulleys, while sometimes she seemed to lie sideways on to the great breakers. Spray and wind attacked our faces as we surged through the opening and into semidarkness. Morandi Pag was roaring with laughter, almost enough to drown the sound of the waves, as he guided us through and out into the relative calm of the ocean proper.

Jermays the Crooked hopped up and down in glee. He was

in the prow, capering and shouting his approval at every minor shift in the boat's direction.

Morandi Pag moved his muzzle in a peculiar expression, as if expressing satisfaction with his skill. "It has been too long," he said. "I have not the youth for this. Now we shall go to Adelstane."

We crossed the ocean rapidly, seeing the great black mountains rising all around us. The little harbour was reached and the boat tied up. After that it was a matter of a few minutes to walk to the opening where we had first been admitted.

Not a quarter of an hour later we stood once more in the comfortable library, filled as usual with incense, while the Ursine Princes greeted their long-lost peer. It was a most tender sight. All of us were forced to wipe away tears. The creatures had a wonderfully gentle way of behaving with one another.

At length Groaffer Rolm, still very emotional, turned from thanking us for restoring his brother to him, and said: "We have heard from the Princess Sharadim. Her army awaits only the opening of the gateway. Whereupon it will enter our realm, not a mile from Adelstane itself. The other army, we are told, also marches, using our old canal paths, and will be here within the day.

"I take it, Morandi Pag, that you agree with these Mabden. Sharadim means us harm."

"These Mabden speak truth," said Morandi Pag. "But they must be about their business. They have to reach the Maaschanheem. From there they must go via Rootsenheem and Fluugensheem to the Nightmare Marches."

"The Nightmare Marches!" Faladerj Oro was genuinely horrified. "Who would volunteer to venture there?"

"It is a matter of saving all Six Realms from Sharadim and her allies," said von Bek. "We have no choice."

"You are heroes indeed," said Whiclar Hald-Halg. She laughed to herself. "Mabden heroes! Now there's a pretty irony. . . ."

"I will take you to the first gateway myself," Morandi Pag told us.

"But what of Sharadim and her armies? How shall you deal with them?"

Groaffer Rolm shrugged. "We are all together now. And we have our ring of fire. They'll be hard put to enter that. And should they breach Adelstane's defences, they must find us. There are many ways we can delay them."

Jermays the Crooked helped himself from a jug of wine. "But she infects all the realms," he said. "She can alter her personality to appeal to any culture she encounters. What is happening in this realm also happens, in a different way, elsewhere. How shall that be countered?"

"It is not our business and neither do we have the capacity to fight the wars of the other realms," said Groaffer Rolm. "We can only hope to hold her off in Adelstane. But if Chaos breaks through and makes itself her ally, then we are doomed I think."

We made our farewells to the Ursine Princes and Morandi Pag took us along the ancient canal banks of the great slow river, climbing slowly into the heavy shadows cast by mountain walls on all sides. Here at last he paused and was about to speak when it seemed the very mountains shivered and the darkness began to fill with a white radiance which, as it gathered in strength, could be seen to contain all colours. Gradually there formed in that clearing beside the river a set of six pillars which formed a perfect circle and had the appearance of a temple.

"It's miraculous," said von Bek. "I am always amazed."

Morandi Pag passed a white paw over his old brow. "You must make haste," he said. "I can sense that the Mabden armies close on Adelstane. Will you go with them, Jermays?"

"Let me remain here," Jermays said. "I have to see if my old trick of travelling has returned. If it has, I will be of greater use to you. Farewell, Champion. Farewell, beautiful lady. Count von Bek, farewell."

Then we had stepped into the space between the pillars and almost at once were looking upwards. Then we were moving in the direction we faced.

The sensation of movement was stranger still without the apparent solidity of a boat. We were not entirely weightless. Instead it was as if we were borne on a current of water, though water which did not threaten to drown us.

Ahead I could see a misty grey light. My head began to spin and for a few seconds my body felt as if it had been plucked up by a gigantic and gentle hand. Seconds later I was on firm ground, still surrounded by the pillars of light. Alisaard stood beside me and, nearby, a fascinated von Bek. The German count shook his head in wonderment again. "Fasci-

nating. Why are there not gateways like this between my own
world and the Mittelmarch?"

"Different worlds have gateways which take different
forms," Alisaard told him. "This form is native to the Worlds
of the Wheel."

We stepped out of the circle of light and found ourselves in
the familiar, overcast landscape of the Maaschanheem. Everywhere was coarse grass, reeds, pools of water, glinting marsh.
Pale water-birds flew overhead. As far as we could see there
was only flat ground and shallow water.

Alisaard reached into her pouch and drew out a small book
of folded charts. She squatted to consult one of these charts,
spreading it on the relatively dry ground. "We must seek The
Wounded Crayfish anchorage. This is The Laughing Pike. We
have no choice but to try to walk there. A way is possible,
according to this map. There are trails through the marsh."

"How far is The Wounded Crayfish from here?" asked von
Bek.

"Seventy-five miles," she said.

In somewhat depressed spirits, we began to trudge north-
wards.

We had not gone more than perhaps fifteen miles when we
saw ahead of us on the low horizon the dark outline of a great
travelling hull. It seemed to be making rather more smoke
than was usual, yet it did not seem to be moving. We guessed
that it might be in difficulties. I was for avoiding the vessel,
but Alisaard felt that there was a small chance we could get
some sort of help from them.

"Most peoples are inclined to trust Gheestenheemers," she
said.

"Have you forgotten what happened aboard *The Frowning
Shield?*" I reminded her. "In helping von Bek and myself you
infringed the most sacred codes of the Massing. My guess
would be that your folk are not at all welcome anywhere here.
What diplomatic harm you did was doubtless made use of by
Sharadim, who would have done all she could to win allies
here and poison minds against you. And as for us, we are
probably fair game for any party of Binkeepers who happens
to spot us. I would be disinclined to hail that vessel."

Von Bek was frowning as he peered ahead. "I have a feeling it does not represent danger to us," he said. "Look. That's
not smoke from her funnels. She's burning! She's been attacked and destroyed!"

Alisaard seemed more shocked than either von Bek or myself. "They war amongst themselves! This has not happened for centuries! What can it mean?"

We began to run over the soft, uneven ground, heading for the ruined hull.

Long before we reached it, we could see what had happened. Fire had gone through the entire vessel. Blackened bodies in every posture of agony lay against the charred rails, upon the smoking decks. They hung like broken dolls in the smashed timbers of the yards. And from everywhere came the stink of death. Carrion birds swaggered amongst this wealth of flesh, fat as domestic pets. Men and women, children and babies, all had died. The hull lay half on her side, beached, looted.

About fifty yards from the remains of the great hull we saw a few figures rise up from the reeds and begin to move away from us. Several were blind and had to be helped by the rest and this is why their progress was so slow. I called out to them:

"We mean you no harm. What hull was that?"

The survivors turned scared, white faces towards us. They were in rags—wrapped in anything they had been able to salvage from the wreck. They looked half-starved. Most were older women, but there were a few girls and youths in the group.

Alisaard now wore her ivory visor, as a matter of habit. She lifted it, saying softly: "We are friendly to you, good folk. We would offer you our names."

One tall old woman said, with surprising firmness: "We know you. All three. You are Flamadin, von Bek and the renegade Ghost Woman. Outlaws all. Enemies of our enemies, perhaps, but we have no reason to think you friends. Not now the world betrays everything we value. Princess Sharadim seeks you, does she not? And also that bloody-handed parvenu Armiad, her most ferocious ally..."

Von Bek was impatient. He started forward again. "Who are you? What has happened here?"

The old woman raised her hand. "You are not welcome here. You brought the evil into our realm. The evil we had thought exiled forever. Now there is war again between the hulls."

"We have met," I said suddenly. "But where?"

She shrugged. "I was Praz Oniad, Consorte to the Snowbear Defender. Co-captain and Rhyme Sister to the Toirset Larens. And what you see is all that is left of our home hull, *The New Argument,* and all that is left of our families. There is a second War Between the Hulls, led by Armiad. And although you did not begin that war, you were part of its excuse. By breaking the rules of the Massing you brought in every kind of uncertainty."

"But we cannot be held responsible for Armiad's ambition!" cried Alisaard. "That existed before we did what we did."

"I said 'excuse,'" said Praz Oniad. "He claimed other hulls had aided the Ghost Women in the raid on his hull. He claimed that. And next he argued that he must protect himself. So allies came from Draachenheem. Hardened fighters who knew how to kill, how to make war. Before long he had allies, of course, amongst other hulls who feared his strength and did not wish to be destroyed as we and so many more have been destroyed. Armiad now commands thirty hulls and they defile the Massing Ground, turning it into an armed camp, their stronghold, together with their Draachenheemer allies. Now all other hulls must pay tribute and acknowledge Armiad King Admiral, a title which we abolished hundreds of years since."

"How could this have happened in so short a time?" murmured von Bek to me.

"You forget, " I told him, "that time passes at somewhat different rates in different realms. In relation, that is, to one another. It seems several months have gone by since we left the Great Massing."

"We hope to put a stop to Princess Sharadim and her allies," I informed the old woman. "Her plans and those of Armiad were made long before we knew of them. They would destroy us because we know a way of defeating them."

The old woman looked at us sceptically, but a little hope showed in her worn features. "It is not revenge we of *The New Argument* seek," she said. "We would gladly die if it meant a stop to this terrible war."

"War threatens all Six Realms." Alisaard stood beside her now and gently took her hand. "Good lady, this is Sharadim's doing. When her brother refused compliance, she blackened his name and outlawed him."

The old woman looked suspiciously at me. "They say this is not Prince Flamadin at all but a Doppelgänger. They say he is in reality the Archduke Balarizaaf of Chaos, assuming human form. They say Chaos must soon erupt throughout all the Realms of the Wheel."

"Part of what you have heard has substance," I said. "But I assure you I'm no friend to Chaos. We seek to conquer Chaos. And we hope, in that conquest, to bring peace back to the Six Realms. To that purpose, we are on our way to the Nightmare Realm. . . ."

Praz Oniad voiced a sharp, bitter laugh. "No human willingly ventures into that realm. Are these more lies? You would not survive. Your mind would melt. The illusions of that realm cannot be perceived by mortals without those mortals going mad."

"It is our only hope of defeating Sharadim and all her allies," said Alisaard. "Those allies, it is true, include the Archduke Balarizaaf."

The old woman sighed. "What hope is there?" she said. "This is no more than desperate folly."

"We journey to The Wounded Crayfish to find a gateway," von Bek said. "What anchorage is this, good lady?"

"This is The Fountain Overflowing," she said. "Anchorage of *An Imaginary Fish,* also destroyed by Armiad's fire-flingers, the same he got from Sharadim. We have no weapons. He now has many. The Wounded Crayfish is miles from here. How do you travel?"

"On foot," said Alisaard. "We have no choice, good lady."

The old woman frowned, making some sort of calculation for herself. Then she said: "We have a punt. It is of no use to us. If you speak truth, and I would guess you do, then you are our hope. Poor hope is better than none. Take the punt. It will be possible to use the shallows and be at The Wounded Crayfish by tomorrow."

They dragged the flat-bottomed boat from out of the burned hull. It stank of the fire and the destruction, but it was undamaged and floated easily on the nearby water. We were given poles and instructed how best to use them. And then we had left the pathetic little party on the bank while we shoved our punt on towards The Wounded Crayfish.

"Be careful," cried the Lady Praz Oniad, "for Armiad's raiders are everywhere now. They have ships of the Draachen-heem pattern which can easily overtake one of ours."

Warily we continued our journey, taking turns to rest as we poled on through the night. And then at last Alisaard consulted her charts and pointed ahead. In the dawn we detected a shimmer of white light.

The gateway was already there.

But between us and it loomed the huge bulk of another hull. And this one was by no means incapacitated. She flew all her colours.

"There's a vessel ready for battle," said von Bek with a hard set to his jaw.

"Could Armiad or Sharadim have wind of our journey and sent this hull to intercept us?" I asked Alisaard.

She shook her head dumbly. She did not know. We were already exhausted from poling the flatboat and had no means of fighting the huge hull.

All we could do was to beach our boat and make a dash for the pulsating gateway. This we did, stumbling and flailing as we forced ourselves on, up to our knees in marsh, falling when our feet became trapped by clumps of weed. Slowly the gateway came closer. But we had been seen. There were shouts from the hull. I saw figures landing on the headland close to the gateway. They were dressed in dark green and yellow armour and bore swords and pikes. Without weapons, we had virtually no chance against them.

Still we floundered on towards the gateway, hearts pounding, breath panting, hoping for some stroke of luck which would allow us to reach the gate before the heavily armed warriors who now called to each other, spreading out as they ran towards us.

Within moments we were surrounded. We prepared to fight with our bare hands.

I had seen no armour like theirs in the Maaschanheem. To me it resembled Draachenheemer war-gear. When the leader stepped forward, awkward in all that restraining metal and leather, and removed his helmet, I knew why I had thought as I did.

The sweating, unwholesome head which was exposed was familiar enough to me. I had expected Armiad or one of his Binkeepers. Instead I faced Lord Pharl Asclett, whom we had left bound in Sharadim's chambers when we made our escape from her palace. His face was twisted in a kind of snarling grin.

"I am very glad to see you again," he said. "I have an invitation from the Empress Sharadim. She would be pleased to have you attend her forthcoming wedding."

"So she's Empress, eh?" Alisaard cast around her for a weakness in their surrounding ranks.

"Did you expect her to fail?" Prince Pharl's face bore a look of sly superiority.

"And who does the lady marry?" von Bek also played for time. "Yourself, Pharl of the Heavy Palm? I had heard you had no predilection for the fair sex. Or any, for that matter."

The Prince of Skrenaw glared. "I would be honoured to serve my Empress in any capacity. Even that. No, sir, she marries Prince Flamadin. Hadn't you heard? There are celebrations in Fluugensheem. They have elected the Empress and her consort to rule over them since the King of the Flying City crashed his command whilst drunk. Will you come with us, back to our hull? We have waited here for you these past five days. . . ."

"How did you know where to find us?" I asked.

"The Empress has powerful supernatural allies. She is also a great seeress in her own right. Besides, she has stationed captains at many gateways of the Maaschanheem and Draachenheem. This was considered one of those you would be most likely to choose, though I must admit I expected you to appear from the gateway. . . ."

He paused as he detected a sound like distant thunder and, turning his horrible head, gasped at what he saw.

We craned for a glimpse. The great hull was attempting to go about, but it seemed to be tangled in an all-encompassing web. I saw a ball of sputtering fire go up from a deck and be flung back as it struck the net. Now I could see a number of sprightly sailing ships, reminiscent of those I had seen in Gheestenheem, surrounding the hull. It was these which had attacked the vessel. The noise had been from the charges used to shoot the tangle of nets across the entire hull.

Before Prince Pharl could voice an order a wave of warriors suddenly rose up from the ground and attacked our captors. They were led by a small figure who wore only a marsh helmet and breastplate, who carried a gaff twice his height and who capered on the fringe of the fight, waving his weapon and urging on his men, all of whom were in the grey-green armour I had first seen in the Maaschanheem. The figure grinned at me. It was Jermays the Crooked.

"We, too, anticipated the enemy!" he called. He chuckled as his fighters closed on Prince Pharl's men and swiftly overwhelmed them. Pharl himself was captured. He glared in fury at us all. When the warriors pushed up their visors to reveal in their ranks the faces of Ghost Women as well as native Maaschanheemers, he was close to tears.

Jermays came panting up like a happy dog. "Peoples of several realms now band together against Sharadim and her minions. But we are badly outnumbered. You must go swiftly now. The gateway will soon be useless to you. Sharadim rules in Draachenheem. Ottro was killed in battle. Prince Halmad still fights against the Empress. Neterpino Sloch failed to win the Battle of Fancil Sepaht and paid the price. He is now legless. Sharadim has sent Mabden from this realm into Gheestenheem and battle now threatens the Eldren. Meanwhile she seeks to consolidate gains in Fluugensheem and all Rootsenheem, such as it is, is hers. Her creatures lay heavy siege to Adelstane, since the Ursine Princes failed to succumb to her trickery. Much depends on you. Her power is almost great enough for her to summon Chaos, to blend her conquered realms with theirs! Swiftly—swiftly—through the gate!"

"But we go to Rootsenheem!" I cried. "If she rules there, how can we succeed?"

"Give false names!" was Jermays's rather unlikely advice.

And so we ran again, plunging between the columns of light, letting them draw us through into another tunnel. Through this we flew, feeling the elation birds must know when they soar on the air currents, and then at last we saw blinding yellow light ahead of us. Within seconds we stood on warm sand, looking towards a massively constructed ziggurat which seemed, in its carved stones, older than the multiverse itself.

Alisaard spoke softly. "We are, indeed, in the Realm of the Red Weepers. You are Farkos, from Fluugensheem. You, Count von Bek, are Mederic of Draachenheem. I am Amelar of the Eldren. No more speaking. They come." And she pointed.

Already an opening had appeared in the base of the ziggurat. From it came a party of men in strange gear similar to that which I had first observed at the Great Massing.

Heavily bearded, wearing peculiar costumes—a kind of fine silk stretched on wide frames so that their skin was touched hardly at all, large gauntlets, helmets of some light wood supported on a kind of yoke across the shoulders— they stopped a few yards from us, raising both arms in greeting.

I was half expecting another attack, but the men spoke with sonorous gravity. "You have come to the Realm of the Red Weepers. Do you cross the threshold by accident or by design? We are the hereditary guardians of the threshold and must ask these questions before we allow you to proceed."

Alisaard stepped forward. She introduced us by our false names. "We come by design, noble masters. But we are not traders. We humbly ask permission to pass through your realm to the next threshold."

I could now more clearly see the men's faces. Their eyes were wide and staring, rimmed entirely in red. Their helmets shaded their faces but I could now see that under each eye, on a kind of wire frame, was suspended a small cup. With a frisson of nausea I realised that their eyes were constantly exuding a viscous red fluid, a kind of mucus, and that the men themselves stared blindly at us.

"What business, then, are you upon, noble mistress?" one of the Red Weepers asked her.

"We seek knowledge."

"For what purpose shall that knowledge be used?"

"We are charting the pathways between the realms. The knowledge will be for the good of all Six Realms, I swear."

"You will do us no harm? You will take nothing from this realm that is not willingly offered?"

"We swear." She signalled to us to echo her words.

"Your heartbeats suggest fear," said one of the other Weepers. "Of what are you afraid?"

"We have but lately escaped Maaschanheemer pirates," Alisaard told them. "There is great danger everywhere, these days."

"What danger threatens?"

"Civil war and the conquest of our realms by Chaos," she told them.

"Ah, now," said another speaker. "Then you must go quickly about your business. We have no such fears in the Rootsenheem, for we have our goddess to protect us, may she bless you all."

"Let the goddess bless you all," they chorused piously.

I was struck by an instinctive suspicion. "Pray, noble masters, what do you call your goddess?" I asked.

"She is called Sharadim the Wise."

Now we knew why war and disaster had failed to touch Rootsenheem. Sharadim had no need to promote either here.

The realm was already conquered and had doubtless been hers for many years. It was easy to imagine how easily she had deceived this ancient, near-senile people. When she offered the Realm of the Red Weepers up to Chaos, few, I guessed, would protest or even know what was happening to them.

This knowledge, however, gave our mission additional urgency. Alisaard said: "We seek the place you call Tortacanuzoo. Where shall we find it, noble masters?"

"You must cross the desert, travelling due west. But you will need a beast. We shall have one brought to you. When the beast is no longer needed, it will return to us at its own volition."

And thus, on a huge wooden platform fixed to the back of an animal roughly the size and shape of a rhinoceros, we began our crossing of the great desert.

"Soon Sharadim must control all the realms save Gheestenheem," said Alisaard soberly. "And even Gheestenheem could fall, her power increases so. She commands millions of warriors by now. And it seems she has revived the corpse of her murdered brother so as to impress the people of Fluugensheem."

"That I could not understand," I said with a shudder. "Do you know what she plans?"

"I think so. Fluugensheem's legends and myths have much to do with themes of duality. They look back to a Golden Age when a Queen and a King ruled over them and all their cities flew. Now only one has that power and it grows old, for they have lost the knowledge of building new ships. They, too, it seems, came originally from another realm. If Sharadim has been able to force an imitation of life into the body of Flamadin, then this also means her Chaos-borrowed power is greater than it has ever been before. She has doubtless, through her skill at politics, convinced the Fluugensheemers that the stories they heard of Prince Flamadin's being outlawed were false. She is skilled at answering the needs of all she seeks to manipulate. She presents an entirely different face to each of the Six Realms—whatever they would most wish to see in their idealism and their secret yearnings for order and peace. . . ."

"She is in other words a classic demagogue," said von Bek, clinging to the side of the platform as the beast lurched for a moment before correcting itself with a great blustering exhalation of ill-smelling breath. "It was Hitler's secret that he could seem one thing to one group and an entirely different thing to another. That is how they rise so swiftly to power. These creatures are bizarre. They can virtually change shape and colour. They have an amorphous quality and yet at the same time they have a will to dominate others which is unrelenting, almost their only consistent trait, their only reality."

Alisaard was impressed by this. "You have studied your histories?" she asked. "You know much of tyrants?"

"I am the victim of one," said von Bek. "I am to be the victim of another, too, it seems, if we are unsuccessful!"

She reached out to take his hand. "You must keep your courage, Count von Bek. It is considerable and has stood you in good stead already. I have known few as brave as you."

I watched as his hand folded hers in turn.

And again I knew that terrible, unjustified, unwanted pang of jealousy.

They saw that I was disturbed and became concerned about me. But I dismissed their questions. I claimed that I was affected by the heat of the old, red sun overhead. I pretended to be tired and, putting my face in my arms, tried to sleep, to dismiss the appalling thoughts and emotions surging through me.

Towards evening I heard von Bek shout. I uncovered my eyes to see that his arm was now around Alisaard's shoulders. He was pointing to the horizon, where the sun had now dropped so that it seemed to be sinking into the sands of the desert, to be absorbed like blood. Against this scarlet half-globe was the black outline of a single mountain.

"It can only be Tortacanuzoo," said Alisaard. Her voice was trembling, but I could not tell whether it was from the proximity of von Bek's presence or from anticipation of what we were about to encounter.

Lost in private speculation the three of us stared in silence at the gateway to the realm of the Archduke Balarizaaf. We were about to enter the Realm of Chaos and at last were struck by the enormity of our adventure, of how little chance we had of surviving it.

The beast continued to plod on towards Tortacanuzoo. Then, as if in greeting, the ancient mountain gave voice to an almost human roar. The beast stopped, lifting its head to answer. The sound was virtually identical. It was uncanny.

A flicker of flame rose suddenly from the summit, a few strands of grey smoke sailed lazily over the setting sun.

I felt a terrible sensation of terror in the pit of my stomach and I wished with all my heart that we had been captured by Prince Pharl at the gateway into Rootsenheem, or been killed in our fight with the smoke snake.

The others had no direct experience of Chaos. Indeed, as far as I could recall, I had never encountered Chaos as directly as we now intended. They, however, were innocents compared to myself. I at least had some knowledge of the warping, mutating power of the Lords of Disorder, the supernatural entities who on John Daker's Earth would be called Arch-Demons, the Dukes of Hell. I knew that they made use of our most treasured virtues and most honoured emotions. That they were capable of almost any illusion. And that all that was keeping them from pouring forth from their stronghold to engulf so many other realms of the multiverse was their caution, their unreadiness or unwillingness to war against the rival powers of Law. But if we humans invited them to our realms, they would come.

They would come when they had been offered proof of human loyalty to their cause. Proof which Sharadim was even now presenting with every victory she made.

I shivered as the old volcano muttered and fumed. It was not hard to see the mountain as an entrance into the bowels of Hell.

Then I forced myself to action. I clambered off the platform and began to wade through ankle-deep sand towards Tortacanuzoo.

I called back to the lovers, who hesitated behind me.

"Come, my friends! We have an appointment with the Archduke Balarizaaf. I see no advantage to keeping him waiting."

It was von Bek who answered me, his voice puzzled. "Herr Daker! Herr Daker! Can you not see them? Look, man! It is the Empress Sharadim herself!"

10.

IT was Sharadim.

She was on horseback, surrounded by a group of brightly-dressed courtiers. They looked for all the world like a party of aristocrats on a picnic or a hunting spree. They were riding up the mountain ahead of us. Now, above the voice of the vol-cano, I could hear snatches of conversation, laughter.

"They have not seen us!" Alisaard called softly, beckoning me back towards the animal. She and von Bek crouched beside one of its massive thighs. Understanding their caution, I rejoined them.

"They are euphoric in their power and cannot believe themselves under threat in a realm where Sharadim is worshipped as a goddess," said Alisaard. "When they round that bend and are lost from sight again, we must make haste to reach those steps you see, cut into the foot of the mountain."

It was growing momentarily darker. I saw the sense of her strategy and nodded agreement. A short while later the last of Sharadim's gaily clad party turned the corner and was gone. Following Alisaard we dashed for the steps and had reached the protection of the mountain long before Sharadim emerged on the other side. Cautiously, we began to mount the steps, following in the wake of our most dangerous enemy.

As we came round to the other side I saw some costly tents pitched below. A servant was feeding pack animals. It was almost a village in its own right. This was Sharadim's camp. But surely she did not intend to go directly into Hell. Even in her pride and her conquests she could not believe herself so invulnerable as yet!

The pace of the horses grew slower as they approached the summit, while we, creeping on the stairs above the trail, were able to move with relative swiftness until we were slightly ahead of Sharadim and her party, but virtually within hearing distance.

Their voices were louder now. I recognised Baron Captain Armiad of the Maaschanheem, Duke Perichost of the Draachenheem, a couple of courtiers from the palace. Also among the group were thin-faced Mabden with the wolfish look of barbarian raiders, men in outlandishly padded black livery. There seemed to be representatives of all the cultures of the Six Realms, save for the Eldren and the Ursine Princes.

I began to guess at Sharadim's intent. This was to be a demonstration of her power. A means of ensuring that her allies were convinced by her threats and promises.

One I did not recognise rode beside her, in a cowled cape. He had the look of a priest. She was in holiday spirit, laughing and joking with all around her. I was impressed again by her unlikely beauty. It was not difficult to see how she was able to convince so many of her angelic disposition. Indeed, she had even convinced the blind Weepers that she was a goddess, and they had never looked on her face.

We emerged now into a kind of wide amphitheatre which was the top of the volcano. Out in the very centre of the crust was a red, glowing, unstable substance which from time to time gave off a thin shoot of flame and some smoke. The volcano seemed to be at its cooling stage rather than about to erupt, so I felt no danger in this. I was fascinated, however, to see that a great tier of stone seats had been erected on one side. This was reached by a causeway, also of geometrically cut stone. Along the causeway, almost like voyagers about to take ship, Sharadim and her party rode.

At a wave of her hand, Sharadim ordered her courtiers to dismount and take seats in the tier. She remained mounted and, leaning over, put a restraining hand on her cowled companion, making him draw up his horse beside hers.

Above the grumbling of the volcano, Sharadim now began to speak.

"Some of you have expressed doubts that Chaos can aid us in the final stages of our conquests. You have required proof that your rewards will be almost limitless. Well, soon I shall summon one of the most powerful nobles in all Chaos, the Archduke Balarizaaf Himself! You will hear from his lips what you refused to believe from mine. Those loyal to Chaos now, who do not flinch from deeds which lesser creatures deem vile and cruel, shall be raised above all others, save myself. You shall know the expression of every whim, every secret dream, every dark desire. You shall know a complete fulfilment which the weak can never begin to taste. Shortly you shall look upon the face of Balarizaaf, Archduke of Chaos, and you shall know what it means to be strong. I speak of strength capable of reshaping reality to the individual will. Strength which can destroy whole universes if it so desires. Strength which brings with it immortality. And with immortality shall come the realisation of even the most fleeting of whims. We shall be Gods! Chaos promises an infinity of possibilities free from the petty constraints of Law!"

Now she turned with upraised arms towards the volcano. Her voice sang out, sweet and perfect in the still evening air:

"LORD BALARIZAAF, ARCHDUKE OF CHAOS, MASTER OF HELL, YOUR SERVANTS CALL YOU! WE BRING YOU THE GIFT OF WORLDS. WE BRING YOU OUR TRIBUTE. WE BRING YOU MILLIONS OF SOULS! WE BRING YOU BLOOD AND HORROR! WE BRING YOU THE SACRIFICE OF ALL WEAKNESS! WE BRING YOU OUR STRENGTH! AID US, LORD BALARIZAAF. COME TO US, LORD BALARIZAAF. LEAD CHAOS THROUGH AND LET LAW BE FOREVER IN DEFEAT!"

A flicker of scarlet light at the centre of the volcano seemed to respond. She continued to chant in this manner and soon her courtiers were joining in with her. The entire night was infected by their voices as the sun finally set and the only light came from the volcano itself.

"Aid us, Lord Balarizaaf!"

Then, as if bursting through an unseen ceiling, came first one beam of light and then another. These were not white as the gateways we had used hitherto. These seemed to reflect the scarlet of the flame. They glowed. They resembled pillars composed of living, bloody flesh.

One by one these pillars grew in width and intensity until at last thirteen of them were poised between the sky and the volcano and it was impossible to see where they began and ended.

Her face and hands scarlet in the light from the pillars, Sharadim crooned and sang. She called out obscenities and imploring promises. She offered her god anything He might desire.

"Balarizaaf. Lord Balarizaaf! We invite you into our realm!"

Now the volcano shook.

I felt the ground shifting under my feet. Alisaard, von Bek and I looked at one another in uncertainty. The gateway was open. It led to Chaos, without question. But what would happen to us if we tried to enter it now?

"BALARIZAAF! LORD OF ALL! COME TO US!"

All around us there was a wind whistling. Lightning began to crackle upon the brink of the crater. Again the mountain trembled and we were almost thrown off our staircase to the causeway below.

The columns of scarlet light pounded as if they were living organs. An unholy yelling began to sound, far away, and I knew it came from the pillars.

"BALARIZAAF! AID US!"

The yelling became a scream, the scream turned into chilling laughter, and then, blazing with black and orange fire, his unstable features writhing, changing shape with every second, stood a creature no taller than a man but from whose lips there now escaped a deafening voice: "IS IT YOU, LITTLE SHARADIM, WHO CALLS BALARIZAAF FROM PLAY? IS THE TIME COME? SHALL I LEAD YOU TO THE SWORD?"

"The time is almost here, Lord Balarizaaf. Soon we shall have conquered the entire Six Realms. This whole realm shall then become One. A Realm of Chaos. And my reward shall be the Sword and the Sword shall give me—"

"Infinite power. The right to be one of the Sword Rulers themselves. A Lord of Chaos! For only you or the one called the Champion may wield that blade and live! What more must I repeat, little Sharadim?"

"No more, Lord."

"Good, because it is painful for me to stay in this realm until it is truly mine. The Sword shall make it truly mine. Come to me soon, little Sharadim!"

It seemed to me that Lord Balarizaaf gave poor guarantees. But so blinded by the prospect of unchecked power were these people that they were prepared to believe anything they were told.

Balarizaaf was suddenly gone.

Below us, Sharadim's courtiers murmured amongst themselves. There was no doubt of their complete loyalty to her now. One or two were already on their knees.

Sharadim reached towards her cowled companion, beside her on his horse, and she pushed back his cape. She revealed a face which was all too familiar to me!

It was a grey face, a lifeless face, with eyes the colour of pewter staring directly ahead of it. It was my face. I was looking at my Doppelgänger.

And even as I stared at it, its dead eyes met mine. They began slowly to fill with something approximating energy. The lips moved. A hollow voice said:

"He is here, mistress. What you promised me is here. Give him to me. Give me his soul. Give me his life. . . ."

Alisaard was howling at me. Von Bek was tugging at me. They were pulling me with them down towards the causeway. At the far end of this, by the tiers of seats, heads were beginning to turn.

We dashed over the causeway, down smooth rocks, onto the crust of the volcano itself. And then we were running towards the pillars of blood.

"Flamadin!" I heard my pseudo-sister cry.

They were howling like jackals as they came in pursuit of us. Yet they were reluctant to approach too close to the gateway, for they knew it led directly into Hell.

The three of us reached the scarlet pillars and hesitated. Sharadim and her courtiers were still behind us. I saw the puppetlike motions of her creature. "Its life is mine, mistress!"

Von Bek was panting. "My God, Herr Daker. That is the nearest thing I have ever seen to a zombie. What is it?"

"My Doppelgänger," I said. "She has revived the corpse of Flamadin with the promise of a new soul!"

Then von Bek had dragged me back into the circle of the pillars and we stood looking down into the bubbling core of the volcano.

Slowly the crust seemed to widen, revealing pulsing, violent heat, a smell at once sweet and repellent. And then we were being drawn into it. Drawn through the gates of Hell and into a realm whose supreme ruler was Lord Balarizaaf, the creature we had just seen.

I think we were all screaming by the time we were passing through the tunnel of flame. The descent seemed to last forever as the yellow and red fires went past us in every direction.

Then I felt firm earth beneath my feet again. I was deeply relieved to see that it looked anything but abnormal. It was ordinary turf. It did not undulate. It did not burn. It did not threaten to swallow me. And it smelled like ordinary dirt.

On the other side of the columns of light, which had now turned a kind of delicate pink, I made out blue sky, the weight of a forest, and I heard birdsong.

Together with my friends I walked slowly out of the columns and into a glade whose grassy mounds were covered in daisies and buttercups. The forest consisted primarily of large-boled oaks, all of them in their prime, and a little silver river ran through the glade, adding its music to that of the exotically plumaged birds which flew across a peaceful sky or came to perch on nearby branches.

We were like wondering children as we looked around us. Alisaard had begun to smile. I contented myself with breathing in the sweetness of the blossoms and the grass.

We seated ourselves beside the little river. We smiled at one another. This was an idyll from our most innocent dreams.

Von`Bek was the first to speak. "Why!" he exclaimed in delight. "This is not Hell at all, my friends. This truly is the most perfect Paradise!"

But I was already suspicious. When I looked behind me the pillars of blood had gone. I saw instead a scene which was almost exactly the same as our own. I turned and retraced my steps, looking for the gateway. It had not been there long enough, I felt. My suspicion increased. There was something strange about the atmosphere of this place, something unnatural. Instinctively, I stretched out my hand. It struck a smooth, hard wall—a wall which mirrored this paradise but which did not reflect our images!

I called out to my friends. They were laughing and talking, engrossed in their own intimate obsessions. I was impatient with them. This was not the time for my allies to become mooning lovers, I thought.

"Lady Alisaard! Von Bek! Be wary!"

At last they looked up. "What is it, man?" Von Bek was irritated by my interruption.

"This place is not merely an illusion," I said. "I suspect it is an illusion to hide something far less pleasant. Come and see."

Reluctantly, hand in hand, they ran towards me over the soft Arcadian grass.

Now that I was close to the wall I thought I could see beyond the illusion to the other side where dim shapes moved, hideous faces beseeched or threatened, misshapen hands stretched out towards us.

"There are the true denizens of this realm," I said.

But my friends saw nothing.

"It is your own mind showing you what you fear is there," said von Bek. "As much an illusion as the other. I will admit this place is an unlikely one and doubtless is artificial. Nonetheless it is very pleasing. Surely Chaos is not all terror and ugliness?"

"By no means," I agreed. "And that is part of its attraction. Chaos is capable of marvellous beauty of all kinds. But nothing in Chaos is ever just one thing. It is ambiguity. It is illusion disguising illusion. There is no true simplicity in Chaos, only the appearance of simplicity." I drew the Actorios from my purse. I held it up so that its strange, dark rays struck out in all directions. "See?"

I directed the Actorios towards the reflecting wall and quite suddenly the illusion cleared, displaying what had lurked behind the barrier.

Von Bek and Alisaard both stepped back involuntarily, their eyes widening, their faces pale.

Creatures neither beast nor human shambled and slouched amongst filthy huts which seemed to be made of fused flint. Some of them pressed grotesque faces to the wall in attitudes of despairing melancholy. The others merely moved about the village, performing various tasks. Not one of them did not walk with a limp, or drag a distorted limb.

"What are these people called?" murmured von Bek in horror. "They are like something from mediaeval paintings! Who are they, Herr Daker?"

"They were once human," said Alisaard softly. "But in giving their loyalty to Chaos, they accepted the logic of Chaos. Chaos cannot bear constancy. It is changing all the time. And what you see is the change Chaos has wrought in humankind. That is what Sharadim offers the Six Realms. Oh, indeed, some of them may come to experience enormous power for a while. But in the end this is what they always become."

"Poor devils!" murmured von Bek.

"Poor devils," I said to him, "is an exact enough description of them. . . ."

"Would they attack us, if the wall did not keep them back?" von Bek asked.

"Only if they thought we were weaker than themselves. These are not the warlike creatures Sharadim commands. These merely put themselves in servitude to Chaos because they thought it would benefit them somehow."

Alisaard turned away. She drew a deep breath and then expelled it suddenly, as if she had realised the air were tainted.

"This was folly," she said. "This was the greatest folly. We were told to seek out the Centre and there find the Sword. But we are in Chaos. Since nothing is constant, we have no way of knowing which direction we must travel."

Von Bek comforted her. I stood back, again having to force myself to take hold of my emotions. Jealousy had come flooding back again.

"We should count ourselves fortunate," I told them, "that Archduke Balarizaaf is as yet unaware of our presence. We should press on. We should get as far from this gateway as possible. Into those woods."

"But if Balarizaaf rules here, he will find us as soon as he decides to look," said Alisaard.

I shook my head. "Not necessarily. He is virtually omnipotent here, but he is not omniscient. We have a small chance of reaching our goal before he seeks us out."

"This is true optimism!" Von Bek slapped me on the back and laughed, his eyes avoiding the dimming vision of the village. Soon, as we moved away, the reflection had returned.

"I've a mind to be wary of those woods now," said von Bek to me. "But I suppose we have no choice. It's thick, eh? Like one of those old forests from German legend. I suppose if we're lucky we'll find a woodcutter who will direct us on our way and perhaps allow us three wishes, too."

Alisaard smiled, her spirits rising. She linked arms with him. "You speak so strangely, Count von Bek. But there's a kind of music to your nonsense which I like."

For my part, I found his whimsy merely facile.

The oak wood had an atmosphere of permanence, as if it had stood here for a thousand years or more. In the cool, green shadows we saw rabbits and squirrels and there was an air of tranquility about the place which was thoroughly enchanting. But, even without recourse to my Actorios, I knew that it was bound to be something other than it seemed. That, after all, was one of the few rules in Chaos.

We had only gone a yard or two into the wood when we saw, standing behind a beam of dusty sunlight, a tall, armoured figure. It was clad entirely in metal of black and yellow.

At first I was relieved to see Sepiriz here. And then it came to me that this, too, might be an illusion. I stopped. My friends also came to a halt beside me.

"Is that you, Sir Knight in Black and Yellow?" I asked him, folding my hand over the Actorios. "How came you to Chaos? Or do you, too, serve Chaos now?"

The armoured man advanced into the light. His bright livery seemed to glow with its own radiance. He lifted his helm and I saw the impressive ebony features which could only belong to Sepiriz, the servant of the Balance. He was amused by my suspicion, but not dismissive of it.

"You are right to question everything in this realm," he said. He yawned and stretched himself in his metal. "Forgive me, I have been asleep. I slept while I awaited you. I am glad you found the entrance. I am glad you had the courage to come. But now you must call on even greater courage than before. Here in the Nightmare Realm you may find horrible torment or salvation for the Six Realms—and more! But Chaos has many weapons in her arsenal and not all of them are obvious. Even now Sharadim prepares her creature to accept your soul, Champion. Do you understand the implications of that?"

He could see that I did not.

He hesitated and then continued: "The corpse she has animated will be able to take the Dragon Sword—if it possesses your life-stuff, John Daker. Sharadim controls this quasi-Flamadin and so it will be her cats-paw. She risks far less than if she were to take hold of the Sword herself."

"Then she seeks to deceive her ally, Archduke Balarizaaf, who believes that she will handle the Sword for him?"

"He cares not which of you eventually lays claim to the blade—so long as you use it for his purposes. He would therefore prefer you as an ally rather than as an enemy, Champion. That is worth remembering. And remember this, also— death is not what one must fear in the Nightmare Realm. Death as such hardly exists here. But to be immortal in this world is the worst fate of all! And you must also remember that you have allies here. A hare will lead you to a cup. The cup will show you the way to a horned horse. The horned horse will take you to a wall. And in the wall you will find the sword."

"How can such allies exist in a world dominated by the tyranny of Chaos?" Lady Alisaard asked him.

Sepiriz looked down at her and his smile was gentle. "Even in Chaos there are some whose purity and integrity are so complete they are untouched by anything which surrounds them. It is in the very heart of Chaos that those most able to resist her often choose to dwell. This is a paradox enjoyed by the Lords of Chaos themselves. It is an irony which even the grave Lords of Law take pleasure in."

"And is it because you possess this purity that you are able to come and go in the Nightmare Marches, Lord Sepiriz?" asked von Bek.

"You are right to question me, Count von Bek. No, my time in this realm is limited. If it were not, why I should doubtless seek the Dragon Sword myself!" He smiled again. "As an emissary of the Balance I am allowed more freedom of movement than most creatures. But it is by no means un-checked, that freedom. The time comes for me to leave. I would not attract Balarizaaf to you. Not yet."

"Will Sharadim find a way of telling the Chaos Lord that we are in his domain?" I asked.

"She does not communicate with her ally at will," Sepiriz said. "But she could choose to enter the Nightmare Marches herself. And then you would find yourselves in the greatest danger."

"Then we can expect to find no allies here," said von Bek soberly.

"Only the Lost Warriors," said Sepiriz. "Those who wait on the Edge of Time. And their help can be called upon only once. And only then if you have no other recourse. Those warriors may fight once in a cycle of the multiverse. When they unsheath their swords there are inevitable consequences. But you know this already, eh, Sir Champion?"

"I have heard the Lost Warriors," I agreed. "They have spoken to me in my dreams. But I can remember little else."

"How shall these warriors be summoned?" asked von Bek.

"By breaking the Actorios into fragments," said Sepiriz.

"But the stone cannot be broken. It is virtually indestructible." Alisaard's voice rose in outrage. "You play tricks upon us, Lord Sepiriz!"

"The stone can be broken. By a blow from the Dragon Sword. That is what I know."

And Sepiriz reached up and closed his helm.

Von Bek uttered a desperate laugh. "We are truly in Chaos. There's a paradox for you! We can only summon allies when the Dragon Sword is already ours! When we have no need of them!"

"You will decide that when the time comes." Sepiriz's voice was hollow and distant, as if he faded from us, though his armour was as solid as ever. "Remember—your greatest weapons are your own courage and intelligence. Go swiftly through this wood. There is a path which the Actorios will show you. Follow it. Like all paths in Chaos it leads eventually to the place they call here The World's Beginning. . . ."

Now the armour began to dissipate, to fade, to join with the dancing motes of dust in the sunbeams.

"Swiftly, swiftly. Chaos gathers territory with every passing hour. And with that territory she gains a host of souls sworn to her service. Your worlds shall soon be little else but a memory unless you find the Dragon Sword. . . ."

The armour vanished entirely. All that remained of the Knight in Black and Yellow was an echo of a whisper. Then that, too, was gone.

I took out my Actorios and held it before me, turning this way and that.

Then, to my relief, I stopped. Very dimly at our feet there stretched, for a few yards only, a faintly shimmering ghost of a pathway.

We had found the road to the Dragon Sword.

BOOK THREE

Hither, hither, if you will,
Drink instruction, or instil,
Run the woods like vernal sap,
Crying, hail to luminousness!
    But have care.
In yourself may lurk the trap:
On conditions they caress.
Here you meet the light invoked
Here is never secret cloaked.
Doubt you with the monster's fry
All his orbit may exclude;
Are you of the stiff, the dry,
Cursing the not understood;
Grasp you with the monster's
        claws;
Govern with his truncheon-saws;
Hate, the shadow of the grain;
You are lost in Westermain:
Earthward swoops a vulture sun,
Nighted upon carrion:
Straightway venom wine-cups shout
Toasts to One whose eyes are out:
Flowers along the reeling floor
Drip henbane and hellebore:
Beauty, of her tresses shorn,
Shrieks as nature's maniac:
Hideousness on hoof and horn
Tumbles, yapping in her track:
Haggard Wisdom, stately once,
Leers fantastical and trips:
Allegory drums the sconce,
Impiousness nibblenips.
Imp that dances, imp that flits,

Imp o' the demon-growing girl,
Maddest! Whirl with imp o' the pits
Round you, and with them you
*   whirl*
Fast where pours the fountain-rout
Out of Him whose eyes are out:
Multitudes of multitudes,
Drenched in wallowing deviltry:
And you ask where you may be,
*   In what reek of a lair*
Given to bones and ogre-broods:
*   And they yell you Where.*
Enter these enchanted woods,
*   You who dare.*

—GEORGE MEREDITH,
  "The Woods of Westermain"

1.

WE had gone perhaps five miles when the green-wood on all sides began to rustle urgently, as if threatened. We had only the shadow path to guide us. Steadfastly, in spite of the rapidly increasing agitation, we continued to go forward in single file. Alisaard was immediately behind me. She whispered: "It is as if the forest senses our presence and becomes alarmed."

Then, one by one, the oak trees turned to stone, the stone became liquid and, in an instant, the entire landscape was transformed. The path remained visible, but we were surrounded by monstrous green stems and at the top of these stems, far above our heads, were the yellow bells of gigantic daffodils.

"Is this what lies behind the illusion?" said von Bek in awe.

"This is as much reality as it is illusion," I told him. "Chaos has her moods and whims, that's all. As I told you, she cannot remain stable. It is in her nature to be forever changing."

"While it is in the nature of Law," Alisaard explained, "to be forever fixed. The Balance is there to ensure that neither Law nor Chaos ever gain complete ascendancy, for the one offers sterility, while the other offers only sensation."

"And this struggle between the two, does it take place on every single realm of the multiverse?" von Bek wanted to know. He looked around him at the nodding flowers. Their scent was like a drug.

"Every plane, on some level or another, in some guise or another. It is the perpetual war. And there is a champion, they say, who is doomed to fight in every aspect of that war, for eternity. . . ."

"Please, Lady Alisaard," I interrupted, "I would rather not be reminded of the Eternal Champion's fate!" I was not altogether joking.

Alisaard apologised. We continued in silence along the path for about another mile, until the landscape shuddered and changed for the second time. This time in place of giant daffodils were gibbets. On every gibbet swung a cage and in every cage was a scabrous, dying human creature, crying out for help.

I told them to ignore the prisoners and keep to the path. "And this? Is this mere illusion?" shouted von Bek from behind me. He was almost in tears.

"An invention, I promise you. It will vanish as the others vanished."

Suddenly the prisoners were gone from their cages. In their place were huge finches squalling for food. Then the gibbets disappeared, the finches flew away, and we were surrounded by tall glass buildings for as far as the eye could see. These buildings were in a thousand different styles yet were unstable. Every few moments one of them would fall with a great crashing and tinkling, sometimes taking one or more of the neighboring buildings with it. To follow the path, we were forced to wade through shards of broken glass which set up a great clatter as we advanced. Voices sounded now, from within the buildings, but we could see that the houses were empty. Shrieks of laughter, wails of pain. Horrible sobbing sounds. The moans of the tortured. The glass gradually began to melt and, as it melted, took the form of agonised faces. And those faces were still the size of buildings!

"Oh, this is surely Hell," cried von Bek, "and these are the souls of the damned!"

The faces flowed up into the sky, turning into great metal blades in the form of fern leaves.

And still we made our way slowly along the shadow path. I forced myself to think only of our goal, of the Dragon Sword which could take the Eldren women to their homeland, which must not be allowed to fall into the hands of Chaos. I wondered what means Sharadim would use in trying to defeat us. For how long could she maintain a semblance of life in that corpse, my Doppelgänger?

A wind howled through the metallic leaves. They clashed and jangled and set my teeth on edge. They offered us no direct danger, however. Chaos was not in herself malevolent. But her ambitions were inimical to the desires of both human and Eldren as well as all the other races of the multiverse.

Once, in that iron jungle, I thought I saw figures moving parallel to us. I lifted the Actorios. It could easily detect creatures of ordinary flesh and blood. But if someone had been trailing us, they were now too far away for the stone to find them.

In seconds the ferns became frozen snakes; then the snakes came to life. Next the living snakes began to devour one another. All around us was a great swaying and writhing and hissing. It was as if a tangled hedge of serpents lined both sides of the shadow path. I held tight to Alisaard's trembling hand. "Remember, they will not attack us unless directed. They are hardly real."

But though I reassured her, I knew that any of Chaos's illusions were real enough to do harm in the short span of their existence.

But now the snakes had become country brambles and our path was a sandy lane leading towards the distant sea.

I began to feel a little more optimistic, in spite of knowing how false my security was, and had begun to whistle when I rounded a turn in the path and saw that our way was blocked by a mass of riders. At their head was our old enemy Baron Captain Armiad of *The Frowning Shield*. His features had become even more bestial in the time since we had last seen him. His nostrils had widened so much that they now resembled the snout of a pig. There were tufts of hair sprouting from his face and neck and when he spoke I was reminded of the lowing of a cow.

These were Sharadim's retainers. The same we had left behind when we dashed for the gateway into this realm. Evidently they had lost no time in following us.

We were still without weapons. We could not fight them. The bramble hedges were solid enough and blocked flight in that direction. If we wished to flee, we would have to run back the way we had come. And we would easily be ridden down by the horsemen.

"Where's your mistress, Baron Porker?" I called, standing my ground. "Was she too cowardly to enter Chaos herself?"

Armiad's already narrow eyes came closer together still. He grunted and sniffed. His nose and eyes seemed permanently wet.

"The Empress Sharadim has more important business than to chase after vermin when there is the greatest prey of all to hand."

Armiad's remark was greeted appreciatively by his fellows, who gave forth a great chorus of snorts and grunts. All of them had faces and bodies transformed by their espousal of Chaos's cause. I wondered if they had noticed these changes or if their brains were warped as thoroughly as their physical appearance. I could barely recognise some of them. Duke Perichost's thin, unpleasant face now bore a distinct resemblance to that of a starved hamster. I wondered how long, in relative time, they had been here.

"And what's the greatest prey of all?" von Bek asked him. Again we were talking in the hope that the next change in the landscape would be to our advantage.

"You know what it is!" shouted Armiad, his snout twitching with rage and turning red. "For you seek it yourself. You must do. You cannot deny it!"

"But do you know what it is, Baron Captain Armiad?" said Alisaard. "Has the Empress allowed you into her confidence? It seems unlikely when the last she spoke of you she complained that you were poor material for her purposes. She said you would be disposed of when your turn was served. Is it served now, do you think, Lord Baron Captain? Or have you been given what you most desired? Are you respected by your peers at last? Do they cheer their King Admiral whenever his hull passes by? Or are they silent, because *The Frowning Shield* is as filthy and disgusting as ever, but is now one of the last hulls still rolling in the Maaschanheem?"

She mocked him. She goaded him. And all the time she was testing him. I could see that she was finding out what Sharadim's instructions had been. And it was becoming plain, from Armiad's restraint, that he had been ordered to take us alive.

His tiny eyes glared Murder, but his hands twitched on his saddle horn.

He was about to speak when von Bek broke in. "You are a foolish, stupid, greedy man, Baron Captain. Can you not see that she has rid herself of unwanted allies? She sends you into Chaos. Meanwhile she continues her conquest of the Six Realms. Where is she now? Fighting the Eldren women? Wiping out the Red Weepers?"

Now Armiad lifted a triumphant snout and voiced something close to laughter. "What need has she to fight the Eldren? They are gone. They are all gone from Gheestenheem. They have fled before our navies. Gheestenheem is absolutely ours!"

Alisaard believed him. It was plain he did not lie. White and trembling she yet controlled herself. "Where have they fled? There is nowhere, surely, they could go."

"Where else but to sanctuary with their ancient allies? They have gone into Adelstane and crouch with the Ursine Princes behind their defences while my Empress's army lays siege. Their defeat is inevitable. A few fight on, with the pirates of my own realm, but most huddle in Adelstane awaiting slaughter."

"They have used the gateway between Barobanay and the Ursine stronghold," murmured Alisaard. "It is their only possible strategy against such forces as Sharadim commands."

Again Baron Captain Armiad lifted his snout in a kind of laugh. "Conquest has been swift across all the Six Realms. For years my lady made her plans. And when the time came to put them into action, how wonderfully she was able to achieve her ambitions."

"Only because few rational people can even begin to understand such a lust for power," said von Bek feelingly. "There is nothing more puerile than the mind of a tyrant."

"And nothing more frightening," I added under my breath.

The bramble hedges began to curl upwards, forming spirals of gauze in a thousand colours.

Without a word, Alisaard, von Bek and myself dived from the path and into the tangle of rustling linen while at our backs charged the yelling, clumsy pack, made clumsier still by the grotesque distortions of their bodies. Yet still they were mounted and had advantage of us.

We had lost the shadow path. We darted from one piece of cover to the next. Baron Armiad and his companions blundered in pursuit, hooting and bellowing. It was as if we were chased by a pack of farmyard beasts.

There was nothing comical, however, about our terror. All we had was an idea that Sharadim had ordered us taken alive, but in their blind stupidity, these creatures might easily kill us by accident!

Desperately I sought for another shadow trail, holding the Actorios out before me.

The streamers of gauze became great fountains of water, shooting high into the sky. It was between these that we now ducked and dodged. Then Duke Perichost had sighted Alisaard and with a triumphant snort had drawn his sword and was bearing down on her. I saw von Bek turn and try to reach her. But I was closer. I flung myself upwards, grasping the Draachenheemer's wrist and twisting the sword from a hand which now more closely resembled a paw. Alisaard dropped down and picked up the blade even as I threw my whole weight against the duke and forced him off the horse and onto the ground.

"Von Bek!" I cried. "Into the saddle, man." I thrust the

Actorios upon Alisaard, who took it, looking baffled. Now more of the Chaos creatures had sighted us and were charging in crowded formation towards us.

Von Bek swung up and helped Alisaard seat herself behind him. I ran for a while beside the horse yelling for them to go ahead of me and try to find a new trail. I would do my best to find them.

Then I was turning to face the charge of a Mabden barbarian whose lance was aimed directly at my groin. I side-stepped the lance and grasped the haft, dragging it down and to the right, hoping the Mabden was fool enough to hang on to it.

He came off the saddle as smoothly as if it had been greased. And now I had his lance.

In seconds I had taken the barbarian's place on the back of the horse and was riding after my friends. Both von Bek and I were more proficient horsemen than the warriors who came in our wake. Darting in and out of the great fountains we gradually escaped Baron Armiad and his pack. Then another reflecting wall came between us and them. We dimly saw them on the other side. There was no particular reason for the wall to compose itself at that particular point. It was merely a random whim of Chaos. But it proved lucky for us as, sweating, we slowed our pace.

I saw von Bek turn in his saddle and kiss Alisaard. She responded enthusiastically to this. She flung her arms around him, the Actorios stone clutched in one beautiful hand.

And it was Ermizhad who kissed my friend. It was Ermizhad who betrayed me. The only betrayal I had thought impossible!

Now I knew for certain it was she. All along she had deceived me. I had slain whole peoples because of my love for her. I had fought in a thousand wars. And this was how she returned my loyalty?

What was worse, von Bek, whom I had believed a comrade, had no scruples in the matter. They flaunted themselves. Their embraces mocked everything I held dear. How could I have trusted them?

I knew then that I had no choice but to punish them for the pain they now caused me.

Steadying my horse, I lifted up the lance I had taken from the Mabden. I weighed it in my hand. I was skilled in the use of such weapons and knew that one single cast could pierce the pair of them, uniting them in death. A fair reward for their treachery.

"Ermizhad! How is it possible!"

Now my arm went back as I prepared to throw. I saw von Bek's cowardly eyes grow big with disbelieving horror. I saw Ermizhad begin to turn, following the direction of his gaze.

I laughed at them.

My laughter found an echo. It seemed to fill the whole realm.

Von Bek was shouting. Ermizhad was shouting. Doubtless they were pleading for mercy. I would give them none. The laughter grew louder and louder. It was not merely my own laughter I heard. There was another voice.

I hesitated.

A tiny shout came from von Bek. "Herr Daker! Are you possessed? What is it?"

I ignored him. I had come to realise how he had tricked me, how he had deliberately courted my friendship, knowing that he was to keep a liaison with my wife. And had Ermizhad helped him plan the deception? It followed logically that she had. How had I failed to guess all this? My mind had been clouded by other, less important issues. I had no need of a Dragon Sword. I had no loyalty to the Six Realms. Why should I let myself be distracted by these problems when my own wife dishonoured me before my eyes?

I ceased to laugh at that point. I poised the lance for the throw.

And then I realised that the laughter was continuing. It was not my laughter.

I looked to one side and saw a man standing there. He wore long robes of black and dark blue. There was a familiarity about his face I could not place. He had the look of a wise, well-balanced statesman in middle years. Only his wild laughter denied this impression.

Now I knew that I looked upon the ruler of this realm, at the Archduke Balarizaaf Himself.

And without thinking I flung the lance directly at his heart.

He continued to laugh, even as he looked at the haft which protruded from his body.

"Oh, this is fine amusement," he said at last. "So much more interesting, Sir Champion, than conquering worlds and enslaving nations, don't you think?"

And I realised, just barely, that I was victim of this realm's hallucinatory influences. I had almost killed my two best friends in my madness.

Then the Archduke Balarizaaf had vanished and Alisaard was crying out to me to look. With the Actorios she had found another shadow path, dimly visible ahead of us. But of still greater interest was the large brown hare which loped along it.

"We must follow it," I said, even as I began to tremble in reaction to what I had almost done. 'Remember what Sepiriz told us. The hare is our first link with the sword."

Von Bek offered me a wary glance. "Are you yourself again, my friend?"

"I hope so," I told him. I was riding ahead now, riding after the hare which continued, with characteristic insouciance, to lead us along the shadow path.

Soon the track had narrowed and the horses were stumbling on loose rocks. I dismounted, leading my mount. Von Bek and Alisaard followed my example.

The hare appeared to wait patiently for us. Then it moved steadily on.

At last the beast stopped at a point where the trail appeared to go through solid rock. We could see a wide valley below us, a river which looked as big as the Mississippi, a massive fortress seemingly all made of silver. Still dismounted, we approached the hare and the wall of rock. I reached out for the beast, but it hopped away from me. And then, quite suddenly, I was falling into blackness, falling through the melancholy emptiness of the cosmic void. It seemed to me I heard Balarizaaf's laughter again. Had we allowed ourselves to be trapped by the Archduke of Chaos, after all?

Were we consigned to Limbo for all eternity?

2.

I FELT that I had fallen for months, perhaps years, before I realised the sensation of movement was gone and I was on my feet on firm ground, though still in utter blackness.

A voice was calling to me: "John Daker, are you there?"

"I am here, von Bek, wherever here may be. And Alisaard?"

"With Count von Bek," she said.

Gradually we managed to grope our way towards each other and link hands.

"What is this place?" von Bek wondered. "Some trap of the Archduke Balarizaaf?"

"Possibly," I said, "though I was under the impression that the hare led us here."

Von Bek began to laugh. "Aha, so like Alice we have fallen down a rabbit hole?"

I smiled at this. Alisaard remained silent, plainly baffled by the reference. She said: "The Realms of Chaos have many places where the fabric of the multiverse has worn thin, others where worlds intersect at random. They cannot be charted, as we chart our own gateways, yet sometimes they exist in one place for centuries. It could be that we have fallen through one of those gaps in the fabric. We could be anywhere in the entire multiverse. . . ."

"Or nowhere, perhaps?" said von Bek.

"Or nowhere," she agreed.

I still maintained the view that the hare had led us here intentionally. "We were told to find a cup, that the cup would lead us to the horned horse and the horned horse would lead us to the sword. I have faith in Sepiriz's powers of prediction. I think we are here to find that cup."

"Even if it were here," von Bek argued, "we could hardly see it, could we, my friend?"

I bent down to touch the floor. It was damp. There was a mildewy smell about the place. As I ran my hand farther I confirmed my guess that we stood on old, worn flagstones. "This is man-made," I said. "And I would guess we are in an underground chamber of some sort. Which means there must be a wall. And in the wall, perhaps, we'll find a door. Come." And I led them slowly across the floor until at last my fingers found a slimy block of stone. The stuff was unpleasant to the touch, but I soon confirmed that this was, indeed, a wall. So we followed the wall, first to one corner, then to another. The chamber was about twenty feet wide. Set in the third wall was a wooden door with iron hinges and a huge old-fashioned lock. I took hold of the ring and turned it. Tumblers clicked with surprising smoothness. I tugged. There was light beyond the door. Cautiously I pulled it open another inch or two and peered into a corridor.

The corridor had a low, curved ceiling and seemed as old as the chamber. Yet at intervals along it there ran what I recognised at once as ordinary twentieth century light bulbs, strung on visible flexes, as if placed there for temporary use. The corridor ended on my right at another door, but on my left it stretched for some distance before turning a corner. I frowned. I was deeply puzzled.

"We seem to be in the dungeons of a mediaeval castle," I whispered to von Bek, "yet there's modern lighting. Take a look for yourself."

After a moment he pulled his head back in and closed the door. I heard him breathing heavily, but he said nothing.

"What's the matter?" I asked him.

"Nothing, my friend. A premonition, call it. We could be anywhere, I know, yet I have a feeling that I recognise that corridor. Which is, you'll agree, unlikely. One such place is much like another. Well, shall we explore?"

"If you feel ready," I said.

He uttered a faint laugh. "Of course. My mind's somewhat disturbed by recent events, that's all."

And so we stepped into the corridor. We made a peculiar sight, Alisaard in her ivory armour, myself in the heavy leather of a marsh warrior and von Bek in his imitation twentieth century costume. We proceeded cautiously until we reached the turn in the passage. The place seemed deserted, yet plainly was in use, judging by the lights. I peered up at the nearest bulb. They were of an unfamiliar pattern to me, yet clearly operated according to the usual principle.

We were so engrossed in exploring this corridor that we were too late to look for cover when one of the doors opened and a man stepped out. We stood there, ready to challenge him as best we could. Although there was a faint imprecision to his form, he seemed solid enough. The sight of his costume was, moreover, enough to shock me, and as for von Bek, the man gasped aloud.

We were face to face with a staff officer of the Nazi SS! He was engrossed in some papers he carried, but when he looked up it was to stare full in our faces. We said nothing. He frowned, stared again, visibly shuddered and then, muttering to himself, turned away. As he walked in the opposite direction he rubbed his eyes.

Alisaard chuckled. "There is some advantage to our situation," she said.

"Why didn't he speak to us?" von Bek asked.

"We are shadows in this world. I have heard of such things frequently, but never experienced it. We have only partial substance here." She laughed again. "We are what the Eldren have always been called in Six Realms. We are ghosts, my friends! That man believed himself to be suffering from a hallucination!"

"Will everyone here think the same?" von Bek asked nervously. For a ghost, he was sweating badly. He, better than I, knew the implications of being caught by these brutes.

"We can hope so, I suppose," she said. But she could not be sure. "Sight of that man has terrified you, Count von Bek! It is he who should have been afraid of you!"

"I can understand something of this," I told her. "And I believe Sepiriz may have found a way to keep his pledge to Count von Bek whilst also having his own purposes served. You said you thought you recognised this place, von Bek. Now do you recall where you may have seen it before?"

He bowed his head, rubbing at his face with his hands. He apologised for his condition, then straightened his back, nodding. "Yes. A few years ago. A distant cousin brought me here. He was an ardent Nazi and wished to impress me with what he claimed to be the resurrection of ancient German culture. We are in the so-called hidden vaults of the great castle at Nurenberg. We are at the very centre of what the Nazis consider their spiritual stronghold. Of course it would be impossible for an outsider to come here now, but then their numbers were fewer, they were less respectable, they had less power. These vaults are said to be as old as the first Gothic builders, who were here before the Romans. They lie under the main hillside on which the castle is built and were excavated in fairly recent times. When I came here there was much talk of their discovery of the 'foundations' of the true Germany. But I was used to that kind of nonsense by then. I found the place disturbing largely because of the value my Nazi relative placed on it. Very soon after I had visited it, I heard it was forbidden for anyone but the highest of the Nazi hierarchy to come here. Why, I do not know. There were the usual rumours, of Hitler's black magic rites and all that, but I didn't believe them. My theory was that a secret military installation of some kind was being built here. In those days it was still necessary for the Nazis to pretend to be honouring the Armistice agreements."

"But Sepiriz said the hare would lead us to a cup," I said in some bafflement. "What sort of cup are we expected to find in Nurenberg?"

"I am sure we shall discover that in good time." Alisaard had become impatient with this talk. "Let us continue. Remember that much still depends on us. We have the fate of the Six Realms in our hands."

Von Bek looked about him. "I remember that there was a main vault. A kind of ceremonial chamber which my cousin seemed to believe had some kind of near-mystical importance. He called it the hub of the Germanic spirit. Some such nonsense. I must admit I was almost as bored as I was sickened by his talk. But perhaps that is what we should look for?"

"Do you remember the way?" I asked him.

He considered for a moment and then pointed. "It is where we were going. That door at the far end. I'm fairly sure that it opens onto the main chamber."

We followed him now. Two other Nazis passed us, but only one saw us, out of the corner of his eye, and again it was plain he did not trust his vision. If this time was contemporary to von Bek's I could imagine that most of these people were short of sleep and had become fairly used to hallucinations of one kind or another. Indeed, if I had been a member of the SS, I too would probably have been seeing all kinds of ghosts.

Von Bek paused outside a door which was evidently of recent workmanship, though in the Romanesque pattern of much of the rest. "I think this is the chamber I mentioned," he said. He hesitated. "Shall I open it?"

Taking our silence for assent, he reached towards the large

iron ring and tried to turn it. It refused to move. He put his shoulder to the oak of the door and pushed. He shook his head. "It's locked. I suspect there are modern locks on the other side. It hardly gives."

"Could it be that since our substance is, as it were, somewhat diffuse on this plane, we cannot exert enough force on the door?" I asked Alisaard.

She had only a little knowledge of the phenomenon. She suggested that all we could do would be to wait to see how others opened the door. "There could be a trick to it."

Accordingly, we drew ourselves into a nearby alcove and, hidden in the shadows, watched as various Nazi officers came and went in the corridor. There were no armed soldiers here, which led us to suppose that the Nazis felt themselves secure at this level.

We had waited perhaps an hour and were growing impatient with this plan, when a tall, grey-haired man in black and silver robes which resembled the uniform of the SS turned the bend in the corridor and advanced towards us. He looked like some kind of officiating priest, for he carried a small box in his hand. Pausing at the door to the chamber, he opened the box and produced a key which he inserted into the lock. This was turned. We heard various tumblers moving. The door swung open. A musty scent came from the chamber beyond.

Immediately we followed quietly behind the grey-haired man. Plainly he was preparing the chamber for some rite, just as a priest might prepare the church. He lit tapers and with these he ignited large candles. The stones of the vault were certainly ancient. The roof was supported by dozens of arches so that it was impossible to tell its actual dimensions. The flames sent shadows flickering everywhere. It was not difficult for us to hide. When the officiary had completed his task he left the chamber, closing and locking the door behind him.

Now we were free to explore. We realised that the place had been designed fairly recently as a temple of some kind. At the far end was an altar. On the wall behind the altar was the black, red and white of the Nazi hooked cross, surrounded by insignia of equal barbarity, versions of ancient Teutonic symbols. Upon the altar itself was a stylised silver tree and beside it the figure of a rampant bull in solid gold.

"This is the stuff which some Nazis wished to put into our churches," whispered von Bek. "Pagan objects of worship which they claim are the symbols of a true German religion.

They are almost as anti-Christian as they are anti-Semitic. It is as if they hate every system of thought which in any way questions their own mishmash of pseudo-philosophy and mystical claptrap!" He stared at the altar in disgust. "They are the worst kind of nihilists. They cannot even see that they destroy everything and create nothing. Their invention is as empty as the inventions of Chaos I have seen. It has no true history, no concrete substance, no depth, no quality of intellect. It is merely a negation, a brutal denial of all Germany's virtues." Again he was close to tears. Alisaard took his hand. She knew little of what he spoke, but she felt deeply for him.

"Try to consider our purpose here," she murmured. "For your own sake, my dear."

It was the first time I had heard her use such a term. And the stabbing jealousy came again. But I was able to gather my senses once more. I remembered the madness which had come over me such a short time ago.

Von Bek was grateful for her concern and her reminder of his purpose here. "A cup—the Grail—is frequently part of this cult's paraphernalia," he said. "But I cannot see it anywhere."

"The Grail? Weren't you telling me, when we first met, that your family has some connection with the Holy Grail?"

"A legend, that's all. Some of my ancestors were said to have seen it. Others were said to have held it in trust. But the story became too fanciful, I think. One legend even said that we held it in trust not for God but for Satan! I read all this when I was seeking a means of discovering what I thought were old passages to lead me secretly out of Bek without the Nazis realising. That was how I came upon the maps and books relating to the Mittelmarch...." He stopped as we heard a sound from the corridor. Swiftly we withdrew into the dark shadows of one of the arches.

The door opened once more, sending a shaft of electric light into the gloom. Three figures now stood there. None was particularly tall and we could not see their faces because of the high, stiffened collars which framed their heads. The cloaks looked like those worn by certain orders of warrior priests, such as the Knights Templar, and indeed these men carried great broadswords in their gauntletted hands, while under their arms were heavy iron helmets which looked as if they had been forged in the Dark Ages. There was a look of barbaric strength about the three figures which was entirely the result of their chosen costume. As they moved forward towards the altar, closing the door behind them and bolting it, I saw that one was very thin and walked with a limp; another was rotund and wheezed a little as he made his way beneath the arches, while the other moved with a peculiar, artificial stiffness, his shoulders set back in the manner of a short man who wished to appear taller than he was. I put out my hand to hold von Bek's arm. He was trembling. I was not surprised.

There could be very little doubt that we were in the presence of three of the twentieth century's arch-villains. The three men were Goebbels, Goering and Hitler, and everything I had ever read about their bizarre mystical beliefs, their faith in supernatural portents, their willingness to accept the strangest and most unlikely notions, was here proven at last.

Believing themselves unobserved they began to chant lines from Goethe. In their mouths I felt the words were defiled and horribly abused. As with so many other romantic notions, they perverted the German poet's ideas to their own miserable purpose. They might as easily have chanted the incantations of a Black Mass or defiled a synagogue with their filth, the effect was somehow the same.

> *Allen Gewalten*
> *Zum Trutz sich erhalten,*
> *Nimmer sich beugen,*
> *Kräftig sich zeigen,*
> *Rufet die Arme*
> *Der Götter herbei.*

"All powers are granted to souls undaunted, when self-reliant, firm and defiant, then shall the Gods be helpful to thee!"

They abused these words as they abused all words, all the finest ideas and feelings of the German people, turning them into tools to build their own pathetically inadequate ideology. I would not have been surprised to find the ghost of Goethe standing beside me, ready to take revenge on those who so badly misused his work.

Now Goebbels stepped forward to light two huge red candles on either side of the altar.

I could sense von Bek beside me, barely restraining himself from lunging at these creatures. In silence, I held him back. We had to wait. We had to see what would be revealed to us. Sepiriz had wanted us to come here. He had sent the hare to lead us here. We must wait for the ritual to proceed.

I was astonished how banal their own words were. Full of implorations to ancient Gods, to Wotan and the spirits of Oak and Iron and Fire. The light from the candles illuminated their faces—Goebbels, a mask of twisted ratlike glee, like a bad schoolboy relishing his own wickedness; Goering, plump and serious, plainly believing everything he said and, moreover, evidently drunk or drugged into near-oblivion; and Adolf Hitler, Chancellor of the Third Reich, his eyes dark mirrors, his pale face full of an unwholesome luminosity, willing all this to become reality as, no doubt, he sought to will the rest of the world into acceptance of his hideous insanity.

It was a powerful scene and one which I hope never to witness again. This was human perversity which had little to do with even the worst examples found amongst the followers of Chaos. This was so much closer to my own experience, my own time, that I could sympathise with von Bek, who struggled with himself like a chained dog who seeks only to kill, who had seen at first hand the horrors this trio had brought to his nation, whose whole original purpose in linking his fate with mine was concerned with destroying them, of saving his world from their evil.

I looked at Alisaard. Even she sensed the ugly power of these creatures.

"Let the powers of our ancient tribal gods, the gods who lent strength to the conquerors of Rome, be granted to our Germany in these, the hours of her destiny, the hours of decision." This was Goebbels, plainly not really believing what he was saying, but well aware that both Hitler and Goering were by no means as incredulous. "Let us be granted the mystical might of the great Gods of the Old World, filling us with that dark, natural energy which defeated the enfeebled followers of the Judaeo-Christian would-be conquerors of our ancient land. Let our blood, which is the pure, undiluted blood of those fearless ancestors, flow again through our veins with the same sweet thrill it knew in the days before our honest, guiltless forebears were corrupted by alien, oriental religions. Let Germany know a return to her full, untrammeled selfhood!"

More of this nonsense followed, with von Bek growing increasingly restless and Alisaard and I becoming gradually bored and impatient.

"Now we summon the Chalice, the vessel of our spiritual essence, the Chalice, which is that same cauldron Parsifal sought; the Chalice of Wisdom, which the Christians stole from us and incorporated into their own mythologies, calling it the Holy Grail!" Goebbels chanted, shifting his weight from one foot to the other, fidgeting like some malformed dwarf. "Now we summon our Chalice so that we might partake of its contents and be filled with the Wisdom we seek!"

These words were echoed now by Hitler and Goering.

"Now we kneel!" cried Goebbels, evidently relishing every moment of his power over the others.

Obediently the two Nazi leaders went down on their knees, leaving only Goebbels standing, his arms spread as he addressed the altar.

"Here in this most ancient of all places, where the Chalice has resided since the beginning of Time, let us be granted a vision. Let us drink that wisdom. Let us be granted the power of our Old Gods, the knowledge of our old blood, the certainty of our old strength. We must know which way to go. We must know if we are to concentrate our forces on releasing the power of the atom or upon conquering the threat from the East. We must have a sign, great Gods. We must have a sign!"

I shall never know if Goebbels was merely putting on a theatrical act for his less sceptical comrades or if he actually believed the rubbish which fell from his thin lips. I do not know if his incantatory speeches had any part in what occurred next, or if von Bek's presence in the vault was the cause of the phenomenon. His family was associated with the Grail, just as I, in all my guises, was associated with the Sword. And that, perhaps, is why fate had drawn us together, since it was a great and important fight we presently fought. How much of a role Sepiriz played and how much he knew, I still do not know entirely, but it is obvious his powers of perception and prediction had been used to ensure that we would be in that exact place at an exact time.

For now there began a phase of the ritual which, I could tell, took all three by surprise, most of all Goebbels. We heard the sweetest music fill the vault. A scent like roses accompanied it. The music was almost choral. It was in direct contrast to the dark heaviness of our surroundings, to the pagan paraphernalia of the Nazi hierarchy. And then there came a white and blinding light, a light of such loveliness that we could after a moment stare into it without suffering. For at the centre of that white light, the source of the music and the perfume, was a simple chalice, a golden bowl, the like of which I had seen only once before.

This is what Christian legends called the Holy Grail and

what the Celts had called the Cauldron of Wisdom. It had existed for all time, under many names, just as the Sword we sought had existed, just as I, the Eternal Champion, had existed. Beyond the radiance I perceived Goebbels, and Hitler, and Goering, all upon their knees now, looking in utter astonishment at the unexpected vision.

I heard Hitler muttering over and over again some mindless oath. Goering seemed to be hiccuping and trying to raise his fat body to its feet. Goebbels had begun to grin, again like an evil schoolboy who had made a wild discovery. He was almost laughing.

"It's true! It's true!" Goebbels screamed now, addressing himself, his own doubts. "It's true. We have a sign! What shall we do? Must we dispose of the threat from the East before we concentrate our forces on building an atomic bomb or should we attempt to consolidate our gains while putting our energies at the disposal of our scientists? How long can it be before Russia attacks us? Or America and England invade us? What shall we do? Our conquests came so rapidly we are hardly able to think. We need guidance. Are you truly a sign from the Old Gods? Will they truly direct us onto the right path to ensure Germany's dominance of the world?"

"The cup cannot speak to us, Herr Doctor!" Adolf Hitler was suddenly contemptuous, sensing his minister's uncertainty in the face of this actuality. "It must be held. Then the truth will be revealed. Surely that is what it means?"

"No, no, no!" Goering finally lumbered to his feet, panting heavily. His eyes were red, his nose ran, and thin lines of spittle fell from his lips. He drew a great, shuddering breath. "There is a maiden, surely. A maiden who guards the Grail. A Rheinmaiden, eh? I know. From Wagner, eh?" And he giggled.

I could scarcely believe that these were the men who had done so much to influence the course of my own world's history. It now seemed obvious that all of them were drugged in some way. They were acting like silly children. And yet I suppose I should have realised that it is in the nature of all such creatures to be at heart infantile. Only children believe they can achieve enormous power over the world without paying a price for that power. And the price so often is the sanity of the one who seeks it. In a way these three men were even more like grotesque caricatures of the people they had once been than those poor distorted things of Chaos who had pursued us earlier. Did they realise it? And did that realisation actually further their willingness towards their own corruption and descent into utter madness?

"Yes," said Adolf Hitler with a display of almost ridiculous self-importance. "Rheinmaidens. Valkyries. Wotan Himself. This chalice merely signifies their presence."

This ludicrous debate continued for a few moments. I believe they had never wanted this vision. The rituals they performed were a kind of reinforcement of their need to believe in the rightness of their actions. This vault in the depths of the Nurenberg castle, the robes, the incantations, were all a means of revivifying their flagging, drug-dependent energies, a way of making themselves believe in their mystical destiny.

And now it dawned on me that the Grail had not appeared in answer to Doctor Goebbel's summoning. It had appeared because we were there—or, specifically, I guessed, because von Bek was there. I looked at my friend. His face was rapt as he gazed upon the Grail. Plainly it had not occurred to him that the golden cup had a special affinity with him, in spite of his family's legends.

Now Hitler stepped forward, his strange little face suddenly sober as he stretched shaking hands towards the Grail. The radiance from the cup emphasised the horrible pallor of his skin, the unhealthiness of his appearance. I could not believe that such a corrupted being would be allowed even to look upon the Grail, let alone touch it.

Those clutching fingers, which already had the blood of millions upon them, reached towards the singing cup. The eyes reflected the glow, glittering like little stones; the moist lips parted, the features twitched.

"You realise, my friends, that this is the source of energy we seek. This is the power which will allow us to defeat every enemy. The Jews as usual look in the wrong direction for the means of creating an atomic bomb. We have found it, here in Nurenberg. We have found it at the very core of our spiritual stronghold! Here is energy to destroy the entire globe—or to build it again in any image we desire! How paltry is the thing they call science. We have something far superior! We have Faith. We have a Force greater than Reason! We have a wisdom beyond mere knowledge. We have the Holy Grail itself. The Chalice of Limitless Power!" And his hands seemed like black claws reaching into that pure light; reaching towards the Grail; about to despoil something of such wonderful holiness I felt sick at the very thought.

But now the Cup was singing louder. It was almost shrieking its alarm at Hitler's intention. The note changed to one
seemingly of warning. Yet still the dictator made to grasp it.
His fingers touched the glowing gold.

And Adolf Hitler's shriek was louder than the cup's. He
fell backwards. He sobbed. He stared at his fingers. They
gleamed black as if the skin had been fused to the bone. Then,
like a little child, he put the fingers into his mouth and sat
down suddenly on the flagstones of that ancient vault.

Goebbels frowned. He reached out, but more cautiously.
Again the Grail sounded its warning. Goering was already
retreating, covering his face with his arm, screaming: "No,
no! I am not your enemy!"

In tones of placatory reasonableness Joseph Goebbels said:
"It was not our intention to violate this thing. We merely
sought its wisdom."

He was frightened. He looked around him as if he sought a
means of escape, as if he had grown appalled at whatever it was
he had accidentally brought here. Meanwhile his master remained upon the floor, sucking his fingers, staring thoughtfully
at the Grail and from time to time murmuring something to
himself.

Afraid that the cup would now disappear as readily as it
had appeared, I reached forward to grasp it. In the light I
understood suddenly that they could see me. Hitler in particular had focussed on me and was shading his eyes to try to get a
clearer view of me. I thought better of taking the cup. I said to
von Bek: "Quickly, man. I am certain that only you will be
able to set hands upon it. Take it. It is our key to the Dragon
Sword. Take it, von Bek!"

The three Nazis were advancing again, perhaps fascinated
by the shadowy figures they saw, still not absolutely certain
that what they observed was real.

Now Alisaard stepped between them and the Grail, raising
her hand. "No farther!" she cried. "This cup is not yours. It is
ours. It is needed to save the Six Realms from Chaos!" She
spoke to them reasonably, having no knowledge of what they
represented.

Plainly Hermann Goering at least believed he had seen his
Rheinmaiden. Hitler, however, was shaking his head as if trying
to rid it of a hallucination, while Goebbels merely grinned,
perhaps convinced and fascinated by his own insanity.

"Listen!" Goering cried. "Do you recognise it? She's

speaking the old, High German! We have summoned an entire pantheon!"

Hitler seemed to be biting his lower lip, trying to come to a decision. He looked from us to his fingers and back again. "What shall I do?" he said.

Alisaard could not understand him. She pointed towards the door. "Go! Go! This cup is ours. It is what we came here for."

"I would swear it is High German," said Goering again, but it was plain he could understand her hardly any better than she could understand him. "She is trying to tell us the correct decision. She is pointing! She is pointing to the East!"

"Take the cup, man," I said urgently to von Bek. I had no idea what would happen to us if we remained much longer. The Nazis were not stable. If they fled from the room and locked the door behind them we would be thoroughly trapped. It was even possible we would die in that vault before they dared open it up again.

Von Bek responded to my cries at last. Very slowly he reached out his hands towards that beautiful chalice. And the thing seemed to settle into his palms as if it had always been his. The voice grew sweeter still, the radiance subtler, the perfume stronger. Von Bek's own features were illuminated by the chalice. He looked at once heroic and pure, exactly as the true knights of the Arthurian legends might have seemed to those who accompanied them on their quest for the Grail.

I led both him and Alisaard past the uncertain Nazis and towards the door of the vault. We took the chalice with us. They did not attempt to stop us, yet they were not sure whether to remain or to follow us.

I spoke to them as I would speak to a dog. "Stay," I said. "Stay here." Alisaard drew back the bolt.

"Yes," Goering murmured. "We have our sign."

"But the Grail," said Hitler. "It is to be the source of our power. . . ."

"We shall find it again," Goebbels reassured him. He spoke dreamily. It seemed to me that the last thing he wanted to do was to set eyes on either the Holy Grail or ourselves ever again. We had threatened the strange power he had over his fellow Nazis, especially over his master, Hitler. Of the three men in that vault, only Goebbels was truly glad to see us go.

We closed the door behind us. We would have locked it if we could.

"Now," I said, "we must return as quickly as possible to

the room we were first in. I suspect that is the way back to Chaos. . . ."

As if entranced, von Bek continued to hold the cup in his two hands, moving with us, though his attention remained fixed on the Grail.

Alisaard looked at him with a lover's eyes, holding him gently by the arm. And now, when SS men approached us, they fell back, blinded. We reached our destination without difficulty. I turned the handle of the door and it opened onto blackness. Cautiously I entered, then Alisaard followed, leading von Bek, whose eyes had never left the Grail. An expression of rapt sweetness was on his handsome face. For some unknown reason I was faintly disturbed by it.

Then Alisaard had closed the door and the Grail's radiance filled the room. We were all dark shadows in that light.

Yet now I counted three such shadows, besides my own!

The smallest of these now drew its little body closer to mine. He grinned up at me and saluted.

Jermays the Crooked no longer wore his marsh armour. Instead he was clad in more familiar motley. "I note that you've lately experienced what's common for me." He bowed. "And know the power as well as the frustrations of being a ghost!"

I took his offered hand. "Why are you here, Jermays? Do you bring news of the Maaschanheem?"

"I am presently in the service of Law. I bring a message from Sepiriz." His face clouded. He added slowly: "Aye, and news from the Maaschanheem. News of defeat."

"Adelstane?" Alisaard came forward, pushing loose hair away from her lovely features. "Has Adelstane fallen?"

"Not yet," said the dwarf gravely, "but Maaschanheem is completely reduced. The survivors, too, have rallied to the Ursine stronghold. But now Sharadim sends even the great hulls through the Pillars of Paradise in pursuit of them! No realm is free of invasion. Each is violated. In Rootsenheem the Red Weepers are enslaved, swearing loyalty to Chaos or they are slain. This, too, is true of Fluugensheem and, of course, the Draachenheem. Only Sharadim's forces occupy Gheestenheem now. All humans are defeated. The Eldren and the Ursine Princes continue to resist, but they cannot hold Adelstane much longer, I fear. I have just come from there. The Lady Phalizaarn, Prince Morandi Pag and Prince Groaffer Rolm send you messages of good will and pray for your success. If Sharadim or her creature reaches the Dragon Sword ahead of you, it cannot be long before Chaos breaks through and Adelstane is engulfed. Moreover, the Eldren women will never be reunited with the rest of their race. . . ."

I was horrified. "But do you know anything of Sharadim and her dead brother?"

"I've heard nothing, save that they returned to Chaos on unfinished business. . . ."

"Then we must try to return to Chaos, also," I said. "We have the cup Sepiriz told us of. Now we seek the horned horse. But how can we get back to Chaos, Jermays, can you say?"

"You are here," said Jermays the Crooked in some surprise, and opening the door he revealed daylight, a rich, exotic smell, dark fleshy leaves and a trail which disappeared into what was apparently a tropical forest.

And, when we had passed through the archway, Jermays had gone, together with the door and any sign of the Nurenberg dungeons.

It was at this point that von Bek lowered the chalice, an expression of dismay on his face. "I have failed! I have failed! Oh, why did you let me leave!"

"What is it?" cried Alisaard in surprise. "What is the matter, my dear?"

"I had the opportunity to kill them. I did not take it!"

"Do you think you could have killed them in the presence of this cup?" I asked him reasonably. "Aside from the fact that you had no weapons?"

He calmed a little. "But it was my single opportunity to destroy them. To save millions. I surely will not be given a second chance!"

"You have achieved your ambition," I told him. "But you have achieved it obliquely, according to the methods of the Balance. I can promise you that now they will destroy themselves, thanks to what happened in that vault today. Believe me, von Bek, they are now as thoroughly doomed as any of their victims."

"Is this truth?" He looked from me to the chalice. The golden cup no longer glowed, but although it was plain, it still possessed enormous power.

"It is the truth, I swear."

"I did not know you possessed the power of prediction, Herr Daker."

"In this case I do. They can last only a short while longer.

Then all three will die by their own hands and their tyranny will collapse."

"Germany and the world will be free of them?"

"Free of their particular evil, I promise you. Free of everything save the memory of their cruelty and barbarism."

He drew a great, sobbing breath. "I believe you. Then Sepiriz kept his word to me?"

"He kept his word in his usual way," I said. "By ensuring that your ambition and his own coincided. By gaining something which serves his own mysterious ends and which in turn serves ours. All our actions are linked, all our destinies have something in common. An action taken in one plane of the multiverse can achieve a result in quite a different plane, perhaps millennia (and who knows what kind of distance?) apart. Sepiriz plays the Game of the Balance. A series of checks, adjustments, fresh moves, all designed to maintain ultimate equilibrium. He is only one such servant of the Balance. There are several, to my knowledge, moving here and there through all the myriad planes and cycles of the multiverse. Ultimately we cannot any of us know the full pattern or detect a true beginning or an end. There are cycles within cycles, patterns within patterns. Perhaps it is finite, but it seems infinite to us mortals. And I doubt if even Sepiriz sees the whole Game. He merely does what he can to ensure that neither Law nor Chaos can achieve a complete advantage."

"And what of the Lords of the Higher Worlds?" asked Alisaard, who already knew something of this. "Can they perceive the entire scheme?"

"I doubt it," I said. "Their vision is perhaps in some sense even more limited than our own. Frequently it is the pawn who perceives more than the king or queen, by virtue of having less at stake, perhaps."

Von Bek shook his head. Quietly he murmured: "And I wonder if there will ever be a time when all those gods and goddesses and demigods will cease their warring? Will cease to exist, perhaps?"

"There may be such periods in the cyclic histories of the myriad realms," I said. "There could be an end to all this, when the Lords of the Higher Worlds and all the machinery of cosmic mystery shall be no more. And perhaps that is why they fear mortals so much. The secret of their destruction, I suspect, lies in us, though we have yet to realise our own power."

"And do you have a hint of what that power may be, Eternal Champion?" said Alisaard.

I smiled. "I think it is simply the power to conceive of a multiverse which has no need of the supernatural, which, indeed, could abolish it if so desired!"

And at that point the jungle heaved once, turning itself into a flowing ocean of molten glass which somehow did not burn us.

Von Bek yelled and lost his footing, keeping hold of the chalice. Alisaard grabbed him and tried to help him up. A noisy wind was blowing. I made my way to my companions. Von Bek was up again. "Use the Actorios!" I cried to Alisaard, who still had the stone in her keeping. "Find the shadow path again!"

But even as she reached into her purse to find the stone the Grail had begun to sing. It was a different note to the one we had first heard. It was softer, calmer. Yet it held an astonishing authority. And the glassy undulations slowly subsided. The smooth hills of obsidian grew quite still. And we could see a path leading through them. Beyond the path was a sandy beach.

Holding the chalice before him, von Bek led us towards that shore. Here was a force, I realised, far stronger than the Actorios. A force for order and equilibrium able to exert enormous power upon its surroundings. It dawned on me that much of what had happened up until now had been engineered by Sepiriz and his kind. I had already seen that von Bek had an affinity with the Grail as I had with the Sword. Von Bek had been needed to find the Grail. And now he was bringing it into this realm, close to the place called The World's Beginning. Was there significance in this action?

We had reached the shore. Above us were grassy dunes and beyond that a horizon. We tramped up to the dunes and stood looking out over a plain which appeared to be without end. It stretched ahead of us, an infinity of waving grasses and wildflowers, without a tree or a hill to break the flatness. There was a subtle scent all around us and, when we turned, the ocean of glass had gone. Now the plain stretched away in that direction also!

I saw a man approaching us. He strode with a leisurely gait through the tall grass. The light wind tugged at his robes. He wore black and silver. I thought for one wild moment that Hitler or one of his henchmen had followed us into this realm. But then I recognised the grey hair, the patriarchal features. It

was the Archduke Balarizaaf. Almost as soon as I noticed him
he stopped, raising his hand in greeting.

"I will not advance much closer, if you'll forgive me, mortals. That object you carry is inimical to my particular consti-
tution!" He smiled, almost in self-mockery. "And I must admit
I do not welcome its presence in my realm. I have come to
strike a bargain with you, if you'll listen."

"I make no bargains with Chaos," I told him. "Surely you
understand that?"

He chuckled. "Oh, Champion, how poorly you understand
your own nature. There have been times and there will be
others when you know loyalty only to Chaos...."

I refused to be drawn. Obstinately I said: "Well, Archduke
Balarizaaf, I can assure you that I possess no such loyalty at
this moment. I am my own creature, as best I can be."

"You were always that, Champion, no matter what side you
seemed to serve. That is the secret of your survival, I suspect.
Believe me, I have nothing but admiration...." He coughed, as
if he had caught himself in a moment of discourtesy. "I respect
all you say, Sir Champion. But I am offering you the chance to
alter the destiny of at least a full cycle of the multiverse, to
change your own destiny, to save yourself, perhaps, from all the
agony you have already known. I assure you, if you pursue this
present course, it will bring you further pain, further remorse."

"I have been told it will bring me at least some peace and the
possibility of being with Ermizhad again." I spoke firmly. I
resisted his arguments, for all their apparent sense and certainty.

"A respite, nothing more. Serve me, and you will possess
almost everything you desire. Immediately."

"Ermizhad?"

"One so like her you would come to forget any difference.
One even more beautiful. Adoring you, as no man has been
adored before."

I laughed at him then, to his evident surprise.

"You are truly a Lord of Chaos, Archduke Balarizaaf. You
have real imagination. You believe that all a mortal seeks is
the same power as you possess. I loved an individual in her
complexity. I have come to understand that even more since I
have suffered the delusions this place imposes upon the human
brain. If I cannot know again the woman I loved, I want no
substitute. What do I care if I am adored by her or not! I love
her for herself. My imagination delights not in control of her,
but in the fact that she exists. I had no part in her existence. I

merely celebrate it. And I would celebrate it for eternity, though I be parted from her for eternity. And if I am reunited, even for a brief while, that is more than justification for the agony I suffer. You have stated, more concisely than I, what Chaos stands for, Lord Archduke, and why I resist you!"

Balarizaaf shrugged and seemed to accept my statement in good humour. "Then perhaps there is something else you would want from me? All I ask of you is that you take up the Dragon Sword in my name. The Eldren women are virtually finished. Sharadim and Flamadin rule the Six Realms of the Wheel. If you serve me in this one small thing, so that I may consolidate this little fragment of the multiverse under my control, then I will do everything I can to return you to your Ermizhad. The game is over here, Sir Champion. We have won. What more can you do? Now you have the opportunity to serve yourself. Surely you cannot wish to be Fate's fool forever?"

The temptation was great and yet I had little difficulty resisting him the moment I looked at Alisaard's desperate face. It was from loyalty to the Eldren that I fought, that I played this turn of the game. If I denied that loyalty, then I denied all right to being united again with the woman I loved. So I shook my head, saying instead to Count Ulrich von Bek: "My friend, would you be so good as to take the chalice a little nearer to the Archduke so that he may inspect it?"

And with a shriek, a ferocious, malevolent and terrific noise which denied all the sweet reason of his earlier tone, the Archduke Balarizaaf fell backwards, his very substance beginning to change as von Bek approached him. His flesh seemed to boil and transmogrify on his bones. In a matter of moments he revealed a thousand different faces, very few of them even remotely human.

And then he had gone.

I fell to my knees, shuddering and weeping. Only then did I realise what I had been resisting, how much I had been tempted by his invitation and his promises. My strength had gone out of me.

My friends helped me up.

The cool wind flowed through the grass and it seemed to me that this was not a production of Chaos at all. This was, temporarily at least, the result of the Grail's influence. Once more I was impressed by the cup's power to bring order even in the heart of Chaos!

Alisaard was speaking softly to me. "It is here," she said. "The horned horse is here."

Trotting towards us through the grass, its head lifted as it uttered a whinny of greeting, came a beast whose coat flashed sometimes silver, sometimes gold. From its forehead there grew a single horn. Like the Grail it bore a strong resemblance to something from my familiar Earthly mythology. Alisaard was smiling in delight as the beast came up to her and nuzzled her hand.

From behind us a voice came. It was a familiar voice, but it was not the voice of the Archduke Balarizaaf.

"I will take the cup now," it said.

Sepiriz stood there. There was something in his eyes which suggested pain. He reached out his great black hand to von Bek. "The cup, if you will."

Von Bek was reluctant. "It is mine," he said.

Sepiriz displayed a rare flash of anger. "That cup belongs to nobody," he murmured. "That cup is its own thing. It is a singular object of power. All who attempt to own it are corrupted by their folly and their greed. I had not expected you to say such a thing, Count von Bek!"

Chastened, von Bek bowed his head. "Forgive me. Herr Daker says that you made it possible for me to initiate the self-destruction of the Nazis."

"That is so. It is now woven into the pattern of their destiny, by your courageous actions here and by what occurred when you sought out the Grail. You have achieved much for your own people, von Bek, I can assure you."

And with a great sigh, von Bek handed Sepiriz the Grail. "I thank you, sir. Then what I meant to accomplish is done."

"Aye. If you wish, you can return to your own plane and your own time. You have no obligation to me."

But von Bek looked tenderly at Alisaard and he smiled at me. "I think I will stay to see this thing through, win or lose. I have a mind to see how this particular phase of your Game ends, Lord Sepiriz."

Sepiriz seemed pleased with this, though his eyes still spoke of some secret fear. "Then you must follow this horse," he said. "It will lead you to the Dragon Sword. The forces of evil are gathering even greater strength now. It will not be long before the Realms of the Wheel collapse completely, reduced to the stuff of Chaos. For this particular realm is stabilised, to the extent that it is stable at all, by those which surround it. If they are consumed, then pure Chaos will be the result. A mass of horrifying obscenity at which these Nightmare Marches merely hint. Nothing will survive in anything like its previous form. And you will be trapped within it forever. Forever prey to the whims of a Balarizaaf a thousand times more powerful than he is at present!" He paused, drawing in a great breath. "Do you still elect to remain here, Count von Bek?"

"Naturally," said my friend, with characteristic and almost comical aristocratic aplomb. "There are still a few Germans in the world who understand the nature of good and evil and where their duty lies!"

"So be it," said Sepiriz. He folded the chalice into his robe and was gone.

Not knowing what we must face when we got there, we followed the unicorn. Already the influence of the Grail was fading. The grass first turned a peculiar shade of yellow, then of orange, then of red.

The unicorn now waded across a shallow lake of blood.

Waist-deep in this, and shivering with horror, we pressed on.

It was as if we walked through the blood of all those who had died thus far in service of Sharadim's lust for a perverse and immortal power.

3.

THAT horrible lake stretched in all directions, filling all our horizons. Save for the unicorn leading the way and the three of us, there were no other occupants, it seemed, in the entire Realm of Chaos.

For some reason I could not rid my mind of the idea that we were, indeed, wading through the blood of countless murdered souls. It seemed to me, as time went on, that perhaps this was not blood shed by Sharadim or the Lords of Chaos. It could as easily be blood which I had spilled as the Eternal Champion. I had slaughtered humanity. I had been responsible for the deaths of so many others, in all my myriad guises. I felt that even this vast plain of blood was only a fraction of it.

Again my two friends had linked arms, like lovers. I was slightly ahead of them, still following the unicorn. I began to see reflections in the red liquid. I saw my face as John Daker, as Erekosë, as Urlik Skarsol, as Clen of Clen Gar. And the action of that cool wind seemed to bring words with it.

"You are Elric, whom they shall call Womanslayer. Elric, who betrayed his race, just as Erekosë betrayed his race. You are Corum, killed by a Mabden woman, whom you loved. Remember Zarozinia? Remember Medhbh? Remember all those you betrayed and who betrayed you. Remember all the battles you fought. Remember Count Brass and Yiselda. You are the Eternal Champion, eternally doomed to fight in all mankind's wars and in all the Eldren's wars, just and unjust. What meaningless actions are yours . . ."

"No," I told myself, *"there is a point to it. I must do positive penance in my remorse. I must redeem myself. And in that redemption I shall discover peace. I shall know some small freedom. . . ."*

"You are Ghardas Valabasian, Conqueror of the Distant Suns, and you have no need of anyone. . . ."

"I am the Eternal Champion, bound by cosmic chains to a duty still undone!"

"You are M'v Okom Sebpt O'Riley, Gunholder of the Qui Lors Venturers, you are Alivale and you are Artos. You are Dorian, Jeremiah, Asquiol, Goldberg, Franik. . . ." And the list of names went on and on and on. They rang in my ears like bells. They beat in my head like drums. They clashed like weapons of war, filling my eyes with blood. A million faces assailed me. A million murdered creatures.

"You are the Eternal Champion, doomed always to fight, never to rest. There is no end to the battle. Law and Chaos are relentless enemies. There can never be reconciliation. The Balance demands too much of you, Champion. You grow weak in its service. . . ."

"I have no choice. It is what I am destined to do. And all of us must fulfil their destinies. There can be no choice. No choice . . ."

"You can choose whom you fight for. You can rebel against that destiny. You can alter it."

"But I cannot abolish it. I am the Eternal Champion, and I have no doom save this doom, no life save this life, no pain save this pain . . ."

I felt a hand on my shoulder. I shook it off. "I am the Eternal Champion. I have no life, save that. I have no means to alter what I am. I am the Champion. I am the hero of a thousand worlds and yet I have no true name of my own. . . ."

"Daker! Daker, man! What is happening to you? Why are you mumbling so?" It was von Bek's voice, distant and agitated.

"I am pursued by destiny. I am the toy of Fate. The Chaos Lord spoke truth in that. Yet I shall not weaken. I shall not serve his cause. I am the Eternal Champion. My remorse is complete, my guilt is so great, my doom is already set. . . ."

"Daker! Take hold of yourself!"

But I was lost in my monomaniacal self-absorption. I could think of nothing but the dreadful irony of my predicament. I was a demigod in the Six Realms, a legendary hero throughout the multiverse, a noble myth to millions. Yet all I knew was sadness and terror.

"My God, man, you are going thoroughly mad! Listen to me! Without you Alisaard and I are completely lost. We have

no means of knowing where we are or what we are supposed
to do. The unicorn leads us to the Sword. Remember that?
Herr Daker, do you remember? The Dragon Sword. Which
only you among us can bear, just as only I could take hold of
the Grail?"

But the war drums continued to sound in my ears. My
mind was filled with the clash of metal. My heart was consumed by melancholy at my own dreadful fate.

Von Bek's voice broke in again. "Remember who you are,
man! Remember what you are doing! Herr Daker!"

I saw only blood ahead of me, blood behind me, blood on
every side.

"Herr Daker! John!"

"I am Erekosë, who slew the human race. I am Urlik Skarsol who fought against Belphig. I am Elric of Melniboné and I
shall be so many others. . . ."

"No, man! Remember who you really are. There was a
time you told me about. A time when you had no memories of
being the Champion. Was that some kind of beginning for
you? Why are you still called John Daker? That is your first
identity. Before you were summoned. Before they named you
Champion?"

"Ah, how many long cycles of the multiverse have passed
since then."

"John Daker, pull yourself together. For all our sakes!"
Von Bek was yelling, but his voice sounded still very far
away.

*"You are the Champion, who bears the Black Blade. You
are the Champion, Hero of the Thousand Mile Line. . . ."*

The blood was lapping about my chest. Somehow I was
sinking deeper and deeper into it. I was about to drown in all
that blood I had spilled.

"Herr Daker! Come back to us. Come back to yourself!"

The blood was at my chin. I grinned. Why should I care? It
was only fitting.

A cold, small voice spoke to me. "John Daker, this will be
your only real betrayal, if you betray that identity. That which
is truly yourself." It was von Bek speaking again. I shrugged
him off.

"You will die," I heard him say, "not because of your
human weakness but because of your inhuman strength. Forget that you were the Eternal Champion. Remember your ordinary mortality!"

The blood lapped against my lips. I began to laugh. "See! I drown in this concrete reminder of my own guilt!"

"Then you are a fool, Herr Daker. We were wrong to trust you as a friend. And so were the Eldren women. And so were the Ursine Princes. And so was Ermizhad foolish to trust you as a lover. It was John Daker she loved, not Erekosë, the monstrous tool of Fortune. . . . "

The blood was in my mouth. I began to spit it out. I rose gasping. I had been on my knees. The level of the lake had not risen. It was I who had fallen. I stood up, staring blankly for a moment at Count von Bek and Alisaard. They were holding me, shaking me.

"You are John Daker," I heard him say again. "It was John Daker whom she loved. Not that relentless sword-swinger!"

I coughed. I could still hardly understand him. But then gradually it dawned on me that what he said had meaning. And as the meaning grew clearer, I thought that perhaps he spoke the truth.

"Ermizhad loved Erekosë," I said.

"She might have called you that, for that was the name King Rigenos gave you. But whom she really loved was John Daker, the ordinary, decent mortal who was caught up in a web of hatred and appalling destiny. You cannot change what happened to you, but you can change what you have become, John Daker! Don't you see that? *You can change what you have become!*"

It seemed to me at that moment these were the wisest words I had heard for many a year. I wiped the liquid from my face. It was not blood at all. I shook the drops from my eyes, from my hands.

Ahead of us, the unicorn waited patiently. I realised that once again I had lost my grip on reality. But now it was clear I had somehow lost a little of my real identity in all my cosmic adventurings. I had been discontented as John Daker. My world had seemed grey to me. But in some ways it had been richer than all the wild, fantastical spheres I had visited. . . .

I reached out and shook von Bek by the hand. I was smiling at him. "Thank you, my friend. You are the best comrade, I think, that I have ever had."

He, too, was smiling. The three of us stood there in that crimson lake and we hugged each other, while overhead the sky began to boil and smoulder and turn as angry a red as the waters below.

Then it seemed to us that the ocean of blood rose up to meet the falling sky, forming a single vast wall of glittering crimson crystal.

We looked around us for the unicorn, but it had vanished. Now ahead was nothing but that vast crimson cliff. And then I remembered the vision we had been shown at Morandi Pag's. And staring into that wall I saw it, imbedded there, like an insect in amber, a green and black blade in which a tiny fragment of yellow flickered.

"There it is," I said. "There is the Dragon Sword!"

My friends were silent.

It was only then that I realised the liquid had solidified completely. Our legs were as perfectly set in crystalline rock as was the sword. We were trapped.

I heard the sound of hoofbeats. The rock in which my legs were encased trembled as the horses grew closer. Twisting my body round I looked over my shoulder.

Two figures rode towards us on identical horses. On bright, black horses. They were dressed in gaudy finery, matching surcoats and cloaks, matching swords and banners. And one was Sharadim, Empress of the Six Realms. And the other was her dead brother, Flamadin, who sought to drink my soul and make it his own.

Now, standing at the base of the great red cliff, the Archduke Balarizaaf, again in the guise of a sober patrician, folded his arms and waited. He was smiling. He disdained to look at me. He called instead to Sharadim and Flamadin. "Greetings, sweet servants. I have kept my promise to you. Here are three little morsels, stuck like flies on a paper, for you to do with as you will!"

Flamadin threw back his gaunt, grey head and a hollow laugh escaped it. His voice was, if anything, more lifeless than when I had last heard it, on the edge of the volcano at Rootsenheem. "At last! I shall be complete again. And I have learned to be wise. I have learned that it is folly to serve any master save Chaos!"

I looked for a sign of real intelligence in that poor, dead face. I saw nothing.

Yet I still felt that I looked into my own features. It was almost as if Flamadin were a parody reminding me what I as the Eternal Champion was in danger of becoming.

I felt sorry for the creature. But at the same time I was deeply afraid.

The two slowed their horses and advanced towards us at a walk. Sharadim looked at Alisaard and smirked. "Have you heard, my dear? The Eldren women are driven from their own realm. They hide like rats in the warrens of the old bear-folk."

Alisaard looked back at her with a firm eye. "That news was offered by your lackey Armiad. When I last saw him he had grown to resemble the pig he always was. Do I detect a similar coarsening in your own features, my lady? How long can it be before your affinities with Chaos begin to show?"

Sharadim glared and urged her horse on. Von Bek smiled at Alisaard. Plainly she had struck a good blow. He said nothing, merely ignoring the two riders as best he could. Sharadim snorted and rode towards me.

"Greetings, Sir Champion," she said. "What a world of deception it is! But then you would know that best of all, since you posed as my brother Flamadin. Do you know they already have a legend in the Six Realms, amongst those few who remain unkilled or uncaptured. They think Flamadin, the old Flamadin of the stories, will return to help them against me. But Flamadin is now at last at one with his sister. We are married. Had you heard? And we rule as equals." She smiled. It was a dreadful, evil smile.

Like von Bek I chose to ignore her.

She rode up to the crystal wall and peered into the rock. She licked her lips. "That sword shall soon be ours," she said. "Are you looking forward to holding it in your two hands, brother?"

"My two hands," said Flamadin. His eyes were empty. He was staring upwards at nothing. "My two hands."

"He is hungry," Sharadim said in pseudo-apology. "He is deeply hungry, you see. He lacks his soul." And she looked with vicious, smiling cruelty directly into my eyes. I felt as if knives had been driven into my sockets. Yet I forced myself to stare back at her. I thought: *"I am John Daker. I was born in London in 1941 during an air raid. My mother's name was Helen. My father's name was Paul. I had no brothers. No sisters. I went to school...."* But I could not remember where I went to school first. I tried to think. I had an image of a white, suburban road. We had moved after the Blitz, to South London, as I recalled. To Norwood, was it? But the school? What was the school's name?

Sharadim was puzzled. Perhaps she could tell that my mind

was elsewhere. Perhaps she was afraid I had some hidden power, some means of escape.

She said: "I suppose we need waste no more time, Lord Balarizaaf."

"Your creature," he said, "it must contain the Champion's essence, if only for a short time. Failing that, Sharadim, you must keep your word to me, and take the sword yourself. That was your bargain."

"And your bargain, my lord, should I be successful?" For a little while, at least, she had some kind of power over this god.

"Why, that you should be elevated into the pantheon of Chaos. To become one of the great Sword Rulers, replacing one who has been banished."

Balarizaaf looked at me, as if he regretted my failure to accept his offer. It was obvious he would prefer me to do what was needed. "You are a powerful enemy," he said reminiscently, "in any guise. Do you remember, Lord Corum, how you fought my brothers and my sisters? Do you remember your great War Against the Gods?"

I was not Corum. I was John Daker. I refused all other identities.

"You have forgotten my name, I believe, my lord," I said. "I am John Daker."

He shrugged. "Does it matter what name you choose, Sir Champion? You could have ruled a universe by any of your many, many names."

"I have only one," I said.

This forced him to hesitate. Sharadim, too, had become curious as to my meaning. Thanks to my recent experiences and the help of my friends I was able to speak with authority. I was determined to consider myself a single individual and an ordinary mortal. I felt it was the key to my own salvation and that of those I loved. I looked into Balarizaaf's eyes and I peered into the abyss. I turned my gaze from him to Sharadim and saw in her face the same emptiness which possessed the Lord of Chaos. Flamadin's poor, blank stare was as nothing compared to what I beheld in their faces.

"You will not deny, I hope, that you are the Eternal Champion," said Sharadim sardonically, "for we know that you are."

"I am only John Daker," I said.

"He is John Daker," said von Bek. "From London. That is

a city in England. I do not know what part of the multiverse, I fear. Perhaps you would be able to discover that, Lady Shara-dim?" He was reinforcing me and I was grateful to him.

"This is a nonsensical pastime," Sharadim said, dismounting from her horse. "Flamadin must feed. Then he must take the sword. Then he can strike the blow which will set Chaos free upon the Six Realms!"

"Should you not wait, my lady," said von Bek coolly, "so that your retainers should witness this? You promised them a spectacle as I recall. . . ."

"Those cattle!" she was dismissive. She grinned as she directed her remarks at Alisaard. "They proved themselves useless here. I have thrown them against Adelstane. There they are happy, running at the walls. Soon those who survive will be having their way with your kinswomen! Now, Flama-din, dear, dead brother. You will dismount. You remember what you must do?"

"I remember."

I kept my eyes upon him as he got off his horse and began to shamble towards me. I saw Alisaard hand something to von Bek, who was closest to me. Sharadim had not noticed. Her whole attention was on the resurrected corpse of the brother she had murdered. As he drew closer I detected the stink of corruption about him. Was this the body my soul was expected to inhabit?

Von Bek's hand touched mine. I opened my palm and accepted what he gave me. It was the pulsing warmth of the Actorios stone. It was the only shield we had against sorcery in this realm.

Flamadin's dead fingers reached my face. I threw up my arms to defend myself, still unable to pull free of the solid rock encasing my lower legs. There was a peculiar, meaningless grin on Flamadin's lips, more like a rictus of death than an expression of humour. The breath from his mouth was foul.

"Give me your soul, Champion. I must eat it and then I shall be whole again. . . ."

Unthinkingly I brought up the Actorios and smashed it against that half-rotten forehead. It seemed to sear into the flesh. There was a stink of burning. Flamadin merely stood where he was, making a kind of gulping noise. There was a blazing mark in his head where the stone had struck him.

"What's this? What's this?" shrieked Balarizaaf in a voice

of frustrated malevolence. "There is no time for delays. Not now! Hurry. Do what you must do!"

Again Flamadin reached out for me. I prepared myself to strike a second blow, but then it occurred to me to try something else. With the writhing Actorios I drew a circle around myself in the red crystal.

"No!" cried Sharadim. "Ah, the Actorios. He has an Actorios! I did not know!"

The rock around me began to bubble and heave, giving off a pinkish vapour. I pulled myself free and stood upon the solid crystal. I threw the Actorios to von Bek, telling him to imitate what I had done, and I began to run towards the crimson wall. Behind me lumbered Flamadin while Sharadim screamed: "Lord Balarizaaf! Stop him! He will reach the sword!"

Balarizaaf said reasonably: "It matters not to me which one of you reaches it, so long as it is used for my purposes."

This gave me pause. Was I inadvertently falling into a trap set by the Lord of Chaos? I turned. My friends were running towards me, but Flamadin was ahead of them. His fingers again reached for my face. "I must feed," he told me. "I must have your soul. No other will do."

This time I did not have the Actorios. I pushed at his cold body, trying to keep him away. But with every touch I felt something of myself ebbing out, being drained by him. I tried to move back, but I had reached the crystal wall.

"Champion," said Flamadin greedily. His eyes had begun to take on a semblance of life. "Champion. Hero. I shall be a hero again. . . . I shall have what is my right. . . ."

Even as I fought with him my energy was being sucked from me. My friends reached us. They tried to pull him back, but he was stuck to me like a leech. I heard Sharadim laughing. Then Alisaard pressed the Actorios against Flamadin's throat. He gave a great choking roar and tried to throw her off him. Fire seemed to burn my own neck. I was horrified by the degree of symbiosis I now experienced. I was sobbing as I still struggled to free myself from him.

Flamadin's ruined flesh was glowing with my life. I felt my vision dimming. There was a flickering sight of myself from Flamadin's viewpoint.

"I am John Daker!" I cried. "I am John Daker!"

I managed to restore something of myself by this reminder. But wherever, in her panic, Alisaard applied the Actorios, I still burned.

At last I fell to the ground, completely weakened. My friends tried to drag me farther away from the Chaos creatures, but I begged them to stop Flamadin. Even now he was flattening himself against the crystal near where the sword was imbedded. I could see that inch by inch he was himself being absorbed by the rock. Then he had gone completely into it. I felt that I, too, was wading through the crimson crystal. I saw my own hand reaching out for the hilt of that great black and green sword with its runecarved blade, its flickering yellow flame.

Meanwhile, through John Daker's eyes, I saw Balarizaaf smiling. He was content with what was happening and made no move to interfere.

Only Sharadim was uncertain. She could not tell how much of my substance had been sucked into the Doppelgänger. My own point of view shifted back and forth. Part of the time I was Flamadin, reaching still for the great blade. Part of the time I was John Daker being helped up by my friends who looked wildly about them for some means of escape, or at least a weapon of defense. We had the Actorios. It occurred to me that neither Balarizaaf nor Sharadim were overeager to move against us while we had that stone.

Inch by inch Flamadin waded through the crystal. I was in intense pain. I murmured over and over again that I was John Daker and only John Daker. Yet my decrepit fingers reached for a sword and proved that I was also Flamadin. I groaned. I wanted to vomit. There was a kind of whispering echo in my head which I came to believe was Flamadin's mind struggling for life, recalling some argument which perhaps his sister had tried to instil in him before she resorted to murder.

The Sword can cure the evil at source. . . . The Sword can bring harmony. . . . The Sword is an honourable weapon. . . . But not in the wrong hands . . . The Sword used in defence is actively good. . . .

"No!" I cried, addressing whatever vestiges of the original Flamadin remained. "It is a deception. The sword is still a sword. The sword, Flamadin, is still a sword! Touch that blade, Prince Flamadin of the Valadek, and you are condemned forever to Limbo. . . ."

I heard Sharadim urging him on. I saw her, with John Daker's eyes, take a step farther towards the crystal cliff. Flamadin's hands were almost upon the sword's hilt now.

Within that ghastly body I struggled to hold back the hand.

But there was a desperate will at work. What had been Flamadin was greedy for life, greedy for the rewards it had been promised.

All around me the red light glowed. All around me were shards, fragments, reflections. I thought I could see a thousand versions of myself.

I was weakening.

"I am John Daker," I moaned. "I am only John Daker. . . ."

Flamadin touched the sword. The blade moaned a little, as if in recognition. He clasped the hilt. It did not resist him. It did not give him pain to touch it. Now I was almost entirely Flamadin, exulting in this power, this strange version of life I had achieved.

I drew the sword up. I displayed it to those who peered through the crystal, watching me.

As John Daker I was slowly dying as the last of my soul began to merge with Flamadin's.

I wrenched myself from that mind. I was whimpering and crying as I reached out for the Actorios which Alisaard still held. "I am John Daker. This is my reality." The same hand which enfolded the Dragon Sword now also enfolded the Actorios. I heard screaming. It was myself. It was Flamadin. It was John Daker. I was both of them. I was being torn into two.

Now John Daker made one huge effort to pull his soul free from the body of Flamadin. I recalled my childhood, my first job, my holidays. We had rented a thatched cottage in Somerset, not far from the sea. Which year had that been?

Flamadin was weakening a little. His viewpoint became hazy while John Daker's grew stronger. In recalling my common humanity, by rejecting the role of hero, I had the chance to free myself from the burden which had fallen upon me. And in freeing myself, I might possibly help others.

I was sure that John Daker was winning the struggle, but now Sharadim was joining in the fight, and Balarizaaf, too. I heard them urging Flamadin to use the sword, to do what he had sworn to do.

I fought against him. But his arm swung back. I tried to stop him, even then. His arm came forward, the Dragon Sword slicing into the stuff of the crystal wall. He was carving a gateway for Chaos!

I moaned in my weakness as John Daker. Having dragged

my soul back from Flamadin, now I sought to return, so that I could put a halt to what he did.

The Dragon Sword rose again. It struck the crystal wall again. Rosy light flared. Rays burst in all directions. And through the rent made by the sword I saw darkness. And in the darkness was another world. A world in which I glimpsed white towers gleaming. A familiar world.

They had planned this exactly! The gateway into Chaos would be the gateway into the vast Adelstane cave, where Sharadim's army laid siege to the last defenders of the Six Realms!

I shouted out my horror. I heard Sharadim's laughter. I turned, as John Daker, and saw Balarizaaf seem to swell to twice his height, an expression of sublime satisfaction on his features.

"He is cutting an entrance into Adelstane!" I told my friends. "We must stop him."

Whatever now animated Flamadin was not my soul. I had reclaimed it all. But even as my strength returned I saw the red crystal flow and dissipate, filling the sky again, turning to liquid again. And that unholy radiance was pouring through into the gigantic cavern.

Without thinking, I ran after Flamadin, still seeking to stop him. But he had passed through the narrow gateway he had carved. I saw him striding to where, on the floor of the cave, Sharadim's armies were camped. There were stone huts now and tents, and here and there were the massive Maaschanheemer hulls, pressed into service against Adelstane.

Alisaard and von Bek were with me as we clambered down rocks to the cave. Flamadin was shouting something to the warriors, many of whom had plainly been touched by Chaos already. They had the warped, bestial features I had seen on Armiad and the others.

"For Chaos! For Chaos!" cried Flamadin. "I have returned. Now I shall lead you against our enemies. Now we shall know true victory!"

I half believed that Flamadin was animated by the sword itself!

The armies were both dazzled and baffled by the crimson light suddenly flooding into the cavern. Sharadim and Balarizaaf were not yet through. I knew that soon the gap must widen farther and allow the whole of Chaos to come through, to infect, mile by mile, gentle Barganheem and, eventually,

the whole of the Six Realms. And I could see no way now of
stopping this encroachment.

"WE ARE THROUGH! OH, WE ARE THROUGH!"

This was Sharadim's voice behind me. She had remounted
her black charger. She had drawn her own sword. She was
riding after us.

Flamadin, flailing and stumbling like a scarecrow, was
making for the nearest hull. A terrible stink came off the vessel. The smoke which curled from its chimneys was if anything even more foul than before.

Flamadin clambered up the side, waving the sword and
mouthing some sort of victorious battle cry. I saw men come
to help him over the rail.

My only thought was to reach him before Sharadim caught
up with him, to wrest the Dragon Sword from him and try to
do what I could to save those who survived in Adelstane. I
knew my friends shared my ambition. Together we began to
climb up the hull, choking back our nausea at the stench. All
around us now the hosts of Chaos were beginning to stir,
grunting, yelling, pointing. Then, as Sharadim rode out of the
crimson glare, a great cheer went up.

I looked towards Adelstane and her fiery ring, which still
held, her delicate lacey white towers, her superb beauty. I
could not let this be destroyed, not while I still had life. As the
three of us reached the rails we saw on the main deck the
Baron Captain Armiad himself, lifting his own sword in salute
of Flamadin. Whether by chance or by destiny, we had arrived
back on *The Frowning Shield!*

So engrossed in their triumph were they that they did not
see us come aboard. We were horrified at the condition of the
vessel. The few inhabitants who remained were in a wretched
state, evidently enslaved to do the work of war. Men, women
and children were in rags. They looked starved. They looked
beaten. Yet I saw more than one face which held hope when
they saw us.

We were able to run for the cover of one of the houses.
Almost immediately we were joined by a bony wretch whose
dirty features still bore the traces of youth and beauty. "Champion," she said, "is it you? Then who is that other?"

It was Bellanda, the enthusiastic young student we had first
met aboard this vessel. Her voice was cracked. She looked
close to death.

"What is wrong with you, Bellanda?" whispered Alisaard.

The young woman shook her head. "Nothing specific. But since Armiad declared war upon those who opposed him we have been made to toil almost without rest. Many have died. And we of *The Frowning Shield* are considered fortunate. I still cannot believe how swiftly our world changed from one ruled by justice to one dominated by tyranny. . . ."

"Once the disease takes hold," said von Bek gravely, "it spreads so rapidly that it can rarely be checked in time. I saw this happen to my own world. One must be forever vigilant, it seems!"

I watched Armiad lead Flamadin to the stairway of the central deck. Flamadin continued to hold the Dragon Sword above his head, displaying it to all. I looked across the floor of the cavern and saw Sharadim riding towards the hull, calling out to Flamadin, who ignored her. He was enjoying his own strange triumph. The corpse's features were twisted in a hideous parody of mirth. He swung up from the central deck into the rigging of the main mast, so that he could be seen by all those gathered below.

I knew that I had a few minutes to get to Flamadin before his sister. Without further consideration, I began to climb, planning to use the network of spars and ropes to reach him, just as I had once used them as a short cut when moving about the ship.

Hand over hand I went up the spiderweb of greasy ropes, then swung myself closer to the central deck.

Flamadin stood upon a platform now so that he could again display the Dragon Sword. His poor, ruined flesh seemed about to fall from his bones. The gesture, as he raised the blade, was almost pathetic.

"Your hero," he cried in that bleak, dead voice of his, "has returned."

Even as I worked my way towards him I could not help but see him as a telling parody of what I myself had become. I did not like the picture. I continued, while I crawled along a spar over the heads of the gathered warriors, to remind myself that I was John Daker. I had been a painter of some description, I seemed to recall, and had had a studio overlooking the Thames.

Flamadin sensed me even as I made to drop down on him. His corpse's eyes looked up. He had the appearance of a startled child whose new toy was about to be taken from him.

"Please," he said softly. "Let me keep it a little while. Sharadim wants it, too."

"There's no time," I said.

I let myself go. I dropped beside him. Holding the Actorios before me I reached for the Dragon Sword. I could see the yellow flame flickering at its heart, behind the runes.

"Please," begged Flamadin.

"In the name of what you once were, Prince Flamadin, give me that blade," I said.

He winced away from the Actorios.

I heard a commotion below. It was Armiad. "There are two of them. Two the same! Which is ours?"

My hand closed on his wrist. He was far weaker now than he had been. The sword's strength no longer filled him. Indeed, it was as if the blade called back its energy and took what was left of Flamadin's also.

"This sword is not evil," he said. "Sharadim told me it is not evil. It can be used for good. . . ."

"It is a sword," I told him. "It is a weapon. It was made to kill."

A crooked, miserable smile came on his corrupted features. "Then how can it ever do good. . . ."

"When it is broken," I said. And I turned his wrist.

And the Dragon Sword fell free.

Armiad and his men were climbing up the rigging. All were heavily armed. I think they understood at last what was happening. I looked back into the cavern. Sharadim was almost at the hull and there was an army following her.

A peculiar sobbing sound came from Flamadin as he watched me retrieve the Dragon Sword. "She promised me my soul back, if I bore the blade for Chaos. But it was not my soul, was it?"

"No," I said, "it was mine. That was why she kept you alive. In that manner you deceived the Dragon Sword."

"Can I die now?"

"Soon," I promised.

I swung around. Armiad's men had reached the platform. The Dragon Sword was shouting in my two hands. In spite of all I had gone through, all I had decided for myself, I found that I was joining in its song, that I was filled with a wonderful wild glee.

I lifted the blade. I sheared through the necks of the first two raiders. Their headless bodies fell onto others below them and all tumbled down to the distant deck in a tangle of gouting blood and jerking limbs.

With the sword in one hand I reached for a trailing rope and swung out over my antagonists, slashing at them as I went. I slid down to the deck, behind Armiad, who had been one of the last into the rigging.

"I believe you wished to settle an account with me," I told him, laughing.

He looked in horror at my sword, at my face. He mouthed something as he shrank back against the mast. I stepped forward, then placed the tip of the Dragon Sword into the wood of the deck. "I am here, Baron Captain. Settlement is due, I'm sure you'll agree."

Reluctantly, his pig snout twitching, he returned to the deck. All his men were watching now. Their bestial faces were intent on the scene.

Suddenly there was a monstrous roar from behind me. I glanced over my left shoulder. The crimson light was flaring still brighter. The gap was growing wider. I saw movement behind it: huge grotesque figures mounted on even stranger steeds. Then I had to return my gaze to Armiad.

Sword in hand, he reluctantly advanced. I thought I could hear a kind of whimpering coming from his fluttering snout.

"I'll kill you quickly," I promised him. "But kill you I must, my lord."

And then I felt a heavy weight land squarely on my back. I fell sprawling, the Dragon Sword flying from my grasp. I struggled to get up. I heard Armiad give a great snort of startled glee. I felt cold lips on my neck. I smelled fetid breath.

Looking up I saw Armiad and his men begin to close around me. I tried to reach the Dragon Sword but someone kicked it away.

And Flamadin, still straddling my back, said through rotting lips: "Now I shall feed again. And you, John Daker, will die. I shall be the only hero of the Six Realms."

4.

ON Flamadin's orders, Armiad and his men seized me. With his strange, awkward movements, my Doppelgänger walked towards the Dragon Sword and picked it up again.

"The sword will drink your soul," he said, "and then it will in turn invigorate me. I and the sword shall be one. Immortal and invincible. I shall know the admiration of the Six Realms once more!"

He seemed to wince as he grasped the blade, staring at me almost with regret. It was impossible for me to understand what terrible, cold fragments of a soul still moved him, how much of the original darling of the Worlds of the Wheel remained. His sister had been able to stay the progress of his body's corruption, but now he was disintegrating before my eyes. Yet he hoped for life. He hoped for my life.

Armiad grunted with pleasure. His clammy hands now held my arm. "Kill him, Prince Flamadin. I have so longed to be witness to his death, ever since he first impersonated you and brought upon me the mockery of my fellow captains. Kill him, my lord!"

On the other side of me was something I dimly recognised as Mopher Gorb, Armiad's Binkeeper. Now his nose had elongated and his eyes had grown closer together so that he resembled some kind of dog. His grip on my arm was tight. Saliva flecked his muzzle. He, too, was enjoying my anticipated death.

Flamadin drew back his arm until the point of the Dragon Sword was a few inches from my heart. Then, with a kind of sob, he made to thrust.

The entire cavern was a mass of noise and moving warriors, all bathed in that same crimson light. Yet I heard one sound above the others. A sharp, precise crack.

Flamadin grunted and paused. There was an inflamed hole in his forehead. From it oozed a substance which might once have been blood. He lowered the Dragon Sword. He turned to look behind him.

There stood Ulrich von Bek, Count of Saxony, with a smoking Walther PPK 38 in his hand.

Flamadin tried to stagger towards this new assailant, the Dragon Sword still half-raised. Then he had fallen to the deck and I knew the final vestiges of life had deserted him.

Yet Armiad and his men still held me. Mopher Gorb produced a long knife, plainly intending to slit my throat. He gave a strange little grunt and dropped the knife. Another wound blossomed, this time in the side of Mopher Gorb's head.

Armiad dropped his hold on my arm. The rest of the ghastly crew began to back away. But now Alisaard had leapt forward, snatching up Mopher Gorb's sword, and she was thrusting, thrusting at the Baron Captain, who defended himself both ferociously and well against the Ghost Woman, but was no match either for her grace or her skill with a sword. She had pierced his porcine heart in moments, then turned her attention on the others. I, too, fought with a borrowed sword. There were too many between me and Flamadin's corpse. I fought as best I could, trying to reach it. And von Bek, too, had a sword. The three of us were at last standing together.

"Bellanda kept your gun for you, I see!" I cried to von Bek.

He grinned. "I now don't regret asking her to look after it. I thought I'd never see it again! Unfortunately, there were only two shells left."

"Well used," I said gratefully.

Suddenly we realised that we were surrounded entirely by dead men. All Armiad's disgusting crew were defeated. A few wounded crawled here and there, attempting to escape. Von Bek uttered a cheerful yell of triumph, but this was swiftly cut short by a scream from Bellanda for, making an impossible leap on her great black stallion, came the figure of Sharadim, landing full on the central deck, the hooves pounding like battle drums above the corpse of her brother, the Dragon Sword still in his hand.

I began to run then, trying to reach the blade before she

could dismount. But with a great billowing of her cloak she was off the back of the snorting beast and had reached down to wrest the Dragon Sword from her brother's deathgrip.

As she took hold of the Dragon Sword, she gasped with pain. She was not meant to hold it. Only by an effort of will did she lift it. Yet lift it she did, and she maintained her hold upon it.

I continued to be struck by her extraordinary beauty. As she carried the Dragon Sword back towards her horse, apparently unconscious of any who observed her, I thought she resembled more than any woman I had ever seen the goddess it was her ambition to become.

I stepped forward. "Princess Sharadim! That sword is not yours to carry!"

She had reached her horse now. She looked round slowly, frowning in irritation. "What?"

"It is mine," I said.

She put her lovely head on one side and stared at me. "What?"

"You must not take the Dragon Sword. Only I have the right to bear it now."

She began to climb into her saddle.

I could think of no other action but to take out the Actorios and hold it up before me. Its pulsing, writhing light made my hand glow black, red and purple. "In the name of the Balance, I claim the Dragon Sword!" I told her.

Her face clouded. Her eyes blazed. "You are dead," she said slowly, through gritted teeth.

"I am not. Give me the Dragon Sword."

"I have earned this blade and all it stands for," she told me, pale with rage. "It is mine by right. I have served Chaos. I have given the Six Realms to Lord Balarizaaf to do with as he will. At any moment he and all his kind will come riding through the gateway I, by my actions, created. And I shall receive my reward. I shall be made a Sword Ruler with dominion over my own realms. I shall be immortal. And as an immortal I shall hold this sword as the sign of my power."

"You will die," I said simply. "Balarizaaf will kill you. The Lords of Chaos do not keep their promises. It is against their nature to do so."

"You are lying, Champion. Go away from me. I have no use for you as yet."

"You must give me that sword, Sharadim."

The Actorios pulsed with stronger light. It was almost wholly organic as it sat in the palm of my hand.

I stood beside her now. She clasped the blade to her. I could tell that everywhere it touched it gave her intense pain, but she ignored the pain, believing that soon she would never experience physical agony again.

I could see the little yellow flame flickering back behind the runes carved into the black metal.

The Actorios began to sing. It sang in a small, beautiful voice. It sang to the Dragon Sword.

And the Dragon Sword murmured a response. That murmur became a strong, powerful moan, almost a shout.

"No! No! No!" cried Sharadim. Her skin, too, reflected the peculiar, writhing light. "Look! Look, Champion! Chaos comes! Chaos comes!" And laughing she swept the blade round so that the Actorios was struck cleanly from my hand. I dived towards it, but she was swifter. She had raised the blade, yelling in her pain as it burned her hands.

She meant to destroy the Actorios.

My first instinct was to dash forward and save it at all costs, and then I remembered something Sepiriz had told me. I stepped back.

She grinned at me, the loveliest wolf in the world. "Now you realise there is no defeating me," she said.

She brought down the blade with incredible ferocity, striking accurately at the shining stone which lay there, pulsing like a living heart.

She screamed as the blade connected with the Actorios. It was a scream of complete triumph which turned, all in the space of a second, to bafflement and then to anger and then to nothing but agony.

The Actorios was shattered. It burst into fragments. It exploded in all directions.

And each fragment now contained an image of Sharadim!

Each fragment of the Actorios was bearing part of Sharadim away into Limbo. She had thought to make herself all things to all people. Now it was as if each persona had separated and was imprisoned in a splinter of that peculiar stone. Yet Sharadim herself still stood there, frozen in her final act of destruction. Gradually her expression of enraged pain changed to one of terror. She began to shiver. The Dragon Sword moaned and wailed in her hands. Her flesh seemed to boil on her bones. All that astonishing beauty was vanishing.

Von Bek, Bellanda and Alisaard made their way towards me but I gestured for them to go back. "There is great danger still to come," I shouted. "You must go to Adelstane. Tell the Eldren and the Ursine Princes what is happening here. Tell them they must wait and watch."

"But Chaos comes!" said Alisaard. "Look!"

The figures I had seen in the redness were larger than before. Grotesque riders led by Balarizaaf himself. The Lords of Hell were riding to claim their new kingdom.

"To Adelstane. Hurry!" I told them.

"But what will you do, Herr Daker?" asked von Bek. His face was full of concern for me.

"What I must. What has become my duty." I thought he would understand those words.

Von Bek inclined his head. "We shall await your presence in Adelstane." It was clear that all three of them thought themselves as good as dead.

The huge rent in the cosmic fabric was growing wider still. And the black riders waited patiently for it to become large enough to admit them.

I stopped and picked up the Dragon Sword. It made a small, sweet sound, as if recognising a kinsman.

All around the blade the fragments of the Actorios were whirling, like planets around a sun. In some of those fragments as they went by, I saw one of Sharadim's many faces staring out, with the same expression of horror she had worn just before her body collapsed.

I looked down at her shrivelled corpse. It lay across that of her brother. One had represented the evil of the world, the other the good. Yet both had been defeated by pride, by ambition, by a promise of immortality.

I watched as von Bek, Alisaard and Bellanda disappeared over the side of the hull. The camps of Sharadim's army were in confusion now. They seemed to be awaiting their leader's command. There was a fair chance that my friends could reach Adelstane unhindered. They had to go there. They could not, I knew, survive what was yet to come.

Now I lifted up the sword and I set my mind into a particular pattern. I remembered Sepiriz telling me what I must do when the Actorios was shattered, what power I could call upon. I could hear them chanting in the back of my brain. I could hear their despairing voices as I had heard them a thousand times in my dreams.

"We are the lost, we are the last, we are the unkind. We are the Warriors at the Edge of Time. And we're tired. We're tired. We're tired of making love. . . ."

"NOW I RELEASE YOU! WARRIORS, I RELEASE YOU! YOUR MOMENT HAS COME AGAIN. BY THE POWER OF THE SWORD, BY THE DESTRUCTION OF THE ACTOR-IOS, BY THE WILL OF THE BALANCE, BY THE NEED OF HUMANKIND, I SUMMON YOU. CHAOS THREATENS. CHAOS SHALL CONQUER. YOU ARE NEEDED!"

Now, on the far side of the cavern, above the wonderful white city of Adelstane, I saw a cliff. And on that cliff was lined rank upon rank of men. Some rode horses. Some were on foot. All were armed. All were armoured. All stared fixedly towards me as if in sleep.

"We are the shards of your illusions. The remains of your hopes. We are the Warriors at the Edge of Time. . . ."

"WARRIORS! YOUR TIME HAS COME. YOU MAY FIGHT AGAIN. ONE MORE BATTLE. ONE MORE CYCLE! COME! CHAOS RIDES AGAINST US!"

I ran to Sharadim's stallion, which panted and snorted near the corpse of its mistress. It did not resist when I climbed into the saddle. It seemed glad of a rider. I turned it towards the rail of the hull and I galloped forward, leapt clear over the side of the vessel and landed on the rocky floor of the cave where Sharadim's soldiers came forward in a flood of flesh and metal to cheer me. I had thought them my enemies. I was baffled for a moment until I realised with a kind of ironic delight that they knew only of Flamadin and Sharadim. They thought me their Empress's brother and consort! They were waiting for me to lead them against Adelstane in the name of Chaos.

I looked backwards. The huge crimson wound was swelling larger and larger. The grotesque black shapes were growing.

I looked towards Adelstane.

"Warriors!" I cried. "Warriors, to me!"

The Warriors on the Edge of Time had awakened. They were pouring down from the cliffs above Adelstane, running along invisible paths towards me.

"Warriors! Warriors! Chaos comes!"

There was a wind howling now. A crimson wind. It blew upon us all.

"Warriors! Warriors of the Edge! To me! To me!"

The stallion reared under me, hooves flailing. It uttered a

great snort of pleasure as if it awaited this moment, as if it lived only to gallop into battle. The Dragon Sword was alive in my right hand. It sang and it glowed with that dark radiance I had known so many times before, in so many different guises. And yet it still seemed to me that there was a quality in it which was not quite the same as any I had known before.

"Warriors! To me!"

They came in their thousands. In all manner of war-gear. With every strange weapon it was possible to conceive. They marched and they rode and their faces had come to life, as if they, too, like the stallion, understood only battle.

I felt that I, too, was never more truly alive than when I bore my blade in war. I was the Eternal Champion. I had led vast armies. I had slaughtered whole races. I was the very epitome of bloody conflict. I had brought it nobility, poetry, justification. I had brought it heroic dignity. . . .

Yet within me a voice insisted that this must be the last such fight. I was John Daker. I did not wish to kill in any cause. I wished merely to live, to love and to know peace.

The Warriors of the Edge were forming ranks around me. They had unsheathed their many weapons. They were yelling and animated. They knew joy. And I wondered if each of these had once been like me. Were they all aspects of heroic warriors? All aspects, even, of the Eternal Champion? Certainly many of their faces had a certain familiarity for me, so much so that I dared not look at them too closely.

The Princess Sharadim's soldiers were now in confusion. The Warriors of the Edge turned hard, killers' eyes upon them, yet they did nothing. They awaited my orders.

Now one of Sharadim's generals came riding through the ranks. He was very fine in his dark blue armour, his plumes, his spiked helm, his full, black beard.

"My lord Emperor! The allies you promised us. Are they all assembled?" His face was bathed in the crimson light. "Does Chaos come to aid us in our destruction? Is that our sign?"

I drew a breath and then I sighed, poising my sword. "Here is your sign," I said. I swung the blade in a single movement which sheared off his head so that it fell with a heavy clanking to the ground. Then I cried out to the assembled army which Sharadim had raised to conquer the Six Realms.

"There is your enemy! In fighting Chaos you stand some

small chance of salvation. If you stand against us, you will perish!"

I heard a babble of questions but I ignored them. I turned my black stallion towards the widening crimson wound. I lifted my sword in a sign to all who would follow me.

And then I was charging at full gallop towards the Lords of Chaos!

There was a sound behind me. A mighty yell which could have been a single voice. It was the battle shout of the Warriors at the Edge of Time. It was an exultation. They had come to life. They had come to the only life they knew.

Now through the crimson gateway the massive black figures rode in. I saw Balarizaaf, powerful in armour which flowed about his body like mercury. I saw a creature with the head of a stag, another which resembled a tiger, while many others bore no likeness at all to anything which had ever walked or crept upon any realm I had visited. And from them came a peculiar stink. It was both pleasant and horrible. It was both warm and cold. It had an animal quality about it, yet it could also have been the smell of vegetation. It was the pure stink of Chaos, the odour which legends said rose always out of Hell.

Balarizaaf reined in his scaly steed as he saw me. He was stern. His voice was kindly. He shook his huge head and when he spoke his voice was a booming reverberation. "Little mortal, the game is over. The game is over, and Chaos has won. Do you still not understand? Ride with us. Ride with us, and I will feed you. I will let you have creatures to play with. I will let you remain alive."

"You must go back to Chaos," I said. "It is where you and your kind belong. You have no business here, Archduke Balarizaaf. And she who made a bargain with you is dead."

"Dead?" Balarizaaf was disbelieving. "You killed her?"

"She killed herself. Now all the different women who were Sharadim, who deceived so many of her kind, are scattered through Limbo forever. It is a harsh fate. But it is deserved. There is no one left to welcome you, Archduke Balarizaaf. If you enter this realm now, you disobey the Law of the Balance."

"How do you see that?"

"You know it is true. You must be called, whether there be a gateway or no."

Archduke Balarizaaf made a noise in his huge chest. He

put a hand the size of a house to his face. He scratched his nose. "But if I enter, what can stop me? The invitation was there. A mortal prepared the gateway. Those realms are mine."

"I have an army," I said. "And I wield the Dragon Sword."

"You spoke of the Balance? It is a fine point, I think. I do not recognise your logic. And I believe that the Balance would not recognise it. What does it matter to me if you have raised an army. Look at what I bring against you." And he swept his monstrous arm to show not only his immediate liegemen, lesser nobles of Chaos, but a seething tide which could have been animals or humans or neither, for their form was hardly constant. "This is Chaos, little Champion. And there is more."

"You are forbidden to cross into our realm," I said firmly. "I have summoned the Warriors of the Edge. And I wield the Dragon Sword."

"So you persist in telling me. Am I to praise you? Or how must I be impressed? Little mortal, I am an Archduke of Chaos and I was summoned by mortals to rule their worlds. That is enough."

"Then it seems we must do battle," I said.

He smiled. "If that is what you wish to call it."

I pointed my Dragon Sword forward. Again came the great shout from my back.

I was riding resolutely into the teeth of Chaos. There was nothing else I could do.

The rest was battle.

It was like all the battles I had ever fought made into one. It seemed to last for eternity. Wave upon wave of belching, whining, barking, squealing, stinking things were thrown against me; some with weapons, some with teeth and claws, some with imploring eyes which begged a mercy they could never return. And yet, all about me, like an impervious wall of hardened flesh, of muscle and bone which seemed tireless, I saw my allies, the Warriors of the Edge. Each of these fought as skillfully as I. And some fell, engulfed by the creatures of Chaos. But there were more to replace them.

The tide of Chaos came, wave after wave, upon us. And wave after wave it was repulsed. Moreover, some of the humans fought with us. They fought with a will, glad no longer to be in Sharadim's service. They died, but they died knowing that they had, in the end, not betrayed their own kind.

The Lords of Chaos had kept back from all this. They disdained to fight more mortals. Yet it grew plain, as the hours wore on, that their creatures could not defeat us. It was as if we had been destined for this one great fight, trained in every arena of war the multiverse could provide. And I knew that in some sense this was my last fight, that if I succeeded in this, I might know peace, if only for a while.

Slowly the ranks of Chaos were growing thinner. My blade was encrusted with their life-stuff (it did not seem the same as blood) and my arm grew so tired I felt it would fall from its socket. My horse bled from a hundred different cuts and I, too, had received several wounds. But I hardly noticed them. We were the Warriors at the Edge of Time and we fought until we were killed. There was nothing else for us to do.

Now Archduke Balarizaaf came riding through his forces again and he was not disdainful. He did not laugh. He was grim and he was fierce. He was angry, but he no longer mocked me with his gaze.

"Champion! Why fight so hard? Call a truce and we'll discuss terms."

This time I turned my horse towards him. I summoned energy for myself and my sword. And I charged.

I charged into the face of the Archduke of Chaos. I flew, my horse's hooves galloping on air, straight towards that huge and supernatural bulk. I was weeping. I was shouting. I wanted only to destroy him.

Yet I knew I could not kill him. It was, indeed, likely that he would kill me. I did not care. In a fury at all the terror he had brought to the Six Realms, at all the misery he had sown and would always sow, at the wretchedness he had created wherever his ambitions took him, I hurled myself and my sword at his face, aiming at his treacherous mouth.

From behind me I heard again that great exultant battle shout of the Warriors. It was as if they recognised what I did and encouraged me, celebrating my action, honouring whatever it was which moved me to attack the Archduke.

The point of the Dragon Sword touched that suddenly opened maw. I felt for one moment that I must be swallowed by him, falling into his red throat.

The saddle of my horse was no longer under me. I sailed directly at Archduke Balarizaaf's head.

And then it had vanished and I felt earth beneath my feet. The crimson wound was closing before me. I looked and saw the piled corpses of our enemies and the corpses of our allies. I saw the bodies of ten thousand warriors who had died in that battle whose memory was even now fading from my mind, it had been so terrible.

I turned. The Warriors of the Edge were sheathing their weapons, wiping blood from their axes, inspecting their wounds. They had expressions of regret upon their faces, as if they had been disappointed, as if they wished to continue the fight. I counted them.

There were fourteen still alive. Fourteen together with myself.

The crimson wound in the cosmic fabric was healing rapidly. It was now hardly large enough to accept a man. And through it stepped a single figure.

The figure paused, looking back to watch the gap close and vanish.

It was suddenly cold in the cavern of Adelstane. The fourteen warriors saluted me, then marched into the shadows. They were gone.

"They rest until the next cycle," said the newcomer. "They are allowed battle only once. And those who die are the fortunate. The others must wait. That is the fate of the Warriors at the Edge of Time."

"But what is their crime?" I asked.

Sepiriz removed his black and yellow helm. He made a small gesture with his hand. "Not a crime exactly. Some would call it a sin, perhaps. They lived only to fight. They did not know when to stop."

"Are they all former incarnations of the Eternal Champion?" I asked him.

He looked thoughtfully at me, sucking his upper lip. Then he shrugged. "If you like."

"Surely you owe me some more substantial explanation, my lord," I said.

He took me by the shoulder. He turned me towards Adelstane and we began to walk over stone slippery with the blood of all those dead thousands. Here and there the wounded were tending to one another. The hulls and the tents and the stone shanties were full of the dying now.

"I owe you nothing, Champion. You are owed nothing. You owe nothing."

"I can speak for myself," I said. "I have a debt."

"Would you not say it is fully paid now?"

He stopped. He opened his mouth and he laughed at my confusion. "Paid now, Champion, eh?"

I bowed my head in acceptance. "I am weary," I said.

"Come." He walked on through all those corpses, all that ruin. "There is work still to do. But first we must take news of your victory into Adelstane. Are you aware of what you achieved?"

"We fought back the encroachment of Chaos. Have we saved the Six Realms?"

"Oh, yes. Of course. But you did more. Do you not know what it was?"

"Was it not enough?"

"Possibly. But you were also responsible for banishing an Archduke of Chaos to Limbo. Balarizaaf can never rule again. He challenged the Balance. Even then he might have won. But your act of courage was decisive. Such an action contains so much that is noble, so much that is powerful, so much that affects the very nature of the multiverse, that its effect was greater than any other. You are truly a hero now, Sir Champion."

"I have no wish to be a hero any longer, Lord Sepiriz."

"And that is doubtless why you are such a great one. You have earned respite."

"Respite? Is that all?"

"It is more than is allowed to most of us," he said in some astonishment. "I have never known it."

Chastened, I let him lead me through the fiery ring of Adelstane and into the arms of my dear friends.

"The fight is over," said Sepiriz. "On all of the planes, in all of the realms. It is over. Now the healing and the changing must begin."

5.

"WE shall know a better peace now," said Morandi Pag, "for those who remain in the Six Realms. There must be building, of course, and replanting. But rather than withholding our ancient knowledge and retreating into our caves, we, the Ursine Princes, will do our best to help. So, too, shall each of the races give their special skills to the common good."

The white city of Adelstane was tranquil once more. The remains of Sharadim's army, who had fought with us against Chaos, had returned to their different worlds, determined to ensure that their future would never again allow the rise of a tyrant. Never again would they be deceived by such as Sharadim into making war upon one another. New Councils were being formed, drawn from all the races, and the time of the Great Massing would not now be merely a time for trading.

Only the Lady Phalizaarn and her Eldren women had not returned to Gheestenheem which, we had heard, had been razed by Sharadim's warriors. They were making specific preparations for their own departure.

Bellanda of the Maaschanheem had gone back with her people, aboard *The Frowning Shield*, promising us that if we should ever return to the Maaschanheem we would experience better hospitality than any we had previously known. We bid her farewell with special affection. I knew that if she had not kept the gun in trust for von Bek all those months I for one would probably not be alive.

Alisaard, Phalizaarn, von Bek and myself were guests in the comfortable study which the Ursine Princes used for their own conferences and gatherings. Again the clouds of incense filled the fireplace and drifted throughout the room as, discretely, the bearlike people did their best to disguise their distaste for our smell. Morandi Pag had already declared his decision not to return to his sea-crag, but to work with his fellows towards the improvement of communication between the Six Realms.

"You have done much for us, you three," said Groaffer Rolm with a wave of his silken sleeve, "and you, Champion, will be remembered in legends, that is certain. Perhaps as Prince Flamadin. For legends have a habit of mingling, transforming and becoming something new."

I inclined my head, saying politely: "I am honoured, Prince Groaffer Rolm, though for my own part I would be glad to see a world free of heroes and legends. Especially heroes such as myself."

"I do not believe that is possible," said the Ursine Prince. "All one can hope for is that the legends celebrate what is noble in the spirit, what is honourable in deeds and ambitions. We have known ages when the legends have not celebrated what is noble, when the heroes were self-serving, clever creatures who improved their own situation against the interests of the rest. Those cultures are usually ones which are close to decay and death. Better to praise idealism than denigrate it, I think."

"Though idealism can lead to acts of unspeakable evil?" asked von Bek.

"That which is valuable is always in danger of being devalued," said Morandi Pag. "That which is pure can always be corrupted. It is our business to find the Balance...." He smiled. "For do we not echo, in our domestic actions, the war which rages between Chaos and Law? Moderation is, in the end, also survival. But this is what we learn in middle age, I suppose. Sometimes the proponents of excess must triumph, sometimes the proponents of restraint must win. That is the way of things. That is what maintains the Balance."

"I do not believe I have much of a care for the Cosmic Balance," I said, "nor for the machinations of Law and Chaos. Nor for gods and devils. I believe that we alone should control our own destinies."

"And so we shall," said Morandi Pag. "And so we shall, my friend. There are many cycles yet to come in the great history of the multiverse. In some of them the supernatural shall be banished, just as you banished Archduke Balarizaaf from this world. But our will and our nature is such that at other times those gods, in different guises, will return. The power is always ultimately within ourselves. It depends how much responsibility we are prepared to take. . . ."

"And that is what Sepiriz told me, when he said I should know respite?"

"It seems so." Morandi Pag scratched at his grizzled fur. "The Knight in Black and Yellow travels constantly between the planes. Some even think he has the power to travel through the megaflow, through Time, if you like, between one cycle and the next. Few have such great power or such terrible responsibility. Occasionally, it is said, he sleeps. He has brothers, according to what I have heard, all of whom share with him the duty of maintaining the Balance. But I understand little more of his activities, for all my own studies in the matter. Some say he even now sows the seeds for the salvation of the next cycle as well as for its destruction, but perhaps that is too fanciful a notion."

"I wonder if I shall see him again. He said his work was done here, and that mine was almost done. Why should there be such a peculiar affinity between certain people and certain objects. Why is it that von Bek can handle the Grail and I can handle the Sword and so on?"

Morandi Pag made a grunting noise at the back of his throat. He put his muzzle into the fireplace and took a deep breath of the fumes, then he sat back in his armchair. "If certain schemes are set at certain times, if certain functions are required to ensure the survival of the multiverse, so that neither Law nor Chaos shall ever gain full command of it, then perhaps certain creatures must be matched, as it were, to certain powerful artefacts. After all, every race has legends concerning such things. These affinities are part of the pattern. And the maintenance of the pattern, of Order, is of paramount importance." He cleared his great throat. "I must look into this further. It will be an interesting way of passing my final years."

The Lady Phalizaarn said gently: "The time for leaving has come, Prince Morandi Pag. There is one last great action to be taken, then this particular stage in the Eternal Game is completed. We must go to rejoin the rest of our people."

Morandi Pag inclined his head. "The ships we hid for you are ready. They await you in our harbour."

Von Bek, Alisaard and I were the last to go aboard the slender Eldren vessels. We remained, almost reluctantly, making our final farewells to the Ursine Princes. Not one of us said anything of meeting again. We knew it was never likely to be. And so it was with a special regret that we parted.

We three stood on the high aft deck of the final ship to sail out of the harbour, leaving the massive cliffs of Adelstane behind us, sailing beyond the whirlpool crags where Morandi Pag had lived for so long.

"Good-bye!" I cried as I waved to the last of that noble race. "Good-bye, dear friends!"

And I heard Morandi Pag call to me. "Good bye, John Daker. May your rest be all you desire."

We sailed for a day until we came at length to a place where great beams of light pierced the clouds and stroked the rolling sea: rainbow light forming a circle of great pillars, a kind of temple. We had come again to the Pillars of Paradise.

The triangular sails of the Eldren vessels filled with wind as, one by one, the clever sailors drove their ships between the columns. One by one they vanished until we were the last ship remaining.

Then Alisaard took the helm. She flung back her head and shouted her song. She was full of joy.

It seemed again to me that Ermizhad stood there, as she had stood beside me in all our adventurings so long ago. But the man whom this woman loved was not Erekosë, the Eternal Champion. It was Count Ulrich von Bek, nobleman of Saxony, exile from the Nazi obscenity, and that he returned her love was clear. I no longer knew jealousy. That had been an aberration brought about by Chaos. But I knew a deep loneliness, a sadness which could never, no matter what befell me, be dismissed. Oh, Ermizhad, I mourned for you then, as the Pillars of Paradise drew us inwards and upwards and out into the glorious, sun-filled seas of Gheestenheem.

We sailed now, our convoy of ships, towards Barobanay, the old capital of the Ghost Women.

The women who crowded the decks and worked the ships were still dressed in their delicate armour of engraved ivory, though they no longer wore the helmets which had once disguised and protected them by means of instilling fear in potential enemies. When we sailed at last into the burned and wasted harbour and looked upon the black ruins of that town which had once been so lovely, so secure and comfortable and civilised, many of those women wept.

Yet the Lady Phalizaarn stood upon the pitted stones of the

quay and she addressed the Eldren women. "This is a memory now. It is a memory we must always keep. But we should not grieve, for soon, if the promise of our legends is true, we shall at last be going to our true home, to the land of our menfolk. And the Eldren will become strong again, in a world which is theirs, in a world which cannot be threatened by savage barbarians of any ilk. We begin a new story for our race. A glorious story. Soon, just as we are united with our men, the she-dragon will be freed and come together with her male. Two strong limbs of the same body, equally powerful, equally tender, equally able to build a world even lovelier than the one we knew here. John Daker, show us the Dragon Sword. Show us our hope, our fulfillment, our resolution!"

At her orders I pushed back my cloak. There on my hip was the sheathed Dragon Sword, where it had been scabbarded since the fight outside Adelstane. I unhooked the scabbard from my belt and held the Dragon Sword up for all to see, but I would not draw it. In my debates with the Lady Phalizaarn we had agreed that I should draw the blade again only once. And then, I swore, I should never draw it again.

If I could, I would have handed it over to the Announcer Elect and let her do what was needed. But it was my fate to be the only one who could handle the poisonous metal of that strange sword.

The Eldren women were disembarking, streaming into the broken buildings, the ashes, the fire-darkened timbers, of Barobanay.

"Go!" cried Lady Phalizaarn. "Bring us that which we have kept throughout our long exile. Bring us the Iron Round."

Von Bek and Alisaard came to stand beside me on the quay. We had already discussed what had to be done. Morandi Pag had offered to try to help von Bek return to his own world, but he had elected to stay with Alisaard, just as I had once been the only human to remain with the Eldren, with my Ermizhad. They linked arms with me, offering me comfort, aiding me in my resolution, for I had made a pact with myself, with John Daker, and I was determined not to break it.

Soon the Ghost Women, their ivory smeared with black dust, came staggering from out of the ruins. They had with them a large oak chest, borne on poles slipped through brass loops set into the brass bands binding the wood. It was an ancient chest, plainly, and spoke of a different age altogether. It was like nothing else the Eldren owned.

To one side of me the sunshine continued to glint on the blue ocean; to the other the breeze stirred the smokey ashes of the razed town. On the quay itself, and on their slender ships, the Eldren women gave me their full attention as the oak chest was opened and out of it was taken the thing they called the Iron Round.

It was a kind of anvil. It was almost as if a section had been cut from a tree trunk and placed upon a pedestal, then the whole turned into heavy, pitted iron. It was like a small table, yet I could see from its surface that generations of smiths had worked their metal upon it.

Into the base of the Iron Round were carved runes and these runes resembled many of those I had seen upon the blade of the Dragon Sword.

They brought the anvil and they placed it at my feet.

Each of those faces held expectation and hope. This was what they had lived for all those generations, breeding as best they could from the poor stock provided them, resorting to an artificial way of life which they found distasteful, yet maintaining their dream that one day the cosmic mistake which had cost them their menfolk and their future would be corrected. It was for this day, too, that I had striven. All else had been secondary. Out of love for the race which had adopted me, the woman I had loved and who had loved me with such intensity and depth, I had sought out the Dragon Sword.

"Unsheath it, Champion," cried Lady Phalizaarn. "Unsheath your sword so that we may all look upon it for the last time. Unsheath that power which was created to be destroyed, which was forged for Chaos to serve Law, which was made to resist the Balance and to carry out its destiny. Let this be the last act of that hero called the Eternal Champion. In redeeming us, let him also be redeemed. Unsheath the Dragon Sword!"

I took the scabbard in my left hand. I took the hilt of the sword in my right. And slowly I slid the sheath away so that black radiance began to pour out of the green and black metal carved with so many runes, as if the sword's entire story was written there.

In the bright air of the Gheestenheem, before the assembled women of the Eldren, I held the blade up high. I let the scabbard fall. I took the Dragon Sword in my two hands. I raised it so that all might look upon it, upon the dark, living metal, upon the little, yellow, flickering flame within.

And the Dragon Sword began to sing. It was a wild, sweet song. It was a song so ancient it spoke of an existence beyond Time, beyond all the concerns of mortals and of gods. It spoke of love and hate and murder, of treachery and desire. It spoke of Chaos and of Law and of the tranquility of perfect balance. It spoke of the Future, the Past and the Present. And it spoke of all the myriad millions of worlds of the multiverse, all the worlds it had known, all the worlds which remained to be known.

And then, to my astonishment, the Eldren women also gave voice. They sang in perfect harmony with the blade. And I found that I, too, was singing, though I knew nothing of the words which left my lips. I had never believed myself capable of such wonderful song.

The chorus built and built. The Dragon Sword throbbed with an ecstasy of its own, an ecstasy reflected in the faces of all who witnessed this ceremony.

I lifted the blade above my head. I cried out, yet I did not know what it was I said. I cried out, and my voice held all my own dreams, all my longings, all the hopes and fears of an entire people.

I was trembling with exquisite delight, with awe and with something akin to fear, as I began to bring the blade down, in one clean, sweeping motion, upon the Iron Round.

The anvil which had been all that these women had possessed to remind them of their destiny now seemed to glow with the same strange light given off by the Dragon Sword.

The two parts met. There was a huge sound. A sound like the breaking of every planet, every cosmic barrier, every sun in the entire multiverse. A monstrous sound, yet a beautiful sound. It was the sound of fulfilled destiny.

And now the sword, which had been so heavy for so long, was light in my hands. And I saw that the blade had broken, clean in two, that for a moment one part of it was imbedded in the Iron Round, while the other remained in my grip. I shuddered at the incredible sensation of delight which permeated my entire body. And I gasped and I continued to sing my song, the song which the women sang, the song of the Eldren, the song of the Dragon Sword and the Iron Round.

And as we sang, something like flame erupted from the anvil, something which had been released from the sword and yet which, for a short while, had also inhabited the Round. It curled and it writhed and it, too, was singing. The singing became a roar, echoed in the throats of all those women, and the flame grew fiercer and stronger and it began to take shapes to itself, and colours to itself, and it seemed to me, as I fell away from its enormous might, that this was altogether a more powerful force than any I had witnessed before. For this was the force of human desire, of human will, of human ideals. It grew and grew. The shard of the sword fell from my hand. I was upon my knees, looking up as the presence took form, roaring still, curling and writhing still, blotting out the sun.

It was a huge beast. A dragon whose scales rippled in the glow of the sun. A dragon whose crest burned with the richest colours of the rainbow. A dragon whose red nostrils flared and whose white teeth clashed, whose coils rose skyward with exquisite grace, whose wings spread wider and wider, beating strongly as the beast ascended into the clear, blue sky.

Yet still the song went on. Still the dragon and the women and I all sang. Still the anvil sang, though the sword's voice grew fainter now. Up, up, it beat, that wonderful creature; up until it turned, weaving and diving, skimming the waters, spearing up again into the sunlight, rejoicing in its strength, in its freedom, in its pure animation.

Then the she-dragon roared. And her breath was warm upon our faces, bringing us, too, fresh life. She opened her vast mouth and she clashed her teeth in an orgy of release. She danced for us. She sang for us. She displayed her power for us. And we knew a complete rapport with her. I had known this only once before and the memory of that time was gone from me. I wept with the pleasure of it.

Then the she-dragon was turning. Her multicoloured wings, like the wings of some enormous insect, began to beat with a different purpose.

She turned her long, saurian head and she stared at us from out of wise, tender eyes, and again the breath steamed suddenly from her nostrils, and she was calling to us, calling us to follow.

Von Bek took my hand. "Come with us, Herr Daker. Come with us through the Dragon Gate. We shall know such happiness there!" And Alisaard clutched my arm. She said: "You will be honoured by all the Eldren now. Forever."

But I said sadly that it was not to be. "I know now that I must find the Dark Ship again. That is my duty and my destiny."

"You said you had no further desire to be a hero." Von Bek was surprised.

"That is true. And I will be a hero, will I not, in the Eldren world? My only hope to rid myself of this burden is to remain here. I know that."

All the women were now aboard their vessels. Many were already putting out to sea, over the white tipped waves, in the wake of the she-dragon. They waved to me as they left. And still they sang.

"Go," I told my friends. "Go and be happy. That will console me for any loss, I promise you."

And thus we parted. Von Bek and Alisaard were the last to go aboard the final ship which left the harbour. I watched as the wind filled their triangular sail, as the slender prow made a cleft in the gentle waters.

The great she-dragon, which had been released at last, according to legend, described a complete circle in the sky overhead, seemingly for the sheer joy of flying.

But where she had gone the circle remained. A blue and red disc which gradually widened until it touched the waters below. The colours became more complex. Thousands of rich, dark shades shimmered above the water. And through this circle now passed the great she-dragon, vanishing almost at once. Then came the ships of the Eldren. And they, too, were swallowed up. They had rejoined their kind. The dragons and their mortal kin were reunited at last!

The circle faded.

The circle vanished.

I was alone in a deserted world.

I was alone.

I looked down at the two halves of the sword, at the anvil. Both seemed to have sustained enormous forces. It was as if they had melted yet held their shape. I was not sure why I had this impression.

I stirred the hilt of the sword with my foot. For a moment I was tempted to pick it up, but then I turned aside with a shrug. I wanted no further business with swords, or magic, or destiny. I wanted only to go home.

I left the harbour behind me. I walked amongst the miserable ruins of the Eldren town. I remembered such destruction. I remembered when, as Erekosë, Champion of Humanity, I had led my armies against a town similar to this, against a people called the Eldren. I remembered that crime. And I remembered another crime, when I had led the Eldren against my own folk.

Somehow, however, the pang of guilt I had known since then was no longer present. I felt that all was now redeemed again. I had made amends and I was whole.

Later, towards evening, I found myself again on the quayside, looking out towards the setting sun. Everything was silent. Everything was calm. Yet it was a solitude I did not relish, for it was the result of an absence of life.

A few seabirds wheeled and called. The waves slapped against the stones of the quay. I sat down on the Iron Round, again contemplating the two shards of the Dragon Sword, wondering if perhaps I should have gone with the Eldren, back to their own world.

And then I heard the sound of horses behind me. I turned. A single rider, leading another steed. A small, ill-formed fellow, all in motley. He grinned at me and saluted.

"Will you come a-riding with me, Sir Champion? I would relish the company."

"Good evening to you, Jermays. I trust you have not brought me further news of destiny and doom." I climbed into the saddle of the horse.

"I never cared much for those things," he said, "as you know. It is not my business to play an important part in the history of the multiverse. These past times are perhaps the most active I have been. I do not regret it, though I should have liked to have witnessed Sharadim's defeat and the banishment of Chaos. You performed a mighty task, eh, Sir Champion? Perhaps the greatest of your career?"

I shook my head. I did not know.

Jermays led the way from the quay and along the shore of the sea, beside the white cliffs. The sun made the sky a wonderful deep colour. It touched the sea. It made all seem permanent and unassailable.

"Your friends have gone now, have they?" he asked as we rode. "Dragon to dragon, Eldren to Eldren. And von Bek, what sort of dynasty will he found, I wonder? And what sort of history will come out of all that went on here? Another cycle must begin before we shall get any hint of the fate of Melniboné."

The name was familiar to me. It stirred the faintest memory, but I dismissed it. I wanted no more of memories, whether they be of past or future.

Soon it was night. Moonlight was pure silver upon the water. As we rounded a headland, with the tide rolling at our horses' feet, I saw the outline of a ship at anchor in the little bay.

The ship had high decks, fore and aft, and its timbers were carved with all manner of baroque designs. There was a broad, sweeping curve to her prow and her single mast was tall, bearing a single large, furled sail. I could see that on each of her raised decks the ship had a wheel, as if she could be steered from stern or prow. She sat lightly on the water, like a vessel awaiting fresh cargo.

Jermays and I rode our horses through the shallows. I heard him cry: "Halloo, the ship! Are you taking on passengers?"

Now a figure appeared at the rail, leaning on it and apparently staring out over our heads towards the cliffs. I saw at once that he was blind.

A red mist had begun to form in the water about the ship. It was faint and yet it seemed to stir not with the movements of the sea itself, but with the movements of the dark vessel. I looked out across the ocean, but the moon was hidden behind clouds and I could see little. It seemed that the red mist was growing.

"Come aboard," said the blind man. "You are welcome."

"Now we must part," said Jermays. "I think it will be long before we meet again, perhaps in another cycle altogether. Farewell, Sir Champion." He clapped me on the back and then had turned his horse and was galloping back through the water to the shore. I heard the hooves thumping on sand and he had vanished.

My own horse was restless. I dismounted and let him go. He followed Jermays.

I waded through the water. It was warm against my body. It had reached as high as my chest before I could catch hold of a trailing ladder and begin to climb aboard. The red mist had grown thicker now. It obscured all sight of the shore.

The blind man sniffed the air. "We must be on our way. I am glad you decided to come. You have no sword now, eh?"

"I have no need of one," I said.

He grunted in reply and then called out for the sail to be unfurled. I saw the shadows of men in the rigging as I followed the blind helmsman to his cabin, where his brother, the captain, waited for us. I heard the sail crack down and the wind tug urgently at it. I heard the anchors raised. I felt the ship pull suddenly and roll and swing out to sea and I knew that once again we were sailing through waters which flowed between the worlds.

The captain's bright blue eyes were kindly as he indicated the food prepared for me. "You must be weary, John Daker. You have done much, eh?"

I stripped off my heavy leathers. I sighed with relief as I poured myself wine.

"Are there others aboard tonight?" I asked.

"Of your kind? Only yourself."

"And where do we sail?" I was reconciled to whatever instructions I might be given.

"Oh, nowhere of any great importance. You have no sword I note."

"Your brother has already remarked upon that. I left it broken on the quayside in Barobanay. It is useless now."

"Not quite," said the captain, joining me in a goblet of wine. "But it will need to be reforged. Perhaps as two swords, where it was once one."

"A new sword from each part. Is there enough metal for that?"

"I think so. But that will not concern you for a while, at any rate. Would you sleep now?"

"I am tired," I said. I felt as if I had not rested for centuries.

The blind helmsman led me to my old, familiar bunk. I stretched myself out and almost immediately I began to dream. I dreamed of King Rigenos and of Ermizhad, of Urlik Skarsol and all the other heroes I had been. And then I dreamed of dragons. Hundreds of dragons. Dragons whom I knew by name. Dragons who loved me as I loved them. And I dreamed of great fleets. Of wars. Of tragedies and of impossible delights, of wizardry and wild romance. I dreamed of white arms locked around me. I dreamed again of Ermizhad. And then I dreamed that we had come together again at last and I awoke laughing, remembering something of that dragon song which the Eldren women had sung.

The blind helmsman and his brother the captain stood there. They, too, were smiling.

"It is time to disembark, John Daker. It is time for you to go to your reward."

I got up, then. I was dressed only in a pair of leather

breeches and boots. But it did not feel cold. I followed them out into the darkness of the deck. A few yellow lamps gleamed here and there. Through the red mist I saw the suggestion of a shoreline. I saw first one tower and then a second. They seemed to be spanning a harbour.

I peered through the darkness, trying to distinguish details. The towers looked familiar.

Now the blind helmsman called to me from below. He was in a small boat waiting to carry me to land. I bid farewell to the captain and I climbed down to the boat, seating myself on the bench.

The helmsman pulled strongly on his oars. The red mist grew dimmer still. It seemed close to dawn. The twin towers had a bridge spanning them. Elsewhere were thousands of lights gleaming. I heard the mournful hoot of what I thought at first was a great waterbeast. Then I realised it was a boat.

The helmsman shipped his oars. "You are at your destination now, John Daker. I wish you good fortune."

Cautiously I stepped onto the slippery mud of the shore. I heard a drone from above me. I heard voices. And then, as the helmsman disappeared back into the red mist, I realised that I had been in this place before.

The twin towers were those of Tower Bridge. The sounds I heard were the sounds of a great modern city. The sounds of London.

John Daker was returning home.

EPILOGUE

MY name is John Daker. I was once called the Eternal Champion. It is possible I shall bear that name again. For now, however, I am at peace.

By summoning up this identity—the original, if you will —I was able to resist and ultimately defeat the powers of Chaos. My reward for this action is that I be allowed to resume my life as John Daker.

When called by King Rigenos to be humanity's champion, I had been discontented with my life. I had seen it as shallow, without colour. Yet I have come to realise how rich my life actually is, how complex is the world I inhabit. That complexity alone is worthy of celebration. I understand that life in a great city of my world's twentieth century can be just as intense, just as satisfactory as any other. Indeed, to be a hero, forever at war, is to be in some ways always a child. The true challenge comes in making sense of one's life, of imbuing it with purpose based on one's own principles.

I still have memories of those other times. I still dream frequently of the great battle blades, the chargers, the massive fighting barges, the weird creatures and the magical cities, the bright banners and the wonder of a perfect love. I dream of riding against Chaos, of bearing arms against Heaven in the name of Hell, of being the scythe which cut humanity down. . . . But I have discovered an equal intensity of experience in this world, too. We have merely, I think, to teach ourselves how to recognise and to relish it.

That is what I learned when I faced the Archduke Balarizaaf, Princess Sharadim and Prince Flamadin at The World's Beginning, when we struggled for the Dragon Sword.

It is ironic that I saved both myself and those I cared for by recalling, at the crucial moment, my identity as an ordinary mortal. There are subtle dangers to the role of hero. I am glad I no longer have to consider them.

So John Daker has returned home. The cycle is complete; the saga finds a form of resolution. Somewhere, doubtless, the Eternal Champion will continue to fight to maintain the Cosmic Balance. And in his dreams, if nowhere else, John Daker will recall those battles, as he will sometimes recall a vast field of statues, all of which seem to bear his name. . . . For the present, however, he need take no further part in battles, nor wonder at the significance of that field.

I still long, of course, for my Ermizhad. I shall never love anyone as I loved her. I believe I must surely find her, not in some bizarre realm of the multiverse, but here, perhaps in this city, in London. Does she look for me, even now, as I search for her? It surely cannot be very long before we are reunited.

And when that time comes there is no sword forged, in this world or any other, which will divide us!

We shall know peace.

Though our span of years be those of ordinary human beings, they will be our own years. We shall be free of all cosmic designs, free of destinies and grandiose dooms.

We shall be free to love as we were always meant to love; free to be the flawed, finite, mortal creatures which from the first was all we ever wished to be.

And, for those years at least, the Eternal Champion will be at rest.